W9-BNT-224

TITANSHADE

TITAN SHADE

DAN STOUT

DAW BOOKS, INC.

DONALD A. WOLLHEIM FOUNDER

1745 Broadway, New York, NY 10019
ELIZABETH R. WOLLHEIM
SHEILA E. GILBERY
PUBLISHERS
www.dawbooks.com

To the person who always found time to read to me
from my favorite book.
Even when it was the dictionary.

This book has my name on it, but it should have hers as well.
Maryann Stout

I T WAS THE BACK SIDE of Friday and I sat at the bar of Mickey the Finn's. My hands laced around a cup of warm joe as I kept silent time to the jukebox, eyes fixed on the clock where it hung by a single crooked nail above a row of liquor bottles. Its minute hand crept ever closer to that magic hour: the moment when my shift would end, and I'd be free to order something stiffer. I was a few ticks away from paradise when the pager in my coat pocket began buzzing. I fished it out and squinted at the faded green display. The three-digit code read 187. Homicide. I flagged down the bartender and asked for the phone.

He brought it over, untangling the cord and dropping it on the bar top hard enough to jangle the ringer. I spun the rotary dial and waited for Dispatch to pick up.

I jotted the details down in my notepad. Room 430 at the Eagle Crest Hotel. I hung up, dropped enough change to cover my coffee, and with an ache I felt in my bones, pulled myself off the cracked vinyl seat of the barstool.

As I left the Finn's I paused at the door, my hand over the geo-vent in the floor. Warm air streamed up, tinged with the strong rotten-egg smell of sulfur. I could tell the imps were really giving the big guy hell that day. Though I'd long ago stopped believing he could hear us, I mouthed the traditional prayer of departure.

For your suffering, which brings us safety and warmth, we thank you. My pager buzzed again. Code 21: All available units to report.

Prayer time was over. I walked out the door and onto the filthy streets of Titanshade.

The sidewalks seethed, the customary sea of pedestrians making walking difficult but not impossible. Street traffic was almost standing still, slowed to a crawl by a funeral procession. A long line of Therreau folk trailed behind a wagon-wheeled hearse driven by a team of matte-black horned beetles. The wide-brimmed hats and bonnets of the Therreau shaded smooth faces plucked free of any hair. They were on their way to the Mount, to perform a sky burial. A taxi would only get stuck behind the beetles, and I had hopes of making it back to Mickey the Finn's that night. So I decided to hoof it, breaking into a fast stroll to cross the street ahead of the procession.

It was winter, and the shortened day was already dissipating into twilight. Although the sky was darkening, the evening air grew warmer as I moved toward the mountain at the northeast edge of the city. I unbuttoned my overcoat and shoved my scarf into a pocket as I dodged panhandlers and slower pedestrians. Other travelers moving mountwise did the same, shedding layers as they walked toward warmer air, while those heading leeward slipped into jackets or zippered sweaters.

The crowd was relatively calm, with only a few obscenities and lewd gestures thrown around as we all jostled for position on the sidewalks. There was a daily chaotic madness to my town, a blue-collar work ethic still visible regardless of how many coats of oil money had been slapped over it the last fifty years.

After a few blocks the pager urged me on once more. I pulled my overcoat off and draped it over an arm, ignoring the aches in my legs and speeding my pace even if I didn't think it was needed.

Dispatch had said homicide, but that was probably an overeager patrolman's report. A death in the Eagle Crest Hotel was far more likely just another suicide, some middle manager trying to escape the shame of financial ruin as one more oil well ran dry beyond the city limits.

So maybe I didn't hustle over as fast as I should have. But at the time I had no way of knowing what was waiting for me. If I had, I would have run as far and as fast as I could. Though in which direction, I couldn't say.

As it was, by the time I arrived at the scene and made my way to the fourth floor Angus was already there, trying to look like he was in charge. He stood outside the door of room 430, hands on hips, suit coat arranged just so, frozen in place like he was hoping the newspaper flaks would suddenly appear and snap his photo.

A born publicity hound, Angus always dressed to the nines. Today he wore a three-piece suit, and the hard, fleshy plates covering his skull had been polished to a reflective shine. He was buttoned up tight, but like all Mollenkampi he wore his tie loose due to anatomical constraints. When he saw me, he jerked his head toward the door, and the oversized, jagged teeth jutting from his biting mouth clattered with the motion. His voice rose from his second mouth, a round void nestled above a shirt collar sharp with starch.

"Go check it out, Carter. But I was on-scene first. My case." The folds around his eyes crinkled with amusement.

I was too tired to think of something clever and I didn't give a damn who claimed the case, so I kept my mouth shut and tried to brush past him. He leaned in and grabbed my arm.

"Close the door quick," he said. "We don't want any photos hitting the papers." The slender mandibles on either side of his biting jaw quivered when he spoke, and his grip was tighter than necessary.

I smirked. "Just keep the press back. Give 'em a big smile." I eyed the rigid plates lining his head and his expressionless biting jaws. "Best as you can, anyway."

I shook off his grip and entered the room, immediately pulling up short. I almost forgot to close the door after all.

Over two decades on the force and I'd never seen anything like the mess in that hotel room. I muttered a prayer that I wouldn't have to see something like it again. Then, like the department shrinks taught me, I paused to collect myself, closing my eyes and taking a deep breath. That's when the odor hit me. I stepped back, struggling to reconcile the scene before me with a scent I associated with breakfasts and baked goods.

The murder scene smelled of cinnamon.

That meant the vic was a Squib. I'd seen a few of them before, but only a few. I opened my eyes and began to process the scene. Human-size bipedal frogs, Squibs rarely came this far north. There was no way to tell if this one had been male or female, no way to tell much of anything. The body was . . . well, "in pieces" probably gets the point across. Chunks of the Squib's skin were underfoot, globs of fat and muscle smeared in the fibers of the carpet and stuck to the wall. The sight was oppressive, but the smell overrode the visuals. I swallowed, distantly surprised that I didn't have the cotton mouth associated with shock.

I stood still, unable to walk more than a few feet into the room without stepping in viscera. The walls and couch were covered in a berry-jam kind of smear. I took another breath. Now that I'd had time to process it, the smell was more complex than cinnamon. It had undertones of something sweeter, like whipped cream melting into a latte, or the way spices bloom when a pastry is bursting with readiness in the oven. Memories of shepherd's pie flooded over me as I saw pieces of flesh hanging in the curtains.

My stomach clenched from a combination of revulsion and appetite. I hadn't been hungry when I walked in, but I was ravenous now.

I tried to look away, but there was nowhere to rest my eyes that hadn't been touched by the gore. I swallowed again, my head reeling like a rookie on his first day scraping up the remains of joyriders who'd miscalculated one of the hairpin turns on the tight roads up the Mount.

Afraid I was the only person struggling with the scene, I glanced at the other cops in the room. There were a handful of techs stepping carefully through the suite. They wore respirators, but still managed to look queasy.

I swallowed a third time, and I realized my mouth was watering. Disgust at my own reaction hit me hard: standing in the middle of a horror show, I was reacting like a starving man at a buffet.

I must have been visibly struggling, because one of the techs walked over to me, slipcovered shoes squishing with each step.

"You okay, Detective?"

I nodded. "It's this smell." I wiped a sleeve across my mouth. I was almost drooling.

The tech stooped to put a tape measure against a smear of blood. "Yeah, I've heard of Squib stink before. Never thought I'd get hit with it firsthand, though."

"Me either." My head swam, and I focused on what he'd said. Squib blood released a pheromone when exposed to the air, and it had a strange effect on some humans. I was clearly in that population. I felt like punching someone—anyone—and I had a perverse desire to squeeze the viscera between my fingers. I shook my head fiercely, and the tech's voice grew more concerned.

"Maybe you oughta get a respirator. We got some more coming down with another crew."

"Reinforcements?" I forced a smile but couldn't tell if it was returned behind the tech's mask.

"It'll take days to process everything," he said. "The bathroom's not bad, though the tub's got some crusty brown residue."

"Killer washed off?" I asked.

He looked back at the bathroom, as if considering the idea. "Maybe. Doesn't look like bloodstains, though. We'll take a sample and see what the lab says."

I wanted to get a feel for the place before anything was moved, but I couldn't think straight. I noticed the techs were only snapping photos and taking notes.

"You're not tagging and bagging."

The tech shook his head. "Just cataloging. Dispatch says a DO is headed down, and we won't move anything till she gets here."

That was good. Sorcery was expensive and most homicides didn't rate a divination officer on site. But this one . . . this one clearly would.

It was possible that this killing was the start of something bigger. Squib smell was a serious intoxicant for some humans, with no way to determine who was susceptible before exposure. There had even been isolated cases of Squibs being killed and eaten when someone made the mistake of taking them to human-staffed hospitals for minor wounds. My stomach gurgled at the thought, and I spoke up to cover the sound.

"Where's the rest of the body?" I asked.

The tech swung a hand, twisting at the waist to take in the whole room. "You're looking at it. Far as we can tell, it was pulverized."

"Come on," I said. "The whole body? That's not possible."

He shrugged. "Squibs are cartilaginous. No real bones. And with this amount of matter spread around . . ."

Looking away from the tech I got another glimpse of the viscera that marked the room. The image of cherry pie popped into my head and I smiled again, broader this time, my lips pulling back from my teeth uncomfortably. I almost slapped myself.

"I'll be back after I get a mask," I said.

Walking away from the nightmare in the hotel room, I slammed the door shut behind me, never so glad to leave a crime scene. In the hall, Angus was waiting for me. The first photographers had shown up, hoping to sell a snapshot to one of the papers. The glare from their flashbulbs lit up the speckled, sea-bass coloration of his skull plates. Angus smirked.

"Problem, Carter?"

I stared back. I'd seen his discomfort earlier. Angus was spooked, and giving me grief was him trying to reassert a sense of control. Reading him that way didn't make me hate him any less, but it let me keep my cool.

"I'm going to survey the exterior," I said.

While I was close, he threw in one more remark the reporters couldn't overhear.

"No appetite for it?"

Without answering I shoved past him and through the scrum of photographers. Let them get a shot of Angus, the most photogenic cop on the case. I needed to get out of there.

Back on the streets the spires and skyscrapers of Titanshade opened around me, and I could breathe again. At least the bustle of the crowd covered my internal, thrumming voice of self-loathing. The press of bodies rose and fell in waves, punctuated by the rumble of car engines and the blare of horns as drivers bellowed their frustrations into the night. Gradually the fog and noise started to wash away the sickness and shame at my reaction to the murder.

Death bothered me, sure, but it wasn't the first murder I'd seen and I doubted it'd be the last. But none of them had put me through what I'd just experienced. Angus could have whatever had happened in that hotel room. Let others deal with that nightmare. For once, I'd simply walk away. I wanted no part of it.

Decision made, I felt a great weight drop from my shoulders. I loosened my tie and took a deep breath. It looked like I'd make it back to Mickey the Finn's after all.

But it was a long walk back through the city and the ache in my leg bones wasn't going away. Reaching into my inner coat pocket I retrieved a small prescription bottle. A brief struggle with the childproof cap and I had two largish blue pills sitting in my palm. Before I could swallow them, a small car pulled up to the curb, and a square-shouldered woman got out. She motioned the driver to find a parking spot and turned her eyes on me.

I palmed the pills and bottle, dropping them discreetly back into my pocket while raising the other hand in a salute. "Hey, Cap."

Captain Bryyh squinted at the Eagle Crest, deep crow's feet etching across dark brown skin as she took in the profile of the building. "You been up there yet?"

"Yeah," I said. "It's bad."

"What are you doing? Scouting the perimeter?"

I considered giving her a line, but it's always a risky thing trying to pull one past Bryyh. I settled on the truth, as far as it went.

"Sorta. I had to get out of there."

"Messy?"

"Yeah, but . . ." I gave her a hangdog grin. "Don't go in there without a respirator."

Her nostrils flared. I wondered if she'd encountered Squib smell before.

"You look like you're getting ready to go somewhere," she said.

"Angus is first on-scene."

"So?"

"So there's nothing for me to do."

She frowned. "You got a page, right? You weren't ordered here by accident."

From somewhere came the rattle of wooden cartwheels on cobblestone, threatening to distract me. I ran my tongue over my teeth and chose my words carefully.

"A murder in a pricey hotel means money. The vic is a Squib, and if it turns out they were tied to the wind farms, it means politics. Either way, the press'll be all over it. You don't want to see my face on the evening news."

She pursed her lips, as if considering that. She was a good actor on occasion.

"You finished with the Reynolds case?" she said.

"Handed it over to Kravitz this afternoon." It had taken me days of nonstop work, but it was done. "He made the arrest this evening. I was waiting on a celebratory drink when I got called up here."

"So you're available. And there's plenty of work here that won't put you in front of cameras."

"Alright. But look—"

Bryyh took a step closer, tightening her tone as she interrupted me.

"You seem to think this is a discussion," she said. "It is not. This is me telling you what's going to happen. I've got every asshole with brass on his shoulder headed this way, and you're here because I want you here." The sharp edge faded and she beckoned me toward the crime scene. "Now come on. We'll find you something useful to do."

I wiped a hand across my face. The brass was headed in to make their appearance for the cameras. Money *and* politics.

The sound of rolling carts got louder. Behind Bryyh's back the

Therreau funeral procession approached. They had caught up with me, the shrouded corpse-wagon pulled by slow-moving tibron beetles twice my size. Methodical and never-stopping, they carried their burden to the mountain.

Bryyh headed toward the hotel. I rolled my head in a slow loop, stretching the tendons in my neck. The tension in my shoulders was building back up, and the pain in my bones wasn't going to go away by itself. But I put one foot in front of another, and walked back inside that hotel.

2

BRYYH WAS RIGHT ABOUT THE brass. Within twenty min-utes of our conversation, everyone over the rank of lieutenant in the TPD began making an appearance. I guess they all went to the same PR class that Angus had attended. They put on somber faces and shook their heads at the crime, then nodded in agreement when each one, in turn, stated their determination to find the killer. Maybe they meant it, or maybe they just wanted to gawk at the victim before going back to their safe homes and comfortable offices, where they could brag to their country club friends about the time they'd gotten a whiff of Squib blood.

Despite her promise, Bryyh never did find something for me to do. She was immediately swept up in dealing with her superiors and the press, and when I revisited room 430 Angus informed me in no uncertain terms that he didn't need my assistance.

"The offer's appreciated," he said as he looked over my shoulder at the stream of influential brass entering behind me. "But I'm first on-scene and we should keep it thin up here. Too many cooks and all." His eyes lit up. "Alvin! Good to see you." He stepped to the side, distancing himself from me as he welcomed an older man in a dress uniform who I'd never seen in my life.

Unable to leave and barred from the crime scene proper, I might have been forgiven if I'd simply found a vacant corner and grabbed some shuteye. Instead, I figured that if I couldn't be relaxing with a drink, I might as well do the only other thing I'm good at. Lucky for me, a hotel is an extremely convenient place to investigate a murder.

Most people don't know this, but death is a frequent visitor to the hospitality industry. Suicides who don't want their corpse to be discovered by their families, addicts who want some privacy to get high and end up overdosing, countless illicit deals gone wrong, and secret affairs whose passions burned too bright. You'd be surprised how often death slips past the numbered doors of a hotel guest room.

Accordingly, hotels have policies to deal with such uncomfortable situations. They cover everything from standardized forms to polite requests for the coroner to come in by the back stairs. This is totally understandable. After all, they have a business to run, and these unpleasant events can be accompanied by headaches.

Headaches like me.

The general manager of the Eagle Crest was a petite man with perfect cuticles and a scar on his upper lip. He had returned to the hotel after getting word of what was found on the fourth floor of his fine establishment. Considering how fastidious the rest of his appearance was, I figured that he had some plastic surgery in mind to take care of the scar. I made a mental note to subpoena his bank accounts and monitor for any large deposits that might indicate a payoff. Everyone's a suspect when you begin a murder investigation.

"I would appreciate a little consideration," he said for the third time. All I'd done was ask if he'd seen anyone with large amounts of blood on their person. Granted, I'd asked from across the lobby, but still—he seemed jumpy.

"I'm sure we can get you the information you need," he said, "*if* you can keep your voice down."

"Amazing thing about voices," I said. "The happier I am, the quieter mine gets."

I wanted the security video. Somewhere on that tape, mixed in with all the other people who had been in and out of the building, we had the killer's photo.

The manager grimaced, but didn't say anything else as he retreated to the back office. Alone at the front desk I stuck out like a black dog on a snowfield. I was the only cop in the lobby. Angus had directed the tech cars to the rear of the building and was running all the crime scene crews in through the employee entrance. He's always been very accommodating to management. That's probably why he gets so many commendations.

While I waited for the manager to return I tasked my weary eyes with finding the complimentary coffee stand. I was headed its direction when a new police cruiser pulled up to the hotel's front door. The passenger side opened and a woman rolled out, tall and skinny with unnaturally white hair done up in elaborate curls. My old man hadn't left me with much to remember him by, but one of his sayings came back to me as I watched her stroll into the Eagle Crest Hotel: "Never turn your back on an ice-plains wolf, and never trust anyone who's hungry by choice."

The newcomer was dressed for an evening out, but as she walked she slipped a dark cloak over her shoulders. It had the look of velvet, and was lined with iridescent symbols that disappeared when I looked directly at them. This had to be the divination officer. Seeing a DO was rare enough, but this one was even more unusual—I'd never seen her before, and I'd gotten into screaming matches with pretty much every ranking officer in the department. I decided to introduce myself.

Stepping into her path, I flashed my badge. "Detective Carter," I said. "I'll take you up to the scene."

She stepped around me without slowing.

"No need. I'm to meet Detective—" She glanced at the palm of her left hand, where something was written in ballpoint pen. "—Angus. He is the detective on-scene, correct?"

I kept pace with her. Divination officers tend to be assigned to high-profile cases, which are the kind that I generally never get near. Accompanying the DO would give me a chance to see a little sorcery being done, and better yet, a way to get back into room 430 to spite Angus.

"Is he expecting you?" I asked.

"It doesn't really matter."

We reached the elevator lobby, and she jabbed the call button. As the elevator descended, the DO looked me over for the first time. I was suddenly very conscious of the wrinkles in my suit and the stains on my shirt. I decided to try a different tack.

"This crime scene," I said. "It's pretty bad. You'll want a—"

"A respirator. I called and confirmed there's one available, thank you." She glanced at the elevator indicator light, then back at me. "How long have you been on shift?"

I attempted a shrug of indifference. "I had a double yesterday. This call came in right before I rotated out. Thought I'd stick around and help out."

She arched an eyebrow. "Even though another detective was first on-scene?"

If I was going to lay it on, I might as well lay it on thick.

"I'm sort of a team player."

"Well. I admit you've got the lobby well guarded."

The elevator arrived with a ding, doors opening to reveal a gleaming metal interior. She walked inside and turned to face me. Her voice didn't soften, but she gave me a respectful nod and said, "Go home, Detective. I've got this covered."

The elevator doors pulled closed, and for the briefest moment I thought I saw someone standing behind her. I wedged my hand into the opening, prying the doors open, and saw my own face over her shoulder. I'd been spooked by my reflection in the polished brass of the elevator cab. Brown eyes ringed by dark circles stared back at me, and a whisker-covered jawline drifting toward middle-aged softness worked open and closed as I muttered an apology. I stepped back, embarrassed. But there was surprisingly no rebuke from the DO.

"Get some rest," she said. "There'll be plenty more to do tomorrow." The elevator doors drew closed once more.

I heard a cough from the direction of the front desk and I turned around. The manager was back. He leaned over the edge of the front counter so he could see me where I stood in the elevator lobby.

"It seems the security tapes have already been confiscated. A young Mollenkampi officer collected them."

I ran a hand through my hair, skirting the edges of the bald spot I tried to pretend didn't exist, while the manager kept talking.

"You realize that if you'd spoken with your own people, we could all have been saved a lot of trouble." With that he turned and retreated into the back office.

He was right. The DO was right. I was dead on my feet—useless. And down in the lobby there wasn't even anyone I could be useless for. I realized the sensible thing would be to go home, where I could at least be useless to my cat.

Instead I jammed the elevator button and waited for my ride up to the fourth floor.

When I approached room 430 there was a patrol cop at the door, a Mollenkampi named Cardamom who I knew from the Borderlands beat. She was doing her honest best to stand tall in her crimson uniform, but her eyes showed that mixture of boredom and disgust that comes with standing for hours next to a grotesque display of violence.

I sidled up next to her and muttered from the side of my mouth, "Anyone run out to puke yet?"

Her eyes perked up as she recognized me. "Not lately," she said, the words coming from the small opening in her throat. "But give it time and it'll happen."

I laughed and asked about her family. Cardamom was a good cop stuck on a crap detail, and she appreciated even a brief distraction. A Mollenkampi was a natural choice to choose as a guard, as they weren't affected by Squib smell, but it still wasn't pleasant standing with your back to a slaughterhouse while the detectives came and went like visitors at a freak show.

I was about to crack a joke when the door opened and a human jogged out wearing a respirator. He yanked off his protective shoe covers as he passed, trying not to tread blood on the hotel carpet. I couldn't see the face behind the mask, but from the pace he set I figured he was looking for somewhere to be sick.

Cardamom watched the sickened man stagger down the hall. "Told you there'd be one sooner or later."

Laughter tinkled through the rows of needle-sharp teeth lining her speaking mouth. Mollenkampi's expressions are conveyed by their eyes, their tone of voice, their body language. Clear enough if you knew what to look for, but to humans farther south the Mollenkampi were stone-faced warriors, a baffling blend of delicate, songlike speech and the intimidating sight of heavy biting jaws erupting from the taut skin of their faces like some mythical creature shedding its human skin.

In Titanshade the general greed and economic plenty of the oil boom had worked to smooth over relations, but tensions still simmered. From skin tone to favorite sports team, there's never been a shortage of excuses to hate other people—human or otherwise.

I pointed at the departing detective. "No shame in it," I said. "Just shows he's not dead inside." I glanced over Cardamom's shoulder, through the now-open door to room 430.

The crew was mostly Mollenkampi, with a few respirator-masked humans in the mix. The DO was there, a respirator flattening the curls in her shock of white hair. She paced back and forth in white slip-on booties already stained scarlet. Those were standard issue in high-contamination sites. Disposable, waterproof slip-ons that would be discarded each time an officer left the scene. There needed to be a store-case of them nearby; a few paces down the hall sat a plastic bin. Lifting the lid, I found respirators and slip-ons rolled in pairs. I snagged one of each and turned back to Cardamom.

"Listen, I know Angus told you not to let me in . . ."

"I don't know what you're talking about," she said. "He told me not to let specific people in. I don't know who you are behind the respirator. All I see's a human with a badge." Her eyes crinkled, and her mandibles twitched.

I smiled back and slid my respirator on. A moment later I walked into room 430.

Angus was splitting his attention between showboating for the DO and bullying the junior detectives present. A plastic tarp stretched across the floor, piled with the Squib's remains. Trying to be inconspicuous I stayed close to the entryway, where the gore hadn't quite reached. Beneath my feet, through the clear plastic laid out to protect the crime scene, I could see imprints on the carpet. A sharp curve and two short, straight lines. I pushed at them with the toe of my shoe. Something heavy and round had sat there recently, maybe with a pair of wheels. Any further observation was cut short when Angus raised his voice.

"DO Guyer is going to conduct a reading of the body," he announced to the room, lecturing like a tenured professor.

Behind him the DO stared at the contents on the tarp.

"Is this all that's left?" she said. Angus nodded and she shook her head. "Well, Hells below, I need more than this."

Angus was silent, though one mandible twitched. He was probably about as tired as I was. *Poor baby*, I thought.

The DO stared him down. "I'm serious. Reading entrails involves reading entrails, not random chunks of Squib. I have no idea what I'm going to get from this."

Angus jerked his chin at her—a truly intimidating gesture when backed by Mollenkampi incisors— but dropped his gaze. "Do what you can. This needs to be wrapped up ASAP."

Guyer sighed and pulled off her latex gloves with a snap. A tech held up a plastic bag, and she tossed the gloves inside. "Well, this is where it gets messy."

She held up a vial and I recognized the substance inside immediately.

Manna is the only liquid that shimmers with all the colors of the rainbow, an ephemeral effect like an oil film on a puddle of water. That tiny vial of manna probably cost more than a year of my salary.

The DO took a breath. I was glad I couldn't smell the reek of cinnamon through my respirator, but thinking of it made my stomach gurgle.

"What's his name?" Guyer asked.

Angus consulted his notepad and read, "Garson Haberdine."

I recognized that name from the desk registry.

Guyer nodded and dipped a finger into her manna vial. She touched a drop to her lips then spread it across them with her tongue. She rubbed the manna into her hands, stretching the precious material as far as it would go. A hundred years ago there'd been enough manna to fuel engines by the gallon. After the Shortage left the world with a fixed amount of manna it had become increasingly valuable. What stores remained were closely regulated by governments and a few wealthy private concerns. That scarcity combined with advances in magical theory meant that a small amount could—and needed to—go a long way.

Spreading her arms, the DO threw back her head, her cloak billowing out like the fins of a great sea creature. The cloak's runes were easily visible now, dancing with tiny sparks of light that trailed afterimages across my retinas. With all eyes on her no one noticed me sidling in for a better look.

Bending, she shoved both hands into the mass of viscera and raised her arms. Coagulated chunks of the victim rained down in an arc.

"Speak to me, Garson Haberdine." Through her manna-touched lips her voice took on a richer timbre and echoed more than it should have in a thickly carpeted room. "Speak through this fellow walker of the Path. Make my hands your own so we may seek justice in your name." She leaned forward and spread the entrails around like a toddler playing with finger paints. Several of the spectators pulled back, disgust or decency making them turn their heads. I stepped in closer, my desire to see the results of the spell outweighing the twinge in my gut as Guyer handled the entrails. I realized I was on the verge of pushing past Angus and forced myself to step back.

The scattered viscera formed a pattern as it passed through the DO's manna-laced fingers. Angus looked over her shoulder and asked what we were all wondering.

"What's it say?"

The DO snorted. "It says dick-all."

Angus blinked, then looked from the bloody smear on the floor to Guyer.

"What?"

Her eyes tightened, and I thought that if it weren't for the respirator she would have spit in the middle of the remains. "It's gibberish. It doesn't make any sense."

She pointed at the beginning of the pattern. "Here it says 'In my time I know the way,' then nonsense, then 'the patch the broken spear.' And this—" She poked at a particularly random-looking blob. "This isn't even words. This is . . ." She picked up a bloody piece of the mess and stared at it before flicking it away. "That's a toenail. Dammit, I told you this is an incantation to read entrails." Guyer glared around the room. "Toes aren't entrails, are they, Detective?"

She straightened and stormed away from the mess. I looked in the direction of the discarded flesh and tried not to think about whether Garson Haberdine had any family and how they might feel if this scene had played in front of them. You have to compartmentalize your emotions to stay sane in this job. It comes easier to some of us, I guess.

"Someone give me a towel." Guyer snatched a terrycloth piece of fabric from a young Mollenkampi detective and scrubbed the mess off her hands. She tore off the respirator and tossed it and the towel aside. The younger detective snagged them out of the air and handed them to the tech with the bag. The kid had fast hands.

Angus rounded on her with as much vitriol as I'd ever seen him show a superior. "So what? You're saying you can't do anything?"

"Oh, I'll get the answers. But I'll need fresh blood to do it. Right now, I've got a dinner party to get back to. I'll see you tomorrow, Detective." She pushed past me on her way out and up close the electric power of the manna radiated from her like heat from an open oven. Anyone could use manna to power a machine, but sorcerers had the ability and training to focus it, amplifying and transforming it into something extraordinary.

Angus turned on a bootie-covered heel and stared at the pile of gore on the tarp. The group of detectives and techs milled around, waiting for orders. I moved to leave, but paused before entering the hallway. On the room side of the entry door a Do Not Disturb sign hung from the handle. That was normal, but what caught my attention was a small piece of glittering red sticker attached to the bottom of the sign. The kind of sticker often used as a signal that while the room may be off limits to hotel staff, it was open for another kind of business.

If a sex worker or other person had been in this room, then we either had a witness or a lead on the killer.

I slipped out the door, disposing of the booties but shoving the respirator into my suit coat pocket. It strained the fabric and slapped against my side as I jogged to the elevator. I was just in time to see the doors whisk closed and hear the cab start its descent. I wasn't going to get another crack at talking to the divination officer that night.

I went home to shower, feed the cat, and ponder how long I'd have to put up with this nightmare of a case. I got the answer to that question when my pager buzzed at six a.m. the next morning. The three-digit code in the display face told me all I needed to know: report to HQ.

3

WHEN I ROLLED IN TO the Bunker it was busier than I'd ever seen it. Reporters clustered outside, waving hands and asking for quotes, and in the hallways a buzz of excitement ran through the staff. In the Homicide department all non-police personnel were banned from the floor as Captain Bryyh called us into a large open area ringed by desks, the Bullpen where homicide cases were organized and duties distributed.

We packed in, two dozen bleary-eyed detectives in rumpled suits and ties. Except for Angus, of course. He looked like he'd stopped at the dry cleaners on the way to the office.

Captain Bryyh stepped into the middle of the circle, a gas station coffee in one hand and a manila folder in the other.

"All right, all right. Cut the noise already." Her tightly braided hair had long since gone to gray, and a pair of reading glasses perched on her forehead.

"You all know what we're here for." The last of the background noise dropped away. "The Squib killing is this department's A-1 priority. All—and I mean ALL—available resources are to be redirected to this case until otherwise ordered. Detective Kravitz is on point."

She motioned to a tall man with a lengthy beard who inclined his head in acknowledgment. Bryyh continued, "All roads lead through him, got it?"

There was a gentle murmuring, to which I added my own grunt of assent. Kravitz was a competent detective, maybe even good. He excelled at being even-tempered and thorough, and he had the organizational chops to run a big investigation. Of course, the fact that he'd just closed a big case didn't hurt. The Reynolds case was something he could hang his hat on. Even if I was the one who'd done all the footwork. But I told myself it didn't matter who got the credit, or the promotions, as long as the bad guys got locked up. And it had the bonus of stripping Angus of his lead detective status.

Bryyh deferred to Kravitz for the case brief, a summary for anyone who didn't already know the basics. The victim was a Squib environmental scientist named Garson Haberdine. Middle-aged, no known criminal habits. Last seen by hotel staff earlier that night. The security tapes had been confiscated and would be reviewed shortly. None of this was news to me, and I thrummed my fingers while I waited to hear something I could use. I thought the findings of the DO would be next on the agenda, but there wasn't so much as a peep about them. Instead, Kravitz looked up from his report and chewed on his beard.

"Haberdine was a member of the Squib delegation negotiating the wind farm project."

The room was silent. With each oil well that went dry, the city's economic position grew shakier. The mayor's office, along with the feds, was desperately trying to set up foreign investors to fund alternative energy options. The only plan that had gained any traction was converting the oil fields to wind farms. But building all those turbines would require a massive influx of cash, and the Squibs were the only interested party with deep enough pockets.

If this murder derailed the talks, Titanshade could be reduced to a ghost town within a generation.

"Expect press coverage on this one, ladies and gentlemen." Bryyh paced a tight circle as she spoke. "So remember the three Bs. Be polite. Be professional. Behave in public." She scanned the crowd but got no dissent from us.

"I'm not going to lie. There is strong political pressure on this case. We are going to present a unified face to the city and to the Squib delegation. To that end we will be working in pairs. One human, one Mollenkampi." That caused a stir. Detectives got to work alone. It was a perk of the job.

I looked to my right and made eye contact with Angus.

Oh, Hells, I thought. Across the room, Angus rolled his eyes. At least he didn't want this to happen any more than I did. But at that moment, it seemed all but inevitable.

Bryyh read the first pair of names. "Coriander and Jenkins."

A human and Mollenkampi raised their hands, glanced at each other, and looked back at the captain.

"You're sorting through the tips."

Some joker quipped, "Good luck."

High-profile cases saw hundreds of tips flood the call center. This one would likely break all previous records. I shot Jenkins a jealous look; I'd have gladly worked my way through an encyclopedia's worth of tips if it meant I didn't have to spend an extra second playing nice with Angus.

Bryyh kept working her way through the list of pairs. "Andreeson and Torvold . . . Robinson and Alonso." Finally she came to me.

"Carter . . ." she paused. "And whoever drew the short straw."

My esteemed colleagues chuckled through mouthfuls of coffee. My reputation has always preceded me. Bryyh pointed at a young Mollenkampi who had only recently transferred to Homicide. "Ajax," she said, "that would be you."

I looked at my new partner. Like all male Mollenkampi, his name started with an A. That's the reason some people called them A-holes. Well, mostly the reason.

Ajax returned my look with an expression I couldn't quite identify. It took me a minute to place it, but as he rubbed the leathery plates along the side of his head I realized what it was. That snot-nosed newbie was wearing the same expression I had on my face when I thought I'd be paired with Angus. What little expectation I had for this partnership idea tanked quickly.

The captain finished the roll call of names, then began to hand out assignments. I pulled away from the larger group to introduce myself to young mister Ajax and see if we needed to establish the pecking order.

He greeted me with a polite "Detective," and I returned the pleasantry as we sized each other up. He was young, even for a Mollenkampi, who were shorter-lived than humans. His face plates shone like soldier's boots, and his nostrils flared slightly as we made eye contact. I had a few inches of height on him and I figured I could take him in a fight. That made me feel better. His eyes carried a certain confidence, and as he looked me over I could see him thinking he'd come out on top in that same hypothetical fight. That made me feel better, too. I like to be underestimated. I decided that if I ever needed to, I could fake an injury then take him out at the knees. You never want to hit a Mollenkampi in the face. As a general rule of thumb, never shove your hand in a blender, and don't punch a Mollenkampi in the jaw.

Captain Bryyh pushed her way between us.

"You'll have time to measure them later." She handed me a manila envelope. "Carter, you still know the class acts south of the Estates?"

I nodded. There was a healthy sex industry catering to the off-duty roughnecks and their oil rig paychecks. The cops in Vice kept things from getting out of hand, but there was no shutting down the trade completely. I'd worked that department for three years before transferring to Homicide, and I didn't miss it. Hunting down the average, run-of-the-mill psycho is far less depressing than working sex crimes.

"Good," said Bryyh. "The envelope has photos of three likely candies who were picked up on the hotel's security footage."

I tore open the package. From the top photo Talena Michaels stared back at me with sad eyes and pouty lips.

"Any of them look familiar?" asked Bryyh.

I slid the photos into my suit pocket. "These are fresh faces. None of them were on the street when I transferred out of Vice."

Bryyh grunted. "Alright. Find out who they are and where to find them. Talk to them, their pimps, anybody potentially related. Type up a brief and send it to Kravitz." Assignment delivered, Bryyh walked over to another pair of detectives who were giving each other the stink eye.

I adjusted my coat and glanced at my new partner. "If you're ready, Ajax?"

He was already moving toward the door, a rolling stride that was barely interrupted when he called over his shoulder, "Call me Jax. It's less formal."

His voice harmonized as he spoke. Mollenkampi can create undertones in their biting jaws while speaking through their eating mouths. Their native language is tonal and musical, almost impossible for humans to replicate, which is why all the Mollenkampi on the force spoke our language. But some of them still used tonality as a matter of style.

The elevator slid downward, and I glanced at my new partner. Ajax wore a brown suit and tie not too dissimilar from my own. It occurred to me that we looked depressingly like twins. Well, apart from the six-inch tusks sticking out of his face.

"You're new," I said.

He nodded. "Moved here a couple weeks ago. I was down in Kohinoor previous."

"That's to the south, right?" It's an old joke. Everything's to the south of Titanshade. He didn't laugh. "How long since you made detective?" I asked.

"Just before I moved."

Not only had I been given a partner, he was fresh off the bus with almost zero job experience.

"When we check out the crime scene, you may want to take a pass. That's okay," I said. "It's a rough one."

"I know. I was there last night."

A flash of recognition hit me. "You're the one with hot hands."

"Excuse me?"

"When the DO threw her—" I waved it off. "Doesn't matter."

He squinted his eyes, one mandible curling in thought. "You were in the room? Angus made a big deal of keeping you out of there."

I didn't respond.

"Not in so many words," he said, pausing as the elevator's ding announced our arrival in the garage. "But yeah. You weren't supposed to be there." He tilted his head in a slight salute. "But you got in anyway."

I held the elevator doors open but didn't leave the cab.

"You oughta know," I said. "If you want your face in the papers,

I'm not the person to be working with." The smell of diesel and grease rolled in from the garage. "In fact, if you want a pat on the back from the brass, or even a healthy career, you shouldn't be anywhere near me."

"So I've heard," he said.

He didn't elaborate, and I'd pretty much tapped out my social skills, so I stopped talking and led the way into the garage.

We were assigned our car. It was standard issue: two doors with a small storage space that the marketing department at Hasam Motors insisted on calling a backseat. Cars tend to be small in Titanshade to accommodate the narrow, winding streets. That was fine in theory, but if we made any collars we'd have to call for a wagon to pick them up or ride back to the Bunker with a killer on our lap. I glanced at the dash and was happy to see that it had an 8-track.

I took the keys from the attendant and twirled them around my finger.

"Feel free to call shotgun," I told Ajax, and got behind the wheel.

4

OUR LITTLE CAR HUGGED THE corners as I slalomed us through the early morning traffic. The nice thing about cop cars in Titanshade is that the boys in the shop keep them tuned nice and tight. I glided up to a stoplight and paused, waiting for the light to turn green.

Our destination lay straight ahead. But while I stared at the red light the thought of Talena's photo and that small sticker remnant on the Do Not Disturb sign whirled in my mind.

When I took a sudden right turn, Ajax looked up from fiddling with the radio.

"We taking the scenic route?"

"Just a quick stop before we talk to the candies."

"Yeah? Where's that?"

A heavily filtered bass line bounced from the Hasam's speakers, followed by a trumpet's trill. I slapped Ajax's hand off the dial.

"No disco," I said. "They can make us work together, but I am *not* listening to disco."

Ajax sat back, and I spun the dial to the other end of the spectrum, tuning in to WYOT, where I knew my favorite DJ wouldn't let me down. We were immediately rewarded by a slinky guitar riff dripping with reverb. I turned up the volume and pointed at the radio.

"Now that," I said, "is music."

"If you say so." Ajax rolled down his window. "Where are we headed?"

"Place I know called the Hey-Hey."

He didn't push for details, so I didn't volunteer any.

A few minutes later we pulled up to the Hey-Hey, parking in the glow of a flickering neon sign that declared with eloquent simplicity: "Liquor."

We were in the Borderlands, the mist-shrouded edge of Titanshade, where the thermal vents were fewer and the buildings farther apart. Farther leeward, away from the Mount, were the ice plains, the zone where no vents shared the life-giving warmth of the fallen god's agony, and where no one could live without expensive electric heating. The Borderlands carried enough chill to keep most city residents farther in-mountain, but for roughnecks accustomed to ice-shrouded machines on frozen oil fields it was a tropical paradise.

"Alright," I said. "Keep your eyes and ears open. Once we leave this car, we've got no connection with dispatch or other patrol cars."

Ajax eyed the entrance of the bar with obvious suspicion. The heavy steel front door sported a number of dents, several of which looked fresh.

"What are we doing here?"

"Reconnaissance," I said.

"Reconnaissance on what, exactly?"

I opened my door. "Watch and learn, partner."

We walked in and I tipped my head to the bartender. I didn't know her but she nodded back, making me as a cop even if she couldn't remember my name any better than I could remember hers. She'd leave us in peace.

Ajax looked over the thinly populated interior. Titanshade

never sleeps, but at this hour even the average Hey-Hey patron was hard to find. There were maybe a half-dozen rough-looking customers slumped in booths or at tables, either nursing a hangover or trying to keep the drunk from last night going strong.

"Reconnaissance, huh?" he mumbled.

"Reconnaissance," I said. By then I'd spotted who I was looking for, and I made a beeline for Simon, the big green man of the hour.

Squibs were a rarity in Titanshade, and I didn't know much of anything about them. But Gillmyn were plentiful, known for their strength and prized as workers on the oil rigs. They hailed from the southern hemisphere, roughly the same area as Squibs. I was hoping that one of them would know something useful. We had a few Gillmyn on the force, mostly beat cops doing community relations in areas with high Mollenkampi/human strife. I could've talked to one of them, but since this was outside our assigned duties, I thought it'd be best to keep things informal. And the talk I planned on having with the Gillmyn in the khaki pants and ribbed thermal shirt was about as informal as it got. I tilted my head in his direction, and he cursed and looked away. Simon never liked being seen with cops, but that wasn't really my problem.

The girl sharing his table stood and walked away as we approached, and I saw Simon's big hand tighten around his beer bottle. That made me smile. I sat down in a chair across the table from the Gillmyn. Ajax stayed on his feet, watching the rest of the clientele.

I held my hands out, showing that I held no weapon, and put them palms down on the table's edge.

"Been a long time," I said.

"Not long enough." Simon's thickly layered neck gills flared, revealing the purple-to-pink blush of his buccal cavity. His body was being pumped full of oxygen, like a human breathing heavy. Simon was getting ready for fight or flight.

"I've got some questions for you," I said.

"I don't have answers." He looked over my shoulder at Ajax. "Since when do humans and Mollenkampi run in packs?"

"He's my partner," I said.

Simon snorted and took a swig of beer. "Mammals," he said. It sounded like the filthiest slur he could think of.

Ajax's voice tinkled. "We're all just different Families on the Road."

I was surprised by the religious response. I wondered if Ajax was a believer or if he thought it would calm Simon down. If so, it didn't work.

Simon shot Ajax an obscene gesture with his free hand—not the easiest thing to do with webbed fingers. I could feel my partner tensing up. That was no good. I cleared my throat, bringing Simon's attention back to me.

"You got five seconds to talk, big man."

The answer came as a roar, and the Gillmyn's beer bottle whistled through the air. It exploded against the wall, missing my head by a country mile. Simon threw his chair back and pulled himself up to his full height. He doubled over just as quickly when I shoved the table forward and slammed the far edge into his gut. I didn't go full speed, of course. There was no reason to really hurt the big guy.

His head hit the table and I grabbed the back of his shirt collar, spinning him around and shoving him in front of us as I ran him toward the back room. Propelling him forward strained my lower body. Pain danced along my legs and hips. I did my best to make the resulting grimace look like an angry snarl. This was no time to show weakness.

Ajax was beside me, one hand on his revolver, scanning the crowd for hostile faces.

We stormed into the back room, where a small group of men

stood around a pool table. From the dice and scattered bills, it looked like they were in the middle of a game of craps.

"Everyone out!" I barked and threw the Gillmyn down on a chair. The wooden legs creaked in a way that gave me a great shiver of satisfaction.

There was a clatter of fallen chairs and toppled pint glasses as the room cleared. If any of the gamblers questioned how a middle-aged cop could push around a hulking knee-breaker like Simon, they didn't bother speaking up. I kicked the door shut behind them and jammed a chair under the handle. Ajax shot me a look, but he followed my lead. He was practically radiating tension. Now that it was just the three of us, I decided it was time to clue him in.

"Ajax, meet Simon. CI number 287-B."

Simon stood. "I don't know what you're talking about. We're done here."

I couldn't blame him. It's a risky side job, being a criminal informant. To put his nerves at rest I reached into my back pocket and pulled out a wad of bills.

"I told you he's my partner. The kid's clean."

At least I hoped he was. While Ajax had the distinct whiff of honesty about him, I knew that in Titanshade appearances could be deceiving, and innocence was a fragile and fleeting state of existence.

Simon wavered, glancing from the cash to me. Finally his greed won out. He dropped back into the chair.

"What do you want?"

"The usual report," I said, "but I need something additional, as well."

"Fine," said Simon. "Let's make it sound convincing."

I picked up a chair and flung it across the room where it struck the corner with a resounding crash, then sat down on another and pulled out my notebook.

Simon had gotten onto my radar a couple years back when I'd found a dead roughneck in an alley. He'd been the loser in a particularly contentious argument over how to split winnings from a lottery ticket. Simon had witnessed the fight, and had been willing to roll on the guy who walked away in exchange for a few drinks. That had been the start of a long and mutually beneficial relationship as my confidential informant. He was a mid-weight thug in the city's underbelly who did all his business out of the Hey-Hey, and he reported to me every two weeks or whenever I needed a tip.

Simon rattled off a list of recent moves in the underworld, most of which I'd already heard from standing near the water cooler at the Bunker. I jotted them down anyway and listened to him complain about the mood around the neighborhood. Word of the Haberdine murder had spread faster than I'd expected. Rumors were flying, and everyone had a theory about what it meant for the wind farms, for the city, and ultimately for their own ability to make a living.

Simon dragged a hand over the hairless green dome of his head and grunted. "And the situation's not gonna be helped by you guys shaking me down in my backyard. Can't you just use the phone like a civilized human being?" He glanced at Ajax. "No offense. I'm sure you guys are civilized too. Only with more, you know . . ." He waved a webbed hand in front of his mouth. "Tusks, or whatever."

I snapped my fingers in Simon's face, and his watery eyes moved from Ajax to me. "What do you know about Squibs?" I asked. "Habits, temperament . . . anything at all."

Simon huffed out a wet sigh that stunk of algae and fish food.

"What do I look like, a school book?"

Ajax sighed and glanced at his watch.

I turned my head toward the door and screamed an unspeakable insult about Simon's parentage, sure to be heard in the bar. Simon grunted.

"Nice, Carter."

"So," I said. "Squibs."

His long arms spread in a shrug. "Look, I can tell you what I've heard, but I don't know much."

"Just tell us what you do know, big guy." I didn't say it harsh but I didn't say it gently, either.

"Squibs're like frogs." He rubbed his head again, evidently straining to come up with more detail. "They like to stay wet. And wear hard armor."

"Hard armor?"

"Yeah," he said. "Like ceremonial stuff. It's like they enjoy touching firm material after spending so much time in the mud."

Simon seemed to pick up on our disinterest in this piece of trivia, and he hurried to elaborate as he popped a bottle under his boot like a stray beetle.

"Think of a frog, sitting on a log and . . ." He trailed off, then tried again. "Or maybe a rock. A wet rock by the side of the river—"

"We understand the metaphor," Ajax said. "Get on with the story."

Simon grunted and resumed filling us in on everything he knew. I finally had to direct him to the area I was really interested in.

"What about sex?"

He blinked. "Sex?"

"Yeah. Any preferences you know of?"

"Hells, Carter, I don't have any idea. Why're you asking? You thinking about taking a walk on the wet side?"

This was useless. I changed the subject.

"Anyone you know got it out for Squibs? Any pimp or candy that had a bad experience, or someone holding a long grudge, running their mouth off when they're drinking?"

He shook his head. The Hey-Hey sat in disputed underworld territory, a handful of neighborhoods that shifted back and forth between at the overlap of two different outfits: the CaCuri twins and the Harlq Syndicate. It meant Simon was often a useful pair of ears, but in this case he wasn't turning out to be the source of inside information that I'd hoped. Simon didn't seem to be enjoying our talk either.

"You know, you showing up like this is bad for business," he said. "Second time in two days someone's come in here throwing his weight around. Makes me nervous about our little chats staying private." Simon crossed his arms and eyed Ajax.

I leaned in. "You said I'm the second person to come in here. Who was the first?"

"One of the CaCuri twins."

That could be useful. I motioned for him to continue.

"Thomas made the rounds last night, gold on his fingers and running his mouth, telling everyone that this is a CaCuri neighborhood whether they like it or not."

"How'd that go over?"

Simon's gills flared. "Couple people mouthed off as they were leaving. CaCuri ran after and talked to 'em outside."

That explained the new dents we'd seen from the car.

"Any of the Harlq boys come around to set him straight?"

Ajax spoke up quickly. "This is Harlq turf?"

I'd said it "Har-lek," the best I could manage with human vocal chords, but Ajax pronounced it more accurately, with a deep thrumming undercurrent of menace. He'd also slid one foot back and dropped his shoulders. Almost, but not quite, a fighting stance.

"It ebbs and flows." I filed away his reaction for later reference. "Depending on who's got more money and drugs that week."

I turned my attention to my informant and repeated my question. "Did the Harlqs come by?"

Simon shuffled his feet.

"Naw," he said. "Seemed like CaCuri almost wanted 'em to, but they didn't show."

Maybe that meant they were busy killing a diplomat. Maybe CaCuri was working hard to establish an alibi. Maybe it all meant nothing.

"And the other twin?" I asked.

"She wasn't around," he said. "Which was fine by me. She's the scary one."

I grunted. Gangster types doing gangster stuff didn't give us much to go on.

"Alright. That's it for now," I said. I slapped Simon on the shoulder and tucked the wad of cash into his shirt pocket.

Ajax turned for the door.

"Not quite yet," I said.

Simon groaned. "Dammit."

I scratched the side of my nose. "You know we need to do it."

He stared at the ceiling for a long beat, then sighed. "Alright."

"Where do you want it?" I asked.

Simon tapped the space between his right eye and nose, a delicate stretch of skin on a Gillmyn that would swell and bruise dramatically without any real damage. The butt of my gun followed a moment later. We crashed one more chair for good measure, then let ourselves out. Simon stayed behind, his rapidly swelling face a testament to the way he'd refused to talk to the cops. I dropped a small wad with the bartender as an apology for the damages. I'd turn in a receipt for the expense account later. Confidential Informants are a standard expense.

Jax kept tight to my side as we held our hands over the entrance vent, the remaining clientele staring daggers at our backs. Once we were outside he turned to me with fire in his eyes.

"You want to tell me what all that was about?" His voice crackled, the needle-sharp teeth in his speaking mouth tapping together.

I walked away, putting a little space between us as I pulled the car keys out of my pocket.

"Just getting background," I said.

He closed the gap again. "Yeah? That Gillmyn give some insight we needed to talk to candies?"

I spread my arms as we approached our ride. "You never know when we're gonna run into some Squibs, is all."

My new partner grabbed my outstretched arm and spun me so that I fell against the rear of our car. I found myself staring into livid eyes, deep-set above powerful jaws with teeth more like horns than molars. His biting jaw was still, but his mandibles clenched as his voice rose from the sharp-toothed hole in his neck.

"Squibs have a parliamentary system," he said. "They eat a largely vegetarian diet supplemented with occasional fish. Their monarch is a figurehead, but she's immensely popular, and the nobility still pulls most of parliament's strings." He tapped me in the chest, flipping my tie to one side. I didn't move, and he kept talking.

"They have shorter lifespans than we do, and significantly shorter than humans. They put great pride in the longer-lived of their species, and elders are venerated."

"Alright," I said, "point taken. It was a wasted trip."

"Oh, no. I think that it was certainly worth the risk of pissing off a bar full of half-drunk lowlifes in order to find out Squibs wear 'hard armor.' It's not like we couldn't have picked that up from the royal seal—the one with their queen in full plate mail. Because after all, we probably would have assumed that they preferred some of that *soft* armor that's so popular lately."

I adjusted my tie, keys jangling in my hand. "In my opinion sarcasm is unprofessional."

"Apologies. It's a bad habit I picked up in college." Ajax leaned forward, bringing his biting jaws closer to my face as he plucked the keys from my hand. "You know, where I took poli-sci courses about the Southern Crossing cultures, like Squibs. Or you would've known"—he held my gaze—"if you bothered to ask me what I could contribute to this case."

Jax turned away and unlocked the passenger door. Before entering he turned back to me. "My point," he said, "is that the next time you think we need intelligence, you ask your partner what he knows first." He slid the keys across the roof of the car. "Now are you driving or what?"

I know when I'm beaten. I didn't say a word, just got in and started the engine. There was no more putting it off. It was time to visit the candies, and Talena's photo still weighed heavy in my pocket.

5

BRYYH HAD TOLD US TO go to the Estates, a former old money neighborhood teetering on the verge of gentrification. Up there the candies were high class and didn't prowl the streets. Her order made sense, given the fashionable way the candies in the photos had been dressed. But I knew better. So instead of the Estates we drove along the south end of the Borderlands, where the air was colder and the tricks came cheaper.

Young men and women for sale stood in carefully rehearsed poses, some swooping or parading while others teetered on the cobblestones, drunk or high on whatever was easiest to get that week. Some of them had probably been out here since last night. When the roughneck crews rolled into town the derrick workers could blow through a month's wages in a night or two. The entire illicit economy of the city had evolved to take advantage of that opportunity. Titanshade never sleeps, and it has no shame. Which is why we could count on open prostitution even in the early morning.

Ajax scanned the crowd, absently scraping the side of his left tusk with one mandible. "How often does Vice sweep down here?"

"When they get enough complaints. But it doesn't change anything. The candies aren't the problem, it's the pimps."

"And the johns."

"And the johns," I conceded. "No matter what way you cut it, the wrong people get arrested down here."

I parked the car in a fire zone, pulled out the three pictures of candies the captain had given us, and spread them on the dash of the car. I tapped the picture of Talena. Frosted blond hair pulled up in fashionable curls, she wore layered clothing topped by nice furs.

"When we find her," I said, "I'll do the talking."

"Yeah?"

"Yeah."

There was a pause while Jax looked at the photos. Each showed a young, well-dressed woman, two humans and one Mollenkampi. Both the humans' hair was done up immaculately, and all three would have looked comfortable walking into a high-end hotel like the Eagle Crest.

"It's the layers that give them away," I said. "If they could afford rooms in a place like the Eagle Crest, they wouldn't be wearing that much clothing."

Like almost everything in the city, the weather got colder and less genteel the farther you got from the mountain. Most people in Titanshade dressed for the neighborhoods where they lived or worked. It made it easy to distinguish the haves from the have-nots at a glance. Only the truly rich could afford to wear a single layer of thin fabric, while people who moved from neighborhood to neighborhood wore layers that could be peeled off or replaced as needed. People like cops, or candies who made visits to posh hotels.

Ajax looked from the photos to the bleary-eyed candies milling around on the streets.

"I don't think we're going to find these girls in the Borderlands."

He kept his voice neutral, but the newly minted detective was uncomfortable with ignoring Bryyh's direction. I couldn't blame him, considering I'd already pulled him along on one unexpected stop.

"She'll be down here." I pointed at Talena's photo. "And she can tell us where to find the other two."

"You know her?"

I ran my tongue over the dry edge of my lips. "I knew her mom."

There was a slight hum from Jax's speaking mouth. It was a soft, sympathetic sound. I saw him glance from Talena's photo to my profile, looking for family resemblance.

Smart, I thought.

I took a breath and prepared to launch into an explanation, but his oversized jawbones clicked together, and I held my tongue. He'd done the math, knew she couldn't be my kid.

Even smarter.

"Alright," he said. "When we find her, you do the talking."

I'd expected a little more pushback from him after the dustup at the bar and was grateful that I didn't get it. But I wanted to be clear about something.

"Look," I said, "Talena's no candy."

Jax nodded.

"Sure," he said.

"I mean it."

He shrugged. "I'm not arguing, Carter."

I saw his glance drop to the picture of Talena on the dash. Even well-dressed and done up, to a cop's jaundiced eye she clearly had an air about her that said "for sale." I gave up.

"You'll see when you meet her."

∞

We prowled up and down the Borderlands' strips in the Hasam, keeping an eye out for the faces in our photos. Candies peered back at us from the usual spots: shaded in doorways or shadowed under the awnings of closed buildings, dark figures in silhouette, only legs and the bottoms of shorts showing, clothing that was slightly too skimpy for the chill of the fog in the air.

The candies were a mix of Mollenkampi and humans, in roughly the same ratio as their clients. Some johns and janes liked to cross species lines, and human and Mollenkampi parts are compatible, but there was no chance of reproduction. "About the same odds as you getting your gym sock pregnant after one of your more romantic nights in," the sergeant had told me on my first day working Vice.

I passed on that nugget of wisdom to my new partner, and he snorted.

"You shouldn't judge," I said. The slow parade of flesh continued past our windows. "Sex is ninety percent mental, kid."

"Maybe at your age."

I shot him a disapproving glare.

"I wasn't judging," he said. "People take solace where they can find it."

I glanced over at his massive jaws and the thick plates that covered his hairless head.

"Right," I said, and shifted in my seat. "Anyway, that's why I asked my CI about Squib preferences. If our vic had some company in that room, I'd like to know about it."

"Isn't that a better question for the candies themselves?"

"Sure, but here's a tip from an old cop: Whenever possible work in some questions you already know the answer to. It'll help separate out who's full of crap."

From down the street someone screamed a string of blisteringly vile curses, and I knew we'd found Talena. At the other end of the block a corner had cleared except for a man and two women. The guy was human, early twenties, heavy acne, denim jeans, matching vest, and raw rage in his eyes. The kind of guy who preyed on the vulnerable and fragile. One of the women he yelled at did look fragile. The other, standing between them, was Talena.

Talena was a ray of light. She wasn't a candy or a cop. She wasn't even a social worker, trying to help people limp through a broken system. She was an activist. And she thought she could change the world.

As we pulled over, the guy's face had turned red from bellowing obscenities at Talena. She kept her cool, though. It was when he reached for the candy behind her that she snapped.

The guy had thirty pounds and a couple inches of reach on her but Talena didn't hesitate. She attacked like she had to tear him apart. Underdogs don't have the luxury of pulling their punches.

It was the opposite of the show I'd put on at the Hey-Hey. No shouting, no swearing. Just strikes backed by every muscle in her body, landing where they'd have the most impact. The assault threw her opponent off balance and he fell back. Talena kept coming, relentless. Exactly like I taught her.

By the time we got to them, the guy had curled in on himself, head tucked between his hands. But he was still on his feet, so she hadn't let up. Each blow staggered him more. Knee strikes to his thighs were followed by elbows to the back of his head. He wasn't going to be standing for much longer.

"Police!" I waved my badge in the air and the spectators melted away.

Talena spun, hands up, ready to deal with the new threat. When she saw me her lips pulled tight and she turned her back.

"I don't want to press charges!" She said it loud, so that everyone on the street could hear. Beating up a pimp or violent john is one thing, being seen as a snitch is another. Especially when he'd likely be back out on the street that same night.

I went to the trouble of reciting a toneless, "Sir, do you need assistance?"

The acne-faced man was already moving down the street. He waved us off without looking back, limping and drifting to one side before he disappeared into one of the city's countless winding alleyways. I guessed he didn't want to press charges, either.

Talena squatted down and gathered up the pamphlets she'd dropped when the fight started. I cleared my throat and she glared over her shoulder at me.

"What the Hells do you want, Carter?"

I didn't have time to reply before she stood and pointed a bruised finger at me.

"I don't even need to ask. You're here to round up candies to pacify some politician's election run, rather than actually get off your ass and do your job for a change."

Jax took a step back, surprised by the onslaught. I'd tried to tell him she was no candy. I counted to three and started over.

"I need to know where you were last night."

She stared at me. I stared back.

"Why?" she asked.

I pulled the photo of her from my pocket. Her eyes narrowed as she recognized herself. I tried asking again.

"Where were you last night, what were you doing, and who else was there?"

"Let me see that." She snatched the photo from my hand and examined it before looking back up at me.

"If you have camera footage then you know where I was. I was doing exactly what you think, and it's none of your damn business who was there." She barely paused as she glanced at Ajax. "Who are you?"

Talena wore conservative clothes. Thick flannel and boots that indicated she had no intention of going in-mountain today. The only jewelry she wore was a lapel pin in the shape of a sideways figure eight, the sign of the Infinite Path. Her hair was dark brown and pulled back in a ponytail rather than elaborate curls. Only her profile resembled the girl in the security footage.

I made introductions. "Talena, this is my partner, Detective Ajax. Ajax, this is Talena Michaels, activist and missionary."

"Missionary?" Jax's voice chirped, and his mandibles twitched. He glanced toward the alley where the pimp had disappeared.

"Is that so surprising?" Talena popped a hand on her hip and clutched her pamphlets to her chest. "You think that this world doesn't need missionaries?"

Jax's biting jaws opened and shut. "No," he said. "I just—"

"You thought that a woman in this part of town is more likely to turn a trick than turn a life around? Or maybe you were too busy picking out which of these kids to shake down for extra spending cash to notice someone who's actually trying to make a difference? Because I can tell you that I am damn tired of having to justify my work to pimps and cops who'd just as soon rob a widow as help her across the street."

Eyes darting from me to Talena and back, Jax shook his head. "No! No, I was—" He jerked a thumb over his shoulder and took a step backward. "You know, I'm actually going to wait by the car."

I watched my partner retreat, then faced Talena again. She was staring daggers at me.

I took another deep breath and let it out as a sigh.

"It's good to see you, kiddo."

The steel in her glance softened a little.

"Good to see you, too."

I pointed after the dispersing crowd. "You sure you don't want me to—"

She crossed her arms. "No. Dwayne's a little shit, but if you arrest him now it'll blow months spent building bridges out here."

I held my breath as a bus trundled by, kicking up a gray cloud of exhaust and street dirt. The sideboard advertising proclaimed in bold letters: OIL MADE US GREAT. OIL WILL KEEP US GREAT. Behind it, cars continued their slow prowl up and down the street.

"Look, this thing at the hotel," I said. "You heard about it?"

"Everyone's heard about it."

"It's a real nightmare. And I want to make sure it doesn't bite you. Now, what were you doing at the Eagle Crest?"

"The usual."

In other words, putting the "active" back in activist.

"You're still running your own stings." I shook my head. "You're going to get killed that way."

Talena and the other members of her activist group sometimes posed as candies, wearing a wire to record johns, then threatening to expose them if they came back to the neighborhood. The odds of running into an angry pimp or psychotic john were stupidly high, and she knew it. But she still tried to justify it.

"It's not a sting," she said, and stood a little straighter. "It's an intervention. And you never had a problem with it when you were down here."

I dropped my voice. "I didn't arrest you. That's not the same as giving you my blessing."

"What we do is economics. If the demand dries up, the pimps and candies shut down."

"No, they relocate. They move two blocks over and set up shop again."

She jerked a thumb over her shoulder, pointing at the candies lounging in doorways or approaching stopped cars. "I'm making a difference."

"You're making yourself a target. And if you think you're changing things out here you're kidding yourself."

She pulled back. "How do you go to sleep at night knowing there's this kind of violence going on all around you? I'm not willing to accept this is how it has to be. And if you think you can scare me off—"

I raised my hands.

"Yeah. I got it. And I know I can't stop you. But this is a dangerous game you're playing."

She closed her eyes and spoke in the affected cadence often used by human religious types. "To create change, you must become change."

I could tell she was quoting something, and my best guess was scripture. I knew I wouldn't win if I went down a rabbit hole. She had the fervor of youth and something else that was beyond me: faith.

A musical voice tinkled from behind us.

"Signposts may line the road, but they can only guide those who read them."

Ajax had moved in closer. Eavesdropping while staying out of Talena's fire. The kid had good instincts. I just wondered how much he'd overheard. If he'd picked up that I'd covered for Talena in any of her shakedowns, it could be a problem.

Talena opened her eyes and looked him over, a tight smile curling one side of her mouth.

"That's right," she said. "You can get all the signs you can handle, but if you don't take their advice, you'll find yourself wandering off the One Path."

Ajax nodded. "Maybe Carter and I are signs on your personal Path. Someone was killed in that hotel while you were there. The powers that be are demanding that someone be strung up for it, and the longer it takes, the less picky they'll be about getting the right one. You might end up in the crosshairs."

Talena's posture sagged, and for a second she looked young and vulnerable, a little girl standing at the edge of a haunted forest. The way she always looks in my mind.

"Alright," she said. "What do you want to know?"

"You went down there posing as a candy?" I asked.

"Yeah. There were two johns there."

"Both human?"

"Yeah." She shifted her folders from one arm to the other, and scanned the streets. Always looking for another lost sheep.

"What room were you in?"

"You're the one with photos."

"Speaking of which . . ." I held out my hand.

She rolled her eyes and fished the security photo from where she'd tucked it in amidst her papers. One of the now crumpled pamphlets stuck to the edge of the photo when she handed it to me. It wouldn't come free, so I slid them both into my jacket pocket.

"We only got photos of the lobby," I said. "The hotel doesn't record people coming and going from rooms. For 'privacy reasons.'"

Talena laughed. "That's so considerate of them. Room 324."

I breathed a little easier. The Squib had been found in room 430.

"Good. Now the names of the johns."

She smirked. "You've gotta be kidding."

"The names."

"My threats to expose them don't work if I actually give their names to the cops."

"I don't care about what you told those johns, I don't care about your shakedowns—"

"They're not shakedowns!"

"And I don't care about your friends. I just wanna make sure you're not caught in deeper shit than you already are," I said. "But you don't need to tell me that. You don't need to tell me anything. What you do with your life is up to you—I fulfilled my promise to your mom years ago." I hoped she couldn't read the lie on my face.

She rolled her eyes and looked away. I'm not sure if it was the mention of my promise to her mother, but something in my speech worked. She rattled off a description of the most bland, boring johns imaginable. I felt a tension drain from my chest. It sounded like she and her friends wouldn't be caught up in any of this madness. I asked my traditional parting question.

"Anything else stick with you from that night?"

"There was one thing." Talena shuffled her folders again. Restless. "I saw Stacie there, a girl from up in the Estates I've been trying to get out of the life. She was coming out as I was going in, and she was steaming about losing some high-paying job. Said she was going to have it out with her madame, because she'd come all the way down there to do kink work for some ambassador but it got canceled at the last minute."

Shit.

I heard Ajax move closer. No more than a step, but I knew his ears were glued to the conversation.

"Ambassador. You're sure she said 'ambassador'?"

"Yeah. Sounded like she'd been scheduled up for some weird service. She's got a higher tolerance for strange customers." She shook her head, angry at a world where that was a marketable skill. I couldn't blame her. "Anyway, might be useful with all your 'powers that be' problems."

I asked Talena for a description of Stacie, and it matched one of the candies from the surveillance photos. I flipped the photos in front of her, and she confirmed one as Stacie, though she didn't recognize the Mollenkampi girl. While she spoke she turned her head, watching one candy in particular emerge from the shadows, a teenage boy with a wicked purple bruise running across his cheek.

"Dammit." Talena's shoulders pulled back. "I've got to go."

"If we need more information—"

"Yeah, okay. Take care of yourself, Carter." She walked away with her folders full of pamphlets and scriptures, one hand in the air, yelling out, "Hey, Jermaine! We need to talk!"

Without taking his eyes off of Talena, Ajax mumbled, "So the 'ambassador' thing . . ."

"That's a big deal."

"What's this mean?" he said.

"We need to call this in to Kravitz." I paused, then added, "I want to be the one to talk to these diplomatic weasels."

So we called it in. We double parked at the corner of Sinclair and 23rd and sauntered up to the pay phone. I stuck a coin in the slot, and while the line rang I unconsciously fingered the change return for any neglected coins. I saw Ajax take note and I pulled my finger back, cheeks reddening at the idea he'd seen me scrounging for loose change.

Kravitz answered, already sounding worn down on the first day of the investigation. Ajax and I crowded in close so we could both hear the reaction when we delivered the news of Talena's scoop. Kravitz didn't exactly burst at the seams.

"Did you find this Stacie girl?" he said.

There was a pause while Ajax and I stared at the phone held between our ears.

"That's it?" I said. "How about some accolades for a major break?"

Ajax tugged the phone lower so it could pick up his voice. "The witness didn't know the girl's current whereabouts."

I pulled the phone back. "But it doesn't matter. We got enough to poke the politicians and see if they give anything up."

The phone twisted out of my hands as Ajax reclaimed it. This was exactly the kind of reason I didn't want a partner.

"What we're trying to ask is do we have permission to talk to the Squib delegation," Ajax said, then held the phone where we could both hear Kravitz's answer.

"No, you don't. Detectives Angus and Bengles met with the Squib delegation this morning."

There was silence on our end.

"Instead," Kravitz continued, "what I would like you to do is talk to the nice people at the AFS and see what you can find on this lead your candy turned up."

I clenched my teeth. "She's not a—"

Ajax interrupted. "Roger that," he said. "Do we have a liaison in the diplomatic world?"

"As a matter of fact we do," said Kravitz. "Roll back here and write up a full brief. I'll line up someone to talk to you at 1 Government Plaza."

I pulled the phone back to my mouth.

"This 'someone' has to be able to answer questions. I don't want to waste our time with some PR stooge who's only cleared to say 'no comment.'"

There was a pause, with only the crackle of a typical bad connection coming through the line, then Kravitz spoke again. "I'll get an appropriate interviewee, Detective. But I'm glad you mentioned PR. While you're in there, Ajax does the talking. Carter, you're cleared to listen."

"Wait a minute," I said. "I've got years of experience working the—"

"You've also got years of experience burning bridges, and right now we're all walking through a political minefield. These partnerships weren't assigned by rolling dice, Carter. Detective Ajax is there to cover your rear. I will set up this interview, but when you get there you will take notes and nod your head politely. You understand?"

I had a whole list of thoughts that I wanted to share with the good Detective Kravitz, but I pressed my lips tight and didn't say any of them. The phone's static crackled again.

"Carter?"

I pushed a knuckle against my teeth, trying to contain the vitriol that boiled up inside me. I almost pulled it off.

"Been meaning to congratulate you," I said. "For that Reynolds case." The one that I'd broken for him. "That was some fine detective work. Set you up for a nice promotion for this Haberdine thing."

I listened to the static pop and hiss in the long silence that followed.

"Just get your asses back to the Bunker," he said. "I'll have an answer when I have an answer." The line went dead and I slammed the receiver home hard enough to generate an extra ring of protest. I stared at it, seething, because I didn't trust myself to face Ajax yet. I closed my eyes and let out a breath, like the department shrinks had told me to do, then turned and looked at my partner. I saw a cop with decades less experience than me, who was apparently my assigned babysitter.

We stood in silence for a five count. He was the first to speak.

"You know you've got a reputation."

I braced myself.

"How's that reputation go?" I asked.

"You get in trouble. You act like you don't care about any of your cases, but when you latch on to one you'll obsess on it until your health breaks. You've got a temper, and you're a smartass. And you're honest."

"And?" If he'd heard that much about me, then he'd heard the worst of it as well.

"And you used to get your share of headlines. But not anymore."

"No," I said. "Not anymore."

His voice was strong and steady, emerging from the speaking mouth in the center of his throat. "And I know that it was a long time ago, but you still make people uncomfortable."

I looked away. I didn't want to dig up old memories. Not when they already haunted me every day.

It made me defensive, and I've found there's only one good response when I feel defensive. Go on the attack.

"Alright. You wanted me to ask about you," I said. "So tell me, Ajax: Who the Hells are you?"

His gaze was level, hands easy at his hips. "I grew up in Kohinoor. Went away to school." The teeth in his speaking mouth clicked, as if he were choosing his words with care. "Didn't work out. Came back home and joined the force. That didn't work out either."

"So now you're here."

"Now I'm here," he said.

"A backwater town like Kohinoor is a damn long way for Bryyh to find me a babysitter."

"Could be everyone local knew better than to take the job."

"Or maybe they didn't like the idea of snitching on other cops."

He threw his head back and groaned. "No one's snitching on you, Carter."

"Fine. You're not making reports." I said it with a laugh, showing him that I knew it for a lie. "Maybe you're just providing stories for Angus and his buddies back at the Bunker to snicker at."

Ajax crossed his arms and took a deep breath. He must have talked to the same shrinks I did.

"You know," he said. "For a guy who always gripes about being hated, you sure seem to have a lot of friends."

My fists clenched and I fought the urge to close in on him. Any reminder that some people still trusted me was a reminder that sooner or later they'd be burned. *Deep breaths,* I reminded myself. Captain Bryyh still trusted me, and she was the one who put Ajax and me together. Disappointing her on a regular basis was bad enough. I couldn't break my new partner's face before lunch.

I looked down as my hands disappeared into my pockets. Still clenched, but holstered for the moment. Ajax was the picture of calm. Maybe his shrinks were better than mine. *Or maybe . . .* I looked at him through squinted eyes, thinking of the ease with which he'd quoted scripture to Talena.

"That college you went to," I said. "What's it called?"

Now it was his turn to drop his eyes. I'd hit some kind of nerve. "Trelaheda."

"Imp's blades," I muttered, anger receding, though not quite evaporating. "You went to a *seminary*?"

"It's not a seminary," he said, anger finally creeping into his voice. "It's a full university. That also happens to have a . . ." He shifted his feet, trying to regain his composure. "A very strong theological program." He rubbed his forehead. "I studied political science, remember?"

I gave him an exaggerated frown. "If I look in your locker, am I gonna find a staff and frock hidden behind your jacket?"

"Oh, for—" His arms flew out to his sides. "I'm not a guide," he said. "I didn't even graduate!" He shrugged, and dropped his eyes again. "Like I said, it didn't work out."

We stood for a moment, him staring at the ground and me staring at him. I was starting to believe he might be genuine, a kid whose sincerity I'd mistaken for deceit.

"So," I said, breaking the silence. "A smartass with a temper. That's my reputation, huh?"

"More or less," he said.

"You've heard a lot of talk for someone who's only been here for two weeks."

"I guess I have," he said, and looked me in the eye. "But I think they're right about one thing—I do believe you're honest."

"Honesty." I coughed. "What do you know about honesty?"

"I know you've got a wad of cash for your CI in your pocket, but you're still checking for change in a pay phone. That tells me you're not skimming."

I spit on the sidewalk and walked away, toward our car. Ajax was showing his hand. A man carrying cash might scrounge for loose change if he's honest, or he might do it if he's obsessively greedy. The fact that my new partner went straight to the optimistic interpretation told me a lot. Ajax was a man of faith and optimism.

The city would cure him of both before too long.

WE PUSHED THROUGH THE DOUBLE glass doors of the Titanshade Police Department like two old-time lawmen entering a saloon. The Bunker was a hive of activity. It was always busy, but the Squib killing seemed to energize even the admittance clerks and security guards at the front desk.

The floor mural of the Titanshade city crest was less scuffed than usual, as if the cleaning crew had recently been by, and the flags of Titanshade and the Assembly of Free States hung on either side of the hall. Which flag hung higher was a point of constant contention, and varied with the political climate. Currently the AFS flag rode higher, a nod to the perilous position the city held if we couldn't come to an agreement on the future of the oil fields.

We made our way up to Homicide on the third floor. We took a minute to move our desks side by side, a tiny island in the chaos of the Bullpen. Around us some of our fellow detectives were hacking out reports in triplicate on clacking typewriters while others were on phones, the pigtail curl of handset cords wrapped around tense fingers as they yelled or cajoled their way through the waves of leads that were coming in, almost all of which were entirely a waste of time. Once we were set up we wrote a report of our own, a one-pager on what we'd learned that day. Then we took it to Kravitz.

The lead detective sat at the edge of the Bullpen behind a desk piled with papers, chewing on a yellow pencil as he listened to a pair of our peers make a plea for assistance as they worked through the list of every guest checked into the Eagle Crest the night of Haberdine's murder. He interrupted them with a wave of his hand.

"We don't have the people," he said. "And if we did, they'd be put on another part of the case first." He wiped an arm across his forehead. His sleeves were rolled up and sweat stains discolored his shirt along the edges of his suspenders. "Keep on it. Don't stop until every name on that guest book is accounted for."

He glared at us, and I bit my tongue and looked away.

"Well?" he asked. There was already another pair of cops behind us, waiting to talk to him.

Ajax summarized the report and made our pitch for interviewing the AFS diplomatic corps.

"Alright," Kravitz said, giving his beard a tug. "You two grab some lunch and I'll think on it."

It's not unusual to wait around for orders like that. Much of police work is hurry-up-and-wait, punctuated by moments of abject terror. But at least it comes with a pension.

We turned to go, and Kravitz cleared his throat.

"Carter, hang back a second."

Jax drifted to the Bullpen's big board, a patchwork of chalkboard and cork that laid out the Eagle Crest crime scene photos and the list of notable persons related to the case. He stared at the chart of which detectives were tracking each lead, allowing Kravitz and me some privacy.

Kravitz rubbed the side of his nose and started to speak, but was interrupted by a muffled yell from the far end of the room. Captain Bryyh was in her office, barking into her phone. I wasn't sure who she was raking over the coals, but I was glad that for once it wasn't me.

I looked to Kravitz. "That what it sounds like when I'm on the other end of the line?"

Kravitz considered, then shook his head. "Not enough swearing."

I chuckled. Kravitz looked around and spoke in a low voice.

"Look, that Reynolds' case was good work."

"Yeah," I said. Carmen Reynolds was a banker who'd funneled immense wealth away from her clients, and received a lead slug in her skull in return. Turned out to be one of her coworkers who'd done the deed.

Kravitz chewed his lip. "You did the lion's share of labor closing it up," he said.

Since I'd done everything but cinch the cuffs I figured that was an understatement, but I didn't point that out.

"It's a damn shame, the way you gotta hide in the shadows."

"The price of fame," I said. It was how all my jobs worked, the result of the permanent stain I carried from my earliest days on the force. Anything I handled was handed off at the last minute for another detective to take credit.

When he started to say more I interrupted him. "Not your fault. It's just the way it is."

Maybe he felt like he owed me one. Maybe he resented me for it. Probably both.

"I'm gonna go eat," I said. "Just let me know when we can talk to the AFS people."

Neither of us brought up the earlier phone conversation. But we'd at least got to a point where we could ignore it, so we left it there. Sometimes that's the best you can do.

Ajax and I made our way down the back stairs of the Bunker and out the less ostentatious side entrance that emptied onto Lestrange Ave. There were always food trucks pulled up along Lestrange, catering to a police force that went long hours between meals and often craved comfort food to help salve the stress of crime scenes and corruption. The food trucks were a never-ending source of deep-fried pastries and processed meat wrapped in artificial cheese product. Unhealthy food for unhealthy cops. The job may have come with a pension but it was a wonder any of us lived long enough to enjoy it.

Running between the Bunker and the sidewalk was a raised bed of grass, or at least grass-looking weeds. There were even a few benches where it was possible to sit and enjoy a meal while gazing up at the skyline and the mountain behind it all. It wasn't a bad way to spend a lunch break.

As we walked down Lestrange we saw two lanky figures in suits, one Mollenkampi and the other human. The Mollenkampi had one foot propped up on a bench as he brushed a scuff from his shoe. It was Angus, of course. The human was a tall woman who I took to be his partner. She bounced up and down on the balls of her feet, like a boxer keeping loose before the starting bell.

Angus spotted us as we approached. He straightened and put his hands on his hips, spreading his sport coat in a vee that looked straight out of a catalog advertisement. He called out to us, or rather, to me.

"How did chasing candies go? Turn up anything useful or just add a new STD to your collection?"

Angus lacked the empathy to actually care what happened to a few candies. Which was fine by me. I still hoped to avoid the notion that candies might be involved. Or anyone associated with candies. Like an idealistic activist who sometimes blackmailed johns. Or an ex-vice cop who didn't bend over backward to get them to stop.

I made a show of scanning the area. "You look like you've had a productive morning out here guarding the benches from pigeon bombing raids."

Angus turned to the woman at his side. "Bengles, this is Detective Carter."

Bengles jerked her chin at me in acknowledgment and flashed a grin so full of teeth and gums that it verged on caricature.

"Heard'a you," she said before greeting my partner. "Ajax, right? Guess Bryyh wasn't joking when she said you pulled the short straw."

Ajax shrugged. "It's possible she didn't measure right."

Bengles's smile grew even wider. "We'll see." She held her suit coat over one shoulder and the cuffs of her new shirt were folded up, exposing tattoos and sinewy muscle. The woman's grin was unnerving. Combined with her constant movement, it gave her the air of someone ready to lash out at any moment and with little warning. Judging from her frame and the way she rolled on her feet, I didn't want to be on the wrong side of her when that happened.

"What did our young friends on the street have to say for themselves?" asked Angus.

"Not much, and not that it matters. I don't see some frail kid doing that kind of damage, anyway."

Angus's mandibles stretched and contracted. "Could be a connection," he said. "Wealthy politico gets his own room apart from his colleagues? Could be he had a discreet get-together planned, then something happened to make things go deadly."

I needed to change the subject. With Angus, that meant using his ego as a distraction.

"Heard you talked to the Squib delegation." I let a note of jealousy creep into the edges of my voice.

He didn't disappoint. "We did," he said, giving his tie a pompous tug. "Can't talk about it, though. So many sensitive topics—you understand."

Just like that, he'd forgotten the candies completely.

"We're about to eat," I said. "Are you two gonna stay out here for long? Cause I don't want to lose my appetite."

"Relax. We're headed inside," he said. "Watch out for the pigeon shit on the benches. I couldn't stop them all."

Jax and I watched the sharply dressed pair walk back to the Bunker. My partner rubbed the plates on the back of his head.

"What's your deal with him, anyway?" he asked.

"Angus?"

"Your archnemesis."

"He's not my archnemesis," I said. "He's just a dick."

"You seem to hate each other in an archnemesis kind of way."

"Nah, he's not evil, he's just . . . I don't know."

That was a lie. But how do you say that someone is the embodiment of everything you were always told to be? Clean, polite, presentable, respectable. I didn't like Angus because he managed to be everything I couldn't hold together, and Angus didn't like me because I was successful without using the trappings he did. Maybe we just threatened each other's sense of self. But that's not really something you hash out while standing in line for a food truck with someone you've known for less than a day. So I changed the subject again.

"Did you notice his partner's clothes?"

Jax snorted. "Yeah. Her outfit still had new-shirt folds in it. You think he took her clothes shopping first thing?"

"I think Angus tries to make everything around him fit his persona."

"That includes people?"

"People, clothes . . . facts." I sneezed into the crook of my arm. "What do you want for lunch?" I scanned the options. "Looks like you can choose between grilled sausage links or boiled sausage links."

Seated on a bench with grilled sausages and coffees, I craned my head back to stare at the mist-shrouded form of the Mount looming on the edge of the city, steady and impassive as always. Looking at it made you feel like nothing about Titanshade would change. One more lie the city told about itself. Even its name was suspect. Titanshade sat to the south and west of the Mount, which meant that we were always in the sun's glare, never the shade of the mountain. But then we drive on parkways, so who am I to judge?

Schoolteachers had another explanation, that the name was a shortening of "Titan's hade." A Barekusean word with two meanings, "*hade*" might refer to a type of ghost or the whispering sound of melting snow filtering through a still solid snowbank. Movement of hidden liquid below the frozen surface carries an otherworldly sound, one that the Barekusu say mimics the murmurs of lost spirits trying to sway travelers from—or back to—the One True Path. And if ever there was a city where the cry of temptation filled the air, it was Titanshade.

"Carter?"

Ajax's voice intruded on my thoughts.

"I asked if you think we'll get a crack at following up on that ambassador lead," he said.

"Hope so. But our killer won't be one of those jokers." I massaged the sides of my knee. The pain was coming back. A deep, tugging ache that circled my bones, almost as if I were at the end of a string being pulled toward the Mount.

"No?" he said. "Why not?"

"Look at it this way." I turned from the skyline, biting my tongue to hold in a groan. I needed more pain meds, but I also needed to wait until Ajax wouldn't see. That was one report I couldn't have getting back to Bryyh. "What kind of person has a motive to kill a diplomat?" I asked.

"Another politician?"

I nodded. "Could be. Or a business tycoon, or a commercial banker with a fortune on the line."

Titanshade had been a tiny community until the discovery of oil in the ice plains beyond town ushered in a boom had lasted for decades. With the petroleum reserves failing, money drained from the city's coffers as fast as the wells drained the last drop of oil from the ground. Wind turbines had begun to pop up on the tops of buildings, a sight that was inconceivable ten years ago, and their blades cut through the sense of desperation hovering in the air. It was the kind of climate that might make a white-collar criminal turn violent.

"But that's not who we're looking for," I said. "Not with that crime scene."

Ajax considered it. I could practically hear him turning it over in his head.

"That Squib smell was harder to deal with than I'd expected." I suppressed a cringe as I remembered the crime scene. "But the killer was able to keep his head together and not leave physical evidence. That's remarkable."

"So we're looking for a Mollenkampi," said Jax. "Or a human who's not affected."

"You saw the body," I said. "Or what was left of it. You really think anyone could do that if they hadn't lost control?"

I did my best to put the images from my mind and rolled back the foil from my lunch.

"Besides, would a politician or tycoon do the dirty work themselves, or hire it out?" My voice muffled as I took a bite. "Whoever tore apart that Squib knew how to avoid all the ways that we catch bad guys. Which means . . ."

Ajax whistled. "Our killer's a pro."

I flicked a finger against the breast of my suit coat, a dull *thunk* sounding as I struck the badge hidden inside.

"Or a cop," I said.

He stared at the ground, processing what I was saying.

"Luckily," I said, "I happen to know someone who's both."

"Oh?" Ajax looked up. "Is this something you'd share with your partner?"

He unwrapped his lunch, and I turned away. Nothing helps my thinking as much as seeing the people of the city go about their business. And nothing distracts me more than having to watch a Mollenkampi eat.

"You ever hear of a cop named Flanagan?" I said over my shoulder.

"Sounds familiar."

I grunted while chewing. "Bad cop. Got busted a few years back. Probably while you were in college." I swallowed. "Real asshole. He was shaking down every criminal who crossed his path for a piece of their action, and killing the ones who didn't pay for protection."

"So he's in lockup."

"Not anymore. Case against him fell apart. Witnesses recanted. Prosecutor admitted hiding evidence, then fled for parts unknown."

The driver of a passing car leaned on the horn and the continual flow of pedestrians in the crosswalk parted slightly to let the vehicle pass. Ajax grunted.

"Seems like a lot to happen all at once."

I nodded. "Some would call it unbelievable."

I could hear him chewing and kept my eyes on the street. A street performer wailed on a saxophone, far enough away that the notes that reached us were broken and disjointed. A fitting soundtrack for the city.

"And now this Flanagan's off everyone's radar?"

"Not mine," I said. "Never from mine." I closed my eyes for a short breath, gathering my thoughts. "And wherever he is, he's keeping a low profile. But if you were a psychopathic killer and needed money, what kind of work would you be doing?"

I made the mistake of looking over at Ajax.

His mandibles flexed as he chewed, like spider legs spinning a web. With quick, jerky movements, they tapped and repositioned the bites of sausage in his biting mouth until it was ground up and covered with saliva from his nasal cavity.

I'd looked at the worst possible moment and saw one mandible impale a round ball of mashed sausage and bun, then bring it down to the opening above his collar. There, with a delicate touch, the inward-curving needle teeth of the eating mouth pulled the mashed sausage off the claw of his mandible.

Ajax looked thoughtful as he swallowed. "A killer who won't get caught." A napkin was tucked into the top of his collar, protecting his shirt and tie from any accidental spills. I didn't care how tidy he was. Watching a Mollenkampi eat was still like watching someone play with their food after they've been chewing it.

"Anything link him to this mess?" he asked.

"Other than a crime that would take a pro's expertise to pull off?" I shook my head. "Not yet. We can pester Kravitz for forensics when they're available, tell him we've got someone in mind. But Flanagan's got the skill set and complete lack of a conscience required to do the job."

I kept my eyes on the pedestrians, and away from the finger-sized sausage being torn apart by those imposing teeth. It didn't bother me to see a Mollenkampi drinking, or eating soup. Liquids simply pour into their eating mouths, same as humans, though Mollenkampi prefer glassware that tapers at the lip, to accommodate their smaller mouths. Glasses and utensils in Titanshade use this design by default, since humans can use them just as well. But the chewing . . .

"The divination officer said she was going to take another stab at it," said Jax. I could tell he was still eating because his voice didn't have the musical dual tonality while his biting mouth was full.

I stood up and tossed my napkin in the trash. "I'd like to be there for that."

The foot traffic had lightened, though the sidewalks were still packed. The crowd was a mixture of humans and Mollenkampi, with the occasional Gillmyn in the mix. Most of the pedestrians dressed in layers, though a few wore thin, almost sheer clothing. People of all colors and castes were represented. The city was a mixture of immigrants. Other than the original Therreau religious settlers, we were all the children of newcomers, dreamers who'd hoped to strike it rich in the oil business one way or another.

Ajax pointed at a pair of especially lightly clad pedestrians carrying shopping bags with high end labels printed on their sides.

"Never saw anything like that where I grew up," he said. "Still throws me. That and the sulfur smell." He looked around as if he could see the odor of the thermal vents.

"Rich folk didn't flaunt their money in Kohinoor?"

"No," he said. "Assholes are everywhere. I mean the lack of cold weather gear. Right outside Titanshade it's colder than anyplace else on Erekusu, but here in the city center people dress like it's a resort town."

"The city's a strange place," I said. "Lots of people, lots of secrets. Learn how it operates and it'll open right up to you."

Ajax said, "I'll file that one away." But there was some thought in his voice, like he might mean it.

We sat in silence for a long stretch. I could tell he was getting ready to circle around to the day that had put my photo all over the newspapers for the first time. Finally he got on with it.

"This Flanagan. He was SRT?"

"Uh-huh." The Special Response Team was often called in to deal with potential shootouts and hostage situations.

"Was he there when you . . ."

"Yeah," I said. "He was."

Jax seemed like a good kid, but if Bryyh had assigned him to keep an eye on me, then maybe he'd also been prepped to probe my mental state.

"The shrinks tell you to ask me about that?" I said.

"Nope."

"They tell you to report back if I talked about it?"

He didn't answer.

I turned from the trash can and faced him. He was wiping off his tusks with the napkin. I took a sip of coffee.

"Well, you can tell them that I acknowledged the trauma and confirmed the ongoing struggle of an officer's duty."

"I'm not entirely sure that's what you said."

I cleared my throat and said in a loud, clear voice, "I acknowledge the trauma and confirm the ongoing struggle of an officer's duty."

"Okay, now I can report what you said in good conscience."

I belched, and Ajax tsked.

"You're gross, Carter."

His eyes wrinkled and his mandibles shook with amusement at his joke. I was working on a witty retort when our pagers buzzed simultaneously. Code 187. Homicide.

We chucked the last of our meal into the trash and headed for the car. Killers never have the decency to let cops work on one case at a time.

7

WHEN WE ARRIVED THE HOUSE was already cordoned off. Crime scene tape the same crimson as the patrol's uniforms marked the perimeter, easily visible to anyone passing by. Part of the parade and activity around a crime scene is always a show. It's there to let the public know we're present and that all will be well. Judging from the anxious faces on the crowd of on-lookers, we were falling more than a little short of that goal.

It wasn't the number of people in the crowd that bothered me. There will always be a mix of concerned passersby and gruesome lookie-loos hoping to catch a glimpse of a corpse. But this crowd was more intense. Restless. I made a mental note to check what the papers had been saying about the Squib killing.

The patrol cops recognized me and lifted the tape as we approached, allowing us to slide under it like boxers entering the ring.

The house was a cute two-story thing typical of middle-class neighborhoods this distance from the Mount. The neighboring homes were full of white-collar folks with jobs as accountants and dentists. The kind of people who hide their crimes below the surface rather than pinned to their sleeves. The home looked well built, but with signs of neglect. Paint was beginning to flake, and the garden gate showed signs of rot that had been ignored rather than repaired. A patrol cop walked by and I flagged her down.

"Any detectives here yet?"

"You're the first. There's a bunch of techs here, though. They're in with the bodies."

I shook my head. As first responders we'd be assigned the lead on this case. Just when we were needed on the Squib killing. I stalled, hoping someone else would show up and take responsibility.

Pointing to the house I asked Ajax, "What do you know about plants?"

He rolled his eyes. "Why are we out here?" he asked. "The dead people are inside."

"Always scope out the perimeter first. Get an establishing shot. You can learn a lot at a distance."

"If you say so."

I rubbed my forehead in an exaggerated *kids-these-days* motion.

"How 'bout this," I said. "If we can get a potential motive by just standing here, looking and thinking, you write up the full report. Deal?"

Ajax eyed me for a moment. He had the look of a man who knows he's being set up but can't rein in his curiosity.

"Deal," he said.

"Great." I pretended to crack my knuckles. "I understand you went to college. Maybe did some studying about the Southern Crossing. You know anything about plants?"

"Political science classes don't really drift into botany."

"Yeah, well stretch your intellectual muscles, okay? Look at the landscaping."

He took a breath and scanned the exterior. Land was too valuable in Titanshade not to be split up as tight as possible, and the yard consisted of a narrow strip of cement separating the home from its neighbors. But sections of that strip had been broken out. In those spots lush, leafy plants clustered alongside the house.

"What am I looking at, exactly?"

"This neighborhood is called Old Orchard. You know why?"

"There used to be an orchard here?"

"Absolutely not," I said. "We're surrounded by ice plains with three feet of permafrost on them. There haven't been native trees here since the continents were still separated. The neighborhood's called Old Orchard because people like to dream about what they don't have." I pointed at the greenery by the home. "So where do you think those plants in particular came from?"

He took a long look. Finally he said, "They're tropical."

I nodded, encouraging him to proceed.

"They must have been imported," he said. "Mail-order seeds."

"Nope." I pointed at the front of the home. "That siding looks about six or seven years old. Any seedlings in that section would have been trampled when the siding was installed. Those plants and trees are newer than that, and if they're that size . . ." I trailed off.

"They were bought grown," he said, catching on. "Which is expensive."

I waved a hand at the surrounding houses. "More expensive than this neighborhood warrants. Whoever lived here had enough money to purchase and routinely water tropical plants. And people with that kind of money generally use gardeners. Look over there."

At the side of the house a small shovel and dirty pot sat tucked against the foundation. Finger extended, I drew an imaginary circle around them. "But they have their own gardening equipment. No gardener."

"Some people like to garden," he said, still skeptical.

"Look closer." I spiraled the invisible circle tighter, centering his attention. "Those are cheap tools. No love for the work, just necessity."

I gave him a beat to take it all in before I continued.

"So all this makes me think—" I stopped using my finger as a pointer and tapped it against my temple. "There had been a gardener when the plants were purchased, they out-spent their neighbors, and now they're cutting back. Certainly the owners are low on cash. And so we've got a possible motive—overdue debts. Could be an insurance money issue or crossed loan sharks."

Jax looked at the building with its expensive tropical decorations, then at me. "Okay, fine. You win."

"I told you at lunch," I said. "Know the city and it'll open up to you."

Ajax harrumphed. "I'll figure it out."

"I'm not disputing that you're smart, kid. Your education needs to be broader, is all."

He crossed his arms and didn't speak, but one mandible scraped at a tusk in sudden, irritated bursts.

"Okay," I said. "You've got a poli-sci degree. Great. But you need a degree in these neighborhoods. You gotta know that a kid wearing a T-shirt in the Borderlands is slumming, and that a Mountside preppie is the best pick if you need someone to roll on a bookie."

I rubbed my chin, which was covered with enough stubble that it rubbed back.

"It takes time to learn the rhythms of the city. There's no class for this, no syllabus with reading assignments. You gotta learn by living here, by being one of us. The cops who see themselves as separate, they're the ones who burn out. Or go rotten."

"Uh-huh."

"Know the city, know the victims." I swung my hand at the onlookers nearest us like a model unveiling a new car. "Know the victims, and you'll know the killer."

The crowd had a surprising number of angry faces looking our way. It wasn't the kind of thing normally seen at murder investigations. At least, not before we started asking uncomfortable questions.

Ajax sighed. "Speaking of victims, can we go inside now?"

I tapped him on the shoulder and pointed out a woman who stood on this side of the scarlet tape, talking to a member of the patrol. She was shaking and looked on the verge of hyperventilation.

"Tell me, college kid, what do you think her story is?"

He looked her over and ventured a guess.

"I don't know. Friend or family." He looked from her to the crowd on the other side of the caution tape. "She's wearing similar clothes to the onlookers, so she's probably from this area. Maybe she showed up and they let her through, maybe she saw something."

I tugged my lower lip. "She found the body."

He didn't ask how I knew. I liked that. I watched his eyes move up and down as he studied her, taking in her posture, her light tan jacket, her nervous gestures, even—

"Her shoes," he said. He looked at me sideways. "There's blood along the sides of her shoes."

I felt the urge to smile. "There's no way the patrol would let a civilian into a homicide scene, so that means . . ."

"She was in there before they showed up," he said. "She must've let herself in, so she's a friend of the family." Jax stared at the woman. Her hands were clasped over the lower half of her face and she looked around with red-rimmed eyes. "Or family herself." His voice trailed off, maybe picturing himself stumbling on the bodies of people he cared about.

"We'll need to talk to her," I said. "You up for it?"

Ajax's mandible clicked against a tusk apprehensively.

"Look, guessing about motives based on the size of the bushes—"

I shrugged. "It's a parlor trick that helps set the stage for real detective work. Talking to people, understanding where they're from." I pointed at the woman with blood on her shoes. "Wading through emotion to find facts that can be proven. That's what breaks cases."

"I was a cop before I came here. You know that, right?"

I waited.

Jax sighed. "I'll talk to her."

I gave him a soft punch to the shoulder. Better him than me.

"And you?" he said. "Are you going to keep stalling out here while you hope someone else shows up to claim the case?"

That was a little too close to accurate for my taste.

"I'll meet up with you inside," I said, and walked toward the front door. Halfway there I turned back and called to him, "I'll take good notes. It'll make it easier when you do the write-up."

I crossed the threshold and saw techs already scrambling around. I did my best to ignore them as I looked over the house. It was a standard home for that distance from the Mount. The furniture was a few years old, in the pragmatic style that had been fashionable the last decade or so, with lots of long, straight lines crossed by graceful curves. To me it always looked like a sine wave. I looked away before I got flashbacks to my grade school geometry teacher. The tables and couches showed the wear and tear normal for a house with children.

I approached a dark brown end table and examined the clutter on top of it. An empty candy dish with a few peanut husks still lying at the bottom, and two framed photos. Both pictures were facedown. I turned to the mantel over the fireplace. A carved wooden sign that spelled H-O-M-E was untouched, as was a small guidepost sign, but a framed picture was facedown as well. Fumbling in my overcoat pocket I pulled out a pair of latex evidence gloves and put them on.

I lifted the photo on the mantel. It was of a family of five. I wondered if they were the victims I was about to see. I returned to the end table and turned up those photos as well. The children were older in these pictures.

Family photos turned over. The killer didn't want to see the family's faces? That could indicate he knew them, possibly felt guilt.

A steady stream of techs moved up and down the stairs leading to the second floor. I paused at their foot, fingers hovering above the handrail. Whatever had happened in this home would be found up there. Ignoring the throbbing pain in my legs, I climbed the stairs.

On the second floor I walked past a hall bathroom and pushed the door open with two fingers. The hand towel lay crumpled beside the sink basin, blooms of red staining its fabric. Above the sink the vanity mirror was covered with what looked like bath towels, probably pulled from the cabinets below. I stepped back into the hallway.

At the far end was an open door. The bedroom.

I took a breath and held it as I walked in.

The whole family was in there. Parents and two young boys, four bodies laid in a row. Deep gashes were clearly visible in the victims' torsos, and the blood had drained out, soaking the carpet in a wide area. There were no markings or trails to indicate the bodies had been moved, and there were contusions on the boys' heads, as if they'd been knocked out before they were brought into the room and killed. A set of shoeprints led away from the bodies. The prints were adult-sized but small, maybe from the witness who'd found the victims.

The techs around me weren't wearing respirators. I let out my breath. On the inhale there was no scent of cinnamon. That was a relief, at least.

An entertainment center sat in the corner, a sheet draped over the television. I glanced at the bed, and saw its sheets had been pulled off. Wondering why the family or killer had done that, I turned away and stared at the windows. All the curtains were tightly drawn except one, and through it I could see Ajax talking to one of the patrol cops outside. I moved to the window and rapped on the glass pane. My partner glanced up, and I motioned for him to join me. He headed into the house, and I was left staring at my reflection superimposed over the neighborhood.

A few seconds later Ajax walked into the bedroom. I greeted him with a question.

"You think they were about to go on vacation?"

He looked around, eyes resting on the sheet-covered mirrors and TV, and the framed photos that had been flipped facedown or taken off the wall.

"No," he said. "That was the neighbor outside. She watches the kids some days, the mother's sister does others. She came by at the normal time and when no one answered she tried the door. She confirmed that the victims live here." A slight nod to the bodies on the floor. "Jon and Tara Bell-Asandro and their sons. But I don't know—"

I waved a hand to interrupt him. "Reflections." I turned around and raised my voice to be heard by the whole crew. "Curtains!"

The techs stared.

"Who opened the curtains?" There was a pause that ran on for too long for my liking. "I watched Detective Ajax walk up to this house through the window. The curtains would have been closed when you got here, and now they're open. Who did that?"

Ajax scanned the room, and I heard an intake of breath. "Reflections," he said.

I shot him a fake grin. *Glad you're catching up.*

A particularly pimple-faced tech approached me and held up a hand. "I opened the curtains, sir. We needed the light to take photos so—"

I raised my voice again. "Those cameras don't have flashbulbs? Cause they look like they got flashbulbs to me."

His cheeks reddened and he nodded.

I spoke loud enough for everyone in the house to hear. "Do not move anything until we see it and document it. Is that understood?"

Turning back to the tech I rolled my eyes. "Get back to work."

"So." Jax drew the syllable out and turned it into a musical scale. "Our guy covered anything that would show his face."

"Which means?"

He snapped on his own set of latex gloves. "Guilt," he said. "Superstition."

"Maybe. It definitely means he was here for a while. At least long enough to pull sheets and cover surfaces, probably longer." I made a slow turn, arms spread. "What was he seeing in here?"

A tech stuck his head into the bedroom. His dust mask was loose around his neck.

"You need to see this, Detective."

"Not now." I scanned the room again. I tried to put myself in the killer's shoes, seeing the room as he or she had done.

The tech cleared his throat. "There's a note."

I paused, not certain I'd heard right. "A note?"

He nodded rapidly. "Yes, sir. In the kitchen."

I pushed him aside, and ran downstairs.

The note was written on paper torn from a spiral-bound pad and shoved in the edge of the pantry cabinet. The slogan, "If You Please, Get These Gro-cer-ies" was printed in a purple graphic across the top of the paper. Beneath that, scrawled in thick black marker, were two sentences.

"Warts and all, the greatest treasures are at the greatest depths. I'm sorry."

I read it aloud, then looked at Jax. "What in the Hells does that mean?"

He didn't say anything, and I stared at the writing for a long moment, waiting for pieces to fit together. They didn't all match, but something clicked.

"Hold on."

I jogged down the hall to the living room. Picking up the family photo, I saw two parents, two young children. I dropped it back in place and grabbed another one. Two parents, two small children, and one older boy. A teenager hiding his eyes behind long bangs. Another son who wasn't lying dead in that bedroom. "Jax," I called, "we need a BOLO on the oldest son."

"What's his name?"

"Don't know. I'd say he's . . ." The other two kids in the photo were a couple years younger than their corpses in the bedroom. I added that time to the look of the missing son. "Nineteen or twenty. Call in to the Bunker—"

He nodded, keeping pace with me. "And have them run a records check. Be on the lookout for someone that matches. On it."

"Make sure that BOLO goes out with a note to treat him with kid gloves. Either he's our killer, or there's a good chance he's got no idea this has happened yet."

There was a rattle from Ajax's coat. He fished out his pager, then showed it to me. Code 25: Report in to Dispatch. We hiked out to the car and radioed in together. The dispatcher we got was a veteran named Kelly.

"Yeah, hold on," she said. We waited while she sorted through the pizza boxes and note cards that littered the dispatch office. "Here it is. Detective Kravitz left a message for you. It says 'Good to go on your interview. You're expected at 1 Government Plaza ASAP.'"

"That's great," I said. "But we're on a crime scene right now."

"There's more to the message," she said. "It says 'Drop everything.'"

Make it work. Even if it meant the death of this family went on the back burner. I looked at Ajax.

"This is exactly the reason I wanted someone else to take first on-scene," I said.

I stalked back to the victims' home and told myself to compartmentalize, to push aside my desire to find this killer, so that I could focus on finding another one. I almost managed to convince myself that it worked.

8

I DON'T LIKE POLITICIANS.

Maybe somewhere they're worth a damn, some alternate world where those who govern do so out of a sense of civic obligation instead of greed and a hunger for power. But Titanshade has always had a way of clarifying people's true intentions. There's never been a politician, whether it's our current representative in the Assembly of Free States or the lowliest alderman, who didn't eventually lash out at the people she was supposed to protect, or line his pockets with the labors of those who trusted him. The people of this city have long since surrendered any hope that politicians are in the game of helping others. At this point we just hope they won't do too much collateral damage as they rob the communal till of every last coin they can find.

And diplomats? They're nothing but politicians who can't be bothered to go to the trouble of rigging an election. So the gilded halls and ornate furnishing of the diplomatic corps didn't surprise me. When we were escorted to an ostentatious office decked out with velvet curtains and oil paintings of famous politicians, that didn't surprise me either.

What did surprise me was the apparent sincerity of the woman seated before us when she stared us in the eyes and said, "Find him, Detectives. Find the son of a bitch who did this, and let us know what you need to help you do it."

Her name was Gellica, and judging from her office, she was far from the lowest rung on the ladder.

Jax answered with a polite voice, solid as an old oak table. "We'll do our best, Ambassador. What we need right now is candor."

"If we're starting with candor," she said, "drop the 'ambassador' title." She grinned and continued in a confidential whisper. "I'm technically a diplomatic envoy. The ambassador is my boss."

She pointed to one of the paintings on the wall, a portrait of a steel-eyed human woman with a dimpled chin and tightly cropped dark hair. I recognized Ambassador Paulus from the front page of the papers. She was the Assembly of Free States' representative in Titanshade, and the lead figure in negotiations with the Squibs and other parties to convert the surrounding oil fields into wind farms. As a member city-state, Titanshade had a fair amount of autonomy. But if the rest of the AFS determined that something would happen, our city's lone voice would be overruled and ignored. Paulus was a powerful woman.

Jax pressed on.

"I may need to ask you some uncomfortable questions."

The smile dropped from Gellica's face.

"I know what happened to the Squib delegate." She paused, and I saw the thought behind her words, as carefully calculated as the curve of makeup that accented the upturn of her eyes. "I would say that the whole damn thing is uncomfortable."

Jax nodded and started the interview. I half listened to the first few questions, but since I wasn't running the interview my focus drifted. I found myself paying more attention to this diplomat who didn't care for titles.

Gellica was dressed in a white suit made of quality fabric, expensive but not ostentatious. Her dark hair wasn't curled but simply swept back over her shoulders. For all the appearance of an outfit casually put together, the finished product was striking, and I was sure every element had been chosen for effect. Not so unfashionable as to be an object of scorn, but she wasn't going to be invited to any social-climbing parties mountainside. The office desk was massive and as ornate as the rest of the room, but she didn't hide behind it. Instead she sat on a simple wooden chair across from the small couch that Jax and I shared. There was an antique coffee table between her and us, and though there was a full tea service laid out on it she hadn't made a show of offering us a drink. Overall, she was showing us more honesty than I'd expected.

The basic preamble over, Jax shifted, jostling my elbow as he started the real questioning. "Are you aware of anyone in the diplomatic corps hiring prostitutes?"

"Yes."

That was *far* more honesty than I'd expected.

Jax nodded. He was either less surprised or better at hiding it. "Were any of those envoys in the area of the Eagle Crest hotel last night?"

Gellica reached into an attaché beside her chair and pulled out two manila file folders. She held them out to us.

"Here are dossiers on the only two members of our staff who have such proclivities and whose whereabouts that night are unaccounted for."

I took the folders, and Jax said, "We like to account for whereabouts on our own, Envoy."

She nodded and crossed her legs. The fabric of her skirt pulled against her thigh and I looked away, studying the swell of the velvet curtains. It didn't help.

"Of course," she said. "But any other envoys I might suspect were on active duty or have alibis backed by witnesses."

Ajax eyed the dossiers. "You assembled all this rather quickly."

"We started work as soon as we heard of the murder. It's natural to suspect those closest to the late delegate. The faster you have this information, the faster you can apprehend the guilty party." She laced her hands over one knee. "And if it comes out that we helped the investigation, it will help mitigate any negative publicity."

As a rule, I'm always suspicious when someone offers to do my work for me. Jax seemed to share my sentiment.

"This is a homicide investigation," he said.

Gellica raised a finger, showing off a tightly trimmed nail. It was painted a rich brown a few shades darker than her skin tone.

"It's a homicide investigation with international implications. It will impact trade relations and redirect billions of dollars in unanticipated ways. People may lose jobs, factories may be relocated. Your investigation," she said, "needs to be aided by any means necessary." She looked at Jax for a long beat and even spared a glance for me. "If you need the other names you'll have them. But start here. I don't know about their . . ." She paused. "Preferences. But I expect that they would only call in candies from the Estates."

So Gellica knew the different availabilities of candies. That was interesting. She was either intimately familiar with that trade or else . . .

"Where are you from?" I asked. Jax shot me a look but didn't call me out for breaking my silence.

Gellica didn't smile, though a careless observer might have

thought she had. Half of her mouth twisted up and there was a look in her eyes as though she was remembering something not quite unpleasant. Like the forgotten memory of a too-sweet apple pie.

"I was born here," she said. "I didn't move away till I went to Fracinica for college."

"And now you're back," I said.

"I go where I'm sent."

"You always that obedient?"

"Only to my country."

Jax leaned forward. "Ambassador—"

"Envoy," Gellica and I corrected him in unison.

Jax opened and closed his biting jaw, looking confused. So I asked the envoy another question.

"What part of town?"

Gellica raised an eyebrow. "Pardon me?"

"You said you grew up here. What part?"

"The nice part."

"There is no nice part of Titanshade."

Her smile was genuine this time, and I discovered that I liked being the cause of that smile. White teeth stood out against the rich brown of her skin and she tilted her head back at a slight angle, as if she were dancing on the edge of a laugh.

Jax was getting impatient. He pointed his pencil at Gellica like a man asking to cut in at a wedding dance.

"You're giving us two names. Is there one you suspect more than the other?"

"I have no idea, Detectives. I was kind of hoping you'd ask some probing questions and then put the pieces together." Gellica pinched her jaw between finger and thumb, making the dimple in her chin more prominent.

"Oh, we will," I said. "We'll haul in the killer, no matter who they work for, or who that might embarrass." I tilted my head toward the portraits of politicians hanging on the wall.

I was brought back to reality by a sharp pain in my thigh. Jax had discreetly turned his pencil around and jabbed it into my leg.

"Carter . . ." She rolled my name across her lips as if tasting it. "I've heard of you."

"It's not an uncommon name."

"When our staff spoke with the chief of police, she told us which detectives she was considering to oversee the case. Your name came up."

"Oh?"

"She assured us it wouldn't be you."

"She assured you right. I'm not overseeing anything. I'm just conducting routine interviews."

Jax broke in again. "Actually I'm conducting the interview. My partner—"

"Your partner is completely right." Gellica raised her voice and pointed at the folders in my hand. "I'm not providing that material to encourage you to hush this up. We need to see the guilty party found, arrested, and incarcerated, or we all look like fools."

She shifted her finger to me. "The ambassador and I will do whatever it takes to help your investigation wrap up as quickly as possible. I'm not disparaging you or your work. But we can't have anything, or anyone, taking attention away from this murder. I hope you understand that."

She leaned back and indicated the folders with a casual wave. "Now do you want to interview those two men immediately or at a later date?"

I started to answer but Jax shifted in his seat, sending an elbow to my ribs as he did so.

"Only if they're flight risks," he said. "Otherwise we'll have to go through our department. Do you think they're nervous about why you were asking about them?"

She shook her head. "Neither of the men named in those files believes he is under suspicion. My inquiries were discreet."

"That's quite a trick," I said. "Where did you pick that up?"

"My mother," she said, and the half-smile of unpleasant memories returned. "She still lives in the Hills."

"Oil money?" I asked.

"Yes."

"New or old?"

"Old as oil," she said.

"If you grew up around oil money, then you learned to be suspicious of everyone," I said.

She looked at me and blinked slowly, not sure where I was going. Suspicious indeed.

"I'll—" I glanced at Jax and corrected myself. "*We* are asking you again. Of these two," I said, tapping the folders, "which one do you suspect more?"

I expected another pencil jab from Jax, but it didn't come. He was focused on Gellica.

She breathed in deeply and seemed to give it some thought. "Of these two . . ." Gellica thumbed the top folder. "Cordray is the one I dislike less as a person. Look at him first."

I raised an eyebrow. "You think the one you like better is the killer?"

She gave me an empty smile and spread her hands. "Isn't it always that way, Detective?"

Ajax cleared his throat, a sound not unlike a basket of wind chimes tumbling down a stairwell.

Gellica turned to him. "How else can I help you?"

Ajax flipped a page in his notebook.

"Tell us about the Squib delegation," he said. "How many of them are there? Are there any tensions among them?"

Good man. We'd had to fight to get in to see Gellica, and this was the closest we'd get to a briefing on the Squib delegates.

"There are five members of the delegation," she said. "They're mostly driven by—" She broke off. "Well, how familiar are you with Squib history?"

"As it happens," I said, "my partner has a degree on Southern Crossing cultures."

"Oh?" Gellica looked at Ajax, who was staring daggers at me.

"Poli-sci," said Ajax.

She pursed her lips. "Then you know all about the reason the Squibs are so interested in the wind farms."

Ajax wavered, as if torn between wanting Gellica to answer, and wanting to demonstrate his knowledge after our earlier argument. In the end his ego won out.

"The beach panic," he said. "About seventy-five years ago, Squib researchers found trace manna on their beaches. People went wild. Fresh manna hadn't been seen in over a century, since the Shortage began. And it had obviously never been found outside of a whale."

"Which is exactly where the manna on the beach came from," Gellica said. "The decaying body of a whale. Probably one of the last that ever lived in the wild."

"Maybe," said Ajax. "Or maybe an old manna-powered shipwreck got dislodged by a storm. No one knows, but it was enough to start a speculation frenzy."

"If it was real," I said, "it would've changed everything."

Ajax's eyes crinkled. "That's an understatement."

I thought of the manna-driven machines and factories, wondered how many had been scrapped, and how many were sitting mothballed in museums. What would it take to restart the first industrial revolution?

"So they searched," I said. "And didn't find anything. And now they want to buy windmills?"

Gellica sighed. "If you want to believe something is there, not finding it won't stop you. The Squibs dredged almost every square inch of shoreline they had. They had a tourist economy and overnight their beaches were nothing but mud and boulders."

"Took decades to repair the damage." Ajax hummed a note of remorse. "The reefs never will recover."

"The Squibs are doing fine now," I said. "They've got enough cash to buy up the old oil fields."

"Sure," said Gellica. "Once the beaches were sand covered again, tourists came back, along with their money. And the fallout from the false manna debacle pushed the Squibs into alternative energy. Now they have plenty of cash and the infrastructure needed to make wind farms work. It's the great irony, I suppose: the same pipe dream that crippled their economy has put them in the perfect place to take advantage of the oil shortage here."

"They must be excited to get the purchase closed," I said.

"Oh, they are," she said. "This deal justifies the economic disaster they suffered through for a generation. For the Squibs this is equal parts pride and greed. It makes them motivated buyers, which is exactly what we need." She tucked a stray strand of hair over her ear. "In the end, we all benefit."

"And Garson Haberdine's death?" said Ajax. "Who benefits from that?"

"No one."

Ajax and I exchanged a look.

"Surely there's some—"

Gellica held up a hand. "No one I know of. I can't speak to the personal lives of the Squib delegation . . . but on a political level?" She shook her head. "I can't think of anyone who'd want him dead."

"Maybe it's not him," Ajax said. "Maybe it's the talks."

"There, either. If the talks are postponed there's no money for the landholders who want to sell to the Squibs, there's no income being generated for the city off that land, real estate values drop . . ."

"Someone wants them to stop," said Ajax. "I've seen anti-wind farm ads all over the place."

I was sure he had. They'd started appearing on television, radio, newspapers, even on the sides of buses. Always the same message: keep Titanshade great by turning back the clock and staying true to oil.

Gellica sighed. "That's Harlan Cedrow," she said. "He's been making noise about deep-layer reserves, but there's no geological surveys to back it up. And again"—Gellica held up empty hands—"no deal means no money at all. Harlan has to answer to his investors. The PR push is just posturing for better terms."

"Harlan Cedrow," Ajax repeated, jotting it down. "Is he tied to one of the oil companies?"

It was a blatant reminder that Ajax was new to town. No native Titanshader would need to ask such a question.

"That's Rediron, kid," I said. "They own pretty much everything." My father had worked a Rediron rig, owned part and parcel by the Cedrows, the oldest oil family of them all.

"Rediron holds the majority of remaining oil land," said Gellica, "and they are the largest group still holding out. But they certainly don't own everything."

"The Cedrows are popular," I told Ajax. "The family kicks back to the community. Raises funds, runs charities. I've seen it firsthand." I didn't feel the need to tell him about how exactly I'd seen it. I looked from him to Gellica.

"What about the other landowners?" I asked. "Even knowing they could be shooting themselves in the foot."

Gellica reached down to the tea service and plucked a sugar cube from the serving dish. She slid it into her mouth and pursed her lips, as if considering the possibility.

"You're asking me if anyone would rather go without than see someone else profit more than they do. It's possible. There's no shortage of people who want a bigger piece of the pie." She ran a thumbnail over her dimpled chin. "But this murder threatens to destroy the pie completely."

She sat up straighter, as if secure in her conclusion.

"No," she said. "Everyone knows the wells are running dry. Titanshade powers the nation. The entire Assembly of Free States is on borrowed time unless we can bring the city into a new age, with an alternative energy supply."

"We grasp the situation," said Ajax, tugging at his shirt collar, pulling it away from the speaking mouth in his throat.

"Then you know that the only way out of this mess is forward. I don't know who killed Envoy Haberdine, or why. But I know that stopping the talks doesn't benefit anyone. The world is changing, Detectives. Titanshade is about to enter a new era."

I looked at Ajax. If she was starting to break out sound bites, then we'd gotten everything useful out of her. We muttered our thanks as we stood up to leave. Gellica walked us to the door, but paused before opening it. Even the doorknob under her fingers was heavy with ornamentation.

"Keep me informed about any developments, Detectives."

Jax and I exchanged glances.

"We don't really keep the public up to date with ongoing investigations," he said.

She didn't smile, much as I may have wished she would. "I

mean keep me informed so that I can help you. Whether it's one of our employees or not, you're going to run into some bureaucratic roadblocks at some point. Tell me when you do, and I'll apply pressure best as I'm able. You might be surprised at what the AFS is capable of."

I thought of Talena's friend Stacie, and the offhand comment that had led us to Envoy Gellica and her handsomely decorated office.

I gave her a smile. "We appreciate that, we really do, Ambassad—" I broke off with a chuckle. "Hells, now I'm doing it."

Jax tensed and I half expected another pencil jab, but Gellica waved my comment away.

"That's quite all right, Detective."

"Out of curiosity, though." I circled around to my real question. "Is there anyone else with the title of ambassador other than Paulus? Even informally, I mean."

She frowned. "Not from the AFS. The only member of the Squib delegation with a formal title is Ambassador Yarvis. Why do you ask?"

"No reason, really. That stuff interests me. Titles and ceremonies and so forth."

"Well, the next time we talk I'll see about getting you a book on the subject."

The door opened, and we walked out of her office. From the hallway I glanced back, and was rewarded with one more glimpse of her smile. Then the door closed, and we still had a killer to find.

AT THE BUNKER THERE WERE more people gathered in the street, and the mood was changing from unhappy to unruly. Some held signs, crude drawings of frogs with x-ed out eyes, banners covered with slogans: "Who do you serve?" "Who do you protect?" Oil protectionists screamed at wind farm proponents and they all jeered at the police. Protesters and counter-protesters, they were there because their world was changing and there was nothing they could do about it. It was one step up from a primal scream of frustration, all ready-made for the six o'clock news.

Ajax eyed the growing crowd with unease.

"You get this kind of reaction for all homicide cases?"

"Nah," I said. "Just the ones I'm assigned to."

We were parked down the street from the Bunker, watching the churn in the streets as pedestrians and drivers worked their way around and through the protests. We'd come down to turn over the materials Gellica had given us, but stopped short when we got a look at the crowd.

The killing had the city on edge. If there was no wind farm deal, most of the people walking these streets would be affected. Once the oil ran dry, those lucky enough to still have jobs would be living in fear of a complete economic collapse. And it didn't stop at the city limits. The rest of the AFS depended on Titanshade petroleum to fill their fuel tanks and to manufacture everything from ballpoint pens to toothpaste tubes. Without our oil reserves the central government would have to go crawling to one of the other world powers to ramp up production. It had been a hundred years since the first industrial boom collapsed when the world ran short of manna. Now we might be headed there again. Titanshade usually got lip service from the politicians once an election cycle. But as we teetered on obsolescence, the rest of the world watched and wondered: Would Titanshade's collapse drive the world into another Shortage?

International politics, domestic unease, and basic fear for one's life. They all came together in the Haberdine case, distilled into the waving signs and chanted slogans of the crowd.

We sat in silence, looking at the crowd, the traffic, the slow-moving Therreau wagons that rolled along, never stopping.

My mind kept returning to the gory scene in room 430, and the devastation visited on the Squib diplomat. The attacker must have raged, like a wild animal. Or worse—an animal kills, even eats, but it doesn't shred the carcass into near nonexistence.

Whoever had killed Haberdine had been able to collect themselves enough to escape unseen. Was it someone working alone, or a team? Why would Haberdine let them in the room in the first place? I remembered the red sticker on the Do Not Disturb sign. But the sign had been *inside* the door—

"Hey, do the Therreau always wear masks?" Ajax broke my concentration.

I looked at the Therreau cart. It was driven by somber-faced, hairless humans wearing cloth bandannas tied over their noses and mouths.

"No, those are new," I said.

"You think they're afraid of breathing in Squib smell?"

"I don't know and don't care enough to find out." I looked away from the cart. "More important things on my mind than a bunch of farmers and their lack of fashion sense."

"Seems kind of paranoid. The streets would have to run with blood before the smell got to entire crowds. Their boots would be dripping with the stuff."

I tried to ignore him. A wasted effort, as he kept talking.

"Footprints!" he said.

I clearly wasn't going to get a chance to think in silence.

"Footprints?" I asked.

"The Haberdine murder scene was such a mess we all had to wear shoe covers in the room. But the killer didn't leave any bloody footprints in that hallway."

I grunted assent. "It's why I think a pro's behind it," I said. "One of the reasons, anyway."

"They could've been cleaned up with magic."

It was the overenthusiastic theory of a rookie.

"You saw the divination officer doing her thing after what, two weeks in the city?" I asked. "Most people in this town go their whole lives with only a glimpse or two of real magic."

"And there aren't other sorcerers in town?"

I cut him off with a frown.

"Back in your hometown," I said. "Kodachrome."

"Kohinoor."

"Whatever. How many times did you see people there use manna?" I asked.

I guessed it'd be close to zero. His lack of response told me I'd guessed about right.

"Titanshade's got no shortage of the super-rich," I said, "but that doesn't mean they've got gold toilets. Manna and sorcery are expensive and getting more expensive each day. And that's the legal stuff. Manna for non-government work sells at black market prices." I scanned the crowd. "Magic's always the last option. The day someone figures how to make more manna, that's when we'll start worrying about magical crimes."

Ajax had stopped listening halfway through my speech, opening the glove box and pulling out the map of Titanshade that was included with the car. He unfolded it, tapping the seams out and spreading it across the dashboard. My city painted in primary colors. A complicated grid of streets and alleys, Titanshade was a rough circle with the irregular shape of the Mount blocking out its upper-right quarter.

"Like a moon going into eclipse," muttered Ajax.

"Funny," I said. "I always thought it looks like a cookie with a bite taken out of it."

A human bite, of course. A Mollenkampi would obliterate a cookie.

Ajax ran one finger over the streets until he found what he was looking for. The Eagle Crest.

"Where's the Bell-Asandro home?"

I tapped a spot farther leeward, in the direction of the Borderlands.

"It's not too far," he said.

"Not too close, either. The boundaries around neighborhoods are economical more than physical."

"Still," he said. "It's close."

"Everything's close," I said. "That's the problem. Five million of us piled on top of each other, clinging to the geo-vents like drowning sailors on a life raft. It's no wonder we're all trying to kill each other." The horror of Haberdine's murder scene came rushing back, and for a moment I thought I smelled a whiff of cinnamon in the air. I pinched my nose. I needed a drink.

We delivered the files that Gellica had given us to Kravitz and retreated to our desks to plan our next move. A mail cart rolled around the perimeter of the Bullpen, its progress announced by the wobbly, squeaky wheel that maintenance kept forgetting or just plain didn't care about. When it came around to our desks, the mail clerk dropped a yellow interdepartmental envelope in front of Ajax.

Ripping the seal open, Ajax pulled out a packet of ten or fifteen stapled pages. He riffled through them.

"This is the profile on the Bell-Asandro kids' aunt. The one who split babysitting duty with the neighbor," he said. "Nina Bell."

"She came up in the system? So she's got a record."

"Yeah. Long and nonviolent. Minor thefts, numerous counts of drug possession and public intoxication."

"What's her drug of choice?"

Jax flipped through a second page. "Looks like it varied with whatever was cheap, but I'm seeing lots of chono."

That made sense. Chono had been plentiful and cheap a few years ago. For the price of a meal users could buy a sense of calm confidence, along with a wicked comedown and an overwhelming urge for another fix. The mayor's office fought the epidemic with a series of poorly produced ads that featured wealthy kids in light clothes, always ending with the tagline "Chono? Oh, *no!*" Not surprisingly, it hadn't worked.

"Hard to believe the Bells let a spiker watch their kids," I said.

"No arrests in . . ." He ran a finger down the page. "Almost eighteen months. She may be clean."

"Doubtful," I said, though I hoped I was wrong. I also hoped that the nightmare she was about to go through wasn't going to push her into using. There was always someone waiting to help those in pain escape their reality, and some organizations moved veritable rivers of the stuff. I thought of Jax's reaction to one of them when we were at the Hey-Hey.

"The Harlq Syndicate," I said. "They push it in Kohinoor?"

He nodded once. A curt affirmative that also told me I wouldn't be getting any further details. I moved on.

"So we should talk to this aunt."

Ajax stared at the rap sheet, perhaps still banishing whatever memories my mention of the Harlqs had dredged up. Finally, he slid the report over to my desk.

"You mean you should," he said. "I've got that report on the Bell-Asandro murder to write up, after your demonstration of how to deduce possible motive."

"Aw, kid. I'm not gonna hold you to that."

"Nope," he said. "A deal's a deal."

I rang the doorbell of Nina Bell's townhome, half hoping that she wouldn't answer. Family interviews were a part of the job I truly hated. I'd rather chase down a homicidal roughneck in a dark alley than rattle the cage of someone truly in mourning.

I wished Ajax was there. He had a softer way about him. Surely he could've said something that would make things easier for this woman. Some quote or gentle insight that would be more at home on an inspirational poster than coming from a cop. It occurred to me that maybe this partner thing wasn't so bad after all.

The door opened and a woman with red-rimmed eyes stared at me. Nina Bell wore jeans and a cotton shirt, topped by a loose-knit sweater she clasped tight to her neck.

I displayed my badge and introduced myself. She stood aside to let me in and I walked into the entryway, feeling the blast of her threshold vent against my face. Her home had an unusual smell. I wrinkled my nose as I tried to place it. The air had a salty tang, like a brine or ocean breeze. It was a distinctive odor in a landlocked city far from any non-frozen body of water.

A quick look back at the front door was all it took to solve the mystery. The threshold vent had almost a dozen pine-tree-shaped air fresheners hanging over it. I tilted one toward me. It, like all the others, was labeled Salt Water Taffy.

"Effective," I said. Vent scents weren't unusual, especially among recent arrivals who weren't accustomed to the smell of sulfur that permeated the city. Though having read her rap sheet, I knew Bell was a native Titanshader.

Nina gave a self-conscious shrug, as if she knew what I was thinking.

"It makes me think of the ocean," she said.

She brought me into her living room and I saw that she had a scrapbook out on the couch. Remembering the family. I'll never understand that impulse. Pictures can be horrible things. Frozen images of people you'll never see again, glimpses into happy moments that ultimately remind you of the story's tragic ending. Why tear open those old wounds?

Nina stood by a bookshelf and fingered the knickknacks that covered it like emotional moss. I stayed on my feet as well and flipped out my notebook and pencil. At least I didn't have to break the news to her.

"How did you hear about it?"

"Their neighbor called. Told me that some young detective would be coming by." She glanced at me without comment. But she didn't really need to. I wasn't the poster child for young detectives.

I sucked in my middle-aged gut and pushed ahead.

"Do you have any idea why someone would target your sister and her family?"

"No," she said. "Nothing."

"What about their oldest son, Jermaine? You know where we can find him?"

She squeezed her mouth shut. "Do you think he's in danger?"

"No," I said, though I had no idea.

"If I lost him too . . ." A hitch crept into her voice. "I just don't know."

I changed the subject.

"How about financials? Were they in debt?"

Nina blinked, surprised, but nodded. "Tara was stressed, said they were struggling to pay the bills. But who doesn't?"

"You think anyone would've thought they had more cash than they did?"

"How would I know—"

"You were an addict."

Nina turned from the shelf to glare at me.

"Am." She drew back her shoulders. "I *am* an addict. Addiction doesn't go away just because you stop using."

I gave her a slight nod without dropping my gaze. She was right, but my question still stood. After a couple of seconds, her shoulders slumped.

"You think I did this?" she asked.

"No," I said, and looked her in the eye to let her know I meant it. "But do you have old contacts you still talk to, anyone still needing cash or a fix? Anyone that might've seen your family as easy targets?"

Nina looked down. Her body language was tight, anxious. One hand clutched her sweater while she rubbed her forehead with the other. I couldn't blame her. The rest of her life she'd always have her motives questioned, always be looked at with suspicion when something went missing or when things went wrong. And always, always she'd hear a tiny whisper, reminding her she could escape it all with a syringe's pinch. I told myself I was lucky to not have that struggle, and I ignored the polite whisper of disagreement from the pills that rode in my pocket.

With a loud exhale Nina raised her head.

"I cut off all my friends from that life. You can't keep bad relationships and expect to stay clean." She moved a hand to the bookshelf, bracing herself. "That's one of the things you only realize after you've hit absolute bottom. Clarity's the gift you find when you fall that deep."

She plucked a porcelain tiger from the shelf, gripping it like a child holding a teddy bear.

"I looked at my list yesterday, and I'd made almost all the goals I'd set for myself, so I set new ones, and now today—" She broke off and gulped in a breath. "Today everything went to shit. It's all shit, and I don't know what to do." She slammed the porcelain tiger back onto the shelf and I heard the slight *snap* as its leg broke. A hand went over her face to hide the tears. I gave her a three-count before I started again.

"Can you think of anything out of the ordinary? Anything unusual?"

She looked up, eyes red, and shook her head. "No. Tara and Jon are just normal people."

I didn't correct her use of the present tense.

I ran through the rest of my standard questions quickly. At the end I patted my pockets, finally locating a business card in my suit coat. "If you think of anything else," I said and handed her the card.

"If I knew something, I would tell you. If I thought anyone I knew would do something like . . ." She licked her lips. "Jules was twelve. Peter was nine." She stared at me from the corner of her eye. "Nine! Who does something like that to kids?"

I didn't have an answer. But she took the card anyway, and I walked out of there thankful that I wasn't going to be taking any of my loved ones to the mountain that day.

At the door I paused, my hand in the warm, sulfur-tinged air of the entry vent as I searched for something useful to share. But my internal cop took charge and I asked one more question instead.

"You said you were making lists. Why?"

Nina wiped at one eye. "My social worker. She said to set a goal, complete it, then set another."

I could hear what Ajax would say to that, even down to the musical tones in his voice. "Like one step after another on the Path."

I hadn't meant to say it aloud, but when I did Nina smiled. Embarrassed, I pulled my hand away from the Titan's warmth and left her home. But as I walked to my car it felt like the warmth stayed with me, and somehow the streets seemed a little less dirty on my way back to the Bunker.

10

THE CROWDS AT THE BUNKER had grown and now the media circled the demonstrators, searching for conflict to serve their audience. Television vans formed a loose ring around the group, broadcast antennas raised high, creating a half circle of skeletal aluminum fingers that ringed round the Bunker like an iron crown.

There were so many of them that Kravitz must have let leak some rumor of a break in the Squib case. It was a smart move; when there was big news all the media flocked to the source instead of trawling through the city, harassing cops and victims. It was like chumming for sharks to distract them from nearby swimmers. A good plan. Except now I had to cut through that line of predators.

I circled the building and came at it from the rear, pulling up to the gate that divided the back lot from the police parking garage.

I leaned out the window and punched my code into the security box, when a lanky man jogged out from behind a dumpster and stood in front of my car. As a general rule, I've found that nobody who lurks behind dumpsters is up to anything good.

"I'm with *The Titanshade Union Record*, Detective. You got a minute?" he said.

The *Union Record* was a strong-selling hotsheet that played loose with the facts in favor of whatever topic the public was currently clamoring for. Unfortunately for him, I'd agreed long ago to have as little to do with the media as possible.

I stared past him into the garage. "I need you to move away from my car, please."

A flash blinded me and I shielded my eyes with a hand. My vision cleared immediately and I saw a Mollenkampi in a wool skirt dropping to one knee to get a shot of me from a better angle. I'd reached for my revolver without thought and pulled my hand away to grip the steering wheel instead.

The reporter leaned over the gate arm. "You were at the scene for that family that got sliced up. The Bells, right?"

"You need to back away from my vehicle."

"C'mon. I won't use your name. Just give us a couple details of what it's like being in the slaughterhouse. Was it like the dead Squib?"

"If you don't move, you'll be interfering with an officer."

He held up his hands but didn't back away. From the side came the pop and crackle of the camera flashbulb.

"What about the candies?"

"Candies?" I tried to keep my face neutral.

"The ones that turned up dead today," he said. "Were they like the Bells? All hacked up?"

I reached out and hit the pound sign, opening the gate. The reporter jerked to the side to avoid the fiberglass arm, and I rolled my car forward at an angle. A third flash lit up my profile as I accelerated.

The reporter popped onto the hood of my car then bounced off to the side. I opened my door and stepped out.

"Oh, my goodness!" I put a hand to my lips. "Are you okay?"

The reporter lay sprawled on the ground, with nothing more

serious than scuff marks on the tails of his jacket. I propped an elbow on the doorframe and flashed him my pearly whites. There was another flash, and the Mollenkampi photographer thumbed her frame advance frantically to get in another shot.

I gave her a quick two-finger salute and said, "Have a good day now," before climbing back into my car and entering the garage.

That's where I found Ajax, cracking jokes with the mechanics as I pulled into the bay. He'd been in town two weeks and he already had more friends than I did.

I grabbed him and we headed toward the staff elevator, only to find it taken up by a frustrated tech trying to cram two display easels and an overhead projector mounted on a wheeled cart into the elevator cab. So we opted for the second set of elevators, a path that took us through the public-facing lobby of the Bunker. As we entered the lobby, someone at the front desk called my name. I pulled up short, and the desk sergeant waved us over. Jenkins was a husky guy with a crumb-catcher mustache.

"Kravitz told me to send you up to 5D when you got here," he said.

"You know what for?"

"Nah, he just told me to tell you."

So we headed up to the fifth floor and made our way to interrogation room D.

A patrolman in the corridor waved us into the adjoining observation room. Kravitz and Bryyh were already there, joined by Angus and Bengles. A one-way mirror showed the occupants of 5D: Divination Officer Guyer and a human girl of maybe fourteen or fifteen. The youth was seated at the examination table, but not handcuffed to the custody ring set in the tabletop. She looked anemic and tired, her eyes set behind dark rings.

A cooler sat on the floor, and the table held a length of cloth folded onto itself. Kravitz nodded to us as we came in.

"Carter. Ajax. Glad you made it."

I looked at the DO beyond the glass. "What's going on?"

"You don't know?"

I shook my head.

Kravitz frowned and looked at Angus. The Mollenkampi shrugged.

"I gave the message to Dispatch," he said. "You should have been paged, Carter." His grade school politics were in full gear.

I bit my cheek, but let it slide. "Well, we're here, so tell us now."

Kravitz turned back to me and Jax. "DO Guyer's going to try to turn up more direct evidence from the victim. I want you both to hear what turns up directly, instead of reading it in transcription. Trying to be more efficient."

From his spot across the room Angus huffed, "It'd be more efficient to let Bengles and me work the Haberdine case full time, instead of scraping candies off the pavement."

I practically jumped at his mention of a candy. The reporter had asked about dead candies. Had Angus been assigned to that case? I was already nervous about Talena's possible exposure. The last thing I needed was Angus digging into candy activity.

"What candies?" I asked.

Angus shook his head. "Complete waste of time."

Bryyh walked between us. "We don't have all day." She punched the intercom, bracelets jangling, and said, "When you're ready, Officer Guyer."

In 5D the DO leaned forward and pressed *Rec* on one of the reel-to-reel tape recorders that had become standard issue in interrogation rooms over the last few years.

Guyer wore professional attire, but the outfit was still topped with a sorcerer's cloak. She spoke into the microphone, stating the date and then, "Oracular Tongue procedure, Divination Officer Guyer supervising sorcerer." The term "Oracular Tongue" meant nothing to me, though Bryyh winced slightly at the phrase. Guyer kept talking.

"Assisted by my apprentice, Carla-Jean, we are attempting to contact Garson Haberdine."

Guyer opened the cooler and pulled out a plastic bag. Viscera, undoubtedly from Haberdine's remains. Bryyh thumbed the intercom again.

"Do you need respirators?"

The DO shook her head. "I'm only using a couple drops." Which confused me, since when she'd stormed out of the Eagle Crest she'd been yelling about needing more blood, not less. I glanced at Angus and saw his forehead wrinkle. He was thinking the same thing.

Guyer dipped a thumb into the bloody bag then quickly resealed it. The blood on the remains looked half coagulated. I wondered if they had added some kind of thinner to make it easier to work with. She crinkled her nose and shook her head. Even with that slight exposure it was getting to her. She swallowed and my mouth watered in sense memory. In a quick movement Guyer pressed her blood-smeared thumb to her forehead, leaving a smudged circle that approximated a third eye. Then she grasped her assistant's head, placing one hand on either side of the girl's jaw. Leaning in, Guyer pressed her forehead to the girl's. When they separated, they shared mirror images of the same bloody mark.

The apprentice—Carla-Jean—looked tense. Her breathing was rapid, and she clenched the armrests of the chair as Guyer released her. The DO unfolded the cloth draped over the table, revealing a selection of tools and implements that I couldn't see well. I found myself rising on my toes to get a better view.

Guyer held up a spray bottle no larger than a lipstick case and nodded to her apprentice. The girl's lips tightened, and then almost against her will, she stuck out her tongue. Guyer spritzed the girl's tongue, and although I couldn't see the distinctive iridescence, I was sure it was manna. Carla-Jean left her tongue sticking out of her mouth. I envied the girl for the experience. I was more likely to snack on a platinum and diamond sandwich than taste pure manna.

Guyer then picked up a thin, cone-shaped metal instrument with her right hand, and a pair of locking pliers with her left. The jaws of the pliers were wrapped in cloth. She bent over to look her apprentice in the eye. "Prepare yourself," she said, and grasped her apprentice's tongue with the pliers. Her right hand jerked upward, cutting into and through the girl's tongue from underneath.

The girl writhed, and all of us in the observation room shuddered. Even a bitten tongue bleeds heavily, and this apprentice—this child—was no exception. A jet of blood squirted across the table.

I fought the urge to jamb my thumb into the intercom. Bryyh's mouth was pulled down into a scowl, and even Angus's eyes were wide with what appeared to be shock or disapproval.

Kravitz spoke, a slight quiver in his voice. "The apprentice is here voluntarily. It's part of her training. She can stop it at any time."

For his part, Ajax had actually taken several steps toward the door, as if he intended to storm in and put a stop to this display. I had to admit, the kid was growing on me.

I looked back into 5D. Guyer set the piercing cone aside and slipped the pliers, still clamped on Carla-Jean's tongue, into a short stand in front of her apprentice. The girl's head nestled against a curved chin rest at the front of the stand. It allowed her head to sit level while keeping her ravaged tongue pulled taut.

Guyer held a metal ring with what appeared to be a white silk ribbon tied to it in her right hand. Chanting words that meant nothing to me, she lifted the ring up and through her apprentice's tongue. She grasped it on the other side and pulled, the silk ribbon now drenched in blood. With her left hand she picked up a wooden spindle and raised it above her apprentice's head. She slid the ring onto the spindle, then lifted a cloth with her right hand. Continuing to chant, she turned her left hand, pulling the ribbon through the bloody gash in Carla-Jean's tongue. With each twist of Guyer's wrist the girl moaned, and more ribbon was pulled through her tongue before being wrapped around the spindle. With her other hand Guyer used the cloth as a squeegee, wiping excess blood from the ribbon as her chanting became questions.

"Are you there, Garson Haberdine? Do you hear my call? Are you willing to aid in our investigation into your death?"

There was no answer, but after each question Guyer was silent for a few moments while she continued to curl more ribbon onto the spindle. The young apprentice kept her eyes closed, sweat glistening on her brow.

The DO fired off a litany of what I assumed must be standard questions, then moved on to ones the others must have given her already. Probably by Angus while I had no idea any of this was being planned.

"Was there a prostitute in the room with you the night you died?" A pause. "Do you know the name of the person who killed you?"

The apprentice squirmed, and Guyer gave her a concerned glance. I couldn't imagine that they would keep going for much longer. This time I did jam the intercom button.

"Ask if there was a cop there."

Guyer's forehead creased, but she asked the question as requested. Carla-Jean's whole body was twitching and tears soaked her cheeks.

I reached for the button again.

Ajax murmured, "Carter . . ."

The apprentice was shaking even more, almost spasming.

Angus's oversized partner broke. "Oh Hells below, let the girl stop, would ya?"

Bryyh moved to the intercom. "That's enough," she said.

Guyer took a long step back, then placed the spindle on one of the metal rods that stood upright. She stepped back toward the girl and lifted a pair of scissors. For a dreadful moment I was afraid of what she was going to do, but she only snipped the ribbon off, and the last of the silk snaked through Carla-Jean's tongue.

Cord cut, the girl collapsed. Guyer carefully lifted her assistant's head and looked in her eyes. She whispered something into the younger girl's ear, and Carla-Jean nodded. The DO handed her a small vial of balm, and patted the girl on the shoulder.

Guyer looked toward our group. I wonder what she saw in the mirror. Did she only see her reflection, a white-haired woman with bloodstained hands? Or did she see something more? Because I know that when she stared at that mirror, it was our shock and discomfort that stared back at her.

She straightened her back and smiled.

"You can come in now."

11

WE LEFT THE OBSERVATION AREA and entered room 5D. Despite Guyer's assurances, the smell of cinnamon was in the air, along with the distinctive tang of fresh blood.

By the time our solemn little procession moved into the larger room, the bucket of viscera had been covered and the apprentice had moved off to the side. The girl sat slumped over, her shoulders draped by a blanket. A long string of crimson-tinged spittle trailed down her chest.

Guyer had tied the end of the ribbon to another spindle, this one empty, and was pulling the silk from the one onto the other. She spun them both, and the ribbon reeled rapidly, but there was a pattern visible, dancing along the silken surface. The spindles slowed, and it became clear that the pattern was a kind of writing. When all the ribbon transferred there was a *click* from the reel-to-reel, and I realized that it had been rewinding as well.

Guyer said, "I'll need someone to work the recorder." She turned her head. "Carla-Jean—"

"Leave her be," Captain Bryyh said. "I'll work it." She stepped away from our little group, and I realized that we'd been huddled together as tightly as we had been in the small observation booth. I looked at the shivering form of Guyer's apprentice, and I was very grateful to not be a sorcerer.

Bryyh stuck her head out into the hall and barked at the patrol-man there. "Get a fan to air this room out." She paused. "Check that. Get as many fans as you can find." She walked back into the room and Guyer nodded at her.

"Ready when you are, Captain."

Bryyh hit play, and the DO's voice came over the speaker. I didn't check to see if the others winced at the words "Oracular Tongue" this time, but I know I did. As the recording of Guyer's chanting played, the DO found the spots in the blood-ribbon that matched the recording. At the first question, "Are you there, Garson Haber-dine?" Bryyh paused the tape, and Guyer read the writing from the ribbon.

"*I am here.*" She spoke in a monotone. "*Though I should be gone. I ache to depart. Please. Please, let me go.*"

I was growing to hate every aspect of divination.

Bryyh kept the pause button down. "Did he actually talk like this, 'I ache to depart' and stuff like that?"

Guyer shook her head. "No, it's a . . . kind of a translation."

Bryyh played the tape and we got to the real questions.

There was a disconnect between DO Guyer's matter-of-fact reading and the agonized pleading that filled Haberdine's re-sponses that somehow made the whole experience worse.

"*A discarded candy, wrap on the floor. Intimate oceans of noth-ing. Now I am alone and cold.*" She scanned ahead. "And then it's just screaming for a while."

She went on like that, relating the words of Haberdine's echo. Some of what the victim had to say was useful. He didn't know his attackers, for example. And the response to the question about a cop in the room was "*One yes, one no, one big, one small. Both deadly.*"

In between each question and answer came the same pleas, directed at Guyer: "*Why won't you let me go, why can't I go?*"

I put my hands against the wall and let my weight sink into it.

"What are we doing to this guy?" I surprised myself by saying it aloud.

Guyer's head snapped around. "You want Mister Haberdine to walk the Path eternal? Catch the killer. Till then, I'll keep him where we need him."

Angus rolled his eyes. "We need a description of who was there, some kind of identification more than vague contradictions."

Guyer tucked a white curl behind one ear. "I can pull his echo in closer to us. Creating a link is easier than breaking it," she said. "If we're going to do it, we should do it now, while the Haberdine and my apprentice are still bound."

Beneath her blanket, young Carla-Jean shuddered. Manna bound items like glue—whether it was pre-Shortage factories of wheat threshers and butter churns or the echo of a murder victim and an oracle, it took a sorcerer's skill to sever a magical connection. She would be linked with Haberdine until the DO broke it.

"But if you want clearer communication I'm going to need a lot more blood," Guyer said. "And even with that I can't guarantee the information will be usable. Sometimes the dead don't give straight answers no matter what we do."

Bryyh held up her hand. "No." She stepped into the center of the room. "No one's shedding more blood right now. We're going to review what we learned today." She raised her brows and peered at Guyer. "You look after that girl." Her gaze lingered on the DO long enough to make it clear there would be no more sorcery that day.

Bryyh turned to face us, one hand on her hip, the other pressed against her forehead.

"Haberdine had a candy in his room, or at least wanted one there."

Angus ran a finger along his collar, pulling it away from his speaking mouth. When he spoke it was slow, thoughtful.

"The candy killing Bengles and I got assigned this afternoon," he said. My stomach tightened. "It felt off. The girl had her throat slit. And someone tried to make it look like a robbery. Purse was gone, but her money belt was left behind." His mandibles spread and closed. "A pimp would have wanted everyone to know it was business-related. A real mugger would've searched the body."

Even with those details, Angus hadn't wanted the case. It wasn't political enough for him.

Ajax poured a sip of coffee down his throat and asked, "What was this candy's name?"

Angus grunted and looked at Bengles, who said, "Stacie something."

Kravitz's brow creased and Ajax looked at me expectantly. I couldn't avoid it, so I pulled Stacie's photo from my jacket.

"Was this her?" I asked.

"Yes," said Angus. "Where'd you get that photo?"

"The Eagle Crest security camera," said Bryyh.

Kravitz put the pieces together. "That's the girl your candy told you about."

With no other option, I brought the others up to speed with what Talena had told me about Stacie, and how that had led to the interview with Gellica. At least I got to see Angus's face when he heard we'd interviewed a high-ranking AFS diplomat.

But he was quick to pivot, claiming the more important case.

"The candies could be the key to the whole thing." Angus raked a hand over his plated head like he was mugging for a camera. I could almost see him calculating the potential media coverage if his new case tied into the Haberdine killing. "I'm hearing rumors of a candy blackmail ring from my CIs."

I forced my fist to unclench. *Hells.* I had to get in front of this before Talena's name was dragged into the spotlight. Before mine was.

"Same here," I said. "But I've heard about kids forcing johns to give up the candy habit. Nothing like the kind of thing we saw at the Eagle Crest."

Angus snorted. "Blackmail's blackmail."

"But it isn't murder," I said.

"No, but blackmail creates pressure, which makes people desperate," said Kravitz. "Desperate people do desperate things." I hated him for being right.

Bryyh dropped the hand from her forehead and squinted at me. "What was with the question about a cop in the room? What do you know, Carter?"

I squared my shoulders. "Nothing for sure. Haberdine's killer was out of control, but that scene was picked clean, like a pro had covered it up. Someone who knew how cops operate. An ex-cop who just got out of lockup would be willing to do desperate things to get reestablished."

Bryyh rocked back on her heels. "Flanagan." Her eyes darted back and forth, her mind whirling through the probabilities while also juggling political and press angles that I couldn't imagine.

Angus spoke up. "Everyone knows that Carter's got a hard-on for Flanagan. That doesn't mean he's the one who tore up the Squib."

Bryyh nodded slowly, apparently taking that into account. She said, "He's still a good lead. We know he's violent and we know he could pull off presenting himself as a cop. He's also probably hurting for money." She looked at me. "Do you know where he's at?"

"Gone to ground," I said.

"Hiding from something in particular, or just hiding?"

"Can't say. But it's a strange coincidence that he's disappeared right now."

Bryyh made a low noise. "We need to end this." Eyelids drooping from exhaustion or concentration. "Work every lead you've got."

Kravitz nodded. "That works for me. Carter and Ajax, you take Detectives Myris and Hemingway and a patrol team. Find Flanagan and bring him in for questioning."

I raised a hand. "How fast can we get a warrant?"

Kravitz shrugged me off. "The way city hall's in a panic? For the Haberdine case any judge will issue a warrant on demand." He pointed at Angus and Bengles. "You two, pull Abrams and Bierce off whatever they're wasting their time on, and requisition a patrol squad if you need one. Find these blackmailers. If it's a candy, turn the streets upside down. If it's a Therreau, handle it with the community liaison. Be quiet, but do what you need to. No kid gloves— if the farmers don't like us around they can file a complaint. The whole political thing is already blowing up in our face. Any questions?" He looked at the four of us. "Then get out of here and let's end this thing."

We filtered into the hall and left the DO to tend to her apprentice. Jax and I walked down the hall while the others talked. My stomach ached. Like everyone, I'd grown up on tales of pre-Shortage magicians and mechanical marvels. But the sorcery we'd just witnessed hurt the living and tortured the dead. More innocent lives shredded in the pursuit of justice. Among police there's an age-old technique to cover your own anxiety: making fun of it in others. I decided to carry on that tradition.

I asked Ajax, "You still hoping to see a little magic? Maybe some disappearing bloody footprints?"

"No," he said, not playing along. "I'll be fine if I don't have to see anything like that again." He glanced at the others down the hall, then motioned for me to duck my head closer to his talking mouth so I could hear him whisper.

"You're completely crazy," he said. "We've got nothing on this Flanagan guy but your hunch."

I spoke into his small nub of an ear. "It's not a hunch. It's logic." I dropped my ear to his shoulder level once again. It's much less complicated to whisper strategy with another human.

"We're going to be wasting time."

I stepped back. "You said I've got a reputation." He started to answer but I cut him off. "Is that reputation that I fail to close cases? Or is it that I piss off too many people along the way?"

He gave me a long stare. "There's also the reputation for drinking," he said.

I put on my best pained grin. "Okay, fine—"

"And the one about generally being an asshole."

I swallowed my response when Angus and Bengles came around the corner.

They caught up to us as the elevator doors opened. We climbed in and Ajax hit the button for the third floor. Angus punched the ground floor button and adjusted his tie. I figured he was giving his speaking hole more room to flap. He didn't disappoint.

"You know," he said, "Flanagan's a waste of time."

I shrugged and bobbed my head to the rhythm of the elevator's muzak. "He's a better bet than some street candy barely old enough to hold a gun, let alone tear a Squib to pieces."

"I don't know. Squib stink turns you humans pretty bestial. Judging from your face at the Eagle Crest, I'd have thought you learned that firsthand." Angus glanced at his human partner. "No offense, Bengles." She grunted, though out of consent or disinterest, I couldn't tell. I ignored her and kept my eyes on Angus.

"Only thing I learned there was that you know how to get in front of cameras and you can't secure a crime scene for shit."

Angus's mandibles twitched and his biting jaw clicked. "You know, you're more pathetic than I ever—"

Jax cut him off with a flow of words in the musical Mollenkampi language. A baritone arpeggio of notes from his biting mouth matched by a delicate bird song of melody from his speaking mouth. Angus clenched his fists and leaned forward. Jax didn't back down.

The elevator slowed its descent, and announced our arrival with a *ding* that provided a way to make our exit without coming to blows. I patted Jax on the shoulder and we left the cab. Angus and Bengles continued their ride down to the garage. When the doors closed I gave Ajax a sidelong look.

"Thanks, partner," I said.

I turned around and faced the pool of detectives. They were working phones, shaking trees, hitting countless dead ends but always crawling forward. For the first time in a long time, it felt like I was where I belonged. I had a partner, I had the resources of a team at my disposal, and I was determined to find my man and prove my case. And if things might end badly? Well, that'd never stopped me from seeing it through to the end before.

12

THE NEXT MORNING DETECTIVES MYRIS and Hemingway sat at desks pulled adjacent to ours. It was a makeshift place for our team to strategize. I wasn't sure what was more bizarre: the nature of the crime we were investigating, or the idea that I had a team.

Myris was a Mollenkampi whose foot kept constant cadence to a beat only she could hear. Hemingway was a human with blond hair in a tight ponytail, showing off earrings that were a touch too long for regulations. They were both flipping through the files I'd given them on Flanagan. Their job was to track him down.

"Check with his parole officer," I said. "Be sure to ask where Flanagan would be staying if not at his registered address."

Hemingway popped her gum. "I know how to find a target."

"Yeah. I'm just telling you—"

"How to do my job."

I pointed to my partner. "Jax, can you do something for me?"

Jax nodded his plated head.

"Call Gellica. I want the two envoys she gave us. What're their names—" I snapped my fingers.

"Lowell and Cordray," he said.

"That's them. Get them down here in separate cars. Unmarked. Let's try not to rattle any PR cages today."

Jax hesitated.

"You're thinking Angus has the candy angle," I said. "I don't care about how the envoys are connected to the candies. If Flanagan's the button man on the Squib, then our job is to find out how he's connected to these diplomats."

"On it," he said, and reached for a phone.

I turned to Hemingway and opened my mouth, then looked back to Jax. "While you've got her on the line, find out if we can meet with her again, too. She claims to be eager to help; let's see if we can put her to work."

Ajax punched up an external extension and I pointed at Hemingway.

Myris leaned forward. She had the thinner head plates typical of female Mollenkampi. "We've got the file," she said. "Is there anything you're gonna tell us that isn't already in it?"

I considered her question and dropped my hand.

"No."

"Then let us find your guy. You go prove that he did the crime, and we'll have him on a platter waiting for you."

With the rest of Team Carter occupied, I reached for a phone and dialed Talena's apartment. It was probably my twentieth call since the day before, when I'd heard the news about Stacie.

The phone rang, and I muttered to myself like a gambler urging on a horse from the stands: *Pick up, pick up, pick up.*

People die. Sometimes they kill themselves, sometimes they kill each other. Maybe they overdose or walk in front of a bus. Stacie's death could mean anything, or nothing.

There was a click as the line engaged, followed by the hiss of audio tape. Answering machine.

"Hi. If you're calling me, then you know who I am. Let me know who you are and I'll consider calling you back."

I counted the gap between the end of her message and the beep. Each message left on the tape added to the length of the gap. This one was short, which means she'd checked her messages and chosen not to call me back.

Dammit!

I was about to leave a message about returning phone calls, but Ajax was making his way across the Bullpen.

"They're here," he said.

We received our first guest in one of our nicer interrogation rooms, the kind with no mystery stains on the floor. We even provided a box of donuts. Envoy Cordray looked them over but didn't take one. He was a wiry man sporting a scraggly mustache with a bald spot over his right incisor. He spoke with an extending of the nasal vowels, dragging out words like "need" and "see." I couldn't place the accent, and it bugged me.

"Where are you from, Mr. Cordray?"

"The west coast. You wouldn't know it."

"Right on the coast?" That didn't seem right.

"No. Farther in. A small town no one's heard of, so it's easier to simply say the coast. Most people don't bother to ask." He favored me with a weasely smile that exposed his top teeth.

If that was his idea of a charming grin, it was no wonder he had to frequent the candies.

"Turns out asking questions is my job," I said. "Where exactly is that town?"

"To the east of the Inland Ocean, but not all the way to the salt plains. It's called Alyria."

Jax chimed in. "Alyria? Robeson was from there. The poet."

Cordray blinked. "Yes."

"Beautiful imagery in his work," said Jax.

I tapped my notebook, and he gave me a small shrug as if to say *It's not my fault I'm more cultured than you.*

"Mr. Cordray," I said, "do you know why we're speaking with you?"

"Gellica said you wanted to know more about the Squib delegation. Goals, key personnel, and so forth."

Gellica was proving to be more useful by the day. I gave Cordray an encouraging nod.

"That's true, and that's all helpful information. But we also wanted to follow up on a bit of intelligence that came to light about the victim's sexual predilections."

"Well, I wouldn't know about that, Officer."

"Detective," I corrected. "And no, of course you wouldn't. We were just wondering if perhaps you'd ever seen Mr. Haberdine with any of these individuals."

I slid three photos out of a manila folder. Two were of the candies from the surveillance photos, and one of Flanagan's mug shot. Two more photos stayed in the folder. One of those was of Talena.

Cordray studied them, fingers running over his mustache. I tracked his eyes, which darted between the two girls and barely landed on Flanagan. Finally he shook his head.

"I do not recognize these people."

I pulled the photos back and opened the manila folder again. "Oh. Sorry, there was one more in here. I missed it before." I handed him another mug shot, this one of a candy whose name we'd gotten from Gellica's file on Cordray. In the mug shot, the candy's face was exposed, though the rubber material of her suit was still visible on her shoulders.

"Does she ring any bells, Envoy?"

The color drained from his face as he shoved the photo back at me. "No, I'm afraid not. I'm sorry I couldn't be of help—"

"Oh, you're being most helpful. We've already detained this young lady. Quite the experience for her. I'm not sure she's worn a lot of handcuffs before. I'll be honest, though, my partner—Detective Ajax here, I think I introduced him already—anyway, my partner and I don't think she has anything to do with the case. You understand how these go . . . we round up everyone with even a partial connection, lean on them in the interrogation room until they throw out a name, hoping that'll make us leave them alone."

Ajax nodded solemnly, letting his biting jaw clack slightly as he did so.

"I was really hoping you'd recognize one of these others, since that's who we're more interested in. But"—I slid the photo in a gentle circular motion before him—"sometimes we need to throw fresh meat to the press. I'm sure she can provide us a sacrificial lamb or two."

Cordray folded his hands. When he spoke, his voice squeaked. "Perhaps—perhaps I could have another look at the earlier photos?"

I widened my eyes in mock surprise and shuffled the photos back over to him.

"Anything to be of help to the police," he said.

I nodded to Ajax, who stood and apologized for having to leave early.

He was off to a second interrogation room, where our other interviewee was already waiting. We wanted to make sure that

Cordray wasn't able to circumvent our tactics by getting advance warning to his colleague. I didn't know if they were friendly enough to do so, but it's always better to divide and conquer.

Cordray didn't need to study the photos so long this time. He dropped a finger on one of the candies. Stacie, Talena's friend who'd turned up dead.

"This girl," he said. "I saw her in the lobby of the Armistice."

Very posh. The Armistice made the Eagle Crest look like an hourly rate joint.

"What was she doing?"

"Attending a gala. Lots of the alternative energy executives stayed there and they like to throw events. I saw this girl speaking with Envoy Haberdine. I'm sure of it."

"Who else was there?"

"Oh . . ." He gave an exaggerated sigh. "I couldn't say exactly. The usual crowd. Envoy Gellica, Ambassador Paulus, the Squib delegation, Harlan Cedrow, Alma Johnson, and a few of the other oil landholders. The big players and their support teams."

Anyone else at that party would have seen Haberdine with her as well.

"Where are the Squibs staying during the talks?" I asked.

"The Armistice. They have an entire floor booked there."

"Expensive."

"Very. They're trying to make a statement about how much cash they could bring to the table."

"Nothing like conspicuous spending to get the locals fired up with greed." I retrieved the photos of the candies, but left Flanagan's sitting on the table. "Are you certain that you've never seen this man before?"

Cordray chewed his lip. "Would it . . . help your investigation if perhaps I had?"

It was tempting. With a witness putting Flanagan at the Eagle Crest at the time that Haberdine was killed, I'd have the go-ahead to hunt him down.

"Only if you're sure you really saw him," I said. "Truly sure."

He shook his head.

I sighed and gathered the photos into the manila folder. "If we need anything else, we'll be in touch."

"I'll be glad to help, Officer."

"Detective."

Cordray dropped his gaze and studied the table in front of him.

"Of course. My apologies."

I left Cordray sweating in the conference room and stepped into the hall to gather my thoughts. There was a pause in the coming and going down the hallway, so I pulled a small aluminum-wrapped packet from my wallet and shook free two painkillers. I'd left the prescription bottle at home, in an attempt to be more subtle. I bent at a drinking fountain and washed the pills down to quiet the pain in my bones. Then I went to find my partner.

Ajax had already begun warming up Lowell, the other envoy whose name Gellica had given us.

This man was the polar opposite of Cordray. A big man in a small man's body, Lowell looked like ten gallons of shit stuffed in a five-gallon bag. Wide as he was tall, he didn't show signs of either fat or excess muscle, but rather thick slabs of meat. His face was broad and flat, and a muscle along his jaw twitched as he glared at me. For a moment I wondered if all the science books had been wrong, and it was possible for a human and Mollenkampi to breed. From the look on Lowell's face, if Ajax reminded him of any distant relatives, he'd prefer to take a chainsaw to that branch of the family tree.

The envoy's nostrils were flared and his jaw set. For his part, Ajax sat pleasantly across the table, the sliding tones of his voice trilling away as he chatted about one nonsensical thing after another. It was burning Lowell up to listen to him go on. I turned my back to them as I shut the door to keep from laughing.

Biting the side of my cheek, I turned around and held out my hand.

"Mr. Lowell, I'm Detective Carter, Titanshade PD. My apologies for being late."

He let my hand hang in the air, then with an unwilling jerk leaned forward for a handshake. "It's about time," he grumbled.

I could imagine him grinning widely and nodding in sympathy with a political or business connection, and just as easily see him howling with rage at a hired lover who'd displeased him. I'd been in the room thirty seconds and I already hated him.

"Well, I do apologize. But your colleague Mr. Cordray ended up being a much greater source of information than we expected."

He clearly didn't know how to take that, and remained silent.

I reached into the manila folder and set the photos of the two candies and Flanagan on the table. I dropped the folder on the table as well, near Ajax's notebook, and remained standing.

Lowell glanced over the photos and frowned.

"I came here as a courtesy," he said. "Am I going to regret not having an attorney present?"

"Do you need one?"

Before he could answer I leaned in. "Because we're not charging you with anything. Yet. And it was your boss who suggested you come speak to us. So you might have to explain to Gellica why you lawyered up."

He harrumphed, his cheeks puffing and deflating. I felt the

expulsion of his breath move across my face from across the table. Powerful lungs.

"Is this off the record?" he asked.

"Absolutely not. But we can be on the record here in relative comfort, or on the record after you've been booked. It's really up to you."

His lips curled back. "You just said you're not charging me."

"I said *yet*." I crossed my arms. "Mr. Cordray was *extremely* co-operative."

Lowell hesitated, but eventually his distrust of Cordray over-rode his desire to frustrate us. He dropped his gaze to the photos laid out on the desk.

"Her." He slapped the photo of a candy, sending her spinning across the table toward us. I caught the photo before it fell to the floor. "And him." The photo of Flanagan shot toward us as well, and my adrenaline surged. "This other girl I've never seen."

"And how do you know these individuals?"

He pursed his lips, jutting them at the photo of the candy, a young girl with blond curls and an upturned nose. Stacie again.

"I bought her. For the duration of my stay in Titanshade." He glared at each of us in turn, as if daring us to judge him. But by then I'd long since made my judgment about the esteemed Mr. Lowell. Ajax put pencil to notepad.

"When?" he asked.

"Shortly after I arrived."

According to Gellica's file, that would have been just over a year ago.

"How many times did you see her?" I asked.

"A number of occasions. I favored her."

"And the agency?"

He scowled and said nothing.

I sat down with a sigh. "Who did you book her through? Some would say 'who is her pimp,' but that word's probably too base for a man of your refined tastes."

There was a pause while he decided how much offense to take at that crack. He seemed to lean toward not taking as much offense as I'd like, so I decided to insult his bravery while I was at it.

"I understand that you're afraid of what the pimp will do—"

"Don't be ridiculous." He spread his legs, as if assuming a battle stance. "I'm an official of the Assembly of Free States. I'm not about to be bullied by some frontier town madame with shit on her boots." He still paused before answering, giving lie to his bravado. "Carrington Placements."

I held up Stacie's photo. "Did you ever see this young woman in the company of Garson Haberdine?"

"I never saw her in the company of anyone but myself. If I did, I would hardly consort with her again. I prefer my commitments to be exclusive."

The man was in for a rude awakening when he learned how prostitution worked.

"Wait a minute," said Ajax. "You said you 'bought' her. Do you mean—"

"I mean that I have an exclusive contract for her attention while I am in this town. I have been assured that she has spent no intimate time with anyone else since I acquired her. The girl is mine alone."

My skin crawled.

"When was the last time you saw Stacie?"

"Stacie?"

I twitched the photo back and forth.

"Oh," he said with a snort. "I named her Kellen."

Jax leaned forward, fists held below the table. "You named her?"

Lowell frowned. "I bought her, I can call her what I like."

I had to change the topic before one of us lost our composure. I held up the photo of Flanagan. "And this man? Where have you seen him?"

"That one I did see talking to Haberdine. About a week ago, he was outside the Armistice."

"You're sure it was him?"

"He stood out. He was dressed for cold weather and was obviously uncomfortable that close to the mountain."

That sounded like it could be true. If Flanagan had come in quickly, especially if he'd been called in unexpectedly, then he wouldn't have had time to change from warmer clothes to something more appropriate for the center of Titanshade.

"How would you describe the conversation between him and Haberdine?"

"It didn't seem heated, if that's what you're implying. It only stuck in my mind because of what the man was wearing."

"Winter gear?"

"That's what I said. But it was the type of gear. Antiquated. Simple. Like your religious folk here."

"Therreau?"

"Yes, them. But the man hadn't plucked his face. He still had hair on his head, eyebrows, everything. It stood out, you see, because it was unusual."

"Did you ask Haberdine about him?"

"I am trying to facilitate the Squibs' visit," he said. "It would have been disrespectful to interrogate him. Something you wouldn't understand." He swiveled his neck and stared above our heads.

Jax shot me a look. If Flanagan was living on a Therreau farm but not shaving his hair, he ought to be as easy to track down as a polar bear in a mud field. And if Lowell was the connection between Garson Haberdine and the mysterious Stacie, then the malignant lump of a man across the table had turned out to be our first real step forward.

WITH MYRIS AND HEMINGWAY ON the hunt for Flanagan, Jax decided to cozy up to an AV cart and review the Eagle Crest security tapes. That was fine by me. I had a personal errand to run. I took the Hasam down to the Borderlands and parked outside the eight-story walkup that Talena called home.

The building's bottom floor was commercial space, small shops that announced they were open for business by rolling their overhead gates up. From tiny storefronts wares spilled out onto the sidewalk, racks of T-shirts and poorly made electronics fought for space alongside small tables and junior-sized chairs that allowed customers to eat without being so comfortable that they lingered.

A couple of the food stalls were cranking out meals for the late breakfast crowd, and the scents mingled in the air. First I caught the smell of broiled cracklefin fillets, probably caught in Blacknall Bay. From frozen, of course. With transportation costs what they were, fresh fish was a luxury only the very wealthy or very finicky enjoyed. Behind the fish came the rich, mossy scent of proilers, a hearty fungus that grew easily on the cool and misty fringes of the city. They grilled up nicely and made good stew stock.

My stomach growled, reminding me how long it had been since my last meal. I considered grabbing an open-face proiler sandwich, until the cook threw a healthy dash of cinnamon across it. My appetite quickly faded.

I headed inside, where the smells were distinctly less pleasant. The narrow stairwell was lined with trash and the occasional sprawled form of someone who thought the stairs were as good a place as any to pass out. Skyrocketing real estate prices meant buildings like this one were crammed with more tenants than they'd ever been designed for. Somewhere a city inspector was enjoying a nice meal bought with bribe money. But griping about corruption wouldn't make my hike any easier. I eyed the stairs and flexed each leg in turn, warming the muscles and hoping to lessen the aches. Then I stepped around the first sleeping figure and began my climb to the seventh floor.

As a rule of thumb in Titanshade, the higher the floor the more affordable the rent. The thermal vents that made the city an oasis in a frozen desert didn't have the pressure to rise more than a couple of floors. As a result, upper levels were never as comfortable without the expensive installation of booster fans.

The pain built as I climbed, an ongoing burning that wrapped around the bones of my legs and hips. Before long I was gritting my teeth and mumbling curses with each step. Seeking a distraction, I busied myself with studying the doors I passed and conjecturing on the lives hidden behind them.

Every third or fourth door on the march upward was decrepit or showed signs of repaired kick-ins from burglaries or domestic disputes, but the rest were well maintained, and probably cozy beyond their threshold. Struggling neighborhoods aren't as unpleasant as you see on the news. Politicians and the media have a vested interest in keeping people afraid of each other. I try not to think about whether that's true of cops as well.

When I reached unit 7A I rapped my knuckles on the door and

stepped back so that I could be identified through the peephole. She opened it anyway, which I appreciated.

Talena stood with one hand on the door, the other tucked in the pocket of her jeans. She wore a zip-up sweater over the top of an open flannel shirt, untucked, with a plain green T-shirt as a base. Easily removed layers perfect for moving around the city's microclimates.

"Twice in three days," she said. "A new record." She may have attempted a smile. If so, it didn't make it to her face. "Why are you here?"

She sounded tired.

"Your friend Stacie. She's dead."

I expected her to stiffen, to turn away. Instead she nodded.

"I know," she said.

"They think it's a—"

"Her pimp's dead, too." She rubbed her eyes. "Butterfly Carrington. She was a proper bitch, but no one should go out that way."

She already knew. I paused, uncertain how to proceed. My major conversational gambit involves annoying people into revealing more than they intended. It was a skill set that left me sorely unprepared for talks like this.

I stood there sweating and unsure, trying to ignore the pain in my legs and the discomfort in my gut as she decided what to do with me.

After three long breaths she stepped aside. "Well, come on in, then."

I followed her inside, trying to remember the last time I'd seen her apartment. Three years? Four? I hadn't helped move her stuff when she left her grandparents' place. That was after Jenny went into the hospital for the last time. After I couldn't afford the rent on our apartment. After I fell off the wagon.

"I'm getting ready to head out," she said. "Can you make it fast, whatever it is?"

Talena's apartment was more workspace than home. The furniture was bohemian-chic, fabrics and oversized pillows stashed around low-slung thrift store tables. Every wall was decorated with paper hangings and every available surface was stacked with pamphlets like the one I'd taken from her the other day and that still sat crumpled in my suit coat pocket. Scattered around were a few personal mementos, including photos of Talena and her mother. I wasn't in any of them.

I turned, not letting myself dwell on the many reasons I'd given her to want me out of her life. Instead I focused on the wall decorations. They weren't photos or posters. I stepped closer. Each one was a thank-you letter.

Dozens of letters, all from people thanking Talena for helping them get off the streets or change their lives. Some were from families of people who she'd tried to help but failed. Hung in groupings of eight, many of the letters had an infinity sign beneath the signature, a nod to Talena's faith.

I looked from the letters to Talena. There was a glint of metal at her collarbone. A stylized eight hung on a simple chain around her neck. The number eight was sacred. Turned on its side, an eight became a ba, the symbol of the infinite One Path, which was walked by eight Families—the eight intelligent species that populated the world. Eight constellations made up the horoscope, and eight continents had once been scattered over the globe before joining together to form Eyjan.

"Well?" she said.

It occurred to me that I didn't know when she'd picked up religion. We'd never prayed much when she was a kid. The occasional thanks to the Titan, but that's tradition, a holdover from old ways that predated the Path. Her faith didn't bother me; I respected her convictions. I was just never that good at saying it out loud.

But introspection is tough to keep up when you're in pain, and my legs were killing me. I fished my aluminum packet out and pulled two pills free. It didn't matter if Talena saw them or not—she wouldn't be reporting to the department shrinks.

"Look, can I get a glass of water?" I loosened my already slack tie.

She hesitated, staring at the tiny, tightly wrapped packet between my fingers. I realized that it didn't look too far from the illicit packages she saw change hands every day on the street.

"Oh, come on," I said. "They're prescription. From Al Mumphrey."

She raised a brow. Skeptical. "Your poker buddy?"

"He's a doctor," I said. "Got a diploma on his wall and never lost a patient."

"He's the medical examiner. His patients are all corpses."

"Except for me," I said. "And I'm not dead yet."

She almost smiled. "If you say so."

I shifted my weight from one aching leg to the other. "How about that water?"

Talena stepped to the kitchenette and ran the tap. As she did, a strand of hair fell across her face and the light caught her profile just right; I was shocked that I could have forgotten how much she looked like her mother. In that moment I steeled my resolve.

My mom had died on the job when I was a kid. I never got to say good-bye, but I also didn't have to watch her go. Talena had been a young adult when she watched Jenny wither on the vine as cancer ate her bones. I didn't want either of us to see the other caught up in the madness that was growing around the Haberdine case. I may not have been a good father figure for most of Talena's life, but I could at least help her stay clear of the coming storm.

Even if she wouldn't want the help.

I shot the pills and chased them with a swig from the tapered cup Talena handed me.

"You need to leave town," I said, and she answered by rolling her eyes.

"I told you the Squib murder was bad." I handed her the empty cup. "It's getting worse. Now there's talk in the Bunker about blackmail being involved." I did my best to appeal to her sense of reason. "You oughta disappear. At least until things blow over."

She smirked. "I don't run away. That was always more your thing."

I opened my mouth, meaning to tell her I was proud of her, meaning to say I didn't know how I'd ended up being just as absent as my own old man had been. But that's not what came out.

Instead, I heard myself using her recently murdered friend to prove my point.

"You saw what happened to Stacie."

Her lips pulled back, and her hands laced around the empty cup, fidgeting with excess energy. Her temper was rising.

"I did." She dropped the cup in the sink with a rattle. "And if we turn our backs it'll keep happening to women every day, in every neighborhood in this town."

She grabbed a stack of papers off a table and rapped the edges, knocking them into tidy order before moving on to another stack. It was a quirk she'd picked up from her mom. The house was never more organized than when Jenny and I fought.

"Talena—"

"You want to run?" She ran her hand across her bookshelf, bringing the spines to order. "Fine."

She turned and struck her chest. "Not me. I'm the person who runs toward the sound of sirens, to see if I can help."

"The world needs people like that," I said. "Trouble is, sometimes the real works gets done in the dark, where there's no flashing lights and sirens to draw attention."

Talena's face flushed and she grimaced, as if biting back her response. Turning away, she gathered an armful of pamphlets. She was getting ready to hit the streets and save more souls. That's when I saw my mistake.

I'd come to warn her off, and I'd only managed to rile her up. If I laid out the full scope of risk she was facing, Talena wouldn't retreat to fight another day. She'd charge in and sort out the details later, probably while sitting in the hospital or a jail cell. Or both.

And who did that remind me of?

If she wasn't going to take my advice, then the only way I could see to get both of us in the clear was to wrap the case up quickly. And that meant moving on Flanagan.

"Alright, I warned you. Mission accomplished." I backpedaled, then changed the subject. "Have you heard anything about Stacie? Any idea who would've wanted her dead?"

She exhaled and shook her head. "Nothing you'd credit. People are saying that it's the Squib Stalker."

"The what?"

"Read a paper." She threw one of the local fish wraps at me. I caught it and popped it open. The headline screamed "IS NO ONE SAFE?" above an utterly indecent photo of Stacie's corpse and another photo of her as a young bombshell. The story was several columns of speculation about a killer driven by Squib rage to slaughter everyone in his path.

"Bunch of crap," I said. "It's nothing like the Haberdine killing." A few questions at the Bunker had confirmed that already. Stacie and her pimp had each been shot and tossed off the roof of a building on the outskirts of town. Brutal, but not out of line for a Titanshade homicide.

"That's not the word on the street," she said. "People are scared. They think any human who looks strange has got Squib rage." She walked to the door and opened it. "Okay, so you delivered your message. Thanks, I guess. Now I've got work to do."

She moved out of the apartment and I followed, waiting as she latched the eight deadbolts on her door. We walked down the stairs together in an uncomfortable silence. My mind chewed on the puzzle of what to say. I was afraid that if I said too little she'd be at risk, and if I told her too much she'd do something stupid. I thought about it all the way down the stairs. I thought about it as we walked through the doors. And then we were on the street and I saw the press of people, the hundreds of lives passing by, and I wondered how many of them might be touched by what she was doing. And I realized that maybe instead of puzzling out what to say, I should just say something.

"Hey," I said. She was already walking away from me. "Do some good out there today."

Talena barked out a laugh, and called over her shoulder, "Since when do you care about what happens to kids on the street?"

"I always have," I said. But she was too far from me to hear.

I said it again, this time to myself.

"I always have."

In my mind a single, obsessive drum pounded. *You gotta get Flanagan. The only way to save her is to find Flanagan.*

By the time I got back to the Bunker, Ajax had heard back from Gellica's assistant. Our meeting was scheduled. We rode out that afternoon and were ushered to a small balcony overlooking the courtyard in the center of 1 Government Plaza. Below, vendors hawked street food and federal employees milled about, enjoying the green space. This failure to squeeze in an extra parking lot or office space was mind-boggling in a city where every available inch of real estate teemed with families and would-be oil boomers. The tiny park was a declaration of power and wealth, eloquent in its simplicity. And it all seemed below the attention of our host, as Gellica sipped iced tea through a straw and looked at Ajax and me expectantly.

"Well? What have you found?" she asked.

I looked away from the litter-free courtyard long enough to give her a non-answer.

"I'm sure you understand that we can't comment directly on an ongoing investigation."

She waved me off. "Fine. I'm not looking for state secrets. But I do want to know if you're making progress, and if there's anything else our department can do to help."

We'd released both Lowell and Cordray, though I had a plan on the back burner to make sure neither one of them walked away from this mess unscathed.

"The information you already provided was very helpful," I said.

"Hmm. I sense this is a lead-in to a request, Detective."

"Your senses are refined, Envoy."

She smiled around her straw. "Well, ask away."

"How much do you track your employees' activities?"

"We have security measures. We deal with sensitive information on a regular basis and can't allow any kind of security breach. But we're not in the habit of spying on our own people, if that's what you're asking."

In the courtyard diplomats and administrators were enjoying the weather. Separated from the rest of the city, there were no hustlers selling knockoff watches, no games of three-card monte running on top of overturned cardboard boxes. But I wasn't fooled by the beauty of the emerald square. I knew they had their own brand of con men in these neighborhoods. Up here, it was the nonviolent offenders who were the most dangerous.

I pulled out the photos of Flanagan and all the candies we'd shown her subordinates. "Have you ever seen any of these people?"

She leaned forward, close enough that I could see tiny flecks of gold in the brown of her eyes as she pushed the photos back and forth. Finally she tapped a finger on the photo of Flanagan.

"I know him," she said.

"You've seen him? With the Squibs?"

She bit her lip. "No . . . from the news. There was a scandal. Not recently."

"Back a few years," I said. "He hurt a lot of people."

"I read about it. One of the tabloids in the capital ran a piece on the level of corruption in the North. Titanshade is still viewed as the wild frontier down in Fracinica."

The capital city viewed pretty much everything outside its borders as second-class rabble. It was only our oil reserves and the tremendous amount of money they provided the AFS coffers that caused us to register with the central government at all. If the wells dried up before the wind farm deal closed we wouldn't even have that.

"You think this Flanagan was involved in some way?" she asked.

"I do."

Jax interjected. "What about her?" He pointed to the photo of Stacie. "Have you ever seen her?"

Gellica looked again, narrowing her eyes.

"Not that I remember, but I have a feeling that you're about to tell me I have."

My partner let out a short, tinkling laugh. "A wise old man once told me to never ask a question unless I already knew the answer." He nudged the photo closer. "Think again, have you seen her with Lowell at any time?"

She studied it, then shook her head. "I honestly couldn't say. Is she connected in some way?"

"She's dead," I said. Gellica's eyes widened and her mouth dropped.

"And you think Lowell—"

"The investigation is ongoing," Jax said. "The detectives handling that case will be in touch if it's needed. But only if it's needed." He paused, giving Gellica a chance to volunteer more information. She stirred her drink and said nothing.

"Right now, we want to focus our efforts," I said. "We'd like to show this photo"—I indicated Flanagan—"to more of your employees. Anyone who was around the Squib delegation or anyone else involved with the talks. If they remember him or who he talked to, it might help us sew things up."

Gellica took another sip of tea and furrowed her brows. "Of course. But . . ."

"What is it?" asked Jax.

"Well," she said, "I want you to wrap this up as fast as possible."

"We all do," I said.

"And I'd be even happier if you found out that it was this Flanagan person, and had nothing to do with any of our people or their proclivities."

Jax piped in. "So you can leave them in place?"

"Oh, Lowell and Cordray will be fired. But only after you're done with them. Every organization has to deal with some assholes, but there's no point in rewarding this kind of behavior."

"But?"

"But," she said "it seems to me like everything is pointing to a connection with the candies. Haberdine taking a room in a second hotel, away from his peers. Then this girl—"

"Stacie," I said.

"Who you say was connected to Lowell." She paused and shuddered briefly.

I shook my head, intending to change the subject, but Ajax leaned in, interested.

"Say more," he said, wiping clean a tusk with his napkin.

Gellica set down the tea. "Well, Lowell and Cordray may not be long for the diplomatic corps, but even they know better than to kill one of their negotiating partners."

"You told us before that no one benefits from the Squib's death," said Ajax.

"Exactly my point. Harlan Cedrow is the main holdout among the oil landowners. And while he certainly has emotional ties to the oil industry, he's just putting on a show to get a better deal. He can't *actually* want to chase the Squib delegation away. No Squibs mean no Squib money."

She looked from Ajax to me. "The killer must've had a motive to want Haberdine dead," she said. "Prostitution seems like a more violent field than diplomacy."

"That's debatable," I mumbled.

"I'm not the cop, gentlemen. You find this guy and put him away, and I'll gladly let you tell me you were right." She tilted her head back, staring up at the darkening early afternoon sky. Far overhead, a small gray shape swung in lazy circles. It was a condor, one of the birds that made sky burials possible. The sky shepherd had a wingspan wider than I was tall, and a beak capable of crushing bone, but at this distance it was barely a speck. Seeing one this side of the Mount was considered by some to be good luck. Others viewed it as a portent of death.

I dropped my gaze to find Gellica staring at me.

"We'll do whatever it takes to support your efforts, Detectives." She flicked an ice sliver from the lip of her glass, sending it to shatter on the courtyard below. "Whatever it takes."

We stood and thanked her for her time. She shook our hands, and I debated whether she'd held my hand a fraction of a second longer than she'd held Jax's. Descending from the rarefied air of the balcony, we rode the elevator side by side and passed through the lobby, back to the streets of Titanshade.

Through the whole process Jax stayed silent. I'd learned enough about him to know that meant he was sitting on something. I got in the car and leaned over to unlock his door. When he got in I waited for him to turn to me. Finally I said, "What is it?"

"Gellica." He straightened his cuffs. "I think she's right."

"About what?"

"About what?" He stared at me, frozen in mid-jacket adjustment. "About the guy you want to pin this homicide on."

I twisted my mouth like I'd bit on something sour and pulled into traffic. "Like she said, she's no cop."

"Well, I am a cop, and I think she's right."

A box truck pulled up in the adjoining lane, its turn signal blinking wildly. I let it slide in ahead of us, taking our place in the slow-motion dance of swearing and sudden braking we called traffic.

"She's a politician, Jax. She's got an agenda."

"Yes, she does. And she told us what it is, then gave us her advice anyway."

"She seems awfully eager to roll on her people," I said.

"And you seem awfully hesitant to follow any leads that don't line up with your assumptions. Or was it just by accident that your friend Talena's photo wasn't laid out on the interview table for Lowell and Cordray?"

I didn't have a rebuttal for such a brazenly true statement. I kept my eyes on the road, but I could feel his stare, judging, trying to figure if I was fighting to uncover the truth or hide it. I chose my words carefully. I didn't want to lie, but I didn't want to tip my hand, either.

"People get killed for all kinds of reasons," I said. "But the motive I see the most is greed. Haberdine was a key player in one of the richest land grabs of the last century. We'd be crazy if that's not the first thing we look into. Even if the politicians don't like it." I allowed myself a grin and added, "Especially if the politicians don't like it."

I glanced at Ajax. He was nodding slightly, absently tugging his shirt collar away from his speaking mouth. He could hear the truth in what I was saying.

"Besides," I said, "you're only taking Gellica's side 'cause you're sweet on her."

He rolled down his window and stuck his arm outside. "Other way around, Carter. She's sweet on me."

"Now I know you're delusional."

"Am I deluded? Or has my keen investigative mind led me to the realization that you're jealous of my special connection with the envoy?"

I cracked a grin, despite my better judgment.

"Let's go find our killer and call it a day, alright?"

"Whatever," he said. "You just try to convince yourself I'm wrong."

IT ONLY TOOK TWO DAYS for Myris and Hemingway to produce results. Hemingway delivered the news to me personally, dropping the surveillance photo on my desk and not even bothering to hide the smile that said *"On a silver platter. Just like I promised."*

The photo showed Flanagan tending to a pair of tibron beetles. He wore the muted colors of the Therreau, his white cotton shirt and tan pants streaked with mud. In the photo his bald head almost gleamed. He'd obviously plucked his face to blend in with the Therreau since Lowell had seen him. But I immediately recognized the hard lines of Flanagan's nose and brow. It was a face I couldn't have forgotten if I'd wanted to.

I tapped a blurry shape in the bottom of the picture. A satchel hung on the side of the wagon.

"College, is that what I think it is?"

Jax studied the photo, then whistled. "Shortcuts," he muttered.

Hemingway interrupted with a snap of her gum. "What is it?"

"That," he said, "is the emblem of Alargo." Jax pronounced the name of the Squib nation with a slight gurgle. "For all we know," he said, "Flanagan took it right off Haberdine's corpse."

"So we're grabbing him?" asked Hemingway. "We gotta be grabbing him, right?"

"An ex-con who's already gone underground once, was seen with the victim, and has the victim's clothes?" I looked at Ajax, seated at his desk, and then back to her. "Yeah," I said. "I think we'll go get him."

The three of us practically ran across the Bullpen where we found Kravitz wiping down a chalkboard on the big wall, erasing some of the false leads and tips that flooded the station in the wake of increasing press coverage. He looked at us with bleary eyes when we approached.

While we told him what we wanted, Kravitz gave the eraser a squeeze, releasing a small cloud of chalk dust.

"Fine," he said. "Bring him in. Call up the Special Response Team."

Ajax leaned into the conversation. "To get one of their own?"

"He went to jail almost twelve years ago," I said. "I don't think he's got any pen pals on the force."

Kravitz scratched his chin, leaving ghostly chalk fingerprints in his beard. "You're arresting one guy on a farm of religious folk. You'll be fine with some patrolmen." A pause, then he tried to look me in the eye. He didn't quite make it. "Carter, you sit this one out."

"No," I said, my voice rising. "No, no. I'm going. I'll be there when the cuffs go on him."

"You know the drill." He wouldn't look me in the eye. "Nothing that puts your photo in the paper."

I began to snarl out a response, reminding him that it was Flanagan's fault that I was toxic, but I was interrupted by the strange, percussive sound of Ajax clearing his throat.

"I'll be there," he said. "Myris and Hemingway will be there. If anyone needs to talk to the press, we'll handle it."

Kravitz hesitated. Ajax said very calmly, "These partnerships weren't random. You wanted Carter's brain, and you wanted me to be his babysitter. This is what you got."

Shaking his head, a scowl barely visible beneath his beard, Kravitz looked ready to speak. I beat him to it, my tone matching Jax's.

"If you ever felt you owed me anything," I said, careful not to name the Reynolds case directly, "now would be a good time to show it."

There was a long pause, then Kravitz relented. "All right," he said, "just make sure it's Hemingway or Myris who puts the cuffs on him."

I nodded my thanks, then took a breath.

"One other thing," I said. "The Therreau ranch is leased. The land is owned by Rediron." The Cedrow family had a history of donating money and property to the Therreau community, and the company they owned followed suit.

Kravitz turned and gave the blackboard another halfhearted swipe. "Shit," he said. "Any Rediron employees on site?"

I looked at Hemingway. Her gum squished as she spoke. "I don't think so," she said. "Half a dozen families. They all look Therreau. Each in their own house and farming the land together."

"Fine." Kravitz pointed the eraser at me. The tremble in his hand was barely noticeable. "Get in and out quick. Don't do anything stupid, and get that SOB back here as clean as possible." He turned and resumed erasing, smearing temporary letters back in on themselves.

The Therreau ranch sat at the edge of the Borderlands where the thermal vents were sparse and the snow swirled in lazy patterns across the ground. They'd once lived at the foot of the mountain, but progress and rising real estate values had pushed them to the fringes of the habitable zone. A glance over my shoulder and I could still see the fog-wrapped center of business and commerce that nestled against the imposing silhouette of the mountain. The people of the Borderlands were kept separate from the city center by an invisible curtain of wealth as flimsy and tenuous as the fabric that shields first-class passengers from their fellow travelers.

I adjusted the hood of my coat, cinching it tight over my body armor vest as I turned back to the ranch. It was a pretty standard Therreau setup, almost unchanged since they'd splintered off during the Shortage. Refusing to adopt new technology, they still clung to outdated equipment that belonged in museum displays of manna-based equipment. Which made it all the more ironic that it had been a Therreau family who first struck oil in Titanshade.

The settlement comprised half a dozen residences clustered around one large greenhouse where crops were raised. Most of the buildings were emblazoned with a sideways figure eight along the eaves or over the front door. At the settlement's edge tibron beetles harnessed to generator cranks walked in endless circles, providing electricity.

The homes were similar in style, simple but skillfully constructed with thick, heavily insulated walls to keep out the creeping cold. Dark smoke rose from chimneys, a sign that coals smoldered in stoves to supplement the geo-vents. Wood was far too expensive in Titanshade to be used for something as fleeting as life-giving heat. Each of the houses held a family, maybe two, passing through simple lives and trying to make ends meet. Flanagan was in the third house on the right, a cancer in the lives of those who'd taken him in.

The walkie at my belt crackled. The other half of the squad was in place. They had coverage duty, watching the other homes and our backside while we went in the front door. One patrolman stayed with the vehicle, ready to radio in for assistance if things went wrong. I looked around at our small team. Checking and rechecking their equipment, they bounced on the balls of their feet and forced smiles that stretched their cheeks and reeked of bravado. They were young cops displaying that blend of fear and excitement that would never quite fade. It was psychological self-defense. You can't walk into a house knowing you might catch a bullet and not have an adrenaline boost.

I thumbed the walkie's talk button. "Go."

We began the sprint toward the house.

Two of the patrolmen carried a battering ram, a stubby metal bar thicker than my thigh with handles running along its side. Once on the porch they swung the ram back, then slammed it home directly above the handle. The door flew off its hinges and the rest of us stormed in, grinding splinters into the carpet as we passed.

From farther in the house someone screamed. Screams of fright rather than aggressive commands, but we were still on edge. Some of us still remembered seeing the victims of Flanagan's handiwork: Bodies scattering the site of a busted drug deal, product and cash nowhere to be found. Charred corpses, hands and feet still bound with baling wire, gruesome warnings to the rest of his clients to pay their protection dues on time. At the time none of us could have imagined that such cruelty came from another cop. Now we were hunting him again.

Guns held out before us at a low angle, we moved through the front room, then into the kitchen. A Therreau woman in a simple light-blue dress and bonnet stood over a half-formed pie crust, her hands in the air, lashless eyes wide with terror.

"Get down!" one of the patrol barked, and she started to her knees. Another of the patrol pushed her prone and planted a foot on her back to make sure she didn't move as he patted her down and handcuffed her. Her flour-sprinkled bonnet had slipped off when she was forced down. With all the hair plucked from her head, she looked like a terrified infant. I knew that face would come back to me someday, probably while drinking, but I ignored it for now, the adrenaline and sense of purpose pushing me forward. Ajax whipped around me, scanning corners and securing the next room as we moved forward. I was surprised again by how fast he could move. He cocked his head and we traded spots, ready to push into the hallway.

One of the doors cracked open, probably a bedroom.

A voice called out, "I'm coming out. I'm unarmed."

Two hands came through, empty with fingers splayed wide. A man's bald head followed. I recognized Flanagan's scarred and mashed nose, and for a moment I had a sense of disorientation, remembering him at trial, grinning as the worst of the charges fell away as witnesses failed to show.

The disgraced former cop looked at us, assessing the danger. When he saw me he grimaced. He mouthed one word, a soundless expletive that I read easily enough: "Carter."

"Police!" I barked. "Down on the ground!"

Flanagan was big, and his deep-set eyes had none of the fear that the Therreau woman had shown.

"Yeah, yeah." He stared at me as he knelt. "I'm complying. Don't hurt anyone."

He was almost prone when another door opened and a figure appeared in the hall. My gun snapped up, leaving the man unguarded while I responded to the new threat. My finger tightened on the trigger.

A boy of fourteen or fifteen stood in the hallway, staring at us with deep brown eyes that were a match for the woman in the kitchen.

"Down! Down! Down!" Someone was yelling behind me.

From the floor Flanagan called out, "He's a kid!" Then to me, "Don't do it, Carter. Don't do this!"

The boy was frozen. His lower lip trembled as he stared at the hallway full of guns pointed in his direction.

I was frozen, a twenty-three-year-old cop with pistol held in trembling hands as I stared at the wild-eyed shooter. An assault rifle strapped across his chest, thick armored boots and thigh straps. He wore a high-impact military helmet and thick gloves protected his hands. Additional weapons were holstered to his side and back. He had only one exposed area: his face. And tied around his neck in a swaddled sling, a screaming, red-faced infant held tight.

"Get on the floor!" The patrolman's command was frenzied. The lack of control in his voice made my blood run cold and I regretted not having an SRT squad on this run.

I eased my finger pressure and stepped past Flanagan, leaving him at my back. Against protocol, but I kept myself between the boy and the patrol. From the corner of my eye I saw Jax restrain the man we'd come for.

"Suspect secured," he called. "Hold your fire."

The kid was halfway out into the hall, only one hand visible. The other could be holding anything from a shotgun to a toothbrush.

From behind me, Flanagan again: "Benny, get down!"

I drew a bead on the shooter, but the wriggling infant was in and out of my shot. The shooter fired again, and I heard a howl from the SRT team as another of their comrades fell.

Revolver in one hand, I held the other out, palm down, and gestured to the ground, like I would a nervous dog.

"Kid, get on the ground. No one's getting hurt, but I need you on the ground." I kept my revolver pointed at him and tried not to think about what a .38 slug would do to his head. *Please, please, PLEASE, don't make me do this.*

The boy shook, not moving. Keeping my eyes forward, I called out, "Talk to him, Flanagan."

He responded, "It's okay, Benny. Do what they say, and they'll leave you and your mom out of this." His voice was calm, low, and patient. "Okay, son? Just do what they say."

For an agonizing second, the kid still hesitated, but finally he went down to one knee, then prone, with his hands out in front of him.

I could hear Flanagan and his men screaming for help. I pulled the trigger. My revolver bucked, the man went down, and the infant stopped crying. It was a solid shot, a one-stopper that killed the shooter on impact. When I made my way to them, I found the shooter on his back, the infant sprawled on his chest, her arms spread wide as if embracing him. I'd almost pulled it off. But the world doesn't run on "almost."

I stood over them and stared as innocent blood merged with the shooter's before draining out, drip by drip toward the ground, toward the oil, and toward the tortured god whose suffering kept us warm and alive. Toward everything that lay hidden beneath the cobblestone streets of Titanshade.

I stepped aside while the patrol secured the remaining rooms. I stared at Flanagan, facedown and handcuffed on the floor, and I wondered who that infant would have grown up to be in the last twenty years. A doctor? A scientist? Maybe just a good person, trying to pay the bills and get by in the world—anyone other than a dirty cop, preying on the very people he was supposed to protect.

Jax put a firm hand on Flanagan's shoulder. "Is there anyone else here? Tell us now if there is."

"Me, the boy, and his mother. No one else."

The calls from the patrol came from the other rooms, a sequence of "Clear!" as each room was confirmed to be empty.

One of the patrol squad stuck her head in the hallway and gave me a thumbs-up. I holstered my weapon.

"Alright," I called out. "Sit the bystanders in the living room. Detective Ajax, please read our friend his rights." I plucked the walkie off my belt and cranked it live.

"Let's get a tech crew in here. Tell them to go over the whole damn farm. Twice if we have to." For once, Flanagan wasn't going to walk away from the lives he'd ruined. For once, all the deaths he'd caused weren't going to haunt my dreams, pointing at me with accusing fingers.

15

LANAGAN SAT IN THE SMALL interrogation room, hands cuffed to the security ring mounted in the table before him. His eyes were half closed, but his lips were in constant motion, mouthing the words to a prayer that was audible only in bits and pieces. I could make out just enough to recognize it as the Traveler's Prayer. I fought the temptation to smack him across the mouth and stop him from reciting the words of a faith that his actions had made a mockery of.

Instead I stood in the corner, hands clasped in front of me, far enough away from Flanagan that I wouldn't be tempted to shake a confession out of him. I didn't know who was on the other side of the one-way mirror, but I knew they were watching me just as closely as they watched him.

I focused on Flanagan's hairless face. The sensitive skin around his brows didn't have the red, agitated look of freshly plucked hairs. He must have adopted the Therreau's grooming fashion some time ago. Lowell had said that Flanagan had a full head of hair when he'd seen him only a few weeks ago. Of course, the bald head wouldn't be much of a disguise when Flanagan's picture hit the papers.

The media were waiting for us at the Bunker. Some greased palm had resulted in a tip that we were bringing a suspect in, and

they'd gone into a frenzy as some of the old newspaper hacks recognized Flanagan. His picture would be splashed all over the
newsstands and talking heads shows. I knew my picture would be
alongside his. After all, we were forever linked.

I could practically read the headlines now: Deadshot Cop Collars Killer He Saved Years Before

The tabloids do love alliteration. And they love their dramatic
irony.

The first time I ever got my picture in the paper was for saving
Flanagan's life. It was on a gambling house raid. Flanagan and his
SRT crew had done the heavy lifting while I was standing perimeter, still a crimson-clad beat cop. The SRT team came out of the
building and took off their helmets, watching the paddy wagons
haul off the gang members. They were laughing, still shaking off the
tension of the raid when their jokes were interrupted by a cracking
sound, and one of the team's head split open. Blood splashed across
the faces of the officers beside him, and for a split second the dead
man kept his balance—about to share one last joke with his team—
before slumping to the cobblestone street.

I shook my head, banishing old memories and focusing on
Flanagan in the here and now. He had dried blood on a split lip,
probably from one of the beat cops "assisting" him into the paddy
wagon after his arrest. It wasn't enough of a bump to cause problems, so I decided it wasn't worth pursuing.

The light on the wall flashed twice, the signal for me to step out
for a conference. I walked into the adjoining observation room,
where Bryyh and Kravitz stood, each with their arms folded, coffees nestled up close to their chests. Kravitz had dark circles under
his eyes. Working point on such a high-profile case was tough, and
it wore harder on some cops than others. Not that I'd know—my
career as a high-profile officer had ended the instant I killed a

child. After that day I'd been hidden behind the scenes for the rest
of my working life. And when the cop I'd saved turned out to be a
monster, it was decided that it wouldn't be good policy to have my
name in the news again.

"What's Flanagan saying?" asked Bryyh. "Is he lawyering up?"

I shook my head. "He's just mumbling to himself. Unresponsive
to all questions, and no request for council." It was hard for me to
keep the hatred out of my voice. There was a part of me that was
disgusted that Flanagan was even alive. And of course, he should
have died on that day I first met him, when his team was pinned
down, a gunman advancing on them, and a rookie cop was the
only one with a bead on the shooter.

"We're charging him," said Kravitz.

I kept my smile restrained. Gloating is unprofessional. "Okay."

Bryyh pulled her arms tighter. "I don't like it. It's too soon."

I shoved a hand through my hair, fingers circling my bald spot.
"We've got the connection with the Squib. We got the eyes that
place him on the scene. And we can put this piece of shit back
where he belongs."

"You don't have to sell me," she said. "It's a done deal."

I threw my hands in the air. "Then why do you look pissed off?"

"Not my call." Bryyh stared at the suspect. "This is coming
from up on high."

"City Attorney's Office," said Kravitz.

Bryyh nodded. "And higher. I'm sure the mayor's breathing
down their necks, and the AFS contingent, as well."

It was all about how things would play out in the press.

"They want him charged in time to have it run on the evening
news, don't they?"

Neither Bryyh nor Kravitz answered me. I waited and finally
Bryyh caved.

"The press already know he's here," she said. "So the powers that be want to make the most of it. Maybe it'll calm people down."

The three of us looked through the glass at Flanagan, the man I'd once saved so that he could go on to destroy dozens of lives.

"Why'd he stay put on that Therreau ranch?" she said. "Seems like there'd be better hiding spots."

Kravitz forced a cough, a sound both desperate and disgusted. "They were human shields." If his grip on his coffee were any tighter he would have shattered the ceramic mug. "And if they weren't, does it matter?"

I was surprised by how fired up he was. But he hadn't seen Flanagan help talk down the family's son.

"No," I said, trying to tell myself I hadn't seen it either. "Cap, if it bothers you that much . . ." I rubbed the back of my neck. "We could hold him for now. Save the murder charge for when we break apart his story or when we get details on what the techs turn up at his farm."

Kravitz ran his hand through his beard and glared at me. A few long hairs pulled out, dark crinkled things that clung to his hand like bug antennae before dropping to the vinyl tiles beneath our feet.

"You're not doing this." He stepped closer so I'd have to crane my neck up to look him in the eye. Tall guys like to do that, to emphasize their height. On reflex I dropped my gaze to his collarbone, where I could track both his face and hips in my peripheral vision. I knew that my lower center of gravity would allow me to get up underneath him. Not that I'd need to—Kravitz was just frustrated and taking it out on me without thinking. But it made me feel better to know that I could drop him on his ass if needed.

"You asked to bring him in—no, you *begged*." Kravitz pointed at me, coffee spilling over the edge of his mug.

Bryyh sighed, the sound alone enough to separate us. "Do it," she said.

I walked out the door and back into the interrogation area. Flanagan looked up as I entered. For a brief moment I saw that shooter, the one with the crying infant across his chest. In my mind they both had Flanagan's face.

"Timothy Flanagan," I said. "You're under arrest for the murder of Garson Haberdine."

He closed his eyes and continued praying. I took a breath and raised my voice as I recited his rights, that litany unique to cops, and my voice drowned out his prayers.

Later, when I returned to my desk, Ajax was watching the Eagle Crest security footage for the umpteenth time. He'd also coopted a nicer chair from somewhere. Twenty years on the force, and this kid was already more accepted in the department than I was.

There were lots of reasons I wasn't the most popular detective in the Bunker. People think cops close ranks—and they're right. We do it because we know that no one who hasn't worn the pressed crimson uniform of the patrol knows what we face day in and day out. But even when we protect our own, that doesn't mean we're blind to what they've done. We put distance between us and them because every time we see them, we're reminded that it could happen to us, that it could be us with a fraction of a second to decide who lives and who dies.

Everyone liked Ajax because Ajax had never shot a child to save a killer. I'd never completely escaped the cloud of the shooting, even after I was cleared by the internal investigation. And when the cop I saved turned out to be staggeringly corrupt, even by the standards of a town famous for graft and corruption . . . I just hoped I'd be able to put a little bit of my past behind me by taking Flanagan off the streets again.

My partner waved me over. "Remember that gunk in the victim's tub?"

"The brown crust?" I took a seat in my old, uncomfortable chair.

"Lab reports it was mostly salt, with a mixture of herbs and cooking spices."

"Like soup?" I didn't care for the implications.

Ajax kept going, getting excited. "I've been looking at the traffic in and out of the hotel that day."

He tapped the screen, frozen on the paused image of a large figure wheeling out a barrel on a dolly. The blurry freeze-frame lacked detail, and the subject's collar was up and hat pulled low. I couldn't even tell if it was human or Mollenkampi.

"Takes some squinting," he said, "but you can just make out a logo on the side of the barrel. Talbot Equipment Company."

"Great. Call them and—"

"Brine," he said. "They delivered fifty-five gallons of brine to the hotel that day."

"For the kitchen?"

He sat back and twirled his hands, a ringmaster presenting the next act.

"It was marked for delivery to a guest," he said, eyes crinkling. "Garson Haberdine, room 430."

The carpet imprints in room 430 had been a curve and two straight lines pressed into the carpet. The kind of marks that a barrel on a dolly might leave.

"Let's check it out tomorrow," I said. "We charged Flanagan." I didn't say that we had a long way to go before we had a case that would stand up in court. Bryyh had said that we were moving fast to keep the politicians happy, and now we'd have to play catchup.

Ajax whistled and leaned back in his chair, but he didn't voice his concerns. Pressure to solve a case wasn't exclusive to the city. I was sure he'd seen plenty of the same in his hometown. More of it was surely in his Path if he stayed on as a detective.

"So now what?" One mandible pulled away from his jawline and snapped back, tapping a rhythm on his tusks and toothy ridges.

The way things had gone down felt wrong, but Flanagan belonged behind bars. For once I wanted to not look that gift horse in the mouth. For once I wanted to savor a victory, even if it meant drowning the bitter taste in the back of my mouth with a tall glass of cheap liquor.

"Now we let someone buy us a drink, kid."

Hammer Head's was packed wall to wall with cops. Not too unusual, as it was a favorite off-duty hangout. But this night it wasn't filled with embittered patrolmen drinking to shake off the lingering images of whatever horrors they'd survived that shift. On this night it was a place of celebration.

The backslapping came fast and furious, and cops who wouldn't have spared me a second glance the day before were lining up to be seen shaking my hand. All things considered, I'd much rather drink at Mickey the Finn's, where at least I could pretend other people saw me as a regular person. The door opened and closed constantly, with a churn of people who wanted to be near the winning team. There's nothing like a victory celebration to smooth over discontentment in the ranks.

I shot a look at Ajax, and he shrugged. *Hey, if you can't beat them . . .*

The bartender had the taps opened up and foamy heads of beer were cresting and sliding down the sides of frosted mugs as he angled the rabbit ear antennae on top of the wall-mounted television. I let out a sigh and did my best to relax. Someone shoved a beer in my hand and we all quieted down as the evening news began.

The reception buzzed and went to static, but a quick slap by the bartender to the television's side resolved the picture. The anchor was a human woman, as manicured and polished as any news personality could be. The most trusted name in local news, Channel 50's Amear Sandersen, she of the whitest smile and most balanced, perfectly curled hair.

Amear pressed one hand to her ear. "I'm getting word of a breaking development." She paused, then, "We're going live to our field reporter. Janice, can you hear me?"

Another reporter appeared in a split-screen image. She was bundled against the cold, a heavy jacket and ear muffs that crimped her curls to her head. Wherever she was, it was far leeward.

"Amear, shocking news in the Haberdine murder case. I'm here at the St. Alban's Guidepost, and with me is Guide Clemens."

The split screen dropped and showed the field reporter standing next to an older woman in a guide's frock and staff. She too was bundled against the cold.

The reporter continued, "Guide Clemens, you contacted the Channel 50 news team with shocking allegations. Can you repeat them for our viewers?"

The guide nodded and looked at the camera. "Timothy Flanagan was with our community the whole night of the murder. We held a prayer service for a local citizen who has fallen ill, and he was present for the entire service."

"And did you tell the police this?"

"Of course, but they ignored me and arrested that poor man anyway."

"These are serious allegations, Guide Clemens. Do you have any proof that Flanagan was with you that night?"

"We recorded the service so that we could play it for the members of our congregation who are homebound. You can hear Flanagan's voice quite clearly. He was a reader during the service."

"Do you have any idea why the police didn't accept your story?"

"No," said the guide. "The police were here to put a walker of the Path in chains, whether he was guilty or not."

Around me the crowd's silence shifted. What had been rapt attention turned to uncomfortable hush.

The broadcast switched back to Amear in the studio. Over her shoulder was a photo of me walking Flanagan into the Bunker, alongside an older shot, of me on the day I saved his life.

"The arrest of Mr. Flanagan raised eyebrows throughout the city," she said, "and brought new attention to controversial police detect—"

Someone said, "Artie, turn that damn thing off, would ya?" and the television went dead, the image of my past replaced by a single white dot in the center of the screen, fading to black as the last of its energy dissipated.

The beer mug was suddenly heavy in my hand. I set it down on the bar top untouched.

I felt a brushing at my side. The sea of supporters parted, and someone grabbed my arm. It was Ajax. My partner.

His eyes were alight with rage. "This is bullshit."

I didn't respond. I wasn't sure if he meant that it was a bullshit smear campaign or if it was bullshit that I'd dragged him down with me.

Ajax raised his voice. "Flanagan didn't have an alibi. And sure as the Hells are off the Path, he wasn't in a prayer service."

Kravitz stood on a chair, and everyone looked at him.

"Ajax is right," he told us. "This is a hurdle, but we've run into stuff like this before. The important thing is we got our man, and we'll get through whatever issues come up." He seemed calmer now that he'd had a few drinks. Even though he was wrong.

Because we hadn't gotten our man. And the issues that failure raised were not the kind you just "get through."

The pager in my coat buzzed. Then someone else's did as well. I looked across the room and saw Detective Kravitz glance at his pocket. Within moments the only sound in the bar was the rumble of weighted plastic rods in plastic cases. We were being summoned back to the Bunker.

16

WE MET IN BRYYH'S OFFICE for privacy reasons. But there's only so much privacy to be had when the rest of the floor can hear you screaming through closed doors. I was glad that she'd chosen that location over one of the interrogation rooms, though the tone she took with me was not much kinder than we'd have shown a suspect. I sat in one of the comfortable seats across from her desk and she bore down on me, the occasional finger popping up to stick in my face. If it wasn't for the presence of Kravitz and Ajax, I think she may have strangled me. I know I was tempted to strangle her.

As it was, I kept my hands at my sides; white spittle flecked Bryyh's lips when she asked again, "Did you talk to that guide personally?"

"No, one of the patrol interviewed her."

"What exactly did she say?"

"Well, since I wasn't there, I don't know." The words came out with more snarling sarcasm than I intended. I regretted it immediately. Bryyh had looked out for me my entire career, and I knew she'd taken grief for it. She'd always seen something of my mother in me.

Kravitz chimed in. "Don't get your back up, Carter. We're trying to help you."

"You're trying to find out if I buried evidence to hang a murder on someone that I've—" I swallowed the bitter taste in my mouth. "Someone I've got a grudge against." Bryyh was one of my few friends on the force, but the proverbial shit had met the proverbial fan. And every detective in the Bunker had more than enough reason to throw me under the bus. Proverbial or otherwise.

The stress was wearing on the captain, just like the rest of us. Kravitz ran his fingers through his beard continually. I could almost swear he was developing a bald spot on the side of his chin. Bryyh continued her interrogation.

"How much do you hate Flanagan?"

"I don't—"

"Please. I didn't ask *if* you hate him. I know you hate him," she said. "Because I hate him, too." Bryyh folded her glasses, fingers running over the frame. "I hate what he did, and the way he betrayed the badge. I hate that he got convicted of lesser charges, and that he got out early." She slid her glasses back on. "So I know you hate him. What I asked you was, *how much.*"

"Not enough to end my career," I said. "And I'm gonna point out—again—that charging him so soon was your idea." I tore off my tie and shoved it into my pocket. The office was hot with all of us packed into it.

Kravitz stared at me. "We only brought him in because you pushed for it."

Ajax spoke up, arguing the point, and Bryyh talked over him. My head ached from listening to all that circular thinking. I pressed a palm into the side of my head and out-shouted all of them.

"Dammit! I can't prove the guide didn't say what she's claiming. But either she's lying, and we can find out where Flanagan really was, or she's telling the truth and—"

"—And we're screwed," said Bryyh. I couldn't tell if she meant it as a question or a statement. I shook my head.

"No!" I swallowed, forcing down my angry screams. "If the guide's telling the truth now, then she lied when we talked to her. That means there's some kind of . . ." I grasped for a word that wouldn't sound paranoid. "Hells, some kind of conspiracy."

Bryyh turned away and planted her hands on her desk. Her eyes moved to the framed pictures she kept there. Photos of her husband and their kids, both adults now, and her two grandkids. Bryyh chewed her lip, probably wondering how many more hours she'd spend on this case instead of her family.

I tried again, my voice calmer this time. "Cap, there's something going on here. Somebody tore that Squib to pieces. And as soon as we collared Flanagan, someone started the wheels turning to get him busted loose."

Turning to the rest of the room I said, "If he had an alibi, why didn't he just say so? If the guide remembered him, why did she deny it when we asked the first time?"

I was interrupted by a loud knock at the door. Bryyh barked out a gruff, "Not now!" but the door opened anyway. A tiny man with a salt-and-pepper goatee walked in. He carried a bowler hat in one hand, the dark material matching both his suit and his slicked-back hair. Assistant City Attorney Flifex had come slinking in just in time for my public shaming.

"I understand this is the place to discuss tonight's momentous events." He pointed at the empty chair beside me. "May I join in?"

Bryyh nodded. "Where do we stand with Flanagan right now?"

Taking a seat, Flifex crossed his legs and popped his hat on his knee.

"His lawyer hasn't filed a motion yet, but she's contacted us to let us know she'll do so at the start of business tomorrow. We can file the paperwork to stall the process, of course. Though honestly, it's a lost cause with that many witnesses. There's simply no way we'll get a conviction."

"And if we hold on to him the press will camp outside the Bunker and hold a countdown for his release." Bryyh rubbed the bridge of her nose.

I cleared my throat to get Flifex's attention. "You said his lawyer contacted you. Who is it?"

"Emily Jankowski."

Bryyh frowned. "What's that turd Flanagan doing with a hired gun like her?"

"Interesting, isn't it?" said Flifex. "Your friend Mr. Flanagan seems to have some impressive connections, Carter."

I seethed, mentally forcing him to eat the word "friend." In my imagination, he choked on it.

Flifex looked around at each of us in turn.

"The City Attorney's Office has made its position abundantly clear. This whole thing is an embarrassment."

I didn't bother to hide my sneer. "The CA was more than happy to have us charge Flanagan when we had him in hand."

"And now we're more than happy to find a way to keep him. So tell me what you have to hold him on, and we'll go from there."

I squeezed my temples. "He had possession of a satchel with the emblem of the Squib nation."

"Did it belong to Envoy Haberdine?"

"We haven't establish—"

"Has a satchel been reported stolen?"

There was silence in the room.

"Not that it particularly matters. The public isn't clamoring for the arrest of a dealer in stolen goods. What do you have to tie him to the Envoy Haberdine?"

"The AFS witness, Cordray, places him in repeated proximity to Haberdine, both before and on the day of the murder."

"A trait the accused shares with dozens of other people. I do hope you're saving the best for last, Detective."

I shifted in my chair. "Nothing else."

"Well." Flifex ran a thumb along the cloth band of his hat. "That's rather thin soup, isn't it?"

I threw my hands in the air. "Then why the Hells did you insist we charge him?"

Flifex's fingers left his hat and folded into each other as he stared me down.

"Whoever made that decision must have been assuming that when you hauled in your prime suspect in a high-profile case, you did so with evidence to back it up," he said. "Silly us. It won't happen again."

Ajax had been nervously drying his tusks with a hanky while Flifex ranted. The poor kid was probably afraid that his career was over before it began. Now he spoke up. "Hold him on the stolen goods. Give us time to shore up the murder case."

If we can prove it's stolen, I thought.

Bryyh raised her eyebrows. "How would that play in the press?"

"Not very well, I'm afraid," said Flifex. "His camp would play it up as a trumped-up technicality, while reminding the public that a brutal killer still walks the streets."

It was time to throw reason out the window.

"Let him go," I said.

Everyone looked at me.

"Even if we manage to make the stolen goods, having him sit in a cell doesn't tell us how he killed Haberdine, or why, or even if he really did it. That guide has a lot of witnesses. And, yes, they could all be lying, but . . . if we let Flanagan go now, he'll go to ground while we can still track him. He'll lead us to whoever ordered Haberdine killed." I swept my eyes around the circle. "Let him out preemptively. Don't even tell his lawyer so there's no chance for a press conference on the Bunker steps."

Flifex arched his eyebrows and stroked his chin thoughtfully. "It would minimize the press coverage. And if we do charge him later, it'll make a good story."

"That would help the prosecution?" asked Bryyh.

"It wouldn't hurt." Flifex ran a finger over an eyebrow, smoothing any stray hairs. "But letting him go is up to you, Captain. Your career, not mine."

There was a moment of silence while that sunk in. Then Bryyh said, "Alright. Cut him loose and get him out of here."

I stood up. "I'll tell him."

"Carter . . ." began Bryyh.

"Don't worry," I said. "I'll take Ajax along to make sure I behave."

Flanagan was in a concrete-walled general visitation room, the only prisoner in the room. Just him, a soda vending machine, and a picnic table bolted to the floor.

He was playing it calm, sitting passively at the table, hands folded in front of him. The rules of the room were painted behind him.

**NO SPITTING.
NO YELLING.
NO PASSING OF CONTRABAND TO
OR FROM PRISONERS.
IN CASE OF EMERGENCY, CALL FOR A GUARD.**

Flanagan had a lantern jaw and a twisted nose that looked like it'd been broken so many times even he'd lost count. His face wore a look of placid calm that was enough to turn my stomach.

"Look at you," I said as I entered. "The cat that ate the canary." Ajax followed behind me.

Flanagan held his hands out, palms up. "I just keep walking. The Path takes me where it will."

"You know this is bullshit," I said with some heat in my voice. It was important that he not think we were choosing to let him walk. "How'd you get the guide to vouch for you?"

"If someone vouched for me, it was because their conscience told them to do so."

"A conscience or a paycheck. How much did you offer her?"

He was silent, his eyes focused on a point somewhere above my head. I recognized that look. It was the look of someone trying to mellow their way through an interview. The thought of him staying calm and collected when I'd lost so much sleep fixating on everyone he'd killed or ruined since I saved his life was more than I could stomach.

"You lying son of a bitch." I was in his face, close enough for him to smell the remnants of my last meal. "If you walk out of here on a bullshit technicality, I'll—I'll—" I was way beyond acting angry to sell the plan. My hands were shaking, and I clenched them into fists that I shoved into my coat pockets to hide my lack of control.

His eyes shifted, and he looked right into me. His voice took on a gravel-rough tone it hadn't had before.

"Innocence isn't really a technicality, is it?"

"In all the world," I said, "there is no one less innocent than you."

"No one?" His nose had been broken often enough that his

words had a nasal, resonate sound. "You think those idiots by the Mount who've never been cold in their life—"

"Don't give me that," I said. "You shook down anyone with a spare dime. You brought nothing but misery to everyone around you."

"I brought justice," he said, then dropped his eyes. "Or at least I tried. But I was never their lapdog."

Ajax had a hand on my shoulder then, and another on my bicep. He eased me back, and I relented. He whispered something musical and calming through needle-sharp teeth, but I couldn't listen. I was busy telling myself that if I could just keep it together long enough to get Flanagan out of there, we'd be giving him enough rope to hang himself.

With that hope, I managed to pull myself together. We processed the paperwork and escorted him out the back way, making sure no reporters were within spying distance. I hailed him a cab and paid for a trip back out to the Therreau ranch where we'd nabbed him. It wouldn't do for him to be caught wandering the streets near the Bunker.

Before he got in the taxi Flanagan looked at me one last time. He opened his mouth as if he were about to say something. Instead he sneered, shook his head, and climbed inside.

As Flanagan's cab drove off, a small Hasam pulled away from the curb and followed at a healthy distance. The tail was on him. Now we'd play the waiting game until it brought us answers.

On the way back to the visitation room Ajax started whistling a tune. I asked him what it was.

"'Don't Stop, Don't Stop,'" he said.

I gave him a blank stare in return.

"The new Dinah McIntire track," he said. When my expression didn't change he threw up his hands. "Seriously? Do you not listen to music at all?"

"Kid," I said. "Disco's not music."

He spent the better part of a half hour trying to convince me that electronic keyboards and canned string sections could somehow make a decent album. It was a wasted effort. I was about to explain how much more dangerous the streets would be if thugs and killers learned he liked disco when we were interrupted by a rattle at the door. A guard stuck her head inside.

"Detectives? The prisoner's attorney is here."

"Send her in," I said.

Jankowski was in a hurry, and she looked irritated—though not particularly surprised—to see us instead of Flanagan. She had faded orange hair swept up above her shoulders, only a few artfully chosen strands were left loose to fall onto her immaculate suit. She was press-conference perfect, even when she couldn't really expect the media frenzy to begin until the morning. Amazing. She and Angus needed to trade notes.

"Ah. The arresting officer," she said. "So glad I can tell you in person that I expect to be present whenever you speak to my client from this point forward. Not that you'll have much of an opportunity. I believe he'll be leaving in the morning. You'll understand if I ask you to wait someplace else while I talk to him tonight."

Ajax and I looked at each other, then stood up.

"Fair enough," Jax said. "I was just passing the time myself. Did you need a lawyer for anything?" he asked me.

"Well." I turned to Jankowski. "I did have one thing I'd like to know, Counselor. If you don't mind, that is."

"Go ahead. We both know you're going to ask anyway." She set her briefcase upright on the table, an expensive miniature wall of leather and clasps.

"It seems to me that a high-profile attorney such as yourself must charge a reasonable fee for her time. Perfectly fair, considering all the good work you do. But I can't help but wonder—"

"I can't help but wonder when you're going to get on with it."

"Who's paying your fee? Because Flanagan sure as Hells can't afford it."

She didn't answer, only stared and looked unpleasant. But that told me something in itself. If the money were coming from an advocacy group, or the Therreau, then they'd want everyone and their brother to know about it. Her silence told me that whoever was footing the bill for Flanagan's escape wasn't eager to appear as his benefactor. And that carried another implication: Whoever this wealthy person was, they would respond if there was a threat to expose them.

On top of that, dragging this mysterious benefactor into the light might be fun.

Jankowski glanced at her wristwatch. "Can I see my client, or do I need to go revisit Judge Kalis?"

Jax stepped out from the corner. "Oh, you can see your client anytime you like. We released him half an hour ago."

The hired gun smirked.

"Okay. No press conference in front of your building. Fine." She picked up her briefcase. "If you're done with me I'll be going. Lots of other very high-paying clients to tend to."

She walked out of the visitation room and Jax and I waited for the click of the security door latching behind her.

"We need to find out who's paying her bill," he said.

"Yes, we do." I did a slow turn, taking in the visitation area and trying to imagine what it felt like to have this drab, dungeon-like room be the only place you could interact with your family.

"Something isn't right," I said.

Jax kicked a discarded candy wrapper to the side. "With what?"

"With any of it." I looked up at the stained, palsied acoustical tiles on the ceiling, then back to my partner. "The whole thing doesn't make any sense."

I scooped the candy wrapper off the floor and stepped toward the trash, when something about the label caught my eye. I turned it over in my hand. The wrapper had once housed a Black Gold candy bar. Written across its face was a promise of the chocolate and caramel that could be found inside.

Black Gold.

"You know," I said, "there's really only two reasons someone would kill Haberdine."

Ajax let loose a brief whistling sigh and clacked his biting teeth. "A personal vendetta or a desire to change up the wind farm plans."

"What if there's another reason that the oil fields are valuable?"

"You mean the oil fields that are almost dry?" he said. "At which point they'll be vast, uninhabitable swaths of ice-covered rock. Those oil fields?"

I tried to coalesce the half-formed idea in my mind. "The entire city is based on oil." I dropped the wrapper on the table. "Even our candy is named after it. What if its connection runs deeper than we think?"

"If I just admit that I have no idea what you're talking about," he said, "will that make you stop saying it?"

"I'm not entirely sure."

"Goodnight, Carter," he said, and knocked for the guard. "Try to get some sleep, okay?"

∞

I saw my cat when I got home. I scritched his ears and said, "Hi Rumple," and checked his food dish. He had water but no dry food. I looked in the plastic storage bin, but only found a note I'd left reminding myself to buy cat food.

Then I opened the fridge and couldn't find a beer. Or much in the way of food; I was down to a single slice of ham and a bottle of ketchup, but it was the lack of beer that got to me. I'd had a beer in my hand at Hammer Head's— before Flanagan managed to yank it away from me. Or rather his lawyer, or whoever was paying her. Same difference. I swore that the world had gotten between me and a drink for the last time.

I flipped on the stereo, a sleek hi-fi unit with both an 8-track and turntable. The amp popped on with a click as it warmed up. I was hoping to catch the tail end of my favorite DJ's rotation, *The Handsome Hanford Happy Hour*. Instead, the sound of a Rediron commercial filled my apartment. A broken record, promoting their the-past-is-our-future rhetoric.

My stomach growled, returning my focus to the matter at hand. I brought the slice of ham to my nose to make sure it was good. Once it passed the sniff test I tore it into chunks and dropped it into Rumple's food bowl. The bottle of ketchup went on the counter. A few minutes later I had a pan of boiling water. A little salt, a little sugar, add the ketchup, and presto—hobo tomato soup, just like my dad used to make.

I ate my soup sitting at the kitchen table, being careful of the wobbly leg I'd been meaning to fix for a couple years. From the wall a younger version of Talena peered over my shoulder. It was a photo of her, me, and her mother. We were all smiling.

It was a reminder that I hadn't missed every important day in Talena's life. Just most of them. Just like my dad had missed mine.

My father was a lifer on the oil rigs, a man who'd always seemed a little lost when he came home on leave and remembered that he had a wife and kid. He'd tried hard, though, to give me a good life, sheltered from the rough and tumble world of Titanshade's streets. In the end, he hadn't exactly succeeded. I ended up following my mom's footsteps, enrolling in the police academy as soon as I was old enough. To his dying day he swore he'd never understand why I'd go and do such a damn fool thing as putting on a uniform and walking a beat.

Done with supper I flopped on the couch with my shoes still on. Dad would have hated that.

There was a hint of movement, then a furry shape landed on top of me. Rumple had finished his dinner, too. Needle claws tugged at my flesh through my shirt, sharp little pains that I knew would fade as quickly as they appeared. I endured it without complaint. Sometimes, that's what you have to do.

The purring, furry mass finally settled down on my chest. He stretched his paws out as he relaxed, clinging to me like a child. I knew I'd wake to a fuzzy throat-warmer in the morning, but I didn't bother shooing him away. It was nice to be accepted for who I was, even if that was just an occasional roommate who wasn't so great at remembering to buy food.

At least that was something.

17

THE NEXT MORNING THE CROWDS outside the Bunker were bigger and angrier. Even in the morning hours the anxiety was palpable. There was an uptick in the number of crimson dress shirts as the patrol had formed a cordon by the entrance to the Bunker, allowing pedestrian access. On either side of the patrol line the swirl of protest and counter-protest had solidified into two mobs glaring at each other like surly drunks at either end of a bar.

Tensions were climbing, people were scared, and the sudden collapse of our case against Flanagan hadn't helped matters. The city had reason to chafe under the competing tensions. But life went on. People still jostled along the sidewalk across from the demonstration and traffic continued to grind along, the inexorable push of steel and rubber as vehicles made their way to deliveries and destinations. Even tibron-drawn Therreau carts wound their way through the city, though now the drivers wore bandannas, as if they could protect themselves from the sickness that was pulling all of us down.

There was panic in the air, and it smelled of cinnamon.

As soon as I entered the Bunker I was told to report to the glass-walled conference room on the fourth floor, a comfortable room where we often took visitors who wouldn't react well to an interrogation room. Coming down the hall I saw Ajax, Bryyh, and Kravitz seated on one side of the conference table, looking even more haggard than they had the night before. Across from them were two slender, mottled-skin frogs dressed in shades of blue. Cobalt-hued ceramic discs the size of dinner plates ringed their torsos, while smaller pieces lined their shoulders and thighs. The discs sat comfortably on an under layer of chainmail and heavy linen fabric.

The Squibs had come to the Bunker.

When I entered the visitors stood. They were slightly shorter than me, and I'm no more than average height for a human. Bryyh made a gesture of introduction.

"Ambassador Yarvis, Envoy Lanathel, this is Detective Carter."

The one introduced as Lanathel let out a guttural harrumph. The sound of a rock pulling free from its muddy bed.

"Yes, we recognize him," he said. His vibrant green skin tone looked to be younger than Yarvis's duller gray, though I couldn't swear to the way Squibs age. I focused on the older of the pair and cocked my head like a confused dog.

"I was under the impression that no one from the Squib delegation had the title of ambassador."

Yarvis blinked, translucent sheaths flicking over protruding eyes. "Your impression was mistaken, Detective."

We all shook hands, like real civilized adults. It was a nice gesture before I was thrown to the wolves.

"Please be seated," said Bryyh, and Ajax pulled out a chair for me at the conference table. The Squibs were barefoot, and their large webbed feet made heavy whomping sounds on the floor as they took their seats. They weren't going to be moving far outside of the central city without much more significant clothing than they were currently wearing. If anyone was running around to find candies for these frog-men, then it wasn't another Squib.

"We were speaking," said Ambassador Yarvis, "about this man you've let walk free after slaughtering one of my delegates."

My delegates. I couldn't tell if he was possessive of his territory or protective of his people. I decided to push him on it, to see if he would be more defensive of his power or the members of his team.

"What exactly—"

Ajax stepped on my foot, a distinct warning to stop, while Captain Bryyh talked over me.

"This is some kind of desperate ploy strung together by Flanagan's attorney. As soon as we pierce the veil of lies they're putting together, we'll have him in custody again."

She was in full spin mode. I sometimes forgot that she could be a fierce political animal when needed.

Lanathel stopped her with an upraised hand. Sturdy webbing connected large knuckled fingers, and a street map of blue veins was visible beneath translucent green flesh. With his palm out, the pale undersides of his fingers were on display, white breakers on the waves of an emerald sea. The claws were nicely manicured into fingernails suited for polite society, where the backstabbings are done with treaties and bank transfers.

He held up a copy of that morning's *Union Record*, unfolding it and laying it on the table so we could get a clear view.

"And so this," he asked, "is part of your investigation?"

The newspaper's front page featured a picture of me. Shot from a low angle, I looked like a schoolyard bully, towering over the cowering figure of a man in a suit and tie. He was sprawled on the pavement with one hand raised defensively between us. I recognized the reporter from the back gate to the Bunker. The Mollenkampi photographer had clearly earned her paycheck.

Above the photo, in forty-point type, was the headline: Bungled Bust in Bloodbath Slaying.

My stomach clenched, and the back of my mouth burned as bile rose in my throat.

"Is this how you seek our countryman's killer?"

Yarvis pressed a hand onto the paper, and his nails dug jagged slices across my photo. Unlike the younger Squib, his nails weren't trimmed. They were true claws, ragged and dangerous. The kind of claws that might not kill but would certainly infect. I suspected that his rise to power had been very dramatic, coming from poverty or a harsh background. Whatever the cause, he'd intentionally rejected the trappings of success. And now I was in his sights.

"Don't believe everything you read," I said. Ajax practically jumped on my foot.

"What Carter means," said Bryyh, "is that sometimes the perception of a misstep is a strategic advantage."

"Are you saying that you intend to let him walk free?" Bony lips twisted into a frown.

Bryyh hesitated. There was an intake of breath, her lower teeth pulling back her upper lip, like an archer drawing a bow. Telling the Squibs about the plan to tail Flanagan was a breach of protocol and could jeopardize the whole plan. But the reality was, if the Squibs squawked loud enough to the right people, the whole case could get ripped out of our hands.

"Ambassador," she said, "we made a strategic decision to release the prisoner. He is under constant surveillance, and at the first indication that he can lead us to co-conspirators, we will spring our trap."

"But this would not have been your first choice."

Bryyh shook her head. "It's true that we were forced to move faster than we would have liked, but he's only a stepping-stone. It's not often that an opportunity like this comes along."

"Is this man still a suspect?"

"Absolutely. But he's not the only lead we're hanging our hat on," she said. "The charges against Flanagan were to make him twist in the wind, so that he'd turn over any conspirators. Justice won't be served until we root out the true architect of this obscene crime. And we intend to do just that."

I kept my mouth shut. Bryyh was fast on her feet.

"Mister Ambassador." She held out her hands. "Envoy Lanathel. I want you both to know that we are taking every aspect of this case very seriously. We won't rest until we can bring in the monster who killed Mr. Haberdine."

"Words," Lanathel huffed, the younger Squib's vocal sac puffing and slowly deflating. His breath smelled like wet cardboard. "What are you actually doing?"

"I can't reveal too many details," said Bryyh, although she already had. "Other than to say that we are continuing to strengthen our case. The City Attorney's Office is dealing with any headaches from Jankowski."

"Jankowski?" The name bubbled as Yarvis rolled it on his tongue. He sounded thoughtful.

"That's the suspect's attorney," Bryyh explained.

"Emily Jankowski," I said. "You know her?"

Kravitz ran a hand over his face, pulling the flesh of his cheeks taut. He opened his mouth to say something, but Bryyh cut him off.

"I'm not sure . . ." she began.

"We know a Jankowski," said Yarvis. He turned to the younger Squib. "She is involved in the wind farm negotiations, correct?"

Lanathel bobbed his head.

"Involved on behalf of who?" I said.

"Rediron Drilling," he said. "Why do you ask?"

I wanted to say *because I'm wondering what a hot-shot criminal defense attorney is doing on contract negotiations.* But Bryyh shot me a not-now look, and I let it pass.

"Just following all possible leads," I said. "Like the captain says, we won't rest until . . ." I rolled my hand: *and so on.*

"Well, if you've gone on to other leads"—Yarvis leaned toward Bryyh, armor clanking as he moved—"we will collect Envoy Haberdine's remains."

Bryyh took a deep breath. She clearly wasn't looking forward to delivering this piece of news. "We can't release them at this time, Ambassador. Until we have the killer—"

"Our countryman has been slaughtered." Yarvis swiveled his head to take us all in. "His body needs to be returned to his family, not left on some rock"—he raked his claws in the direction of the Mount—"and his bones picked clean by vultures." His description of sky burials and the Mount were clearly meant to get a rise out of us. The rush of heat in my cheeks told me that he'd succeeded. Bryyh was made of sterner stuff.

"And he will be returned to his family," she said without so much as a creased brow. "We all have the same goal, to bring Envoy Haberdine's killer to justice. Please understand."

The Squib ambassador snarled and dragged his hands back, claws raking across the table like nails across a blackboard.

"Understand? I understand more than you'd like. Our people know how humans respond to the smell of our blood."

"Mister Ambassador, I assure—"

"Every Squib who travels beyond the borders of Alargo knows

the risks of associating with humans. You are a violent people who can't be trusted. If there were ever a textbook case of this kind of butchery, it would be the sadistic desecration of our fellow traveler, Garson Haberdine. Some of the people in this city have drifted very far from the Path indeed."

Bryyh tried again. "Not all humans are susceptible to these effects. And I assure you, we are putting our very best and brightest on this case."

Yarvis looked from Bryyh to the newspaper. My picture stared back at all of us.

"But it's true some setbacks are inevitable," Bryyh said. Even to my ears, she sounded less than convincing.

"Perhaps," said Lanathel. "Or perhaps the blood rage is clouding the officers' minds?"

I bit my cheek to keep from responding. The younger Squib pressed on.

"Do you stop to consider Garson's family while you huff in the rage that accompanies his blood?" The broken baritone of his voice got louder as his anger boiled to the surface. "Do you think about that before you laugh and have a drink at night?"

Lanathel swung a finger around the table, accusing all of us of indifference, but his eyes settled on me.

Bryyh placed both her hands flat on the table. "On behalf of the Titanshade Police Department, I can promise you the personal nature of this senseless crime is foremost in our thoughts."

The Squib gave a silent chuckle, the flesh around his cheeks and chin flaring out dramatically. "And on behalf of Her Majesty, I can promise you that we will not forget who works to end this nightmare, and who has been the cause of these 'inevitable setbacks.'"

The paper sat on the table, reminding us who would play the role of sacrificial lamb when things went bad. I didn't see how my standing could get any worse. So I figured I might as well ask what was on my mind.

"Can you think of any reason you'd need a lot of brine? I mean a lot," I said. "Gallons and gallons of the stuff."

Lanathel half stood, throat sac bulging in a display of outrage, or aggression, or some other emotion I didn't quite follow. "What is the meaning of this?" He bellowed the words, a deep reverberation that shook the glass walls of the conference room and caused passersby in the hallway to turn and stare. I blinked. It wasn't the reaction I was expecting.

Yarvis held up a webbed hand and the younger Squib lowered himself back into his chair.

"Why would you ask that?" said the ambassador.

I chose my words carefully. "Envoy Haberdine had a large quantity of brine delivered to the hotel before his murder. Do you know why he might do that?"

The diplomats exchanged a glance, pausing before the elder of the two responded.

"Our people trace our roots back to the coastal marshes," he said. "And many of our practices stem from our times there." He shifted in his seat, anxious, but continued. "Many Squibs prefer to have intimate relations in salt water."

There was an uncomfortable silence. I looked at my partner and found him wide-eyed. Apparently this was something that hadn't been covered back in college.

"But this was . . ." Jax's biting mouth clicked open and shut. "Cooking brine."

Yarvis tilted his head, as if searching for words.

"Some people prefer flavored or spice-infused salt water. It adds an element"—he blinked his lower lids—"of romance."

Bryyh said, "Like scented candles." She dropped her eyes, and I got a feeling we'd just gotten more of a glimpse into her private life than she'd intended.

Kravitz spoke up.

"The, ah, room that Envoy Haberdine reserved had a . . . ah . . ." He fumbled, no doubt searching for the least offensive phrasing. "Extra deep whirlpool tub."

There was another moment of awkward silence.

"How do you think Haberdine's family will react," I said, "to hearing that the deceased was getting ready to play hide-the-tadpole with some hired company?"

"Carter!" Bryyh's voice was sharp, the cracking of thin ice under a boot. She glared at me, a vein throbbing on one temple.

I stared back defiantly. Then I thought of the pictures of grandkids on her desk. I'd known Bryyh for most of my life, and she'd taken the heat for me more times than I could count. I thought of that, and I was the first to drop my eyes.

From the other side of the table, Lanathel broke the silence. "Garson Haberdine left his home to serve his queen. He should be at that site collecting core samples instead of—" Lanathel swallowed, seemingly surprised by his own anger. He glanced at Yarvis, then resumed speaking quickly, as if eager to move the conversation along. "Instead he was murdered in this off the Path town. And you have the gall to drag his memory through the dust?"

Bryyh turned to the Squibs, but Lanathel silenced her with a shake of his head. It was a motion of simultaneous negation and disgust.

"To continue this discussion, we wish only to speak to the Mollenkampi," he said. "The humans should leave us."

There was a pause as everyone waited to see who would speak next.

Bryyh inhaled and ran her hands over the conference table, as if soothing a spooked animal. "Detective Ajax and I would be glad to talk to you—"

The envoy swung his hand as if dismissing a servant. "Him alone. Or another of his kind. At least we know the Mollenkampi are not mad with blood rage."

He didn't spare me a glance as I stood, but not the other Squib, the older, grayer-toned one. That one watched every move as I left the office. I couldn't tell if he was trying to get a measure on me or if he wanted me to know that he was the one calling the shots. It didn't matter to me either way—he could stare at my clenched jaw and bunched fists all he wanted, as long as I didn't have to deal with him any further.

Having been dismissed from the principal's office, I decided I needed to clear my head a little and headed for Lestrange. But when I reached the side door the eating area was deserted, no food trucks in sight. No one wanted to deal with the protest if it spilled over into the side streets. So I simply sat on a bench and stared out at the passing traffic. My stomach growled, and I thought for a moment I smelled cinnamon. I shook my head, angry at whatever hold the Squib blood had over me.

A voice from behind caused me to jump. "Well, that was really something." Ajax stuck his head out the door and looked around. "Not much of a crowd."

"No shit." I scratched my chin. The salt-and-pepper whiskers had gotten longer. I'd forgotten to shave again. "Did your new friends have anything interesting to say after I left?" I did my best to keep my voice level. I wasn't angry with Ajax, but I didn't like being set up as the department scapegoat. I stepped inside and let the door swing shut. Ajax trailed behind. He ran his hands over his head, massaging the leathery skull plates with small, swirling motions.

"I wouldn't call it interesting," he said. "They didn't really want to talk to me. They were mostly just trying to embarrass Bryyh."

We moved through the back offices of the first floor, past the public-facing front desk and the long room where the dispatchers worked the radio waves. From outside it was a tangle of voices describing crimes, announcing successes and failures. Requesting help.

"They were sending a message," I said. "It's what diplomats do."

Jax dropped his hands to his sides with a grunt and stared out over the sea of support staff that kept the TPD running.

"I'll tell you one thing, though," I said.

"What's that?"

"That was some damn fine hard armor they were wearing."

He actually threw his head back and laughed, an amazing sound that tinkled and bellowed all at once.

Pulling a hanky out of his coat pocket, Jax said, "So what's next?" as we headed deeper into the Bunker.

"We wait to hear from the tail on Flanagan. In the meantime, I'm gonna rattle my CIs and see if I can verify whether Flanagan's been on the market as muscle," I said.

As we walked, Jax polished the bone-crushing tusks and serrated grinding teeth that made his biting jaws so intimidating.

"You know what happened to the whales?" he asked as we passed a final set of doors and emerged into the parking garage.

I exhaled loudly, trying to let my breath carry my irritation away, just like the shrinks taught me. It didn't work.

"They got hunted to death," I said.

"They're extinct." He put away the hanky. "Because people wanted the manna in their bellies."

He was delivering a speech, like he'd absorbed a bit too much of his professors' lectures on the Great Shortage.

"Maybe there was a way to sustain manna," he said. "Maybe it was synthesized from blubber at the pressures of great depths. Or maybe the whales ate some kind of deep-sea kelp and it was just a waste byproduct. No one knows, because no one bothered to ask. They were too busy—"

"Hunting whales," I said.

"Hunting whales," he said, slightly louder than I had. "And now?" He waved a hand and sighed. "No more whales."

"No more whales and no more manna." I rubbed my hands together. "Well, this has been fun." I fished the car keys out of my pocket. "Do you have a list of other extinct animals to discuss, or should we take this up sometime when we're not busy finding a killer?"

"It's a metaphor," he said. "Your confidential informants are like whales, and if you keep drawing on them—"

"They'll get killed."

The garage smelled of oil and spilled petroleum. It set my teeth on edge.

"I know the risks involved in being a confidential informant," I said. "And so do the CIs. Sometimes they don't make the best decisions. I think it may have something to do with being criminals more than being informants." I spun the keys on my finger. "But, I could be wrong. Are we done, or do you have some more metaphones you'd like to discuss?"

Ajax walked toward the Hasam.

"Metaphors," he said. "They're called metaphors."

"Whatever." I opened the door, slid behind the wheel, and leaned over to the passenger side. But instead of popping the lock I cranked down the window.

"Listen, I'm gonna take care of a few things. Why don't you see if you can get some traction on the Bell-Asandro case?"

There was silence as Jax glared into the car. It was worse than getting yelled at.

"What?" I said. "I got it covered. You don't have to work the Bell-Asandros if you don't want. Hang here and keep an eye on the Bunker." I couldn't quite look at him when I said it, but I sold it as best as I could. He didn't seem to care.

"I'm not bailing on you," he said.

"Jax . . ."

"Don't get sentimental. You're worried that I'm going to try to distance myself, and I'm telling you that's not going to happen. Besides, I'm committing to follow the truth, not you."

I glanced at the exit gate, and the unrelenting stream of traffic beyond, and felt an overwhelming need to get moving. Ajax was trying to help, but the longer I sat there yapping with him, the more I wanted to scream. But I managed to raise my volume only slightly when I replied.

"You saw how that went down back there. Can you think of any scenario where I'm not the fall guy if things go sideways?" I gave him a second to respond. When he said nothing, I continued. "You want to be standing beside me when that happens?"

Jax kept his hands folded over the passenger door.

"Just who is 'they,' Carter?" he asked. "Who exactly is out to get you? Because as far as I can see, you're good at your job."

"Says the guy who was assigned to babysit me."

"Says the guy assigned to make sure you didn't act like an asshole in public," he corrected. "A task at which I didn't precisely excel."

I smiled and looked away. I'd worked for years on my own. I didn't need a partner to hold my hand. Especially if I was drowning.

"I gotta go," I said, and put the Hasam in gear.

I drove long, winding laps around my city, trying to clear my head. But I couldn't get away from the details of the Haberdine case, from the Bell-Asandro family massacred in their own home. It felt like things were starting to connect, if only in an abstract way.

There was a parking spot along Evendale that I claimed, and then, with the radio turned up so I could hear my favorite DJ Handsome Hanford's morning show, I got out to stretch my legs. I made it as far as the front fender. Taking a seat on the hood I drew a deep breath and wished for a flask of whiskey to magically appear in my hip pocket. But magic was rare and dying out with the last of the manna reserves. My wish wouldn't be granted.

I rubbed my cheek and ran my fingers over acne scars that still pocked my flesh from when I was a teen, felt the whiskers that poked out from the tiny craters. After years of working alone, it had only taken a few days for me to grow accustomed to having someone to talk to about a case. I decided that I'd have to get over it. Much as Ajax may want me to be someone else, I knew I was damaged goods. I didn't want to drag him into things any more than I needed to, and I damn sure wasn't going to call him now.

Set back from the curb, a pay phone stood slightly askew, as if it had taken a knock from a drunk who couldn't park right. I stared at it, at its torn-off phone book and graffiti-covered surfaces. Ajax wasn't there to talk to, so I asked the phone itself.

"Who would pay for an attorney to pull Flanagan's nuts out of the fire like that?"

The Ajax-phone was silent.

"Yeah," I said. "It boils down to who had the most to gain by making us look bad. Or who had the most to lose by seeing Flanagan in jail."

I waited for the phone to magically ring with an answer. No such luck.

"Alright, so the diplomats all wanted the negotiations to go through. . . . But someone obviously didn't. Or they cared more about killing Haberdine than keeping the negotiations going." I tapped my foot against the Hasam's bumper, keeping time to the songs on the radio. "If they only cared about killing Haberdine, then there's no reason to pull Flanagan. Especially if Flanagan didn't do it. So why the Hells would you falsify witnesses in order to spring the man who's in position to take the fall for you?"

The pay phone didn't have any opinions, so I kept on thinking things through out loud.

"Option one." I raised a finger. "Flanagan can turn evidence on the people who really did it. Option two . . . the goal wasn't to kill Haberdine. It was to sabotage the negotiations." I sat up straighter. "Option three . . . he was killed to prevent him from sabotaging the deal."

I jumped off the hood of my car and dug in my pocket for a coin.

"It's time we pushed past this whole everyone's-on-the-same-side line we've been fed." I nodded at the phone. "See? Who needs that college kid?"

I picked up the handset and dialed Gellica's number. It was time I talked to her boss.

18

ARRIVED AT A HOUSE in the Hills about an hour later. I was waved through the gate at the top of the driveway, and pulled up to an ornate multistory home ringed by carefully maintained exotic plants.

Gellica was there, standing by the side of a late-model sports car. It was an Aristarov Mark-VIII, sleek and low-slung. Designed for speed, with only a passing thought given to safety. She took off her sunglasses and gave me an easy salute.

"I didn't expect you to be here," I said.

"I had to pick up some files." She tossed the shades through the open window of the car and fell into step beside me as we approached the house. "Plus it seemed like a good idea to walk you to the office. I had to vouch for you to get you on the schedule."

The early afternoon weather was relatively mist-free, and the property offered a dramatic view, even from the driveway. The day's fleeting few hours of winter sunlight were already fading, and shadows lengthened over the city.

"I was surprised she could see me right away. I thought ambassadors were busy people."

"They are," she said. "My voucher counts for a lot around here." She opened up the front doors, thick wooden things with decorative metal insets. The place looked like it had been designed to withstand a medieval-style siege. "Besides, you're still our best bet to get this horrible situation resolved."

"Am I?"

"I think so. Follow me." She led me through a marble-floored entry area, then up a gracefully curving front stairway.

"As far as best bets go, you're aware that the entire police force is working this case, not just me, right?"

"I'm well aware of that, Detective. I've talked to close to a dozen different detectives about the case and its status."

"You have?" We walked down a hallway lined with oil paintings in thick, finely carved frames. The same aesthetic I'd seen in Gellica's office. Looked like Paulus controlled everything, even down to the office decor level.

"It seems like a dozen, at least. Who's the well-dressed one, Angar . . . Anna . . . ?"

"Angus."

"Yes!" She stopped at a five-panel oak door and pushed it open, revealing a small sitting area with another door in the far wall. "He and his partner came around after you did. Sharp dresser, dull questions. Would you care for coffee or tea?"

"Coffee," I said. And then, "What did he ask about?"

"Lowell and Cordray. He wanted to know if I suspected them of moving funds. He seems to think that someone is blackmailing the clients of some of the city's most desirable candies."

"That's . . . interesting," I said.

"Not half as interesting as who he thinks is doing it. He didn't say it directly, but he implied it's candies themselves who are blackmailing the johns and janes."

I slipped my hands in my pockets and tried not to look nervous.

"Not," she said, "that I wouldn't think it a fair turn of events."

"What did you say?"

"I said it would seem fair for candies to blackmail—"

"No," I interrupted. "What did you say to Angus? About Lowell and Cordray."

Her jaw dropped. "Honestly," she said. "It's like you detectives don't even talk to each other."

"It's a complex case."

"I guess so." She shook her head, sending her hair rippling over her shoulders. "If Lowell and Cordray were being blackmailed, they make enough money to not need AFS funds. Even if they didn't, I doubt they'd be stupid enough to compound their danger by embezzling funds. It wouldn't make sense. Though I'm no cop."

"You've mentioned that before," I said. She handed me a coffee in a thin white porcelain cup. I took it and said, "Been nice of you not to say 'I told you so.'"

"About what?"

"About Flanagan. The candies. All the stuff you said that was probably right."

"Who says I won't? I may simply be waiting for the right moment." Gellica set her weight against the edge of the serving table.

"Didn't you have files to pick up?"

"Yes. I'll get them once I know that you've been to see the ambassador, and that you'll behave yourself."

"I will." I kept a straight face when I said it. "Why are you so concerned about my behavior?"

"Is this where you give me the police psychoanalysis?"

I tasted the coffee. It was good, strong and unsweetened.

"I admit to some curiosity about what drives you," I said.

Gellica almost laughed, arms clasped across her chest as she threw her head back to study the ceiling.

"What drives me? I think I mentioned my mother previously."

"Maybe you did," I said. "If you don't want to talk about it we can say she never came up."

"No, it's okay. She was—is, I suppose—very controlling. I was always under a lot of pressure to succeed, but always at things that had no interest for me."

"Like?"

"Like fashion and social climbing. Knowing who was having an affair with whom, and what members of the currently fashionable elite we were allowed to speak about it with. The better my grades got in economics and poli-sci, the more I excelled at sports, the less interesting I was to her. It was like I had all the wrong skills to be a real woman in her eyes. I never quite forgave her. Or trusted her." She took a breath and exhaled with a smile. "I suppose some people have real problems, but those are my mommy issues. What about you, Carter?"

"Mom died young. My dad worked more often than he was home." I set down my now empty cup. "They didn't leave a whole lot behind for me to remember them. I was mostly raised by the parents of other rig kids. Riggers are rough around the edges, but they care for their own."

She tilted her head and narrowed her eyes. "Where'd your father drill?"

"The Ursus Major rig. About fourteen hours' ride out across the ice plains."

"Huh." She frowned and dropped her eyes.

"Why?"

She looked up, and one corner of her mouth twisted into a smile. "I was wondering if he worked on one of my family's rigs."

I laughed, a deeply genuine belly laugh. "Yeah, the old man

would be over the moon to see his son talking to an oil money diplomat in the heart of some mansion in the Hills."

Gellica tapped the dimple in her chin. "You said they didn't leave much to remember them. What did you mean?"

"I don't really remember my mother. I mostly know her from stories my dad or her coworkers told me. She had a lot of friends on the force. A few of them checked in on me when I was young. Once I became a cop and got to know them as an adult, the stories got a lot less sanitized." I stretched my legs. "Strange to realize that your parents were regular people, just like you."

Her smile faded. I got the impression she couldn't quite relate to that sentiment.

"You still close to your dad?" she asked.

I winced. "All those years of hazard work on the rigs and cheating death on a regular basis," I said, "and my old man goes and has a heart attack while cooking breakfast. He always cooked up a big pan of bacon and eggs in grease." I forced a smile. "Which might explain the heart attack, right?"

She smiled kindly but didn't laugh.

"Anyway, he must have knocked the pan onto the stove during the . . ." I trailed off, let her fill in the details herself. "The fire took pretty much everything he owned. There were a few items, but I didn't keep them. I thought I didn't want reminders of my childhood." I tapped my forehead, indicating that it was probably empty. "I was a stupid kid who didn't value his own history. I regret it."

"I understand wanting to leave memories behind," she said. "And I think your folks would be proud of you."

"Great," I said. "At least I've got a couple ghosts in my corner."

The far door opened, and an immaculately dressed man appeared. He inclined his head in my direction.

"Detective Carter?" he said. "The ambassador will see you now."

I looked back to Gellica and gave her an exaggerated shrug.

"Guess I gotta go," I said.

"Guess so." She pushed off from the desk in one smooth motion. "Be seeing you," she said.

I headed toward Paulus's office.

"And Carter?"

Gellica's voice turned me back around.

"Yeah?"

She smiled.

"I told you so."

Paulus stood when I entered. She had the same fine-boned features and chestnut complexion as Gellica, but her eyes lacked the sincerity of her younger employee. Paulus's smile was professional, a movement as polished as a stage magician fanning a deck of cards. She wore a silk blouse cinched at the waist with a silver buckle, set off by bracelets ornamented with turquoise and gold flake. Tattoos crawled from under the short sleeves of her blouse, black ink peppered with blue highlights, matching her hair.

"Pleasure to meet you." She gestured to an armchair across from her desk. I sat down, and the leather cushions sighed. I could smell leather conditioner and wood polish. Someone spent an inordinate amount of time caring for the items in that room. The office was filled with leather and oak, a palette of scuffed brass and earth tones carefully chosen to give an impression of coziness. It was a place of coldly calculated warmth.

"I have a tight schedule, Detective, if you don't mind making this brief." Her smile never wavered. She cared about her time. I could use that.

Every lock has a different key. And knowing what throws people out of their comfort zones can open a lot of doors.

I leaned forward and opened my notepad, flipping through the pages until I heard the ambassador's sigh of impatience. I was off to a good start.

"I'm sorry, Ambassador, I really am. I'm trying to pull myself out of the doghouse, so to speak, and I've got to cover all my bases. Real by-the-book stuff." I held up my pencil and notepad and gave her a look of apologetic embarrassment.

"No apology needed. Let's just get started." Her tone was crisper now.

"It's just that I need to have all the i's crossed and t's dotted. I'm sure you understand."

"Yes. I understand. Now please continue."

"Okay. . . ." I stared at my notepad. "Ah! Here we are: how well do you know the envoys named Lowell and Cordray?"

"Fairly well, but only professionally. Lowell has been here for five years, and Cordray three, but I knew of both of them before that. They do good work, though their personal habits are about to cause the end of their careers. I know what you're asking, Detective, and the answer is no." Her head angled back, letting her look down her nose even though she was significantly shorter than me. "No, I didn't know that they were engaged in prostitution."

"Oh, that's not what I was going to ask." I stood and took a few steps, trying to give the appearance of a man wandering aimlessly.

"You've got a really fantastic library," I said. "You know, I just love old books."

I walked to the built-in bookcases lining the walls. Paulus sat stone-faced.

"I don't know enough about them the way a collector would, and it certainly looks like you're a collector." I leaned toward the books, scanning titles though not touching them. "No, I wasn't asking about sex trafficking. I was more curious about whether you knew that your envoys are connected to the murders that happened in the Estates."

Her shoulders crept upward. "What?"

"There was a family murdered last night and it seems like both Lowell and Cordray have connections to the victims."

I said it with conviction, though in reality the connections were so tenuous they were practically gossamer. Nina Bell had mentioned someone who might have been Talena, who knew a candy named Stacie who may have heard someone say "Ambassador" after having sex. Three degrees of barely related coincidence. But Paulus didn't know that.

"A murdered family?" She stood and circled the desk, perhaps to intervene if I started touching things.

"An entire family was massacred. Two small children butchered like pigs for market." I hoped the imagery might shake her up.

"Hmm. That's awful." Paulus sounded like she was talking about a picnic canceled by bad weather.

I stretched a hand toward the books. Slowly. Giving her plenty of time to react. Her arm came up and her blouse sleeve pulled back, revealing more tattoos.

"Please don't touch those," she said. The ink-work on her arms were of stylized creatures. Half-animal, half-glyph things that seemed to shift in the fading light of the day.

I held my hands up as if she'd pulled a gun. I turned away slowly.

"I didn't mean to cause offense," I said. "It's just hard to get images like that out of my head."

"Yes. Truly a tragedy," she said. "And if there's anything I can do for you in the future let me know. But for now—"

"Lots of people die," I said, punctuating the statement with a rueful shake of my head. "Every day they get bagged and shipped home for their families to cry over. But these were executions to forward someone's agenda."

There was a large mirror on one wall of the office, and when I turned it showed me the ambassador and myself, with the city as seen from her window spread out behind us.

"There are truly monsters out there," she said. We stared at each other through the filter of the mirror. "But that's the harsh reality of your world, isn't it?"

I turned from her reflection to face her directly.

"It's not just my world. We're all stuck in it," I said.

"The rest of us may live here, but I suspect that your world is quite of your own making." She crossed her arms, and the tattoos pulsed. Not the side-to-side jiggle of muscle, but true independent movement. A snake squeezed its prey, a meal moved farther down a wyvern's throat.

I recoiled and looked away, not sure if I'd really seen that unnatural motion. Taking a breath, I studied the leather-bound backs of her books. They were stained to appear so similar to the leather chairs that they could all have come from one giant animal. It was like everything in her office was connected by death. The cascade of leather and death was like its own world, a world entirely of . . .

". . . our own making," I murmured.

Paulus tapped her dimpled chin. "That's what I said."

I needed to regain control of the conversation. Scratching my neck, I stared at the ambassador from the corner of my eye.

"Just out of curiosity, do diplomats have much in the way of life insurance?"

"What?"

"Well, I don't ask for myself. But a friend of mine, she has a son. And like most kids—he's sixteen, seventeen at most—he wants to do what he wants to do, and there's no putting together anything for him. Anyway, he wants to go into politics. He's a clean-cut kid, so he might get away with it. I never could have, with the amount of trouble I'd caused by his age, you understand."

Paulus circled her desk again, picking up a letter opener from the stacks of paper. It was a heavy, sharp-bladed thing that was far more than was needed for slicing open correspondence.

"You want to know if Mister Haberdine's family would benefit from his death."

"The thought had occurred to me."

"Or"—she paused—"you want to know if anyone else would benefit from the death of this family in the Estates."

"If Haberdine's death derails the talks, it will affect millions."

"It will cost at least that much," she said.

"I meant millions of *people*."

She cleared her throat. "Of course."

I pointed out the window. "There's what, a dozen sizable drilling concerns in town?"

"That depends on your definition of 'sizable.'"

"And how many of them are on board with the switch from oil?"

"We're on the brink of a new age in Titanshade," she said. "The drilling companies want to be on the right side of things. Both for the history books and their bottom line." Fidgeting with the letter opener, she looked like an older version of Gellica, though drained of the younger woman's concern and compassion. I wondered if that happened to all diplomats over time.

"But really, you can get all this information from the newspapers." She glanced meaningfully at the clock on her desk.

"The newspapers say that the owner of Rediron Drilling opposes the move from oil."

"Well, there you go," she said.

"You have insight the papers lack," I said. "Insight into these people's ethics."

"You want to know if any wealthy, powerful executives are the sort to tear apart another living being in a hotel room?"

"That's not what I said."

She gave me the courtesy of a false laugh. "You didn't need to. I'm a diplomat, Detective. *Subtle* is what I do."

"I appreciate that. It's just that I'd also appreciate an answer to the question."

She shook her head, and still dodged it. "I'm afraid you're barking up the wrong tree."

"Could be. But at least I'm barking."

"Yes." The soft brown skin on her knuckles paled as she tightened her grip on the letter opener. "You certainly are doing that."

My pager buzzed and I glanced down at my pocket. It wasn't a number I recognized.

Paulus set the opener down. "I know of no one who would benefit directly from Mr. Haberdine's death, or from the dissolution of alternate energy talks. If there's some back channel path, then I surely don't know what it is."

"What if it was Haberdine who opposed the deal?"

Paulus's lips pressed together. "Say more."

I leaned forward, expensive leather crinkling under my weight.

"You say no one would want to sabotage the deal. Okay. Fine," I said. "I'm not sure I buy that, but let's say you're right. If the wind farm deal is so important that no one would ever dream of sabotaging it then it sorta begs the question. . . ."

Paulus stared at me. Silent. I spread my arms and finished my sentence.

"Would anyone kill to keep them on track?"

Paulus shook her head. "No. Garson Haberdine was working for the trade agreement. He had no reason to sabotage anything."

I scratched my chin. She hadn't exactly answered my question, but I let that angle drop.

"But Haberdine also was favoring candies," I said. "Delivering salt water by the barrel to keep up with his sexcapades. If that were exposed, would the talks have been derailed?"

She tilted her head as if in thought. "Perhaps. It depends on what else was in the news that week. Public perception is a fickle thing." She looked me over. "As you are well aware."

I shifted in my seat, brown suit rumpling around me as I spread my hands wide, giving her my best "what-can-you-do?" look. I resumed speaking immediately, eager to move the conversation along. The same way that the Squib envoy Lanathel had tried to push the conversation along at the Bunker when he'd said something that he'd seemed to regret.

"If so many people would benefit from the talks coming to completion," I said, pulling us back to the question she'd sidestepped earlier, "then it stands to reason that one of them would be willing to kill to see them go through."

She pressed her palms together. "Again—perhaps. It's also true that many people would benefit from the oil economy returning. But that doesn't mean anyone is being sacrificed in the hope of finding more petroleum reserves."

The mention of additional petroleum caused the pieces to click in my mind. Lanathel had grown uncomfortable right after he'd mentioned that if Haberdine were alive he'd be out on the ice, taking core samples.

I leaned forward with a new enthusiasm.

"If the Squibs had no interest in using the ice fields for drilling," I said, "why was Haberdine checking for evidence of more oil?"

There was a knock at the door and Paulus waved off my question.

"While it's a pleasure to assist your investigation, I'm afraid we're quite out of time." The magician's smile appeared again. "Good day, Detective. This has been a most illuminating conversation."

Outside Paulus's office I looked around for Gellica, but she'd disappeared. I asked Paulus's assistant for a phone and he led me to a spare desk. Turning my back to the room, I dialed the number that had been left on my pager. Ajax answered.

"How fast can you get to the butcher's shop on Eubanks?" he said. "I found the Bell-Asandro kid."

The missing oldest son. We had our witness. Or our killer.

19

PULLED UP TO THE butcher's shop to find a well-maintained Hasam Motors vehicle by the curb. It had cop car written all over it.

I walked over and sure enough, Ajax was sitting at the wheel. He nodded a greeting.

"You'll want your armor on for this one," he said, and handed me a vest. He was already wearing one over his dress shirt.

I've learned the hard way to never argue when someone tells you to put on protective gear.

As I strapped in I asked him, "So what's the score with this?"

"Jermaine's in there. The surviving son from the Bell-Asandro family."

The butcher shop's windows were dark, their shades drawn. "How'd you find him?" I asked.

"I decided to do a follow up with the Bells' sister—Nina, the one you interviewed."

"The recovering addict."

"That's the one. I got to her place and no one was home. Couple days' worth of mail was sticking out of her mail slot and newspapers were sitting in front of her entry. I started thinking that she was in danger."

"You entered without a warrant?"

"You kidding?" he said. "I was afraid she'd been attacked by the thrill killer who's been in the news lately. Soon as the neighbors heard that, one of them with a spare key let me in."

Never underestimate the morbid curiosity of the public.

"Clothes and essentials missing from the bathroom," he said. "But there was a set of sheets on the couch."

"She had someone staying with her," I said.

"Neighbors described a young man who matches the profile we've got for the missing Bell-Asandro kid, her nephew. I expanded the BOLO to include Nina Bell and her vehicle. A patrolman spotted her car"—he pointed at a worn sedan down the road—"near her place of employment." He moved his finger, indicating the butcher's shop.

"I tried the door, but it's locked. Kind of unusual for a business to be locked up during the day."

"And where's the butcher?"

He thrummed his fingers on the steering wheel. "I don't know. But this was good enough to get a warrant."

"Pretty good police work, College."

"What, you thought we were all going to sit around while you ran your mystery errand? The world moves on even when you're not in the room, you know."

I looked over the butcher's shop, a two-story brick building that shared walls with neighbors on either side. Commercial space on the first floor, surely living space on the second. Outside the shop the sidewalks were thick with people shopping and running errands.

"We should call for backup."

"I did," he said. "You."

After a beat his mandibles quivered. "I'm just messing with you. Myris and Hemingway are already on the back door. We've got no activity in or out for the last hour."

He lifted the walkie-talkie from the dash. "The old man's here. You guys ready?"

"Really?" I tightened the last strap on my protective vest. "Old man?"

The walkie crackled and Hemingway responded. *"We're here. On your signal."*

"Entry at"—Ajax checked his watch—"ninety seconds from . . . now. Good?"

"Golden."

Ajax looked at me.

"Well, alright," I said.

We walked to the front door of the shop. Ajax eyed his watch, and on his signal I tried the door. As Ajax had said, it was bolted. He turned and delivered a mule kick to the glass body of the door. It was safety glass, and spider-webbed rather than shattering. A second kick knocked it loose enough for Ajax to reach in a hand. I scanned the front of the building as he unlocked the latch and pulled the door open. The entry bell tinkled as we entered.

"Police!" I called out.

The cash register was deserted, and no one stood behind the thick cuts of meat on display in the glass-fronted counter.

Ajax glanced my way, nodded toward the open doorway behind the counter. It led to the back room, out of the public eye. Where the bloodiest work was done.

I circled the butcher's case, moving at a fast walk. The back room was open, the lights on, with stainless steel surfaces and slotted mats to prevent slips. It was a room designed to be hosed down. As far as I could see, it held no good hiding places.

I stopped before I got too far from Ajax. We moved in alternating exposures, covering each other as we progressed forward in short jumps. I paused at one of the cutting stations and nodded the all-clear. With light steps Jax passed me and reached another of the stations. He was heading for the open doorway in the far wall. When he paused, I moved forward again, stopping when my shoulder hit the doorframe. I stuck my head around the corner.

Before me was a hall, maybe twenty feet long with a door at its end and a curtained alcove to the side, about halfway between us and the door. A quick survey of the hall revealed no movement. I tilted my head and Ajax circled around as well. He glanced down the hallway and hesitated before starting in. I couldn't blame him. I didn't particularly like confined spaces either. At least not when armed killers might be the prize at the end of the tunnel.

I looked over my shoulder and confirmed that no one had closed in on our backs. When I looked forward again, Ajax had taken a few more steps and was slowing. The curtain to the alcove rippled as if in a breeze. I hissed a warning, and Ajax froze.

"Police!" I said. "Announce your presence and lay down any weapons."

The curtain rippled again. I knew what was coming.

I yelled to Ajax, "Down!"

The roar of a gunshot swallowed my warning, followed by a second, answering shot from Ajax before he tumbled into the wall. Starbursts flared in my vision, ghosts of the muzzle flash. The ringing in my ears subsided enough for me to realize I was yelling, though I wasn't sure what I was saying. Jax, eyes wide, mandibles slack, leaned against the wall and stared at the curtain as it moved back and forth. His revolver pointed in the air almost casually. Then it kicked back, firing another shot. A section of ceiling tile fell to the ground, followed shortly by his sidearm. Jax's right arm went limp and blood coursed down his shirt, crimson drops collecting at his fingertips, hanging for an impossible moment before letting loose and falling to the butcher's bloodstained floor.

A noise snapped my head around. The entire curtain bowed forward, suspension rod crashing down as a lanky figure rolled out, screaming and bleeding. He was older than in the photos I'd seen at the Bells' home, his eyes red-rimmed and there was the start of a patchy, teenage beard on his cheeks. But I recognized Jermaine as he ran for me, arms outstretched, mouth open in a meaningless roar. And I recognized the sudden slackness on his face when he bucked forward and another gunshot rattled the walls. Jermaine dropped to the ground, revealing Myris's silhouette on the opposite end of the hall, weapon in hand. She came my way, and together we circled the figure crouched in the small alcove where Jermaine had erupted from. It was Nina Bell, the kid's aunt, and the gun she held was still smoking.

"You are going to drop that weapon," I told her. "You will drop it now."

Nina cringed, and held out shaking hands, setting the gun down in front of her. I reached for the walkie. "Hemingway, drop back to your car. Radio to Dispatch we have an officer down, need immediate assistance."

She snapped out a brusque affirmative and was gone.

Myris kicked the aunt's handgun a safe distance away and instructed her to get to her knees. The woman who'd just shot my partner looked at me with tears running down her face.

"I didn't know it was you," she said. "I didn't know, I didn't know."

Myris restrained her and I focused on Ajax. He was bleeding from the arm, but there was a gouge on the vest beneath his armpit. The armor had saved him from a chest wound, ricocheting the bullet sideways, where it buried itself into the meat of his interior upper arm. The danger in that area was a wound to the brachial artery. If that was hit, we'd have to stop the wound or he'd bleed out before the ambulance arrived.

There's some mystery to bullet wounds. A shot to the arm may wound without critical injury, while another a few inches to the side can tear open an artery, leading to massive blood loss and near certain death. So many little things determine a projectile's path and the damage it does.

Jax had lost a fair amount of blood, but it didn't show the pressurized squirting that would have indicated an arterial breech. I was very happy to see my partner was one of the lucky ones.

Jermaine Bell, however, was not. His aunt continued to sob, staring at her nephew as she lay on her side, hands cuffed behind her back. Myris's shot had struck him in the neck, and much of the blood sprayed on the wall was his. That's when I became aware of the warm dampness on my face. Something rolled down between my eyes, clinging to the edge of my nose and refusing to fall to the floor.

Disgusted, I swiped an arm across my face and looked down. My shirtsleeve was red with the boy's castoff blood.

"Myris, what'd you come through in the back of the building?"

"Small kitchen. Stairs to the second level."

"Give me a hand," I said. Myris and I each grabbed an arm and lifted Nina Bell to her feet before the spreading puddle of her nephew's blood reached her. We marched her back to the kitchenette. I sat her down at a small table that was covered with a faded yellow and orange flower print tablecloth. She slumped in the chair, sobbing silently. I grabbed a dishtowel from beside the sink.

"Cuff her to something that won't move," I said. "Make sure there's no knives or anything else that can be used as a weapon near her. Watch her. Keep your ears open, and if you hear anyone else moving, you yell like our lives depend on it."

"I got it. Hemingway'll have that ambulance here in no time."

I ran back to Ajax. His eyes were squeezed tight. Still bleeding, but not so much that I was panicked. I needed to put pressure on the wound, though. Folding the towel, I shoved it in his armpit. He cried out.

"Squeeze on that," I said. "Keep the pressure strong. You're going to be fine."

I looked at him for a response, but his eyes were still shut.

"You ever been shot before, college boy?"

He shook his head.

"Alright, listen. Right now, you're more scared than wounded. We're getting an ambulance, and you're gonna get attention. But you're stabilized. Do you understand me?"

His nostrils flared as he took deep breaths.

"Do you understand me?"

Jax's eyes snapped open, gold-flecked brown sparking with anger. "Yes, you asshole."

"Attaboy, College. Just hold tight."

WHEN THE AMBULANCE WAS GONE and Ajax was headed to the hospital, I walked back into the kitchen.

On the floor by the cabinets, hands cuffed around the soldered metal of the under-sink plumbing, Nina Bell sat staring at nothing. All the cleaning materials kept under the sink had been pulled out and tossed onto the countertop. Myris was nothing if not thorough. I unlocked the cuffs and helped her to a kitchen chair. She rubbed her wrists and stayed silent, eyes on the floor. I looked down and saw bloody footprints across the linoleum. Tracked in by me, judging by the size. I pulled over another chair and sat close, but not too close. I didn't want to intimidate her, but I wanted her to know that I was there.

"Tell me about it, Nina." I leaned in, echoing her words from when we'd last spoke. "What happened before it all went to shit?"

She sucked in a ragged breath.

"The night before you came and talked to me about Tara and the kids," she said, "I heard tapping at my window. I flipped on the outside light and there he was, soaking wet and shivering."

"Your nephew."

She nodded. "Jermaine." She said his name with such sorrow. I remembered photo albums spread across her couch, a makeshift memorial as she mourned her family.

"He wouldn't—" Her lip quivered. The stress and adrenaline of the shooting had evaporated, leaving her on the edge of breaking down. I gave her as much time as she needed to start over. "He wouldn't tell me what happened. Just that he was in danger. He said the people he worked for were after him. That they'd killed Tara and the kids."

"What people? Who did he work for?"

"Doctors."

A voice spoke from behind me, dripping with disbelief. "Doctors?"

Myris and Hemingway stood in the door, staring at the woman who'd shot Ajax. Their rage practically rippled across the room.

"Why would doctors kill his family?" I said, pulling Nina's attention back to me.

"It took a long time to get him to tell me anything. And when he did, it didn't always—" She grimaced. "They did something to him. To his head."

"Where?" I asked. "A hospital? A lab?"

"I don't know." She chewed her lip. "He said some of the equipment had a drill company logo on it."

"Which one?"

She shook her head. "It was all bits and pieces. He'd wake up on the couch, screaming, still sweaty from nightmares, talking about a scar-faced doctor injecting him with rainbows. But it always felt like . . ."

"There was something he wasn't telling you."

"Yeah." She blinked, as if she'd confused herself. "No. It was like there was something he wasn't telling himself." She looked at me, then at Myris and Hemingway.

"I've just—" Nina rubbed her shoulders, hands trembling. A self-embrace to help her focus. "I've known him since he was a baby," she said. "I looked at him and it broke my heart. All I could think about was all the times I'd held him when he cried, or took him to the movies." She turned to me. "You can't know what it's like. Even if a kid's not yours, when you know them all their life you want to protect them."

"I know," I said, and did my best not to think of Talena.

"He was terrified. He couldn't even bear to look at photos of Tara and the kids. When I got out my photo albums he just started shaking and sweating. Poor kid."

A bitter taste rose in the back of my mouth. Realization was setting in.

"Was he using?" I asked.

Nina closed her eyes. "For years. Runs in the family, I guess." She attempted a smile, the weary half grin of someone who knew the weight of addiction. "It's why he still came to see me even after he and his folks stopped talking. He knew I understood."

"Was he selling?"

"Not drugs. Jermaine was . . ." She stared at the kitchen table, hands rubbing like cricket legs. "He was selling himself."

A discarded candy. Like Haberdine's spirit had told us to look for. I flashed back to Talena on the street, walking away from me and calling out to a teenage boy. I tried to picture his face but it wouldn't come into focus.

So instead I focused on the woman in front of me.

"You said he came to you the night that your sister and her family were killed."

She nodded. That was the same night Haberdine had been torn to pieces.

"And he was wet?" I urged her on. I needed to understand the timing. "Water was dripping off of him?"

She hesitated. "No. It was . . . I don't know."

"You said *soaking*."

"He was wet, all right?" Nina wrinkled her nose. "He smelled like salt water."

I remembered the thick odor of brine in her apartment, the salt water taffy air fresheners over her entry vent that I now realized were camouflage.

"He was there when I talked to you." I jabbed an angry finger at her. As if anything I did could make her feel worse. "You lied to me."

She was almost too exhausted to nod. "He said no cops. Never any cops. He said the doctor had cops working for him." Her eyes were empty of anything except honesty. "I had to save my nephew."

"By shooting a cop!" Myris snarled from across the room. Nina Bell flinched, casting her eyes down and hunching her shoulders protectively.

I held my hands up, and spoke in as calm a voice as I could muster.

"Just relax. Nina, take your time. Let's back up." I reestablished eye contact, kept my distance. "Tell me everything you can about the people Jermaine was working for. When did he start?"

"About six months ago," Nina said. "Jermaine said he'd found honest work. Not sex stuff. Said he was working for a doctor. Doing studies."

"Studies." I leaned forward. "Where?"

"I don't know. Some lab. He told me they started giving him stuff that'd trip him out and record his reactions. Things to eat, things to smell, aerosol sprays . . . all kinds of stuff. He said it was a crazy high. Bad, but good. Too good, you know?"

"That's why he always went back," I said. Whoever had done this had selected their victim with care.

Nina's lips tightened. "They shot him up with something and had him wandering the ice plains. They told him it was a treasure hunt. The kind of lie you tell a little kid when you want their help finding your car keys, you know?"

"What were they really doing?" I asked.

Shaking her head, she said, "No idea. But it got worse. They put him in a gas mask, breathing in that smoke, or steam, or whatever. He said it made him violent. He had animal bites all over him. They had him fighting dogs. Dogs!" She opened her fists, and I caught glimpses of the dark half moons she'd dug into her palms. "Who does that to a kid?"

I didn't say anything. Even Myris and Hemingway were silent.

She hesitated. "It scared me so bad to hear him tell about it. They used to ask him weird questions. About politics, about what he wanted to do for the city." She pulled back a lip in disgust. "Like the city ever did anything for him, besides chew him up and spit him out."

Nina swallowed. "There was one other guy he talked about. A Mollenkampi. Big, scary. Like the Mount itself was walking around. Jermaine was terrified of that guy."

"So when you fired at us . . ."

"I saw him through the curtain. The biting mouth, the things . . ." She waved at her face, where mandibles might sit if she were Mollenkampi. "Thought he was coming for Jermaine. To finish what he started with the rest of my family."

Shortcuts and side roads. She'd thought she was saving her last living family member.

Nina rocked back and forth, hugging herself, hair matted with blood and in tangles around her.

"The man you shot isn't big," I said.

"He looked big to me." It was the first thing she'd said with real anger. "He looked big when he sat out there in his damn car and watched us, like we were bugs under glass. And when we heard him break in the front door . . ." She let out a long exhale through clenched teeth. "We hid."

"When you heard us yell 'police'?"

She brought her palms to her cheeks and pressed in, making her eyes look even more hollow. "I thought it was a lie. To make us come out." She looked over my shoulder at Myris and Hemingway, pleading her case.

"I couldn't let them take him. He's my family, I couldn't let them . . ." She trailed off, staring again at the red footprints on linoleum, the marks I'd picked up while walking back and forth over the body of her nephew. Now he'd be going up the Mount with the rest of his family.

I didn't have words to comfort her. Ajax might have found something to say, but he wasn't around. Because this sad-faced woman had shot him. People will hurt anyone they need to in order to protect their family. Sometimes they'll even destroy the thing they love in order to save it.

I pushed my thinning hair back and ignored the bitter taste that wouldn't go away.

All the reflective surfaces in the Bell-Asandro home, covered so that the killer wouldn't have to see himself do the unthinkable. The bodies carefully laid out, treated with near reverence. That wasn't the act of a stranger killing for cash or pleasure. It was done by someone who destroyed for another reason.

"He did it to save them," I said. "From people he thought would hurt them even worse."

Nina stared at me, confused.

There was a snap of gum and Hemingway said, "That is bat-shit crazy."

It took a moment longer to hit Nina.

"No," she said. Her hands rose, covering her eyes, hiding her face. "No, no, no."

I felt the puzzle pieces teeter on the brink, almost pulling together. I walked to the back door, opening it to air the place out—the butcher shop still smelled of those old traveling companions, gun smoke and blood. What could push a teenager into killing his own family? Was it the strange drug he'd been fed, or something else?

I remembered Ajax tapping the map of the city, showing the Bells' home in relation to the Mount and to one of the more exclusive hotels in town. The scene of Haberdine's murder had affected me, even walking in hours after the fact. If Jermaine had seen something like that it might have put him over the edge. Or if he'd *done* something like that . . .

But even if it was true, it didn't really solve anything. Somebody had chaperoned him in and out. A strung-out candy wasn't waltzing into the Eagle Crest on his own. Even if he tried, the fact that he wasn't on any of the video surveillance meant that he'd had help from someone familiar with the hotel. Not to mention whoever had manipulated him into doing it. But all I had to go on were nightmare recollections of a scar-faced doctor and a giant Mollenkampi. There was still so much to unravel.

But right then, there was something else I had to do.

"Nina," I said. She didn't respond so I said it louder.

She looked up and I did my best to soften my voice.

"You shot a police officer."

She nodded.

"I have to arrest you, do you understand?"

Fresh tears started their descent down her cheeks. They collected at her jawline, hesitated a moment, then dropped into a free fall, landing on the butcher's floor, mingling with bloody foot-prints, remnants of her nephew or my partner.

"You didn't know what you were doing but I can't—" I wiped a hand across my face. "I have to take you in."

She sobbed. I felt a pain in my chest, deep inside. To keep my sanity, I ignored it.

"Stand up and place your hands on top of your head."

"I didn't know. I didn't know."

I recited her rights, the words tumbling over my lips like the Traveler's Prayer while I cuffed one hand, then the other, trying not to twist her arms as I moved them behind her back.

"Do you understand your rights?"

Snot and tears clogged her voice as she repeated, "I didn't know."

I sat her down on the chair as gently as I could, and looked over her head. The doorway was empty. Myris and Hemingway had already gone to tell the paddy wagon crew to come in and collect her. While no one was there to watch, I patted Nina on the shoulder, trying to comfort her in my own clumsy way.

Sometimes it doesn't feel good to catch the bad guys.

After I walked Nina Bell through booking, I sat down at my desk in the Bunker and started making phone calls. After those were done I checked the ribbon in the typewriter and started writing up the report. Myris came and stood by my desk, tapping her foot.

"I'm a bad typist, Myris. I don't need you staring over my shoulder."

"So get lost."

I looked at her, waiting for her to explain. With an exaggerated sigh, she tapped her chest.

"I'll do the report. I'm the one who took the kid down. I'll need a statement from you, but I don't need it now." She walked toward her desk. "Go see your partner, old man."

I blinked, unsure how to respond to an offer of help. Then I stood and grabbed my coat. "I don't like the 'old man' thing, you know."

"I know," she yelled back without turning around.

At Wayfinder's Hospital, my badge got me quick access to Ajax in the emergency room. I found him on a luxurious paper-draped examination table separated from other patients by eight feet and a curtain. He sat upright, shirt off, with white bandages wrapped around his arm.

The scaly head plating stopped at the back of his neck, the plates growing smaller and thinner until they blended with the olive complexion of his skin. Although the plates were only on his head, the brown and white spots returned along his collarbone and sternum, sweeping out to trace the lines of his rib cage. Or they should have. Currently they were obscured by dark bruising on his right side, where his vest had absorbed the bullet's impact. The TPD vests were bulletproof, but getting shot is still akin to being hit in the ribs with a hammer. Ajax tensed with every twinge of pain, ropey muscles clenching. The kid was gristle, all sinew and lean muscle.

"No wonder you're so fast," I told him. "You don't have any fat on you at all." I jabbed my pencil eraser in the unwounded left side of his ribcage.

"Stop it!" He swiped at my hand but I pulled back faster than he could catch me. They clearly had him on painkillers.

"Seriously, man. Eat a sandwich or something." I took a seat and Jax twisted to follow me. The paper beneath him crinkled, matching the static that faded in and out of the easy-listening music piped out over the hospital's PA system. My entire visit had been underscored by a muted saxophone-and-oboe duet.

"The aunt," he said. "She talked to you?"

"She did." I filled him in on my working theory. Jermaine had killed his parents and siblings in the grip of some drug. And why I thought he was tied to the Haberdine case.

"The kid's the killer?" he said. "You think he tore someone apart in a hotel room and smuggled himself out?"

"Don't know," I said. "I'm saying there's a chance he was there."

"It's something."

"It's a strong something," I said. "But it could still dissolve."

"There's a witness," he said.

"The dead one?" I snorted. "We've got a secondhand story about mad scientists and huffing chemicals. No specific names or locations. Just a 'maybe' that some of the equipment came from a drilling company.

"Though"—I stretched my arms over my head in an exaggerated yawn—"I did find time to make a few calls before I started in on the paperwork."

"Yeah?"

"I left messages for the owners or CEOs of the largest twenty drilling companies. Said I wanted to ask about information I'd received from a witness we're holding. A former employee of theirs named Jermaine Bell. Thought I'd see if anyone jumped at the mention of that name."

"And?"

I smiled.

"And I've got an appointment to meet the owner of Rediron Drilling in a couple hours."

"Harlan Cedrow?" he asked.

I nodded.

"The guy delaying the wind farms?"

"That's him," I said.

"The one you assured me had done so much for the community? The one with so much to lose if the wind farm deal goes sour?"

He almost chuckled, then laid a careful hand between his wounded arm and his rib cage.

I bit my tongue, glad he hadn't gotten to a full gloat.

"All that still stands," I said. "He helped people at one time, no matter what else happened since." I ignored the flash of memory, Jenny's face, the feel of her hand gripping mine as the Cedrow Care Center doctors laid out a plan of action to ease her pain. A surgery, infusing her cancer-ridden bones with material from a donor. From me.

"I'm going to go have a talk with the man," I said, "and see what he says."

The curtain was pulled aside and a doctor entered. I saw her eyes fall to the badge I'd clipped to my jacket. "Which one of you is . . ."

I pointed at Jax. "Right there, doc."

She peered into my eyes, which I was sure were bloodshot and baggy.

"Uh-huh," she said. "Sit there and catch your breath, and we'll look at you after your friend."

That wasn't going to happen. I already had my pills, and no exam would find anything physically wrong with me. The small scrape on my leg bones, the result of the donor surgery, was insignificant; it shouldn't bother me at all. I didn't need to hear one more doctor explain the idea of "psychosomatic pain." I waited as the doctor placed two X-ray images on a wall-mounted light box, then let myself out as she was explaining to Ajax that his ribs were bruised but not broken.

The nurses' station in the hall was vacant, and I saw a built-in radio tuner next to the announcement mic for the PA system. The source of all the easy-listening tunes that filled the floor.

I asked myself, what kind of partner would I be to leave a disco-loving kid like Ajax trapped with an endless oboe solo?

With a quick glance to either side, I stretched over the counter-top and twisted the dial on the radio. A moment later I entered the elevator with a smile as thunderous guitar riffs echoed down the halls.

21

I HAD JUST ENOUGH TIME to pick up cat food, feed Rumple, and shower before heading to my appointment in clean clothes. I even poured an extra bowl of food, so that Rumple could graze if I was late getting home. Every now and then I can pass for a competent adult.

On my arrival I was led through the offices of Rediron Drilling by a series of lackeys before being deposited outside the big man's office, with instructions to wait until I was called for.

Most of my career had consisted of rousting thugs and roughnecks, or piecing together when marriages went from argumentative to homicidal. In twenty years I'd never sat in more waiting rooms than the last few days. I was done waiting. I walked to the nicely built five-panel door and announced my presence with a fierce knocking.

I heard quick steps, the door opened, and I found myself eye-to-lapel with the single biggest Mollenkampi I'd ever seen. I glanced up and stared into massive biting jaws. He wore a collared shirt open at the neck, and I got a good look at the rippling gleam of his eating-mouth teeth as he spoke.

"Mr. Cedrow will see you now." He took one step back, giving me just enough space to squeeze by.

If Jermaine Bell-Asandro was truly terrified of a massive

Mollenkampi, this character certainly fit the bill. But there was more than one big guy in the world, and when would Jermaine have seen an assistant to one of Titanshade's most powerful people?

Once past the bruiser I found a room the size of the Bunker's Bullpen. Unlike the artificial intimacy of Paulus's office, this place looked like a museum. Display cases ringed the walls, and two large glass-top jeweler's tables displayed an array of documents and objects, lit and labeled for presentation.

At the far end of the room a man sat behind a metal desk, one leg propped up on its corner, steel-toed work boot emerging from the frayed cuff of canvas work pants. Seeing me he threw his hands in the air and shook them like a true believer at a tent revival.

"Mister Detective! Come on in!"

Harlan was lanky, with big hands and jug ears that were sized to match. He had a head plucked free of hair and a toothy grin. He dressed in Therreau fashion, simple fabrics and modest styling, though the accessories were those of a rig-working roughneck. The disparity between his dress and his surroundings was striking.

Harlan was perhaps the last of the old-school oil barons. His family was Therreau, but had left the faith to make their fortune. Harlan had gotten a lot of favorable press for steering the company back to Therreau ideals, though he never took it so far as to switch from trucks to tibron beetles or from electricity to oil lamps and pellet fires. He was famous for his down-home ways and a philanthropic streak that had helped countless families in need, including my own. I'd never forget the way Jenny's pain eased after her surgery, an experimental trial that never would have happened if not for the Cedrow Care Center. The surgery ultimately didn't save her and it had consigned me to a lifetime of aching pain, but it made her last months pass easier. And for that I was grateful. But if he was behind the treatment of Jermaine Bell, then I'd drag him kicking and screaming into the light.

I walked toward him with my hand out.

"Thank you for seeing me, Mr. Cedrow," I said.

"Harlan. Just Harlan." He shook my hand without bothering to stand. I was surprised to feel rough calluses on his fingers and palms. Those work boots weren't just for show.

I sat in a comfortable leather chair that I inched closer to his desk. I wanted to be able to read his face while we talked.

"Detective, you are as welcome as rainfall on thirsty soil." His voice rose and fell in the archaic cadence common among Therreau folk. "What can I do for a fellow servant of this city?"

"I know that when I called I said that I wanted to talk to you about an employee . . ."

"Jermaine Bell, yes indeed." Hushed now, like a whispered prayer.

"But that wasn't entirely true."

Harlan raised a hairless brow but stayed quiet.

"I do want to talk to you about Jermaine, but I have to wait for the docs to clear him for being interviewed."

The oil magnate's jaw tightened, but otherwise he was the picture of patience. I'd have to keep on pushing buttons to get a rise out of him.

"In all honesty, the kid's just a reason to get in here to speak with you." I leaned forward, as if sharing a ripe piece of gossip. "I'm here because I spoke with Ambassador Paulus earlier today."

"Ah . . ." He adopted the same hushed tone of confidences shared. "And how is the ambassador?"

"She sends her regards," I said. "But when I spoke with her, she made it quite plain who would have reason to derail the wind farm negotiations."

"And who might that be?"

"Well, there's a reason you were my next call, Mister Harlan."

That made him laugh. "She is little, but she is fierce," he said in a louder voice. "Though in this matter, she is mistaken."

"Well," I said, "for someone who wants to sell his land, you're spending an awful lot of money advertising against the deal. All those billboards and commercials. 'Oil made us great.'" I punctuated the phrase with air quotes.

"First let me be clear. Oil did indeed make this city great." He ran a thumb over his jaw. "But I have a duty to our stakeholders to make the most out of the opportunity the wind farm proposal presents. Perception is a powerful thing, Detective."

"So you're supporting the deal by attacking it?"

He gave the arms of his chair a lazy slap, a tutor losing patience with his student.

"I'm spending thousands," he said, "to make millions. Isn't there some kind of math requirement at the police academy?"

"If there was, they wouldn't be able to screw us on our overtime pay."

"Well, I'll be sure to say a word to Chief Janus the next time I see him."

He wasn't too subtle with the casual displays of power, that Harlan.

"I don't mean to imply that you'd be suspected of any wrongdoing." I backpedaled, as if afraid to give offense. "Everyone knows that you have a tremendous amount to lose if the talks break down. But she seemed to think you might have some"—I spun my hands as if at a loss for words—"I don't know, some insight into the mindset of whoever would oppose the deal." I pulled out my notepad. "So if you wouldn't mind a few questions?"

With a deep breath and wide-armed gesture, the owner of Rediron Drilling sat back in his chair. "Ask away, friend. As for who'd have the most to lose if the wind farm project evaporated . . . well, I'm sure you and I will get there in time."

"I suppose we will," I said, then tried an abrupt pivot. "In fact, I was wondering about the key players in the negotiations. Did you notice any of the other parties bringing in attorneys who might not be focused on contract law?"

"An unusual attorney?" He rolled the phrase in his mouth. "Did you have anyone in mind?"

I waved my hand in a broad gesture. "I don't know. A divorce attorney would be out of place. A criminal attorney. Someone who didn't belong."

Harlan eyed me, then grinned and wagged a finger like I was a disrespectful child.

"Deceit is a wicked thing, Mister Detective. A wicked thing that rots the heart from inside, sure as a worm burrows through an apple." He tapped his breast for emphasis. "And I think you're flirting with deceit, yes I do. I think you're trying to ask me a question without coming out and asking." He pushed back, his chair gliding easily across the floor. "But I can teach thee, cuz, to spur temptation." He slapped a hand against his knee and swung it into the air. "Tell the truth and *spur* temptation!" His eyes followed his hand as it rose to the heavens. He paused at the apex, arm extended. Then he looked at me and lowered his arm, extending his finger as he did, a slow-motion accusation. "And you, Detective, could use a bit of schooling on telling the truth, don't you think?"

Alright.

"When did you hire Jankowski?"

"There it is!" He clucked his tongue. "Doesn't it feel better to simply come out with it?" Harlan drew close to me again, and glanced around as if we were back to swapping secrets. "I hired her years ago, and I use her to consult on all kinds of matters. Lawyers are expensive, but more expensive still is a lack of them when they're actually needed. And it was clear that Mr. Flanagan was in need."

"He was in need of an alibi. And Jankowski found a guide who could provide one. A guide who didn't remember seeing Flanagan at her service when we interviewed her. What are the odds she found a few extra contributions slipped into the donation box that night?"

"Not from me or mine," he said. "The real mystery is why she forgot the facts when she spoke to your men. Now, why do you think that was?"

"I'm sure I don't know."

"Contributions can cause people to remember things, but they can also cause an amnesia of convenience. And I am not a man who would disparage a guide's integrity lightly, Detective."

"And the source of these contributions? The ones that made her forget that a member of her flock was innocent?"

"Perhaps you should ask your fierce friend Ambassador Paulus."

My stomach clenched.

"You're saying Paulus paid the guide to lie about Flanagan for . . . what?" But even as I said it, I remembered Gellica's doubts about Flanagan's guilt, and the pressure she was under to see the case resolved.

"I'm saying that Attorney Jankowski uncovered the guide's true knowledge. As for the 'who's and 'how's of why it was concealed to begin with . . ." He paused to give me a smile. "That's more in your line of work than mine."

I remembered the cool calculations with which Paulus viewed the negotiations. The thought of a politician covering up inconvenient facts shouldn't have shocked me, but it meant I'd misread Gellica.

"As for my opinion of Mister Flanagan," Harlan continued, "I believe that man is a reformed soul. A true walker on the Path."

"And a tenant of yours."

"Yessir. And proud to have him." He placed a hand over his heart for the second time in our conversation. "I was saddened to hear that the police felt the need to disturb his foster family in such a way. And it did not surprise me that his bonds were burst in so fast and dramatic a manner."

"Did you ever see Mr. Flanagan in the company of Garson Haberdine? Maybe doing something that didn't—"

"That man is the book and the copy."

I straightened my tie. Or at least I moved it around to kill time. "I admit I'm not familiar with that phrase."

"He's bona fide, Detective."

I pretended to write that down in my notepad, repeating it as I did. "Bone . . . a . . . fide. . . ."

Harlan showed me his toothy grin. "Where were you born, Detective?"

"Why would you care about something like that?"

He folded his hands neatly in his lap, looking chastised.

"I care about the Path, the people in my employ, and the populace of this city. In that order." He steepled his fingers. "I am a shepherd. And I'm curious to know the origin of anyone who objects to the way I protect my flock. So I ask you again, Detective . . . where were you born?"

"I was born here."

"A Titanshader born and bred. That's good. We have to take care of our own in this town."

"All five million of us?"

"Eventually." Harlan nodded so deeply his chin nearly clipped his chest. "The One Path is straight and true, but all of us must find our way to it through a rocky and winding road. The huddled masses who dwell in these crooked streets need a chosen few to serve and guide them."

"Like shepherds?"

"Indeed."

"That's a privileged position for someone like you," I said.

"One of privilege, perhaps, but also responsibility. My family has served this town and its people for more generations than you could imagine. I'm meeting with you," he said, "because it's my civic duty to assist law enforcement to the best of my ability. But I cleared my calendar so that you could come in tonight because I care about this town and its people. And I will do anything in my power to protect them."

Harlan grinned and stared at me. Waiting.

"One of those people is an employee of yours. Jermaine Bell."

"Was."

"Was?" I asked. As far as the public knew, we were holding Jermaine for questioning. If Harlan was aware that Jermaine was dead, then he had an agent working inside the Bunker.

"After you called I asked my assistant to check the HR records. Mr. Bell-Asandro was hired in an entry-level position, but we were forced to let him go after repeated no-shows. He hasn't worked for Rediron for over six months. I'd be glad to give you a copy of the paperwork for your files."

I had no doubt that it would all be in order. But my immediate concern receded. The Bunker wasn't compromised. That was at least one ray of good news.

"I think you'll be happy to know that we've got Jermaine Bell-Asandro safely in custody," I said. "He's a little shaken up, but we're getting more and more information out of him."

The grin faltered, and a split second later it was back in place. It happened so fast that I almost couldn't be sure I'd even seen it. But it was my way in. Now I had to play him just right, leave him wondering how much I knew, whose side I was on. I dropped my notepad lower, and held my pencil away from it. A meaningless gesture that many people interpret as a sign the conversation is somehow off the record.

"I'll be honest," I said. "Jermaine is telling us that he worked for you much more recently than that. He says that he performed some rather questionable activities for you."

Harlan's grin danced the line between a smile and a sneer. "There's no shortage of people who'd like to slander our work at Rediron," he said. "It's a side effect of having resources that others would like to raid."

"And you're used to dealing with such people?"

He reached out and tapped two fingers in the center of his desk.

"The eagle suffers little birds to sing. But no sparrow will stand 'gainst the talons of righteous anger." He looked at me for a long, quiet moment. "You may want to write that down in your notepad, Detective."

We stared at each other, then he pulled back. "I am a passionate man. It's one of my failings. If my words have given offense, I apologize." He peered at me, head cocked to one side, sizing me up like I was a prize work beetle about to go on the auction block. "Have you ever even been on the ice plains?" he asked. "I don't mean driven over them in a vehicle. I mean really been out on them and experienced what it's like."

"I have."

He grinned and shook his head. "Walking from a heated motor car into a heated building is not what I meant."

"I've been on the plains," I said, with perhaps more bite in my words than was needed.

"Oh, well, I apologize—" He spread his hands out, as if offering me the world.

"My father was a rigger. On the Ursus Major."

That stopped his mouth from flapping.

"I do apologize," he said, and now his tone matched his words. "If that's the case then I suspect you truly have been out on the fields." He looked me over again. "I misjudged you, and that's a sin I know myself to be prone to." Harlan dropped his gaze and pursed his lips. When he looked up he slapped the leather of his office chair.

"Detective, would you do me a favor and stretch your legs enough to walk over to that display there?"

I followed his pointing finger to one of the many display cases, a walnut monstrosity on the opposite wall.

Harlan made a shooing motion at me. "Go ahead, get up," he said. "I'm not going anywhere."

Curiosity got a hold of me, and I did as he asked. The case was packed with antiques, items from every time in the history of Titanshade's development. With an emphasis on oil discovery and the role Harlan's family had played in extracting it.

"Go on, open it up—that's right." He stood as he gave me directions, urging me on from afar the way an athlete might urge a poorly thrown ball back on course.

"That's the original city charter, and the first land survey my great-great had done. History made manifest, right there."

There was more. There were mementos from almost every rig, Rediron owned or not. Aerial photos of the city's development, pictures of the city's founders, the settlers who'd wanted to escape civilization and found oil, and the oil barons who brought civilization right back to those settlers, whether they wanted it or not. Harlan's family had been among the settlers and oil barons both.

"Your donations to the Therreau," I said. "Is that because your family turned away from its roots? Pushed their own community out into the Borderlands?"

Harlan shook his head, refusing to be baited. "My ancestor was directed to drill in the ice plains. A vision in his sleep guided him, like it has so many other great folks."

"Dream sight?" I asked the question, though I already knew how he'd answer.

"Yes, indeed." Harlan beamed. "A holy vision of another world, showing him men and women drilling far below the ground and finding great treasure. Treasure enough to turn the gears of the world."

"That's something of an advantage."

"Like cresting a hill and getting a glimpse of the Path ahead."

I grunted. Most anyone with an agenda to push claimed dream sight granted them glimpses of other worlds on the Path. Maybe for some it did. But more likely it was smoke and lies. Like the lies a man tells himself as the last mementos of his old life crumble to ash.

Harlan returned to his seat and pointed to the display case once again.

"Now on the second row there's several hip flasks, the kind men and women who work for a living keep on themselves to take a nip from time to time. To keep the cold of the ice plains at bay."

The flasks were spread out in array. There were branded items from all the major rigs, and dozens of the smaller ones. Industrial operations, the names of which any good working-class Titanshade child could recite from memory. Javelin. . . . Imp's Pike. . . . Shelter in the Bend. . . . Ursus Major.

My hand went out unbidden, lifting and examining the flask.

"Know what I think, Detective? I think you do what you do because this city's in your blood just as much as it's in mine."

I stared at the filigree on the flask. Detailed, handmade, covered with tiny dents and scratches that showed it had been used on a job site. I didn't remember my old man carrying one like it, but I could imagine him slipping it into the pocket of his thick canvas work overalls. It was exactly the kind of thing I wished I'd saved. Something to remember him by.

"You take that one on home with you," Harlan called from his desk.

"I can't accept gifts," I said, though I didn't exactly put it down, either.

"That's no gift, that's me returning a belonging of one of my employees to another employee's child. It's wrong that such a fine thing collects dust in a showroom. It should be out in the world, with someone making a difference."

I hesitated. It felt good in my hand. Heavy, with the weight of a well-balanced tool.

There was a squeak as Harlan leaned back in his chair.

"Now, it's empty of course, but I would be grateful if you would take it, fill it up with a spirit of your choosing and enjoy a nip from time to time."

When I didn't respond, he spoke again.

"You asked who wants to derail the oil field purchase, Detective. And I've spoken to you about truth. So here's a bit of truth for you. I'm not looking to derail the talks, Detective, but I'm not hurrying them along, either." Harlan chuckled. "Do I want the money?" He tilted his head. "Of course I do. But turning our back on oil, that changes everything. Lost jobs, lowered wages. Abandoning the work ethic that brought us this far. You think the Squibs will have a place for the roughnecks, for people who work with their hands? For people like your father?"

He raised his callused hands to stop me from answering. "Best hold your tongue, Detective. It might get you in trouble back at City Hall." He favored me with one of his wide grins before continuing.

"When I look at those items"—Harlan pointed at the shelves filled with the history of the city, so much of it entwined with his own family—"I can't help but wonder—shouldn't there be a way for my family to profit without destroying the city that we helped build?" He closed his eyes and dropped his hands to his lap. "I remember where I came from, and it makes me proud. As sure as I walk the Path, I am determined to remember my family's history."

I ran a thumb over the flask in my hands. It was well polished and the sigil of the Ursus Major rig glinted in the light from the display case. I thought of my old man, and how I had so little to remember him by. I wondered how many times he'd taken a break from the backbreaking grind of roughnecking to swig from a flask like this one.

I slid the flask into my jacket pocket and gave Harlan a nod. "Thanks."

"Well, thank *you*, Officer, for doing your best to protect the people of this city." He bobbed his head. "The problem is that the populace of the city doesn't appreciate the miracle that they inhabit. Did you know that almost none of the residents of Titanshade have actually been on the ice plains? With no way to see what they've been saved from, they don't appreciate the sacrifices we make to allow them easy lives. This city," he said with wide, serious eyes, "is hallowed ground."

His toothy grin returned. "And I'm sorry that I need to get back to work. Have a good day, now, and may your Path be smooth and easy traveling." He sat down, calling out as he did. "Ammon! Show the detective out, please."

The door opened, and I walked out of the office, past the

hulking bodyguard. The big Mollenkampi didn't give way as I edged by him in the hall, turning my shoulders so I could slide past. A surprising bit of intimidation from someone whose boss was sending me out the door with a gift. I looked up at him, staring above the intimidating mouth armament to look into his eyes. He kept his biting jaws thrust out, on display. That meant they weren't protecting the soft flesh of his throat. I filed that away for future potential use.

"Tell me," I said as I squeezed by, "have I seen you somewhere before?"

He was silent. But his eyes narrowed.

I snapped my fingers and pointed at him. "I got it! When I worked Vice. Didn't I see you at a roundup?" I moved in and stood close to him, nudging him with an elbow, like a conspirator sharing a taboo confidence. "You can tell me—you got a sweet tooth for the candies, right?"

It was a meaningless question, full of insinuation that led nowhere. But it gave me an excuse to advance in a nonthreatening way. Now that the intentional closeness was at my instigation, the oversized Ammon shied away. He had clearly been trying to intimidate, not assault.

"Not talking, huh? I gotcha. Discreet. I like that." I reached out and patted his arm. His bicep was a steel spring beneath the fabric of his coat. I decided to leave before my luck started to change.

22

THE STREETS WERE STILL CROWDED when I left the Red-iron building, protesters leading chants with megaphones, scuffles breaking out in a few different places. Crimson patrol cops closing in to keep things controlled. I pushed my way through the crowd and tried to distance myself quickly. It was a powder keg waiting for a spark. This wasn't even an organized protest in front of a government building, just scared citizens trying to be heard.

The problem is, when people feel threatened, they do crazy things.

I showed up at Gellica's office without confirming she was there at such a late hour. It wouldn't have been that hard to find her home if I needed to. I'm a cop; finding people is one of the things I'm good at.

When I was shown in past her ornately carved office doors, she greeted me with a smile. It didn't last long.

"Why did you give the guide hush money?" I demanded. I was breathing heavy, a middle-aged cop in a wrinkled brown suit, winded from the trip and seething with anger.

She blinked and capped her pen. "What guide?"

"The guide who came forward with Flanagan's alibi. The one

who's been on the front page of the papers and on every news channel since the case fell apart. That guide."

She was seated. I stood, hands digging into the back of the comfortable guest chair she'd occupied when Ajax and I had first met her.

"Who says I did?" She said it with a scowl, but her face told me all I needed to know. The light chestnut of her cheeks flushed darker, and her lips grew paler as she pressed them together. But I asked again, just the same.

"Did you or didn't you?"

She tossed the pen down. It struck her desk with a clatter.

"Where is this coming from?"

"We made an interesting arrest today."

"The Bell-Asandro murders. What does that woman have to do with me?"

The fire in my gut froze solid. Gellica could have heard about the shooting on the news, but no one had been identified publicly. If she knew Nina Bell had been arrested, there was no doubt that she and Paulus had a source inside the Bunker. The pressure in my head was building but I tried not to let my rage show.

"Did you bribe the guide?" I asked again.

She muttered to herself, "I can't believe this."

"That's not a denial."

She rolled her eyes.

"I formally deny it," she said. "But if anyone did what you claim, it was because you needed it to happen."

I looked away from her. It wasn't the first time I'd heard that logic. It was an old favorite of the kind of cop who planted evidence.

"That's not how it works," I said. "That's not how I work."

"Well, nothing was working, and something had to happen."

I flashed back to the talk on her balcony. My grip tightening on the lush upholstery of the chair. "You warned me about Flanagan. You said you didn't think it was him."

She picked up her pen and slid it into a folder. I pushed the chair aside and leaned across the table, jabbing a finger in the air.

"You didn't just have a feeling. You actually knew he was innocent." I thought of Lowell's smug face as he identified Flanagan, and how the envoy had described him as having a full head of hair, matching the mug shot, but not the cleanly plucked man we'd apprehended.

"'Whatever it takes.'" I spit her words back at her and felt a surge of satisfaction when she winced. "Tell me, is there any part of this case you haven't corrupted?"

"You were the best shot we had at seeing this mess cleaned up quickly. I didn't want to see you fail." She stood. "But as I said, I never bribed anyone."

The Ursus Major flask was an unaccustomed weight in my suit coat, and it prodded me in the chest, a reminder of why I was working the case. I pulled it from my pocket.

"Your family owned oil rigs," I said. "Did they ever work on them? Or just sit at home and collect checks?"

"Your retirement fund owns a stake in dozens of companies," she said. "Have you worked at any of them?"

"The whole damn city's built on the blood and sweat of the people who pull oil out from under the ice." I set the flask on the table between us and pointed at the logo of my father's rig emblazoned on its side. "I don't care how corrupt the rest of you sons of bitches are, they deserve at least one honest cop out there."

There was a tentative tapping at the door. Gellica called out,

"Come in," and a subordinate entered with a stack of papers under one arm. A young, wide-eyed Gillmyn doing his best to look intimidating, almost standing on tiptoes to make himself look bigger. Shouting matches seemed common enough to not burst in alarmed, but not so common that her staff took it completely in stride.

Holding out the papers, he said, "The proposal documents you requested."

"Thank you." Gellica took the stack and began flipping through it. "If there's nothing else, Detective?"

I kept my mouth shut and left, resisting the impulse to shove her assistant into the wall as I passed.

Brooding about bureaucrats and diplomats, I stormed through 1 Government Plaza like I could bring the whole place down with my stomping.

When I got to the lobby I realized the flask was still sitting on Gellica's desk. I cursed and turned back around.

I blew past the staffers and hangers-on, most of whom had seen me enough times that they had stopped outright staring at the appearance of someone who wasn't on any Most Influential Titanshaders list.

Her assistant at least attempted to stop me, standing and asking, "Detective? She's occupied. Hey!"

I ignored him, swung the heavy office door open, and almost collided with Gellica on her way out.

She jumped back and the flask fell from her hands, bouncing on the carpet with a dull thud. At least there was nothing in it to spill. Gellica glared at me.

"I left my—"

She nodded. "I was going to ask someone to run it out to you."

We both bent to recover it, our heads almost colliding. I plucked the flask off the carpet and held it in both hands. We spoke over each other.

I said: "I think we're done," while she said: "Is that all?" We shared an uncomfortable pause, then she looked away.

"Good night, Detective."

I turned and left. I didn't need her to show me the way out.

EXHAUSTION SUNK ITS CLAWS INTO me as 1 Government Plaza dwindled in my rearview mirror. I'd started the day being called onto the carpet by foreign dignitaries, and since then I'd gone toe to toe with an ambassador and a titan of industry, seen my partner shot, and I had nothing more to show for it than a dead, drug-addled kid who'd claimed he'd been experimented on by a mad scientist, and that he was afraid of a big Mollenkampi.

Evening shifted into the uniform darkness of night, and I snaked the car through the streets like a shark along a reef, half afraid that I'd die if I stopped moving. All around me were flagrant violations of any one of the myriad laws on the books, the vast majority of which are only enforced if a cop needed an excuse to bust someone. Solicitation. Open container. A half-dozen jaywalkers and at least two poorly concealed weapons would all have been legitimate arrests. But I ignored the small fish. I was no beat cop looking to make my monthly quota of citations. I was hunting a mad killer.

And to do that I needed a drink and a good night's sleep.

I parked my car and walked into my neighborhood liquor store. The shelves were full of brown and clear liquors, all calling my name. I selected a particularly peaty whiskey and walked it to the counter. I nodded a hello to the clerk as I pulled out my wallet. He was a scrawny kid with an ugly burn scar on the side of his scalp, half hidden by long blond hair that he must have arranged carefully every day. I'd seen him in the store dozens of times over the years. I had no idea what his name was.

"That everything?" the kid said. He started ringing up the bottle without waiting for a response.

It occurred to me that I could ask something innocuous, get to know him, maybe make a friend. Maybe he needed a friend.

Maybe I did.

"Fifteen twenty-one."

As I dug out my wallet the pager in my other pocket buzzed. I handed the kid a twenty and collected my change in silence.

At the corner pay phone I called back the number on the page. I immediately recognized the voice on the other end. It was Simon.

"Carter." His burbling voice was hushed and excited. "Can you meet? You'll wanna hear what I got for you."

"You know, I really don't." My legs ached, my lower back was a mess of knotted muscle, and I had to get home to the bottle I'd just bought. "Tonight I don't want to hear anything."

"You told me to call if anyone mouthed off about Squibs."

My pulse picked up.

"What did you hear?" I said.

"Can you meet me in person?"

"I'll be at the Hey-Hey in twenty minutes."

"No."

"Then where?"

"I don't know." There was the sound of drunken yelling in the background, and he had to raise his voice. "Look, come to the neighborhood. I'll page you when I can talk more."

There was a click, and Simon was gone.

Back in my car, I started the engine and glanced at the paper-bag-wrapped bottle in the passenger seat. Truly, liquor was my copilot.

In the Borderlands I found a parking spot near a phone a few blocks from the Hey-Hey. The candies immediately made my Hasam as an unmarked unit, and gave me a wide berth. I thrummed my fingers on the steering wheel while I waited for Simon's page. That's when the bottle started calling my name. I was in no condition to resist.

I needed a swig and a piss, and the last thing I wanted was someone spotting me boozing on the curb. I took the bottle and the flask down the alley and stepped behind a dumpster. No such thing as being too careful. One more bad headline and I'd be directing traffic for the rest of the case. And if that happened Talena was going to get hung out to dry. No one was gonna hurt that kid on my watch.

I positioned myself to make sure I could keep an eye on the car, then relieved myself on the side of the dumpster. Finished with that task, I opened the bottle and breathed in the sweet nectar of mediocre liquor. I unscrewed the cap from the flask, and thumbed it back on its hinge. Even the hinge worked well. I gave a mental "thank you" to Harlan. I still hoped to parade him out of his building in handcuffs one day, but I appreciated the gift. Carefully I filled the flask with the whiskey, then chucked the empty bottle into the dumpster.

I gave the flask a jiggle, glad to hear the welcome slosh of spirits against metal. Before I took a swig, I glanced back at the street. A familiar figure was storming up to my car. With a sigh of regret I tucked the flask back into my jacket, the contents still untasted.

Of course it was Talena.

By the time I got to the mouth of the alley she was pounding on the window and peering in, as if I were hiding inside. Maybe she thought I was cowering in the backseat.

"Hey."

She spun at the sound of my voice.

"Oh, you son of a bitch!"

"Talena—"

"You son of a bitch! I can't believe you."

A few people stopped to stare, so I pulled back my coat to reveal my badge. And my shoulder holster. They moved on.

I looked back to Talena.

"Look, you got this all wrong," I said.

"The Hells I do. It's all over the papers. You finally went too far. You got tired of dancing on that line and set up some poor SOB and now you got caught, and you . . . you . . ." She waved her hand, trying to put words to her anger and disappointment.

"No. I'm trying to protect someone from getting a frame job."

"You are not," she hissed. "You're manipulating things for your own self-interest like you always have and always will."

"I'm not."

She held up her hands and coated her words with sarcasm. "Oh, that's right. You're actually defending the downtrodden. And who's this poor innocent you're dying to protect? You're about to tell me it's some houseful of widows and orphans, just to make things that much more believable, right?"

"You."

She paused. "What?"

"You're the suspect, Talena. They want to pin the Haberdine murder, the Bell-Asandro killings, the whole damn thing on you." I jammed my hands into my pockets. "And your activist friends. But mostly you. I tried to tell you at your apartment. You need to get out of town."

She got quiet. I was afraid that maybe I'd have been better off telling her everything from the start. Then the clouds moved across her face.

"You're too much. You're too damn much, Carter. You get me to give up information to you, then you frame an innocent man—"

"Flanagan's not innocent," I said, though not with the conviction I would've had two days earlier.

"And then you have the balls to say you're doing it to protect me. Me!" She slapped her chest and stared at me. My stomach felt like I was in free fall.

"I at least thought," she said, "you respected my intelligence enough to not lie to me *about me*."

"Talena, you were at the site of the murder."

Talena bit her lip and shook her head. "That's not enough—"

"That's fact one." I talked over her. "Fact two. You blackmail johns with threats to ruin their reputations. A Squib politician has way more to lose in terms of reputation than most johns. He would have been desperate."

She was still shaking her head, but she'd stopped talking. For some reason that made me raise my voice even more. Louder than I should have, probably, but I didn't care anymore.

"Fact number three: there's an eyewitness who puts candies at the scene."

"Who?"

"The victim. Thanks to our divination officer, the victim has implicated you or your friends in this whole mess. Now Flanagan's got some bullshit alibi, and someone's gotta go down for this thing. You're this close"—I brought my finger and thumb to eye level—"to being specifically called out on this. I know you didn't do it. But if we don't make an arrest soon, then things like guilt and innocence are gonna get a lot more flexible."

She blinked. I could see her work through it, attacking it from all angles. She figured it out fast. Probably faster than I would have in her place. She was a lot like her mom that way.

"Oh, Hells." She turned away from me and sat on the hood of my car. I sat down next to her. We didn't say anything for a while. The small crowd that had gathered drifted away with the end of the fireworks.

"I should've told you," I said. "I tried to. But . . ." I stuck my hands into the pockets of my wrinkled suit. "I should've told you," I repeated.

"Told me what? That I was the center of a conspiracy I don't know anything about?"

"That's kind of elevating your place in things . . ."

A ghost of a smile touched her lips. "No, that's an accurate assessment. Center of a vast conspiracy."

I seesawed my hand. "More like convenient patsy."

She rubbed her temples then pulled back the skin around her eyes. Another habit of her mother's. "I need a drink."

Dammit. I fished into my overcoat and pulled out the flask. "Here."

Talena faked a laugh and took the flask from me. "Well, we have some things in common, right?" She took a long swig. I was happy to at least be able to give her something.

She made a face. "That stuff's awful."

"You have an immature palette."

She took another drink. "So what do we do now?" She didn't return the flask. I held in a sigh and let her keep it.

"You don't do anything," I said. "The lower your profile the better. You're sure you don't have anyone to alibi you for the Squib killing? Anyone you talked to that night?"

She shook her head. "The only people I'd trust for it are involved with my work with the candies. From what you said, they're all on the hot seat as well."

"Yeah, but not as bad as you."

"See? Vast conspiracy." She drew a large circle in the air. "And there's me." She pointed. "In the center."

"Okay, maybe it is all about you."

"Damn straight." She coughed and sipped at the whiskey.

I grunted. Plans to get her out of town started running unbidden through my head.

"So where's your partner?"

"Jax?"

Talena cleared her throat. "Yeah. The cute one."

I dragged a hand through my hair and pretended I hadn't heard that. I searched for some way to change the topic and was saved by the buzz of my pager. It had to be Simon.

"Well, whoever is setting this up—" Talena coughed again. "They'll have made a mistake." She cleared her throat a second time.

"Oh yeah?" I stood up to get a better read on the buzzer's display in the shine of the streetlight. Once I settled things with Talena I could call Simon back and arrange a meet-up.

"Just like the pimps and johns who think they're untouchable. They start thinking they're smarter than the rest of us." She swallowed and took a wheezing breath.

I looked up from the pager.

"You okay, kid?"

She nodded, then shook her head "no" violently. I stuck the pager back in my pocket and felt her forehead. Talena kept wheezing. Her pupils were dilated and as I watched, her eyes rolled back into her head. The flask slipped from her hand and dropped to the street with a clatter. I grabbed Talena and dumped her into the passenger side of the car. I turned the ignition and floored it, sideswiping two cars as I merged into traffic, knowing that the nearest hospital was eight blocks away.

"Hang on, kid. Just hang on."

I never glanced in the rearview, so I have no idea if I crushed the flask under a tire as I drove away, or just left it gleaming in the gutter behind us.

I WAS IN THE WAITING room of Wayfinder's Hospital staring at the word "Emergency" printed on a fire alarm when Jax found me. It took the rookie a few tries to make me hear him. I realized he was there when he turned me around and shook me by the shoulder. I made an attempt to swat his hand away but he held on and I finally heard what he was saying.

"I need you to wake up, old man, because it's all coming down around us right now."

"What is?"

"The whole thing: the case, Flanagan, the embassy, the Squibs."

He'd pulled me into the stairwell so we could speak with at least a light veneer of privacy. His back was to the door and I peered over his shoulder as we talked, watching through the glass pane of the door for any doctors who might appear with news of Talena.

"I about got Talena killed, Jax. I need to fix this."

I told him what happened, from the confrontation with Harlan to rushing Talena to the hospital.

He took it all in calmly, adjusting the bandages on his right arm while he listened. When I was done he asked, "Where's the flask?"

Jaw clenched, I shook my head. "I was kind of preoccupied."

By now it'd likely been collected by a metal scrapper. I only hoped the liquor had drained out, and that a booze-desperate passerby wasn't choking on the poisoned draft.

Ajax grunted. "We can at least request a patrol to swing by and look over the area."

Even if we could find it, there was no link between it and Harlan other than my word. The flask was old enough to belong to my father, and was stamped with the logo of the rig my father used to work. It was filled with whiskey that I'd purchased myself that same day. No one would believe it wasn't mine. If it'd been found in my apartment, no one would've questioned the cause of my death.

"I plucked it from his display case myself," I said. "Five'll get you ten that he wiped his prints clean after setting it there."

"The flask went straight from him to you, to Talena?"

I hesitated. "No. I left it in Gellica's office. She was alone with it for maybe five minutes."

It was clear where he was headed, and my anger boiled over even as he was saying, "So it could have been her."

"What's your theory?" I snarled. "She happened to have some spare poison lying around next to the stapler?"

His wounded arm was held tight by a sling, but he spread his other arm wide.

"And that's less believable than the owner of the biggest oil conglomerate in the world poisoning you when he could've just paid someone to put a bullet in your head from a hundred yards out?"

I clutched my temples and squeezed my eyes shut, fighting to hold in the screams. I wanted a villain, a bad guy I could drag in— mission accomplished and time for a beer. I just wanted a single damn moment of black and white in a world of gray tones.

I took a ragged breath and brought myself under control. I didn't want to say it, but this was why he'd been the first call I made after getting Talena to the hospital. I needed Ajax's help now even more than before.

"Alright," he said. "We'll get there. For now, circle back to Harlan Cedrow. If he had the flask prepped for you, then he already knew where your dad worked."

There was only one way I could see for Harlan to know that. I ran a trembling hand over my face and tried not to think of the look in Talena's eyes while I drove her to the hospital.

"Gellica. She asked me about my family before I met with her boss."

Jax paused, tugging at his collar with his free hand. "You think she's working with him?"

"I don't know. But there won't be enough left of her or Harlan to piece back together when I'm done." I pointed down the hallway. "An innocent girl is in there because of them. Because they tried to kill me. And I want to know if you're going to have my back."

He held my eyes, not looking away but not answering, either. Then I saw motion over his shoulder.

Through the wire mesh glass of the stairwell door I saw a young woman in scrubs looking around the waiting room. She wasn't much older than Talena herself. Jax must have followed my gaze, because he backed away, and I walked in to talk to the doctor. I struggled to breathe as I approached her, my heart racing and vision tightening. When she smiled, it was one of the greatest moments of relief I have ever experienced. Doctors don't usually smile before they tell you bad news.

It was still several hours before I was able to see her.

Outside Talena's room the doctor looked at Jax and myself in turn.

"Five minutes," she said. "She might be in and out of consciousness. Do not try to wake her. You can say her name and hold her hand, nothing else." With that last bit of caution, we walked into Talena's room.

Her color was wrong, far too pale, and the plastic tube that stretched into her nose and down her throat looked strange and unnatural. There was a small fortune's worth of machinery hooked up to her, beeping affirmations of life at regular intervals. I refused to let myself think about how she'd pay for this when we finally got her out of there.

I sat down on the edge of her bed. Jax stood behind me, wearing his own bandages. Gently, I squeezed her forearm, trying not to see how much she looked like her mother in her last days. I focused on Talena, waiting to see if she would respond. The moment stretched on, and I wondered if I'd failed her one last time. Then Talena stirred, groaning like a kid who didn't want to get up for school.

She opened a single eye and looked at Ajax, then me.

"Carter . . ." Her voice sounded strange with the tube down her nose.

"Hey, kiddo," I said. "Don't try to say anything. I just wanted you to know we're here."

"Carter, yuhhr . . ."

"Shhh." I patted her arm.

". . . an asshole," she said, and drifted back to sleep with a smile on her face.

I walked out of that room and Jax had to jog to catch up to me. I brushed his hand off my shoulder and kept walking. In the lobby I jabbed the elevator button and rounded on him.

"I know you're hot," he said. "But you can't go gunning for Harlan Cedrow."

I glared at him, waiting for the elevator to open.

"You don't even know for sure he did it," he said.

I hung my head. In Gellica's office I'd defended Harlan, praised the man as a philanthropist. Because he'd helped someone I loved find some small respite from her pain, I'd blinded myself to the facts. I'd been a fool, and Talena had paid the price. I thumbed the elevator call button again, two quick jabs. Despite the evidence, despite the common sense that should have alerted me that something was wrong, I took the flask because I was grasping for a past that was dead and long buried.

Jax mistook my silence for disagreement.

"You don't," he said, almost pleading. "You told me yourself that Gellica had free access to the flask. She asked about your father. Who's to say she didn't do something to the flask itself?"

I slammed my fist into the call button, rattling the metal panel and sending pain dancing across my knuckles.

"It was Harlan!" I practically shouted. "I don't know what he's playing, but I'm ending all his bullshit. I don't care about his money or his reputation or any other damn thing that gets in my way." I was breathing fast, and I could feel the flush spreading across my face. I'd been running on fumes for days, and I could feel my legs wobble with fatigue as I demanded, "Are you with me?"

My partner took a long, slow breath and tried again.

"It's almost morning," he said. "Let's go in to see Bryyh together."

"Bullshit."

He pointed back down the hall. "Don't you abandon that girl now, Carter."

I took a step toward him.

"Watch what you're saying." I didn't have to fake the ice in my tone.

"She needs you right now. We need you to help bring in whoever did this to her. And we need to get a protective detail on her room."

I reeled a bit at that idea of protection. "They were trying to kill me, not her."

He snorted. "I don't care what their plan was, she's the person who got hit. Now she's a loose end."

I thought about it. "Fine," I said. "I'll call it in."

"And you're going to talk to Bryyh."

"About what?"

"About everything. How you know Talena. How she was poisoned. Everything you told me about Gellica and Harlan."

I wavered. "I got no proof, though, Jax. I got nothing but my word, and a day ago my word got dragged through the mud. Probably will again once today's papers hit the streets, unless some other scandal has come along in the meantime."

"Well, then talking to Bryyh's not going to make anything worse, now is it?"

He winced and shifted his shirt to relieve pressure on his injured arm.

"You can do this alone," he said. "Or you can do it with the full backing and support of the entire Bunker. Which would you rather have?"

"They're not going to listen to me at the Bunker."

"Maybe not all of them. But someone will. Bryyh's on duty in a couple hours. Let's lay it all out and see what happens."

I rolled my head, felt the crackle and pop of the movement.

"I'll be at the Bunker in two hours," I said, then walked away.

I walked aimlessly, following the maze of hospital corridors, with their vinyl floor tiles and sheets of vinyl wall coverings. One foot after the other, I kept walking, eventually passing through the emergency room entry doors, placing my hand in the air stream of the large entry vent and praying as I went. "For your suffering, which brings us warmth and safety, we thank you."

My car was still sitting in the emergency zone, where I'd left it when I carried Talena into the emergency room. All around me was the calm of the ER entryway. There was no activity at all, which is how it would stay until a paramedic team burst in with a dead or dying person on a gurney. It wasn't that different from being a cop. Boredom punctuated by terror and remorse.

I turned and faced the city. The calendar had flipped to a new day since I'd brought Talena into the emergency room, but in Titanshade the sunrise was still a long way off.

At the moment, that suited my mood just fine.

25

THINGS DIDN'T BRIGHTEN UP FOR me at the Bunker.

"Are you saying that *I* poisoned her?" I couldn't keep the anger from seeping into my voice.

Bryyh pinched her fingers as if snapping that line of thought shut. "Of course not. But I can't get warrants issued for people like Harlan and Gellica just on your word."

Ajax and I had briefed her on the developments, and the three of us sat in her office, surrounded by her diplomas and pictures of her kids as the level of tension increased to its normal fever pitch.

"Why not?" I demanded, already knowing the answer.

"Because right now your word isn't worth a bucket of warm piss."

I sucked air through my teeth and managed to keep my mouth shut. Bryyh kept going.

"You think judges don't watch the news? Judge Fox is getting roasted right along with you for signing off on the raid on Flanagan's ranch. Not a single other judge will put a signature on something with your name on it unless it's verified five ways to Friday. And they sure as shortcuts aren't going to okay a fishing expedition on one of the city's preeminent citizens."

"Harlan Cedrow is willing to kill anyone who gets in the way of—" I waved my hand in the air.

She raised an eyebrow. "Of what?"

"Of some plot that's so bizarre that I'm not even sure *he* knows what it is."

Bryyh sighed. "That nutjob happens to be the descendant of a founding family, and closely tied to the Therreau community. And," she said, "he's the biggest beneficiary of the wind farm deal going through. But that's okay"—she leaned in—"because you assure me that he's sabotaging his own deal by killing a foreign diplomat, then working to free the man who he set up to take the fall, and then trying to kill you for not being able to figure it out fast enough? That's the case you want to take to the City Attorney?"

"He tried to kill me because I told him we had Jermaine."

"If he really believed that, wouldn't he have tried to kill the Jermaine kid? What would killing you solve?"

She raised a good point. It was like there were two separate cover-ups of the same crime. I sat back in the office chair and tried to reconnect the dots.

"Are you telling me to let it drop?" I asked.

"No." She exhaled, and her hands shook. She was fighting to control her temper. Normally I would give a damn. Right then I was glad to see her suffer. "Carter . . . no. We are not letting anyone walk from this shit-storm. But we also aren't going to be able to bring in someone like Harlan by storming into his office and accusing him with no proof. You know that, and I think you're being obstinate just as an excuse to be an ass."

That stung close to home.

"I know he did it," I said.

"Oh, for—" She threw her hands up. "Listen to yourself! I don't care what you know. A jury doesn't care what you know. And the CA damn sure doesn't care what you know. The only thing that matters is what you can prove." She stressed "prove" like she was giving a speech to a halfwit rookie who cared more about TV-style justice than learning how to work the system. "And you already admitted that Harlan wasn't the last person in possession of the flask before you."

"So what do we do now?" I said.

"*We* continue the investigation. *You* take a day and collect yourself."

"You gotta be out of—"

"Carter! You are way too emotionally hot right now to think with anything approaching a rational mind. Why is that?"

"It's probably because one rich asshole or another just tried to kill me."

"And failed."

"Yeah."

"But someone else is in the hospital."

I swallowed. "Yeah," I said, quieter this time. "Talena Michaels."

"Who is this girl? Who is she to you?"

"I knew her mother."

Bryyh let out a now-we're-getting-somewhere kind of sigh. She leaned against her desk. "How long have you known her?"

"Since she was six."

Bryyh frowned, but somehow she made it the most sympathetic scowl I'd ever seen. I'd been about that age when Bryyh met me, after my mom was killed. She was there at the funeral, part of the honor guard for a cop killed in the line of duty.

"No," she said. "I can't think of a single reason why seeing her poisoned would make you emotionally skewed."

"Motivated," I said. "It makes me motivated."

"It should make you off the case." Bryyh glared at me.

I leaned forward and opened my mouth, but Ajax got there first. "Captain," he said. "We need Carter in order to—"

"Oh, shut it." She didn't even bother to look at him. "Save your solidarity speech. I said 'should' take you off the case. If I wanted to do everything by the book I'd have moved to some rich city by the Inland Ocean where they don't have more murderers than churchgoers. You"—she pointed at me—"will stay on the Squib case in an advisory role only. And you"—she redirected her finger to Ajax—"you'll be responsible for making sure that role stays advisory."

I raised a hand. "Can you define 'advisory'?"

"It's a word that means 'don't be a pain in my ass,'" she said. "Because if you do, you'll be scraping street pancakes until you retire." She looked at each of us. "That means nothing that gets your face in the paper, nothing that gets me phone calls from the mayor's office, and nothing that involves harassing city fathers without due process—specifically Harlan, or anyone else who has Rediron Drilling on their resume. Other than that, I don't really give a damn how you do it, but you *will* be helping this case come to a rapid close. Are we perfectly clear about this?"

Bryyh asked Ajax to stay in her office after I left, probably to give him instructions on keeping me in line and out of the limelight. I headed toward the exit. After all, I had a day on my own. To "collect" myself.

I turned a corner and almost ran into Angus. He was walking with a cadre of admirers, all of them hanging on every word as he told some witty anecdote. Angus wore a crisply pressed suit and carried a fleece overcoat draped over one arm. He must have recently come from somewhere leeward. When we all came to a stop he'd managed to stand in the single beam of sunlight that broke through the fog that day.

What a dick.

"Carter," he said, his mandibles spread in what I knew was a gesture of welcome. It always made me feel like I was about to be eaten.

He shifted his coat to the other arm, draping it over the briefcase and freeing up a hand to clasp me on the shoulder. "I'm sorry you're going through this thing with the media."

I grunted and dropped my eyes. Angus's nicely shined shoes had an irregular line of dirt along the toes. Even the immaculate Angus couldn't keep clean in Titanshade.

"It'll pass," I said. "I just hope something happens to distract those jackals quick."

"Don't worry. You'll be old news before long."

Classic Angus. He genuinely didn't care about me or my well-being. But he said all the right things, so he was accepted by everyone else. I never understood the line between his type of emotional dishonesty and a sociopath who fakes a conscience in order to function in society. I wonder how many of us fell farther down on the dark end of the spectrum than we'd care to admit?

I cut the empty chitchat short with a shrug and head scratch that said *well, I gotta go, Angus ol' buddy,* and continued on my way. His coterie laughed, and I wondered how long before Myris and Hemingway would be moved to his team, or if I'd be working under him next. But I stopped walking when I heard him call out.

"I think there's a nice scandal brewing that'll distract from your sufferings."

I turned and looked back. The beam of sunlight that he'd been standing in now washed over me. I didn't like it as much as I thought I would. The brightness hurt my eyes, made me squint. I held up a hand to hide in its shade. I was more comfortable in the darkness.

"I've got an angle on one of your little envoys from the AFS. Lowell, the beefy one." He held up his thumb and index finger. "I'm this close," he said, "from hanging that candy murder on him. And if that breaks, who knows how long it'll be before I close up the Haberdine case."

"You still holding on to that pipe dream?" I asked.

Angus kept walking toward me as he talked, leaving his fan club behind. Soon he was close enough that only I could hear his words.

"You don't want any more headaches." His tusks were spotless and his head plates shone with fresh polish, but his breath had the bitter reek of stale coffee. "Stay out of my way or you'll get chewed up in the machine."

He turned on the slick sole of his dress shoe and walked away. I was frozen for a moment, then dropped my hand. The sunlight burned my eyes, but I just took it. Penance for spending too many years in the dark.

When I hit the streets outside the Bunker the protest had grown, both in size and intensity. Chanting crowds blocked the steady flow of pedestrians, choking and constraining traffic. And just like an obstructed internal combustion engine, the system was starting to backfire.

Someone pushed someone else, a push became a punch, and overreactions rippled through the mass of bodies, multiplying as they went. The crowd seethed, twisting and turning in on itself. The chants changed, lost their rhythm, became screams. Fists that had been pumped into the air to show unity now swung out in anger.

A heavy clumping noise rose above the sounds of the chaos, and the patrol force that ringed the crowd faded back to allow colleagues in riot gear to step to the fore. The thick clumping was the sound of batons beating on riot shields.

I retreated. There was nothing I could do in plainclothes that wouldn't get me killed, or at least clubbed into submission. I looked for the easiest escape route when there was a sudden tug on my coattails, and a high-pitched, crackling voice yelled behind me.

"Carter!"

I spun and saw a Therreau youth running down the street, glancing over his shoulder at me. Daring me to give chase. I'm too old to run on demand and I would have chalked it up to a kid getting caught in the wild abandonment of the crowd, but he'd called my name. So I started in pursuit, ignoring the voice in my head advising caution every bit as much as I ignored the pain in my legs.

We crossed Deland Avenue, gliding between cars and leaving a chorus of blaring horns and raised middle fingers in our wake. The youth didn't speed up. He wanted me to follow.

He also didn't turn his head, so I wasn't sure who it was. But I had a guess.

At last he ducked down an alley. When I came around the corner, he'd disappeared. But there, tall and stock-still, dressed in blue and white, with a wide-brimmed hat was the one person who had absolutely no business standing around outside the Bunker.

My throat tightened up and my jaw started to shake. The son of a bitch raised a hand to his shaved scalp in lazy salute.

"You got a minute?" asked Flanagan.

26

FLANAGAN'S SMUG SMILE WASN'T ANY more likable than the last time I'd seen him. I walked farther into the alley, the noise and bustle of the city fading as I focused on the disgraced cop before me.

He was dressed in the Therreau fashion, black vest over white button-down shirt paired with canvas pants and a wide-brimmed, dark hat. But the air of an honest farmer was shattered by the way he leaned on the hood of a late-model coupe. He held the kind of relaxed posture that indicated that he owned the vehicle, everything in it, even the pavement it sat on. None of that was true—I could see a tibron beetle and wagon farther down the alley—but he oozed possession and entitlement. Flanagan stretched his long arms and rolled his neck as I approached, like he was limbering up for a fight. I fought the urge to swing at him first.

"Been looking for you, Carter."

That I believed. He wasn't the type to hang around the Bunker sampling the food trucks.

"You found me," I said. "What do you want?"

He chewed on air, as if he were having trouble getting the words out.

"I want to help."

"So make a donation to the patrol fundraiser," I said. "I can't talk to you without your lawyer present." But I didn't turn away.

Flanagan pushed off from the car. "I heard you put a girl in the hospital last night."

It was the wrong thing to say. I stepped toward him, hands curling into fists. Four inches taller and forty pounds heavier than me, Flanagan didn't flinch.

"You want to assault the guy you unjustly imprisoned? Right in front of the Bunker? Shortcuts." He sneered. "Even you're not that stupid. And not so charmed that you'd get away with it."

"Charmed?" I said. Far as I could see, my career had mostly been cursed.

Flanagan eyed the alleyway opening. He had the look of a man who didn't want to be seen talking to me.

"This girl," he said.

"Talena."

"Whatever. She helped a kid I knew."

"She helps lots of kids," I said.

He shrugged. "I only care about one of them." A pause while he shot a look over his shoulder, deeper down the alley where the cart's driver and the boy who'd drawn me there had the tibron beetle turning tight circles. Always moving, going nowhere.

Flanagan adjusted his hat. "Maybe you noticed I got out of jail pretty damn fast," he said. "Not this last charge. Before that."

He meant the stint he'd done for murder, extortion. His reign of terror.

"I heard you named names," I said.

He cocked a nonexistent eyebrow. "You think I'd snitch?"

"Yes."

He slid a thumbnail between two teeth, fishing out an invisible seed.

"Maybe." He popped his lips. "But I didn't have to. Someone did me a solid. Evidence came under question, witnesses recanted. I walked. Takes money and favors to make that happen. A lot of favors. A lot of money. And a special kind of person."

The kind of person who'd send in a high-priced attorney to pull him out of jail.

I grimaced. "Harlan Cedrow."

He didn't say a word, and that told me everything.

"So now he owns you." I got a spike of pleasure watching Flanagan's face cloud over. "Guess you ended up someone's lapdog after all."

"Think what you want," he said. "There's more than one person pulling strings. This whole town's crooked, and no one's capable of keeping their fingers out of the pie."

I didn't disagree.

"And you?" I asked. "What did these mysterious people want with you?"

Plucked brows pulled together, creating a crease smoother than a baby's rear end.

"To have me in their toolbox." His eyes flashed with anger, but it wasn't directed at me. "These rich sons of bitches sit in their Mount-side mansions and collect people. I got placed with the Therreau and told to blend in. Then I did jobs, small things."

He hung his head and swallowed loudly. On another man, I'd have thought it a sign of remorse.

"One of the things I did was pick up Jermaine Bell. Make sure he got to work on time. He was a good kid. Harmless."

Down the alley, the tibron wagon creaked and groaned as it rolled along. The kid who'd drawn me there perched on the bench, and I finally placed his face.

"The boy at the farm." I searched my memory for what Flanagan had called him, calming him as he stared down our drawn weapons. "Benny?"

"Benjamin," he said.

That was the connection.

"He's not much younger than Jermaine," I said.

Flanagan spoke in a low voice. "If I'd known what they wanted him for, I'd have stopped it."

My stomach clenched. The light in the alley seemed to fade, and I felt myself sway, a flagpole in an arctic wind.

"Stopped what?" I said.

Flanagan wiped at his mouth.

"I don't know exactly what they did to him. I didn't see that. But I saw the changes. Saw the way he changed. Some days he was fine, others he would attack people, go into a blind rage. At the end he was a loaded gun, waiting to be pointed at a target." He shook his head, his lips flirting with a smile. "Even with all that, he used to talk about his family, about the people who helped him, like your friend." His nostrils flared, and color flushed his cheeks. "He was a good kid. Harmless." Flanagan'd started repeating himself, like a man convincing himself he was on the right path.

"What happened then?" I said.

He frowned, hesitating. I gave him time. He'd come to me, there was no need to push him. Finally, he grunted, getting over whatever inner hurdle he'd been wrestling with.

"Haberdine had a sweet tooth," he said. "No real secret. I just dug around until I found out what candy he had his eye on. Turns out it was a girl who worked for Butterfly Carrington."

Stacie. Haberdine had seen her with Lowell at the Squib's soiree at the Armistice hotel, and she must have caught his eye.

"Carrington owed me a few favors," said Flanagan. "I made sure the candy met Haberdine. Next thing you know, they've got a date."

That meant that Flanagan—and Harlan Cedrow—knew when and where Haberdine would be alone.

"And then?" I said.

"Then I told Carrington to call the candy off."

"And that left Haberdine sitting alone in a room, expecting company."

He fell silent.

"Was it Jermaine?" I said. "Did he kill Haberdine?"

"I wasn't there."

I snorted, equal parts disdain and disbelief.

"I told you," he growled. "If I'd been there, Jermaine wouldn't have been involved." He rubbed the back of his neck. "I was at the guidepost the rest of the evening, just like Guide Clemens said. All I did was call off the candy. I didn't know about anything else."

"You did more than that." I stayed very still, watching his reactions. "The candy and her pimp ended up dead."

"I don't know about that, either." He glanced back at his companions while he said it, looking as guilty as a dog who's gotten into the garbage.

"Right," I said. "Come inside and you can make a statement."

"Hells," he said. "I'm here to help, not do your job for you."

"You told me what you know," I said. "Now we need to get it down—"

"I didn't go to the trouble of shaking that tail you put on me just to talk about the Squib. We're just getting started."

Something in his voice gave me pause.

"What's Harlan up to?"

"Something strange," he said. "But there's nothing good that'll come of it."

I spat on the cobblestones. "Sure," I said. "'Nothing good' is kind of your specialty."

"Not anymore. It's something I'm . . ." He stumbled over the words. "I'm working on it."

I'd rather have heard him cackle like a cartoon villain than deliver a halfhearted apology.

"Oh, no." I shook a finger, a futile gesture in the face of a killer. "You don't get to say you're sorry and walk away," I said. "You don't get to forget about the families of the people you—"

"Hey." He raised both hands. "You don't want me here? I'll go." But he didn't move.

"What I got for you," he said, "is bigger than one dead Squib."

Of course Flanagan viewed just a single murder as no big deal. Sighing, half at him and half at my own willingness to listen, I twirled my fingers in a *let's-go* motion.

"Look at this," he said, and pulled a plastic bag from a pocket. Opening it with a twisting motion, he showed me the contents: a dingy white rag. He pushed the sides of the bag, and a familiar smell wafted out. Cinnamon.

I gritted my teeth and swallowed the rush of saliva it produced. I stepped back and covered my nose and mouth with the crook of my elbow. I gagged, but managed to keep my breakfast where it belonged.

"Oh, Carter. This stuff really gets to you, don't it?" He practically leered at me, and I ached to wrap my fingers around his throat. Which is when I realized I was already holding something.

My fingers were digging into the damp fabric of the rag. I had no memory of grabbing it from him, but there it was. The fabric was wet, but there was no blood, no hint of viscera. So where was the smell coming from? The confusion was enough to distract me from my rage.

"What—" My voice was muffled behind the fabric of my jacket.

"It ain't blood, Squib or otherwise," he said. "I've seen it when they soak the rags. It's clear as gin."

"What is it?"

"Don't know." He shrugged, his indifference total. "But they've got us driving around with these rags tied beneath our carts. Especially down here." He jerked his chin toward the roiling crowd. The violence had escalated so much faster than I'd expected. I remembered the ever-present rolling Therreau carts, the plain-dressed religious folk most of the city ignored.

"Flanagan. What is that stuff?" My voice was tense. I already had a guess.

"I told you I don't know." He bared his teeth. "I do what I gotta to survive. If bags of this stuff show up and we're told to parade around the city with them, then that's what I do. The smell doesn't do anything for me, but some people . . . Man, oh man."

I'd had enough. More than enough, and I wanted to ram that damned rag down his throat. Before I knew what I was about to do, I'd grabbed hold of him and wrapped a hand around his neck. He easily shed my grip and stepped back. The heel of his hand caught me on the cheek. The kind of strike a lioness might deliver a wayward cub.

"Stop it," he said. His voice was monotone, no anger or excitement. I might as well have been a toddler taking swings at an adult.

I moved to the side, hoping to get another shot at him. His hand drew back.

"Timothy!"

The call came from the wagon at the end of the alley, a deep baritone that echoed off the buildings on either side of us. Never straying from his course, the driver craned his neck to maintain eye contact with Flanagan.

"That is not our way," the man said. Next to him the boy, Benny, stood with one foot on the buckboard, as if he were ready to spring to Flanagan's defense.

Flanagan's hands went up, fingers outstretched, so that his companions could see him disengage me.

"Not here to dance with you," he said. "Don't keep tempting me."

I threw the rag at him. It struck his chest before falling into his open hand. Flanagan tucked the rag into the bag and resealed it.

"Why did Harlan Cedrow poison me?"

"Side roads." He shook his head. "You don't listen at all. I don't *know* who put your friend in the hospital, but I can guess. You oughta check on what that person would've wanted with a kid from Old Orchard. And this"—he shook the bag—"is some kind of trial-and-error thing. Sometimes it's potent, sometimes not. Real lab rat stuff."

"Really?" I said. "Cryptic hints? This would go a lot quicker if you just spelled it out."

"No, it wouldn't. You'd have hearsay and insinuation, and there's no way a jury would believe what I had to say, even if I was willing to testify." He wiped his mouth with the back of his hand. "Which I'm not.

"Instead," he continued. "I'm telling you where to look. Now pull your dislike for me out of your ears and listen to what I'm saying. Follow the kid's trail. Find out where he worked. You think you can handle that?"

Lips pressed tight, I said nothing. He smirked.

"Good," he said. "You may be an idiot, but you're no lapdog."

The disgraced cop glanced down the alley again and shifted his bulk from one foot to the other. He was anxious to leave. But I had another question for him.

"The cop who shot Jermaine," I said. "Myris. You going to come after her?"

He pursed his lips and pulled his brows together, as if he were puzzled by the question. "She pulled the trigger," he said. "But she's not who killed him. You oughta understand that better than anyone."

The taste of cinnamon still sat in the back of my throat. I spat it out, and Flanagan snorted.

"Spare me," he said, and stepped away from the coupe. He half turned, looking at his companions on the tibron-pulled wagon.

"When guns come out," he said, "some people get shot, and some people walk away. You got a fraction of a second to sort out who's who. Admit to yourself that you're the kind of person who makes those decisions. It's your job and it's who you are. Recognize that, and it'll let you get on with your life." He squinted at me, eyes tight, as though he were staring into the midday sun. "Course, you won't get to sit around feeling sorry for yourself anymore, so you probably won't do it."

"Is that the motive behind this good deed?" I asked. "Are you getting on with your life?"

He frowned, and looked to the Therreau wagon. "I don't like to see these folk put in danger."

"Come on," I said. "Now you're the defender of the innocent?"

Flanagan shrugged. "I got out of prison and was told to live with the Therreau. Prison makes you harder than when you came in. You live with decent folk, maybe that rubs off, too." He slipped off the wide-brimmed hat and ran his fingers over his hairless scalp. "I gave you what I can, now get the job done. Jermaine deserves it. And your girl in the hospital," he said. "She deserves it, too."

"Protect and serve," I said. "It's what I do."

"Good." He stepped away. "You won't see me again."

Flanagan walked down the alley and met the wagon as it circled around once again. In one easy motion he hopped onto the driver's bench and landed next to the older Therreau man, who shot me a nervous glance. Flanagan gave him a pat on the shoulder. Pulled forward by the ceaseless legs of the tibron, they merged into traffic and were absorbed by the city.

I probed the flesh along my cheekbone where he'd struck me as I watched them go. It was already swelling. I'd be hard-pressed to convince Bryyh that I'd been "collecting myself" when I showed up with a black eye.

I didn't care, now the Haberdine killing was coming together. As long as I went the day without taking any more beatings, I'd be fine.

27

MAYBE I SHOULD HAVE REPORTED the conversation with Flanagan immediately. But I'd already been sent home for the day. And besides, what would I say? *Hey everyone! Remember that Flanagan guy we just let go? I wanna rearrest him so he can deny secretly telling me that he didn't do it.* Somehow I didn't think that would go over well. No, to make use of the information Flanagan had just revealed I needed to knock holes in the defenses of the head of Rediron Drilling. And Bryyh had been right about one thing: I couldn't go barging into Harlan's office. That would be both stupid and reckless. I try to only be one of those at a time.

So I followed the tips that Flanagan had dropped and started researching medical facilities. I had Jermaine's history, and his information that he'd given to his aunt. Little enough to start with, but I began to pull the threads together.

I assumed that any facility like Jermaine described would be in a less populated part of town, but not so far out as to make stocking supplies difficult. So I directed my search farther leeward, away from the Mount and the warmth of the geo-vents. I made a few calls to medical supply companies, and asked about their delivery routes.

That gave me a list of twenty sites with potential. Around mid-afternoon I stopped by the vehicle bay and checked out the

Hasam, forgetting to mention to the pit crew that I was supposed to be home "collecting myself." Then I started driving. I made it to the fifth site on my list before seeing something I knew wasn't right.

The place was a nondescript concrete building with tinted windows and a front gate designed to keep out an invading army. Everything about it was too new and too well maintained for the neighborhood. I drove past, knowing better than to try the security gate with its punch code and sturdy steel construction. I circled the block, scoping out the rest of the property and looking for weak spots in its security.

It was on the fringes of the city. Wisps of snow snaked over the streets, and there were even scattered vacant buildings, an almost inconceivable sight closer to the Mount. I parked on the back side of the block, and eyed the medical building. As I watched, a stocky human in a thick coat trudged around a well-worn track on the perimeter of the lot. Clearly he was walking guard duty. I waited long enough for him to make a full circuit, and didn't see anyone else outside in that time. That meant only one guard outside, making the rounds at specific intervals and probably pissed off about it, keeping his head down, not really watching what happened beyond the edge of his coat's hood.

I could work with that.

Stretching an arm into the rear of the Hasam I swept aside the remnants of my fast-food lunch and flipped up the backseat bench, exposing the storage bin below. All police vehicles—and practically all Titanshade vehicles, period—had an emergency kit stored in an out-of-the-way compartment. A stranded vehicle might be inconvenient in most environments, but on the ice plains it meant a death sentence. The Hasam held a medical kit, snow chains, a thermal blanket, and an insulated parka. The parka would be the most convenient item, but it was a bright orange to help stranded motorists be seen by rescuers. No, it'd be the thermal blanket for me.

Coming at the compound from the rear I moved as quickly as I could. Bundled in the thermal blanket, I trailed its long end behind me, obscuring my tracks in the snow that dusted the ground this far from the Mount. We weren't into the truly cold areas, but I couldn't stay outside for long in just a suit and tie. At the chain-link fence I stooped and tugged at its bottom end. The cold ground was hesitant to let the metal fencing out of its grasp, but with a few pulls, it came loose. Then I pushed, pointing the sharp links of the bottom row toward the building and away from me. Perfect.

The ground was hard and frozen. I crouched low, obscured by the blanket and late afternoon twilight as I waited for the big guard to pass by on his rounds. It took some time and I was glad I'd taken a preemptive pain pill as the cold seeped into my joints. Finally the guard came around, his head down, not bothering to study the scenery beyond the lot. He just kept moving and continually cracked his knuckles. First one hand, then the other. Probably trying to move fast and keep warm.

I gave him enough time to get around the corner of the building. Drawing the blanket tight around my shoulders, I rolled underneath the chain link. I dragged the blanket behind me, obscuring my tracks, and jumped into the big man's footprints. I followed in them another twenty feet, then hopped closer to the building. The windows were few and far between. I peered through one, but the bland office and file cabinets told me nothing. If I wanted to learn anything I needed to get inside.

Moving quickly, I followed the outline of the building until I came to a side door, where the guard's footprints had worn the area clear of snow. It had to be the entry and exit point for his rounds. I tried the handle. He'd left it unlocked.

The handle turned, but I didn't pull it open. Crossing the threshold with no warrant, with no reasonable cause meant leaving my authority behind. I couldn't ignore Flanagan's information, but I didn't have enough cause to go through proper channels. Ajax had convinced me to wait, to go the official route. And when I did, I'd been sent home like a misbehaving schoolboy, while Talena convalesced in a hospital bed.

So maybe just a little peek, I told myself, to see if there was anything to Flanagan's talk. I could always come back later with the full weight of the Bunker behind me.

I went inside, immediately searching the utilitarian, antiseptic corridor for someplace to hide. That guard might be coming back at any moment, and I didn't want to risk being caught out in the hallway. I folded the blanket up on itself, so that any melted snow wouldn't puddle on the floor, and moved forward holding my breath, trying to find my way with my ears and my nose as much as with my eyes. From somewhere down the corridor voices echoed. I placed my hand on a door to my left, feeling the handle just as the door to the outside swung open. I walked through the door and found myself in a dark room. I cushioned the door's swing with my fingertips, shutting it silently behind me. In the dark, I stretched out my arms and felt walls to the left and right. Sturdy metal shelves filled with plastic containers. The air was musty with pine-infused antiseptic, and the back of my hand dragged over the knotted cloth strands of a mop head. I was in a maintenance closet.

Footsteps approached from down the hall. The heavy stomps of someone knocking snow from their boots. The guard was coming. I considered covering myself with the blanket and cowering in the corner, but with no light I didn't know how much clutter was in the closet, and if I made a noise it would surely draw attention. I turned to face the door and drew my weapon. If I had to make a noise, I might as well make a damn loud one.

The footsteps grew louder and I heard knuckles crack. First one hand, then another. My finger rested on the trigger. I held my breath. From underneath the door I saw the shifting shadows of the guard's feet. He didn't stop. He didn't even slow down. The footsteps grew fainter and I let out a breath.

Leaving the blanket, I crept back into the hallway. At one end of the hallway was the door I'd come in. With no guard outside it was a safe escape. At the other end the hallway split into a T. I worked my way in that direction, listening for any warning sounds as I went.

A guttural laugh from the left of the T froze me in my tracks. It sounded like my friend Knuckles was watching an early evening sitcom. I pushed on in the other direction, after peeking around the corner to be sure I wasn't seen.

The hallway's bright lighting and flat, white walls left me nowhere to hide. I kept my eyes open for somewhere to lurk, and moved slowly, listening for footsteps. At the end of the hall was a pair of swinging doors, their stainless steel surface polished to a shine. From beyond the doors came another voice, different from the others I'd heard.

I couldn't enter the doors without being seen. Double swinging doors likely led to a large workroom, the kind of place items would need to be wheeled into. To be that big, it would have to curve back the way I'd come, an oversize L that took up the west and north sides of the building.

All of that meant that there was likely more than one way into it.

The hall was lined with doors, and I tried the handle of the one closest to the swinging doors. It opened into a storage room lined with shelves bowing under the weight of their contents. Boxes upon boxes, labeled and organized. I didn't know what was in them and at the moment I didn't care. What mattered was the logo on their sides. Three overlapping capital Cs. A design I'd once associated with kindness and generosity. The logo of the Cedrow Care Center.

There was another door leading out of the storage area, and I hoped that it opened into the larger room at the end of the corridor. I wound my way through the narrow walkways between shelving racks and reached the far door. As gently as possible I opened it just enough to give me a look into the room beyond.

A man stood near a wall, his back to me. The overly styled mop of hair on his head was an obvious wig even from a distance. Heavyset, he was dressed in green surgical scrubs. Was this the doctor Jermaine had talked about?

The room was a large laboratory. It clearly took up most of the square footage of the building. An array of instruments and devices that I vaguely remembered from high school chemistry class lined the tables and walls. Some sections of the room were messy, with vials and beakers strewn about, while others were almost shining in obsessive-compulsive cleanliness. Large cages lined the inside wall, and what looked like office space took up the far end of the room. There was a musky, animal smell in the air, but it was so mixed in with the general antiseptic smell of a hospital that it was beyond identification.

The man nodded, listening to someone on the other end of the line. When he spoke it was with a muffled voice. The strings of a surgical mask clung to the back of his head, though even from my vantage point I could see the clump of green material at his neck that meant his mask was pulled down.

"Have patience, sir," he said. "It will work. All of my projects eventually culminate in success. Some merely require a longer gestation period."

There was pause, and the man said, "Yes. I shall see it done." Then he turned, and I got my first good look at him. His face, from the tip of his nose to his chin, and back to his ears on each side, was unnaturally smooth, almost immobile, and three shades paler than the rest of his rosy face. I recognized the awkward look of extensive skin grafts. But what would burn someone so badly in such a specific region? It was as if he'd been burned in the exact place he wore a surgical mask.

The man's eyes peered out from under thick, bushy eyebrows. His eyes and cheekbones were alive, darting and contracting with excitement, but all motion died abruptly at the scarred line below his nose. The skin graft had left him with no facial hair, but he had taken the time to draw in a luxurious handlebar mustache, thick enough to match his eyebrows.

"With the recently acquired material, we've made excellent progress on the new inhalant." His eyes darted to the cages on the far wall. "I would love an opportunity to display the subjects—"

He stopped abruptly, obviously cut off by the speaker on the other end of the line. He threw his free arm in a dramatic sweep.

"I understand the terms of our agreement quite clearly. But a few words, if you please, about our mutual friend, Ambassador Paulus. If she learns I am here, then her anger wi—"

The doctor's eyebrows peaked, though his dead lips didn't move. Watching him talk was like sitting through the act of a deformed ventriloquist.

"Yes?" he said. Then he chuckled. "That would be perfect. It's as big a stage as I could ever want. Indeed, yes indeed!"

He strode back to the wall-mounted phone and hung up the receiver. He rubbed his hands together and called out to someone in the adjoining office.

"Prepare yourself, Fritz! We have much work to do." And with that, the doctor hustled out of the room, shutting the office door behind him.

I waited a long twenty count for him or Fritz to reappear. But there was no motion, no sound, and eventually I slipped into the larger room.

Big money was evident everywhere I looked. Most of the equipment had functionality that went well beyond my high school chemistry experience, but I could tell it was expensive, and it still gleamed with the shine of a fresh purchase. Presumably Rediron Drilling's funds at work.

There were also signs of strange behavior: a table covered with broken wood, a section of wall that was being used as a notepad had a series of equations that had been overwritten with loopy, hand-drawn spirals. The entire place seemed like madness run with great efficiency.

Around the corner of the L I found a whole other type of madness.

The cages lining the wall were more involved than I'd thought. There was a central area, open and vacant, and smaller cages lining the wall. These individual cages were occupied by dogs, their snouts covered with plastic muzzles, each with a circular opening at its end. Tired eyes watched me, but they were too whipped to even whimper as I walked past the row of cages and to the open shelves at their end. The shelves were filled with dozens of metal canisters, each the size and shape of a can of spray paint. But instead of normal paint nozzles they each had round adapters, threaded like a screw.

I stared at them, unable to imagine what they were for. Then I looked back at the dogs. A few tails wagged tentatively as they watched me, curious eyes peering out from behind muzzle straps. The circular openings at the end of those muzzles were receptors, threaded to accept the canisters. The dogs were test subjects for some kind of gas. I wondered if it was the same kind of gas that had been tested on Jermaine.

There were dozens of the canisters. Maybe as many as a hundred. Were these the next generation of the rags that Flanagan had been using to spread agitation? If they were making aerosol Squib stink, then what could they do with it that *wouldn't* be evil?

I scanned the room, searching for information. The source of the funds that operated the lab, the name of the scar-faced madman running the place, anything that would help me push the pieces closer together. I was aware that at any moment someone could come in through the main swinging doors, or the doctor could come storming out of his office. At that thought I couldn't help but glance at the office door, to make sure it was still closed. On a brass plate "Dr. Alfred Heidelbrecht" was engraved in clear, easy-to-read letters. I'm always amazed what some men's egos will cause them to do.

There was a shuffling sound from around the corner, and the sound of a swinging door being thrown open at the other end of the L. There was no question about what I should do—I needed to get back to the Bunker and raise the alarm. I wished the dogs the best. I couldn't take them with me, and even unlatching their locks would take too long and clue someone in that I had been there. I stepped quickly and quietly to one of the side doors, and departed before I could be seen.

I backed out the way I'd come, looking down the hallway to make sure there were no signs of movement as I silently crept to the back door. I hit the cold outside just in time to see the big human guard rounding the corner on another of his patrols, cracking his knuckles once again. He froze when he saw me, staring with a stupid expression that I almost certainly mirrored right back at him.

Knuckles fumbled at a coat pocket for a weapon or walkie-talkie. Either way, it couldn't be good. I barreled across the distance between us, and tackled him at the waist. He was too big for me to get a lot of lift, but I still managed to get him on the ground. I tried my best to land on his solar plexus, knocking as much air out of him as I could.

It must have worked, because he didn't call for help. With one hand stuck in his coat pocket, Knuckles swung at me with the other. It only grazed the side of my head, but still shook me. The guy had a big punch. I rolled off him, my left shoulder on the frozen ground, my right foot swinging in a short, powerful arc that ended in his crotch.

His legs folded up, and pinned my foot between his knees. I'd hit him hard enough that he might be pissing blood that night, but he rolled with my foot still trapped, and it took precious seconds to get free from his tangled legs. In that time he managed to pull his hand from his coat, clutching the gun I'd feared he was going for. But he fumbled it as he drew, and he held it awkwardly around the barrel.

Both of us still prone, I grabbed his gun hand and rolled into him, so that my shoulder was wedged into his right armpit. With both my arms I pushed down, cracking his hand onto the rock-hard ground. I did it again, and saw the gun clatter from his grip. But I paid for it, as his left hand slammed into my kidney once, twice, a third time. I curled up, half from pain, and half from an attempt to kick his lost gun a safe distance away.

He stopped punching and wrapped his left arm around me, while also curling in the arm I had pinned to the ground. My back pressed to his chest and he held me like a sleeping lover as he fought to reach my throat. I jabbed backward with outstretched fingers. My thumb found his eye socket and dug in, twisting. He jerked away and I rolled again, worming back to maintain leverage.

He lashed out and caught me in the ribs. I jerked away and we were out of each other's reach. I struggled to my feet, while Knuckles raised to a crouch then sprang at me.

I spun, trying to dodge, but he was faster and knocked my legs out from underneath me. I landed on my stomach, the ground hard and unyielding. My head snapped forward, striking the cold ground. I was aware of the non-taste of frozen dirt as it pressed into my lips and up my nose. I turned over as Knuckles scrambled on top of me. Thick fingers clawed at my face.

His thumb caught in my cheek. He yanked up and away, sending a wave of fiery pain across the left side of my face. I shoved my free hand under his jaw and he dropped his chin to protect his throat. As he did, he let up the pressure on my head and I was able to crane my neck and catch his thumb in my teeth. I bit as hard as I could. It might not have been enough by itself, but he pulled away, surprised, and my teeth sliced into his skin. The taste of oil and dirt on his flesh gave way to a rush of warm, coppery blood. He flailed and shook me loose from his hand. I spit a mouthful of blood at him and he backed off. I sat up and stuck a hand under my coat.

Amazingly, my revolver was still in its holster. I pulled it out as he lunged at me again. We were too tight to aim, but I was at least able to swing. Revolver connected with his nose in one of the most satisfying crunches I'd ever heard.

But he didn't go down. One of his big hands struck my temple, and rocked me back on my heels. Somehow I kept my head enough to not fire my weapon, which would have drawn whatever other guards were inside. Or maybe I was just too punch-drunk for it to occur to me.

Everything was spinning. I looked straight ahead, and focused on Knuckles's bloody face. I swung out again with the butt of my gun. The force of the impact numbed my arm.

Knuckles dropped, and this time he didn't move. I spit out a mouthful of blood and took a deep breath, but the world didn't stop spinning. I knew I had to get out of there. I managed one step, then another. I felt good about taking a third. But when I tried it there was no sense of ground beneath my shoe. The night opened up, and darkness surrounded me.

28

I DREAMT OF A FIELD of wheat. Golden stalks covered the land clear to the horizon, the kind of agricultural paradise they showed us in junior high social studies classes. I was in the thick of the wheat, but my perspective was above my own body and I could see me—Carter, the world's worst cop—standing with arms outstretched, letting the stalks of wheat graze my hand as they waved in the power of the wind.

I could see the wind move through the crops, sections of it bowing then straightening, bowing then straightening. It was beautiful, in the way that only nature can be, lulling you into forgetting its poison thorns and venomous fangs.

My dreamer's eye shifted, and in the distance stalks of wheat moved not with the breeze, but in response to the movement of some hidden thing. Something was coming through the wheat, something big, headed straight for dream-Carter. I tried to wake him/me up, but I had no voice. When I opened my mouth there was only a dry, rattling sound, like the pounding of distant jackhammers. The thing kept coming and I tried again to call out, but my voice was still stolen. Nothing more than a *bzzt-bzzt-bzzt*. The wheat stalks nearest to dream-Carter parted, and even though the thing was right there, I still did not know its face, or if it were there to kill my dream-self or beg for help.

Wake up! I thought at myself, while my screams rang *bzzt-bzzt-bzzt* until my throat was raw and bloody. *Wake up!*

I woke to the sound of an insistent buzzing, pulsing through darkness. I tried to look for the source and a crack of light sliced into my vision. My eyes were stuck closed. I fumbled a hand around, scooping snow from my coat and pressing it to my eyes, letting my body heat melt it. The first thing I saw was rust-colored snowmelt dripping from my hand. Blood had covered my eyes, and they had gummed over while I was unconscious.

My pager buzzed, rattling and shaking its plastic case on the hard ground: *bzzt-bzzt-bzzt.*

I tried to sit and pain danced across my body, settling in my kidneys and my spine. I reached out for the pager and saw that one of my fingers bent at a weird angle. I dragged the pager closer, so I could see the display. I didn't recognize the number.

I fought to my knees, then my feet. Knuckles was still sprawled out on the ground. I was glad to see he was still breathing, and even happier to see the dark blush of bruising spread across his face. Every movement was agony, but I patted him down. My bloodied knuckles left red smears across his clothes as I pulled his wallet and piece. I took the wallet to get an ID on him in case it would come in handy later, and I took the gun on the off chance he woke as I made my getaway.

Judging from the snow on my coat and the coagulated blood on my face, I'd been out for a solid fifteen minutes. The good doctor would be expecting Knuckles back inside any minute now. Luck was the only reason I hadn't been discovered while unconscious.

I moved along as quickly as I could, rolled back under the fence, and had never been so happy to see a Hasam Motors vehicle as when I made it back to the car. I drove several blocks before pulling over. I fumbled in the back, shoving aside the top of the bench seat from where I'd left it before. I pushed aside the warm parka, and pulled out the emergency kit. It had the usual items, including wooden tongue depressors, one of which I bit down on as I sandwiched two more against my broken finger. They forced the digit back into a semblance of straightness, then I bound the whole thing with medical tape.

Breathing deep, I took a moment to think about what I'd seen in the lab, and how I could act on it. The guard had assaulted me, but I hadn't identified myself as a cop, and what good would it do me to jail low-level muscle? But what I'd seen and heard was more than enough to start the wheels in motion to bring down Harlan, Paulus, and anyone else who was wrapped up in this madness.

I looked at the pager that had woken me. The number I didn't recognize was followed by the number 2323. That was the code I'd given to Simon for when he needed to talk to me.

Simon. I hadn't even thought of him since Talena had been hospitalized. My priority was to get back to the Bunker, to report on what I'd seen. But I hesitated. Simon never pestered me this much. I thought about what Ajax had told me about the long-extinct whales, and the short life spans of CIs. After a moment I eased the car back into traffic and searched for a pay phone.

Twenty minutes later I was in Old Town, mingling with the tourists and panhandlers. Titanshade is a mix of old and new, a town where close quarters force opulence and poverty to live shoulder to shoulder. Old Town was one of the neighborhoods that highlighted the polarized nature of the city. Dating back to the first days of Titanshade, when the need for an outpost at the northern crown of the world was in question, it had been built by settlers with more stubbornness than common sense. Many of its historic buildings were made of wood, an inordinately expensive building material in a city where every joist had to be imported from the south. Newly minted buildings were made of steel, glass, and plastic. Still imported, but at far less cost.

The heart of Old Town ran on a combination of historic tours and prestige rents paid by lawyers and advertising agencies who wanted to see something old when they looked out their office windows. To my left was St. Ogden's, the oldest guidepost in the city, now more tourist attraction than place of worship. Catercorner to it were the ornate gates that marked Titanshade Public Cemetery #1, the first and only in-ground cemetery in the city. After oil was discovered on the ice plains, the city founders quickly realized that real estate and thermal vents were far too precious to be given over to the dead. Instead, the practice of sky burials or cremation became mandated. For citizens of Titanshade the ultimate worldly destination of the physical body was either funeral flames or the fierce beaks of the condors that lived on the north side of the Mount.

Along this street the city's oldest dead kept watch over the red-and-white embossed compass above the city's oldest place of prayer. And in turn the faithful averted their eyes from the cemetery gates as they walked to service. Life on one hand, death on the other. As if there was a difference.

I turned left, and walked through the doors of St. Ogden's.

Once inside, I mixed with the small crowd of early evening tourists. Simon had given me no details beyond telling me to meet him there, and I scanned the place, looking for his familiar profile. The guidepost was large, with rows of backless trail benches flanking a central aisle that led to the celebratory stand. From there the presiding guide could deliver speeches or lead meditations during service. Private meditation alcoves were set into the side walls, separated by racks of devotional candles and engravings of saints from which the faithful could draw inspiration. The smell of incense and burning candles was heavy in the air, undercut by the heady blend of sedatives and herbs that drifted out of the occupied chambers, as slumbering adherents hoped to be touched by dream sight and granted a glimpse of a world other than this.

I had vivid memories of my parents dragging me to a guidepost, where I'd hear how the Path teaches of many worlds and many walkers. Dream sight is a way to peek into those worlds and draw inspiration. Artists and inventors claimed uncountable creations that had resulted from meditation-induced visions. Of course, the Path also teaches that of all the worlds, this one is special. The guides call Eyjan a spiritual fulcrum, that the paths of other worlds hinge on the ability of the eight Families to live in harmony. I had my doubts; funny how you never hear anyone talk about living in the world that doesn't matter.

In any case, if survival was any indication of authenticity, then the Path had it in spades. The world had once been rich with religions but all had been absorbed by the Path, their multitude of deities and devils transformed into the pantheon of saints, leading us astray or righting our route as we walked our road in this life.

As for me, I kept circling the crowd at the front of St. Ogden's, looking for Simon among the shadows and alcoves. At my back, a guide in full frock and staff regalia rattled off a prepared speech to the tourists. The crowd oohed and ahhed, cameras clicking as they moved from stop to stop. Overhead, stained glass windows stretched to the ceiling, each with its own lesson or historical snap-shot. The one closest to me depicted a pair of shaggy, bison-sized Barekusu teaching a group of other Families. Above and behind them stretched the sideways figure eight of the ba, representing the eternal, winding nature of the Path.

Simon was nowhere to be found, so I slipped away from the tour group and walked through the rows of nearly empty trail benches to the far end of the guidepost. I passed a pair of old women sitting side by side, hands clasped as they meditated together. A few rows away a burly man rocked back and forth, hands obscuring his face. He wore a thick flannel coat, frayed at the cuffs and collar. He'd surely trekked in from the tattered fringes of the city where the warmth of the geo-vents was sparse.

As I drew closer to the celebratory, I looked mountwise. The Mount's silhouette was hidden from view, cloaked in the dark of evening. But I knew where it was. Jenny was up there. After the last efforts of the doctors failed, after the funeral and the tears, after Talena and I said good-bye, Jenny's body had made the trip up the Mount. It was her last wish, so the sky shepherds could help her be reborn and walk the Path in a new form. Some days I missed her so bad it was like a physical tug in my bones, pulling me to-ward her like iron shavings drawn toward a magnet.

A hiss caught my ear, and I turned toward the meditation chambers at the rear of the guidepost. There I found my favorite Gillmyn waiting for me, huddled in a shadowed alcove near a rack of devotional candles and scanning the crowd of tourists for, I guessed, any unwelcome company.

Simon looked me up and down as I approached.

"What happened to you?"

"I beat someone up," I said. When he was silent I added, "No need to ask if I'm okay. I'm sure it looks worse than it—"

"Were you followed?" He wore a black stocking cap and a tight knit sweater, the sleeves pushed up to display his forearm tattoos.

"No."

He said it again, more insistently. "Were you followed?"

"Dammit, no. Now what're you so desperate to tell me?"

We were on the far edge of the seating, and he hunkered down onto a trail bench. I sat beside him, matching his posture, both of us keeping a low profile. The background noise of the tour group provided enough cover for us to speak in hushed tones.

"You asked me about pimps." He peeked over his shoulder as he spoke. "Blackmailed johns and janes."

I straightened up, at least as much as my aching body would allow. "That's right."

"I've heard talk," he said, still peering behind us.

I made a spinning motion with my hand. *Get on with it.*

"First time was the other day," he said. "Some hard cases I never seen before showed up and ran their mouths about problems with candies. They said anyone with a sweet tooth was getting shook down by candies with wires. That the pimps tried to deal with it and couldn't manage, so a client set them straight."

Giving up on looking over his shoulder, Simon slipped back into the shadows of the alcove. He hiked up his blue jeans and squatted down, a move that put his back to the alcove wall and gave him a better view of the crowd. "I tried to get a hold of you, but you never responded."

"I was a little busy with people trying to kill me." I slid over, to the end of the trail bench, giving him some cover from prying eyes. He was spooked bad.

"Whatever." He adjusted his stocking cap. "So I figured you weren't interested."

"Simon. They were trying to kill me. They put a friend in the hospital."

The shadows around him danced to the flickering flames of the devotional candles. "So I never got a hold of you. We never talked."

"I know," I said. "I was there when we didn't talk."

"So today, when a completely different set of hard cases come in and spill the same story, it spooked me."

"Different guys?"

"With the exact same story."

"And when you say exact . . ."

"Like someone had written it out for 'em."

I grew very still. "Someone knows to plant a story with you."

"Worse. They tried a second time. Which means they knew the story hadn't gotten back to you."

Hells below. The only people who would've known that were—

"Your buddies in the Bunker are feeding info to someone who's trying to get a story in the system. Maybe that new guy you brought over. I don't know who. But you understand that I'm screwed, right?" His gills flared, with anger or fear or both.

I tried to process what he was telling me. Someone in the Bunker was leaking, but to whom? And the leak had to be from someone with access to critical information about the case, and about me. It meant I couldn't report what I'd just found in that laboratory, and it meant that my CI was . . . I looked at the big Gillmyn beside me.

"Simon, I'll make this good." It felt false even as I said it. Once a CI was exposed, he or she was living on borrowed time.

"Oh, yeah. You'll make it great," he said. "I'm heading out of town. Don't contact me again."

"Why are you telling me this?"

He huffed and glanced warily over the trail benches.

"I mean it," I said. "You could've just split town. Why did you tell me?"

He looked at me like I'd sprouted another head. "Because of all the low-lives in this town," he said, "you're the one asshole that wouldn't sell me out."

We sat for a moment in the quiet of the guidepost. The tour had ended, and the only sound was the gentle weeping of the burly man, overcome by grief or joy. As if there were a difference.

Simon's eyes still swept back and forth, watching the crowd and the entrance. I tried not to calculate odds on him getting out of town alive. Whoever had ears in the Bunker wanted him to feed me those fake stories, which meant they wanted him alive. But if word about Simon had leaked to the Harlqs or CaCuris or any of a dozen other crews, he wouldn't see sunrise. And with my own people compromised, I couldn't even offer him protection. Not that he'd have accepted it anyway.

"You got enough cash to get out of town?" I said.

He nodded and wiped his hands across his jeans. I jerked a thumb at the exposed tattoos on his forearms.

"You ought to cover those up," I said. "If someone's looking for you, they're distinctive marks."

Simon smiled. "Are you kidding? I'm big, green, and gorgeous. No one needs tattoos to recognize me." He stood up. "Good luck, Carter. Try not to let the bastards kill you."

He headed toward the guidepost's entrance, zigzagging a path past chattering tourists and engravings of long-dead saints. As he disappeared from view, I saw him roll down his sleeves.

I STAYED AT A MOTEL that night, my talk with Simon leaving me too troubled to trust that my home was safe, and too exhausted to defend myself if it wasn't. I visited a drugstore and spent most of the evening sitting on the edge of an uncomfortable mattress patching myself up from my encounter with Heidelbrecht's guard. I left the motel's washcloth stained red, but I was glad to find that the damage wasn't nearly as bad as it looked. Torn lips and brows were as ugly as the swelling along my jaw, but the only injury that'd stick with me was the broken finger.

The rest of the night I spent lying in bed, surrounded by freshly emptied take-out boxes and bathed in the silent flicker of the muted television. All the while I worked with pencil and paper, trying to make sense of the mess I'd found myself in. It took me hours before I found sleep, but when I did I slept hard, and no dreams disturbed my rest.

In the morning I returned to the Bunker, turning heads with my bruised and bandaged face. As I passed each colleague, I wondered if they were the one who'd sold out Simon.

Myris was headed somewhere with a box full of files, but skidded to a halt when she saw me.

"Side roads!" She set the box down. It was probably packed full of research for Angus's investigation into the candies. I wondered if my name was in there somewhere. "What happened to you?"

"Long story," I said.

"Does it have a sequel?"

I wondered if she knew how much her career would benefit by her move to Angus's group. I wondered if she was the person leaking information. But I said none of that. Instead I shrugged, smiled, and kept walking till I got to my desk. It was covered with the usual office debris. I sat down and surveyed the stack. Memos about this or that bit of procedure, files I'd meant to get around to reading. As I stared, a drip of blood fell from my mouth to the blotter below me. My lip had torn open again. I wiped the drip away with a stray memo about dress code policies, then dug in my coat pocket for a fresh bandage. I opened a desk drawer and with a single sweep of my arm sent all the files and folders tumbling inside.

There's nothing like the feeling of getting things done.

I dropped a single folder on my now-clean work area. I flipped it open and revealed the map of connections I'd been working on overnight. It showed Garson Haberdine, Jermaine Bell, Harlan, names I'd learned since I'd been pulled out of Mickey the Finn's, what seemed like a lifetime ago. Gellica, Paulus, Lowell, and Cordray. The envoys were there, as were the Squibs: Lanathel and Yarvis. Flanagan was on there as well. He wasn't innocent, but he wasn't guilty. Not completely. Or at least he wasn't the only guilty one. Next to Flanagan were the names of my fellow officers, at least one of whom was feeding info to another player.

I'd drawn lines in pencil representing the relationships between all of them. An intricate web encompassing the many players on both sides of the law and the hundred tenuous connections that tied them together. Somehow the answers to everything were hidden in that map.

Ajax arrived a little after I did, settling into the desk next to mine. He was on my web too, of course, but as a relative newcomer to Titanshade, he had almost no connections with anyone else that I'd been able to verify. That made him one of the least risky people to trust. But I couldn't tell him about my meeting with Flanagan. Not yet.

Jax eyed my battered face, but kept any comments about it to himself. Reaching to his shoulder he untied the sling and flexed his arm, still bulky from the bandaging under his suit coat. "I hate this thing," he said, and bunched the linen fabric of his sling in one hand before tossing it in his wastebasket. "If anyone asks, it broke."

I grunted my complicity. For him, it was probably a significant act of rebellion. Maybe I was setting a bad example.

"Well," he said, "you're here in an advisory role. You have any advice?"

I squeezed the splint that held my finger straight, biting my lip with the twinge of pain it brought. I wanted to trust him. But I couldn't say anything. Not there, in the middle of the Bullpen, anyway.

A muted rattling broke the silence. I looked at Jax, who shrugged. It sounded again, and I pulled open the drawer where I'd shoveled my desktop. The rattling got louder. I reached in and fished out my pager. I didn't recognize the number, and dropped it back on the blotter.

"What about Guyer?" I said.

"She can't do anything else."

"Can't or won't?"

"Either," he said. "Both. The Squibs took Haberdine's remains."

"For what?"

"To send back to his family. You've heard that some people care when their family members die, right?"

I flipped through my sketch of relationships. "I've heard. Is she sure she can't do anything?"

"She's around here somewhere, ask her yourself."

The phone on my desk rang. I answered it and found myself talking to Talena.

"Why didn't you answer my page?"

I thumbed the page to look at the call-back number. "Didn't recognize it. I had other priorities."

"People are trying to poison me," she said. "Make me a priority until I'm out of the hospital. And why does your voice sound funny? Are you eating right now?"

I dabbed a tissue to my mouth. It came away crimson. "I bit my cheek," I said. "And no one was poisoning you. They were going for me."

"Fine." Her voice rasped, a reminder of the plastic tube the docs had used to pump her stomach. "Either they were aiming for you and they're incompetent, or they were targeting me, and they're skillful. Two different lists. Let's go over them both."

She read me her list. I listened to the whole thing. It was the least I could do. The poor kid had almost gotten killed for the mortal sin of knowing me too well.

When she got to the end I recited a couple of the names back to her—former johns or janes who she'd forced to give up their taste for candies—just to show I was paying attention. I told her I needed to go.

"I'm not going to stop," she said. "My work, I mean."

"I know. Don't ever stop doing the right thing." There was more emotion in my voice than I'd intended, and the line was silent for a moment.

"You sure you're okay?"

"Yeah, I'm sure. I'll take care of things on this end, and I'll swing by and see you soon." I broke the connection and rested my aching head in my hands. There was a rustle of paper and Ajax shoved a report to the side.

"Carter," he said. I raised my head and found him giving me a crinkle-eyed look. "You want me to go talk to Talena? I've got a follow-up at the hospital today anyway." He displayed his bandaged arm. "Unless you think she'd get nervous about having another cop around."

"Nah, she'd love it," I said. "She thinks you're cute."

He froze. "Yeah?"

Uh-oh.

"No. Not really. I only said that to get you to— In fact, don't worry about it . . ."

"Like I said, I've gotta go anyway." He stood up. "Try not to bleed on anything while I'm gone."

Over the next few hours I worked the phones, spinning the rotary dial until my index finger was numb. I leaned on every government connection I had, trying to get some traction on the connection between Paulus, Harlan, and the mysterious Dr. Heidelbrecht. No one had anything beyond the normal political backbiting, and no one had heard of Heidelbrecht. As I hit brick wall after brick wall, my patience got lower and lower. I hung up after yet another futile call and pressed on the bridge of my nose, trying in vain to hold a headache at bay.

"Carter, what are you doing?"

It was Captain Bryyh, gracing my desk with a visit as she stormed through the Bullpen.

"I'm okay," I said. "Maybe bruised up a little."

"You'll be more than that when I'm done with you." She loomed over me, fire in her eyes. Somewhere beneath my bandages, I started to bleed again.

"What part of 'don't be a pain in my ass' did you not comprehend?" One hand rested on her hip, the other clenched into a fist that shook slightly as she spoke.

I flipped my map of suspects facedown.

"You will stop doing whatever afterhours bullshit you're getting up to. And"—she brought a finger up to my face—"you will stop calling city officials."

My suspicions flared. "How do you know who I've called?"

"Because I'm your boss, and when you piss people off, they call me to complain. And that's the kind of pain in my ass you're supposed to be avoiding."

With some of her anger vented, she took a step back and looked me over.

"What incompetent hack bandaged you up? It looks like someone tried to glue you back together with dollar-store tape and cotton gauze." She clucked her tongue, managing to sound both disappointed and amazed. "Did you do that yourself?"

When I didn't answer, Bryyh rolled her eyes.

"Go to the hospital," she said.

"I'll get over there before too long."

"I'm not joking. You will go to a doctor. You will go right now." She pointed to the door. "I do not want to see you in here again today."

"Cap, I think—" I looked around the Bullpen. Detectives scurried all around us, ears listening, mouths ready to whisper what they heard back to some unseen puppet master. Kravitz stood at his chalkboard, and I couldn't tell if he was watching me while he wrote a list of new leads on the relevant persons list. Somewhere Angus and Bengles were slinking around, as well as a dozen other cops I'd irritated over the years. I wanted to tell her about the lab and the dogs, the danger that was simmering in the city. But I couldn't do it.

As much as Bryyh had helped me over the years, as much as her friendship with my mom had protected me, I couldn't count on her; right then I couldn't count on anyone.

"Alright," I said. "I'll be out of here as soon as I turn up some info on a doctor."

"Damn right you will. You've already wasted enough of my time. There are riots in the streets, politicians at my throat, I'm twenty minutes late for my next meeting, and the sun isn't up yet." She stalked away from me.

I was tempted to point out that it was winter, and the sun didn't rise until one p.m., but I managed to keep that observation to myself. I'd have to give the phones a rest for a while, unless I wanted Bryyh to strangle me with the cord. Instead I dug into my pocket and pulled out the photo ID I'd taken off the guard at the lab. Like I'd told the captain, I intended to turn up some information on a doctor.

But first I needed a pick-me-up. I pushed away from my desk and grabbed my empty coffee mug.

I dragged myself into the kitchenette on the third floor of the Bunker, where I knew I could find a fridge, a sink, and some of the only palatable coffee in the building. When I walked through the doorway, I also found DO Guyer.

The divination officer was pouring herself a cup of coffee, wearing khaki pants and a polo shirt, a revolver holstered to her hip. She glanced over her shoulder and offered me a greeting.

"You look like a normal cop," I said. "What's going on?"

"Administrative day. Happens to the best of us." She set the coffeepot down and riffled through the drawers until she found a bag of sugar. When she got a good look at me she froze. "You look like you got worked over by the imps themselves."

I shrugged it off. "Occupational hazard."

"Funny." She peered over my shoulder. "I just walked through a room full of cops who didn't have black eyes. I wonder what their secret is."

I held up my empty mug. "Whenever you're ready."

She filled me up. "I heard about the Bell-Asandro family case."

"Yeah?"

"Yeah. Sugar?"

I shook my head. She poured an unhealthy amount of the white stuff into her coffee. "I heard you wrapped it up."

"That was mostly Ajax." The coffee was bitter and hot, but the scalding felt good and I desperately needed the caffeine.

"Either way, that was well done."

I clasped my hands around the mug, letting the warmth seep into my aching joints. I knew that I should be happy to get the compliment from a DO, but I lacked the energy to even pretend to care.

"They were going to call me in on that one," she said.

"Were they?"

"Yes." Guyer's spoon clinked against the sides of her mug as she stirred in her sweetener. "With all the publicity, they wanted to wrap it up fast."

I thought of Haberdine's echo begging to be set free, of Guyer's insistence that she'd hold him until she saw fit to let him go.

"But you didn't do that."

She sipped her coffee and winced. She reached for the sugar again. I slid it away, and threw a half-spoonful into my own drink.

"You made an arrest. It's no longer an issue."

"If it's no longer an issue, then why are you telling me about it?" She took the sugar back.

"Because we're colleagues. Because I'm stuck in a miniature kitchen while I wait to talk to Bryyh. And because you showed up while I was making coffee."

She mixed in another two spoonfuls of sugar and sipped again. This time she seemed satisfied. I looked at the out-of-date safety posters that hung on the far wall. Something clicked in my head and I turned back to her.

"Do you know Ambassador Paulus?" I held a hand up at shoulder height. "About this tall. Rich. Powerful. Tattoos that move around on their own."

She lounged against the countertop. "I know her. Not well."

"Sorcerous connections? You guys belong to the same country club?"

"We don't bond over coffee, if that's what you're implying." She raised her mug to me in mock salute. "But I've met her. I know of her work."

I'd been standing for a while, and I noticed my legs had a definite wobble to them. While I waited for the coffee to kick in, I sat down at the linoleum-topped table.

"So how much do people like you know each other's business?" I said.

"Paulus and me?"

"Sorcerers in general."

"Surely you know magicians other than me."

"Not as many as you'd think. Detective salaries don't let us run in the same social circles."

"They can't keep up with your lavish lifestyle?"

I gave her a smile and regretted it. Smiling made the bandages crinkle and wounds tear open. "So Paulus's tattoos . . ."

She sipped her coffee. "Are runes, yes."

"Like the ones on your cloak."

She gave a thumbs-up. "Also a 'yes.'"

"But you don't all get together and compare notes."

"No we don't. I make a good living—"

"Glad one of us does."

"—but I'm not in the same tax bracket as your friend the ambassador. She's got her own money."

"From her position?"

"From her holdings."

The term "holdings" only had one meaning in Titanshade.

"Oil," I said.

"Yes. Old money. Her family still lives up in the Hills. Those tattoos are done with ink that's been blended with manna. I don't even want to think about how expensive that was."

"There's manna in your cloak?"

"Sure." She chuckled. "But the amount of manna to coat some thread is minimal. That's nothing compared to what Paulus has sunk into her flesh. More powerful, more expensive. And no matter where she goes it's right there with her." She wagged her head and groaned. "Do you have any idea how long I'm going to be paying off the student loans that covered that cloak?"

I redirected the conversation before we ended up comparing financial woes.

"So if Paulus has all this oil money, why on the Path is she the one running negotiations? Isn't that a conflict of interest?"

"I would assume she had to put her holdings into a blind trust so she doesn't know where she's invested. Most politicians do that. Some financial manager is running it for her until she retires." She glanced at her watch. "It's probably a load off her mind, not having to deal with it directly."

"One more question," I said. "As long as you're here."

"I've nothing but time."

"Just something I always wondered . . . What does manna taste like?"

She laughed. "Not like anything you've had before. You ever drink a really strong whiskey?"

I winced, and her hand flew to her mouth. "Sorry," she said. "I didn't mean it that way." Clearly word had gotten around about my recent experience with poison. She hurried on. "Anyway, that's not the flavor, but there's a bite to it like whiskey. It pinches your tongue." She squinted, considering. "That, combined with cotton candy. Again, not the flavor, more the feeling that it melts away before you can fully taste it."

"Like hospital food," I said.

She laughed, but I hadn't been joking. My last experience with hospital food was at the CCC, when both Jenny and I had been limited to a pasty, flavorless custard before the transplant surgery.

"Could you"—my words stumbled—"I don't know, add it to food?"

"I suppose. It's an oil," she said. "You could fry your potatoes in it, if you had enough spare cash to cover the federal budget . . . and you didn't mind the unexpected consequences. Manna is power-ful and unpredictable." She waggled a finger in the air, warming to the topic. "Without proper training, you're as likely to become a living shadow as you are to achieve anything useful. There're stories of pre-Shortage sorcerers who—"

Hemingway stuck her head in the kitchenette and looked at Guyer.

"Captain Bryyh's looking for you, DO."

"I'll be right there." Guyer raised her cup of coffee in a mini-toast in my direction. "It's been a pleasure."

She walked out but Hemingway stayed, waiting until we were alone to speak in a low voice.

"You might want to check out the interrogation rooms," she said.

Still processing what Guyer had told me, it took a few seconds for me to respond.

"Why?" I asked.

"Remember those white-collar johns from Government Plaza?"

"Lowell and Cordray?"

"They're back."

"Both of them?"

She nodded.

One or the other might be trying to cut a deal to keep any prosecution to a minimum. But scumbags never turned evidence in pairs.

My mug clattered as I dropped it in the sink. "When?" I asked.

"This morning. They said they had more information. Called Angus and came in first thing. Them and their lawyers. Angus and Kravitz kept them isolated. I just found out in a briefing from—" she broke off, uncomfortable.

So she'd been moved over to Angus's task force. So much for Team Carter.

I was surprised to feel a pang of betrayal. I hadn't even wanted a partner, and here I was missing a team. And, of course, it happened when I had too many things to handle on my own. Digging in my pocket, I pulled out Knuckles's ID card.

"I'm sorry to ask you this, but can you pull a sheet on this guy? Ajax is on his way to the hospital, and I've got no one else."

Hemingway gnashed her gum. But she said, "Hand it over," and took the ID from me.

I thanked her, then was out the door.

30

THE BUNKER WAS A BIG place, with far too many nooks and crannies where the envoys could be hidden away for me to search through them all. I could have tried to find Angus, but he'd never tell me where they were.

Instead I moved through the Bullpen, looking for the one person who would both know the envoys' location and could be coerced into giving it up. I spotted his beard from across the room. He was walking toward the elevators, dressed in a loose tie and shirtsleeves, stains spreading across his underarms. He looked almost as bad as me.

"Kravitz!"

He turned and saw me, then kept walking. I broke into a jog, gritting my teeth as my bones grated with the sudden motion. Kravitz gave me a cursory glance as I intercepted him.

"What do you want?" he asked.

"What's Angus doing with the envoys?"

"What envoys?"

I wasn't going to be stonewalled. I grabbed his arm and turned him sideways. He looked at my hand, then at me. He towered over me, shaking his head like he was dealing with a misbehaving dog.

"He recorded statements," said Kravitz. "Gathered evidence. Police work. You should try it some time."

"No one comes in like that a second time. They're trying to play us."

Kravitz winced, as if I'd slapped him.

"Let it go, Carter."

I wasn't sure if he meant the envoys or his arm. Not that I cared—I held on to both.

"Where are they? What rooms are they in?"

"They're done. They made their statements and turned in their materials—"

"Materials?"

Kravitz jerked free and walked away, frowning like he'd said too much. I kept up with him as he reached the elevators.

"What did they give up?"

He ignored me, and entered the elevator as it opened with a ding.

"What did they give up, Kravitz?"

He turned, red-rimmed eyes boring into mine. "Sealed information," he said. "You'll get access when Bryyh clears you."

The elevator began to shut. Kravitz glanced over my shoulder, as if he were scanning the Bullpen for watchful eyes. "You want my advice?" His eyes flicked back to me and he licked his lips. He looked as if he were staring down the barrel of a gun. "Tend to your own, Carter. Fast."

The cab doors closed, and I was left wondering what Kravitz had meant. Had that look on his face been guilt? Pity? Disgust? I didn't know what to think or who to trust, and I didn't have time to sort it out.

I jogged back through the Bullpen. I saw Bryyh behind the glass door of a meeting room. She and Guyer were pouring over a stack of photos with detectives Bierce and Abrams. As soon as I opened the door, Bryyh glared at me.

"Not now, Carter."

I hadn't even opened my mouth to argue before her index finger went up.

"Not. Now."

A few weeks earlier I'd have barged in and laid it all out for the captain and asked for help. But at that moment I didn't know who I could trust and who I had to hold out against. I let the door swing shut and drifted away. There had to be another way to find out what was going on.

Gellica.

I stopped at the nearest desk and scooped up the phone. The junior detective working there looked up and gave me an irate, "Hey!" He was a beefy guy named Greendale who I didn't know well.

"It'll just be a minute," I said.

"Nah, you're done now," he said, and reached out a pencil to disconnect my call.

I snatched his pencil and stabbed the eraser end into the back of his hand. His hand hit the table with a slap, and I held it there. The rubber tip dug into the soft spot between two knuckles while I asked the operator to connect me to 1 Government Plaza. Greendale mumbled obscenities at me but kept his voice down, I suppose in an attempt to save face. He didn't want to be seen getting manhandled by the department eccentric. I let up on the pencil and made a tsk-tsk gesture at him. He turned his back to me and pretended to shuffle paperwork.

"I need to speak with Envoy Gellica," I said. "This is Detective Carter of the TPD, and it's urgent."

If I could talk to Gellica, maybe I could find out why she'd sold me out. Why Lowell and Cordray were pulling this stunt.

They told me she wasn't in. They told me she wasn't expected in that day, and weren't sure when she would be available. They offered to put me in contact with their chief legal counsel if I needed further assistance with the investigation. They all but told me I'd have better luck going home and teaching my cat to sit and stay.

I could smell the backstabbing coming from a mile away.

Hemingway entered the Bullpen with Myris at her side. I hung up and walked over to them.

"You gotta hear this," said Myris, talking in a hushed voice.

"She already told me," I said. "The envoys were here."

"Not just that, they changed their whole story."

"What?"

Hemingway glanced around, then walked over to the board listing relevant names. Myris and I followed, and the three of us looked at it while we talked, making it appear that we were slightly more on focus.

"They dumped entire black books of scandal," said Hemingway. "The names of politicians, and the candies they prefer. The ones who've paid off blackmailers. If what they're spilling checks out, the Squib killing is going to be tied into the candies for sure."

"It will," said Myris, and I knew she was right. They wouldn't have come in if they didn't have corroboration.

Hemingway said, "Lowell and Cordray claim they were both being blackmailed by candies, and that Haberdine was targeted as well. But, Carter—" She paused to snap her gum. "They say that it's been going on for years. That cops with Vice were letting it happen. Helping, even."

Myris tapped the section of the board that still had Flanagan's name. "Didn't Haberdine's echo say something about a cop in the room? *One big, one small. Both deadly.*" She let out a dual-toned whistle. "If a dirty cop was helping the candies shake down johns and janes, then that's gotta be who was in the room."

Hemingway crossed her arms and scowled. "Another Flanagan," she said. "Just what we need."

My head was swimming. If Lowell and Cordray had turned in evidence implicating Talena and her friends, it'd just be a matter of time before someone connected it to me and my time on the Vice squad. Back then I'd turned a blind eye, thinking I was letting victims protect themselves. But it might turn out that I was very slowly laying the groundwork for my own frame-job.

It looked like they'd found their fall guy for the Haberdine killing.

I excused myself with a mumbled, "Gotta make a call," and left Myris and Hemingway staring at the board. I made it back to my desk and grabbed the phone and the pager. I scrolled to the most recent message, the call-back number for Talena's hospital room. I dialed and the line rang through. I had to call twice more before someone picked up.

"Hello."

I recognized the voice. Of course I did.

It was Angus.

WHEN I GOT TO TALENA'S floor at the hospital, Ajax was in the hallway. He looked at me in that wide-eyed way Mollenkampi get when they're surprised.

"I couldn't stop it, Carter."

"I know," I said.

Angus's voice echoed in the hallway as it came from farther down the hall. He stood outside Talena's room.

"Stop what? Stop us from arresting Carter's pet waif?"

I faced him. "Where is she? I want to see her." I took two long steps toward Angus, and his human partner appeared from nowhere, pulling me up short. Angus held up a hand.

"She's still in her room. Where she'll stay until the doctors clear her for transfer." He twisted his head to call off Bengles. "Let him go in. He can spend some quality time before saying good-bye."

I pushed past them.

"Don't take too long, Carter. We'll be wanting to ask you all kinds of questions about your other connections with our murder suspects."

Talena was still in bed, eyes big and brimming wet. Not quite in tears. She was holding those in check, like the fierce warrior she was. Her left hand was handcuffed to the side rail of her hospital bed, and when she spoke her voice was tiny.

"Carter," she said, and she didn't need to say anything else.

I stood there a long moment, looking at the scrawny girl lit from above by a flickering fluorescent light, her wide-eyed face set against white linens and the pale green of the hospital walls. Then Angus called to me from the hallway. I couldn't avoid talking to him, and I couldn't help Talena by standing there slack jawed. So I turned to leave, but when I reached the room's threshold I paused and looked back.

"Hang in there, kiddo," I said. "I'm gonna get this fixed."

She nodded, the door closed, and that was the last time I saw her in that room.

Bengles leaned against the wall, her neck and shoulders touching the paint, one foot kicked back against the wall. She bounced in place, a fast tempo of nervous energy. It reminded me of how Talena used to get while watching early morning cartoons and eating bowl after bowl of Sugar Sweets cereal.

Angus examined his reflection in the glass of an in-case-of-emergency cabinet, where a fire hose lay coiled, snakelike and ready to spit.

He looked at me. "Time to talk."

I stuck my hands in my pockets and waited for him to say more.

He glanced in the hospital room across the hall from Talena. "Looks like this one's free," he said, and held out his hand like a waiter showing me to my table.

The room was half turned over. Sheets had been stripped from the bed, but the previous tenant's belongings still sat around the room. A half-empty cup, a half-full bedpan. I wondered if the occupant had gone home or to the morgue.

Angus and Bengles followed me in, and Jax made a move to do likewise. Bengles blocked his way.

"No chance," Angus told him. Jax looked to me and I nodded, letting him know it was okay. He faded back and the door closed, leaving me alone with Angus and Bengles. I stood by the window, getting a scenic view of the brick wall of the building next door. Bengles stood with her back against the door and resumed her over-caffeinated bouncing. Angus sat in the room's lone chair. Blue vinyl upholstery crackled under his weight, decaying edges exposing the stuffing inside.

"Since you're here," he said, "I assume you heard about the new evidence in the Squib case."

I kept my mouth shut. I wanted him to show as many cards in his hand as possible.

"You've got to talk at some point," he said. "I don't really care if it's now or later, but you should know that I was told I might have to make a call to IA at some point today."

No cop in their right mind wanted to deal with an Internal Affairs probe.

"Fine," I said. "What do you want to know?"

"Who is this girl? Who is she to you?"

She's everything I'm sworn to protect.

"She's the daughter of one of my ex-girlfriends."

"What about the father?"

"What about him?" I raised and lowered the window blinds, giving me something to look at other than Angus's smug face. It was critical that I not lose my temper.

"Does his name rhyme with Barter?"

Behind him, Bengles mumbled something that sounded like "martyr." Angus never took his eyes off me.

"No idea," I said, and it was true. Talena had been six years old when I met her mother.

"I'm wondering what makes you so interested in her."

"Apple doesn't fall far from the tree." Bengles grinned and bounced in place.

"How long were you with her mother?" Angus asked.

Thirteen years. With repeated breaks to build our will back up.

"Off and on. Fits and starts," I said. "You know how it goes."

Angus grunted. He had no idea how it went.

"Why did you break it off?"

I drank too much, she didn't drink enough. We were doomed from the start.

"The job. Lotta stress, being with a cop."

Angus crossed his legs. "When the girl—"

"Talena."

"When she drank the poison," he said, "you said it was meant for you. Is there any chance it was meant for her?"

"No. I would've been dead if she hadn't shown up and drank first."

"Convenient that she happened to be in that neighborhood."

I slid the blinds up. I let them drop down. Using them as a metronome, I kept my breathing controlled even as my temper rose.

"She's an activist," I said.

"The envoys who came in today were very clear about just how active she's been."

"Was there a question in there?"

"Did you know she's been engaged in blackmail?"

"I think a blackmailer would be able to afford something nicer than a seventh-floor walkup like Talena's."

"Answer the question," he said.

I turned away from the window, and looked at him directly.

"How about you ask me the real question?" He didn't respond. "Ask me about the Squib," I said.

"What about the Squib?"

My temper flared, and I fought it back down. "The Oracular Tongue nightmare we watched. Haberdine's ghost or echo or whatever it is that said there was a cop in the room when he was killed. You gonna ask me where I was that night?"

"Where were you?"

"At a bar, waiting for my shift to end."

Angus sniffed. "Sounds believable."

I waited for him to turn on me, but it didn't come. He merely looked at me, and his biting jaws clattered slightly as he shook his head.

"Do you think I'm stupid?" he asked.

"No," I said. He was a lot of things, but stupid wasn't one of them.

"Well, whoever gift-wrapped this package thinks I am." He pulled out a handkerchief and dabbed at his tusks. "I don't like you," he said. "You're a spoiled prima donna who thinks you're better than the rest of the force."

I blinked, the up-down motion of the blinds forgotten. "Prima donna?"

"Your life's a mess, you're a disgrace, and you use your woe-is-me bullshit to get the brass to let you slide on every regulation in the book." His mandibles twitched violently. "If you were helping facilitate some kind of blackmail ring, I'll put you away. And if you interfere with my investigation, I'll roll right over you. But for someone to think I'd believe you tore apart a diplomat in a hotel room?" He looked disgusted. "Please."

He stood up. "I'm not making the same mistake you did with

Flanagan," he said as he walked to the door. "I'm not charging an innocent man, no matter how good it might make me feel in the short term."

Angus pointed at the hall dividing us from Talena. "Now your favorite lost cause in there? I've got plenty to hold her. She'll go down for something. Maybe you will too, or maybe you won't. But just because someone wants me to hang this mess on you doesn't mean I'm going to do it." His biting jaws clenched. "Don't come back here, don't try to make contact with my prisoner."

Prisoner, he called her.

"And when I do break you," he said. "It'll be for something that sticks."

He walked out, Bengles on his heels. I stared after them, and the weight of everything bore down on me. The murders, the Squib smell, Flanagan's arrest and release, my humiliation in the press, my failure to protect anyone. Even Talena couldn't depend on me to keep her safe from my own department. My head ached and I needed to sit down.

I eased myself onto the bed that had so recently held some other sickly soul, and loosened my tie and slipped off my coat. When I did, a crinkle in the pocket caught my attention. I reached in and pulled out the pamphlet I'd taken from Talena the day after Haberdine's murder. I'd shoved it in my pocket to be forgotten, but now I flattened it out and examined it. Laid out in big bold type, it was designed to be easy, inspirational reading for her flock of addicts and candies.

Are you at your Lowest Point?
It may feel like All Hope Is Lost, but Remember:
The Richest of Treasures Are Found at the Greatest
of Depths.

My mouth went dry.

It was the wording from the note at the Bell-Asandro murder site. Jermaine had quoted it after he'd killed his family, and Haberdine's ghost had made an oblique reference to it during the Oracular Tongue ceremony. Somehow Talena, or at least her words, was connected to these killings. I looked up from the pamphlet and stared at the wall that separated me from the girl I'd helped raise.

I didn't have access to Talena to ask her about it, and I sure as Hells wasn't going to hand it over to Angus. There was only one place to learn if Talena had been set up, or if she was actually involved, to find out if Lowell and Cordray were now telling the truth about her, or if they were lying once again.

Gellica was stonewalling but I was going to find her, and I was going to get answers. One way or another.

32

GELLICA LIVED IN A WEALTHY part of town, close to the Mount. The kind of neighborhood where people can leave windows open without worrying that someone will come in and take their possessions. As I stared at her house, I wondered if kicking down her front door would shatter that false sense of security.

It was seven p.m., and the short-lived winter sun had long since set. Streetlights provided illumination, but I saw a shadowed path where I could walk the perimeter of her home and find a way in. The neighborhood was warm enough for shirtsleeves, but I kept my jacket on to cover my shoulder holster. If a neighbor spotted me, I didn't want them to automatically call the patrol.

A window near the back door was unlocked, so I didn't have to kick in anything after all. Hand to the window, I could see the status light of a security system keypad. It glowed a dim green, telling me it was deactivated. Had Gellica left it off, or was she the sort who never got around to activating it in the first place? Was she home? Truth be told, I didn't much care either way. Someone had set Talena up for a fall. If Gellica wasn't home, I'd toss her place looking for signs of collusion. If she was, then I'd confront her directly. In either scenario there was zero chance I'd be giving her a courtesy knock.

I let myself in and stood listening for any signs of activity. The lights were off and I heard no sound, but a television's flickering glow came from a room at the far end of the hall. I moved through the darkened house, stepping carefully and stopping often.

The windows let long shafts of streetlight into the building, and the light splayed across the floor, creeping up the walls at twisted angles, forming distorted doorways along the blank walls. None of those doors led anywhere, of course. False exits, every one. Nothing got out of the city. Not Gellica, who'd traveled from one side of Eyjan to the other, only to get sucked back into Titanshade's vortex. Not Ajax, who'd served in a small town and then come to the city that would eventually chew him up and spit him out. And not me, the native son who always wanted to leave, but somehow never had the guts to board a bus and ride the ice highway south, where the temperatures were warm and the jobs didn't come with a daily dose of self-loathing. There were many ways out of Titanshade, but none of them were real. And pondering the dream doorways that marched down Gellica's home wasn't going to help me bring in a killer.

The hallway led into the living room, and I paused at the threshold. The room was divided into light and shadow by the flicker of the muted TV, a big-screen model that perched on the crown of an entertainment console. It was playing a movie, a trashy classic about a wandering sorcerer who drifts into a small town on the salt plains carrying only a six-shooter and flask of manna, before proceeding to clean the streets of criminals and corrupt officials. The kind of movie that rots kids' brains and makes them think they want to grow up to be heroes.

The unmistakable tinkle of liquid on glass cut through my nostalgia. I turned my head toward the sound and saw a woman sitting in the shadow-cloaked far corner of the room. It wasn't the woman I'd hoped to confront.

Ambassador Paulus locked eyes with me and smiled. In her hands were two ice-filled tumblers and a bottle of whiskey.

I sat in a green-cushioned chair and faced one of the most powerful women in the city, in the darkened living room of her chief assistant.

She'd moved to the couch and set the whiskey on the coffee table between us. Even from that distance I could smell the bite of its aroma. She appraised me for a long, silent moment, swirling the ice and whiskey in her tumbler. The motion left a thin sheen of liquor slowly sliding down the inside of her glass, falling toward the body of the drink. Liquor snobs call those "legs." I call them delicious.

Paulus sniffed her drink as she reclined on the rich leather of the couch. "So tell me, Detective, why do you keep popping up to bother me?"

"I'm not here to bother you."

"No." Her face was heavily shadowed, the television still the only light source in the room. "You're here to bother Gellica, aren't you? You came into her home in the cover of night, uninvited. I wonder why that is."

She was completely relaxed.

"Is that what you were pondering?" I said. "While sitting alone in the dark? Is this a normal way for you to spend an evening? Drinks and a movie in someone else's house?"

"What else would I be up to? Surely you know I'm not out doing despicable things to Squibs in hotel rooms."

"Yet somehow it always seems that you're at the heart of things. You and Harlan Cedrow."

"I'm at the heart of things because I'm at the heart of the negotiations." She tapped a crimson-coated nail on the edge of her glass and let out an exaggerated sigh. "You know, the tragedy is that all I really wanted was for you to do your job. Arrest someone for killing the Squib and let the talks resume. I even tried to hand you the blackmailing candies gift-wrapped with a bow, but you insisted on running off on that idiotic chase after your old friend Flanagan. Disappointing."

"Guess I was concentrating on the 'upholding justice' part of my job."

She sniffed. "Short-sighted."

"I prefer 'focused.'"

"Hmm." She tilted her head. "I suppose you're going to ask me some dramatic question?"

"No," I said.

"Really? You're not going to ask me who killed Garson Haberdine?"

I was silent, giving her plenty of room to talk.

"I have no idea," she said. "And I'd like to keep it that way. I mean, I hear that it was some junkie teenager, but obviously he wasn't the one behind it all." She brought the tumbler to her lips, but paused before drinking. "I don't care who it was. My only concern is that the talks resume. I'd think you'd see the wisdom there. Peace and prosperity and all that."

"His name was Jermaine Bell. The junkie teenager."

"If you say so." She took a swig of her whiskey, grimaced, then gave it an appraising eye. "That's quite good. Bowery blend." She glanced at the remaining glass on the table. "You don't want any?"

"I'm somewhat off gift liquors at the moment," I said.

"That's right." She frowned. "Your incident. And it turns out that poor girl was almost killed instead of you. Of course, I hear she's been arrested. I'm sure it'll be quite the scandal. Bad news for anyone involved with her."

"It wouldn't have happened if Lowell and Cordray hadn't changed their stories. Almost like they were forced to do it."

"The power of a conscience, Detective," she said. "But once someone is punished for Haberdine's death the negotiations can resume. All will be well." She swung her glass, indicating the scope of the darkened city, the oil fields, the entire world beyond the house's walls. "And we can all go on with our lives."

"Really?" I said. "And the protests, the unrest? A single scapegoat and you'll make it go away. Just like that."

"Yes," she said, and slid toward me. "Just like that." She snapped her fingers. "Are you surprised to see that kind of power?" She leaned over the table, getting closer, until I could smell the liquor on her breath and see the flecks of gold in the brown of her eyes. "Real power doesn't play by the rules. Not your rules, not any rules." She waited, as if daring me to contradict her. "Real power *is* the rule."

Another long pause and then, with a smirk, she melted back onto the couch. She smacked her lips as she sipped her whiskey. "Of course, if that Flanagan arrest had stuck, none of this would have come to light. I wonder if you bungled that arrest because you're incompetent . . . or is it because you were distracted by the sincere, pretty Gellica?"

"Gellica." I sneered. "She's a nice tool for you, isn't she? The way you had her pry information out of me. The way you had her deliver your messages—"

"Detective." Paulus's smirk broadened into a grin. "She's an *envoy*. Delivering messages is in her job title."

"But there's more than that. I think I know the story behind the two of you."

"Oh? And what's that?" She stood and stretched, then ran a finger along the top of a nearby lampshade, checking for dust. Rubbing her fingers, she tsked and opened a nearby window. A cool breeze immediately entered the room.

"The reason you brought her back to serve on your staff," I said. "Back to her hometown and the mother she resents. You couldn't stand to let your daughter out from under your thumb, could you?"

She turned from the window with a laugh. "I hope that's not an example of your best deductive logic." Her back was to the television, and the tattooed glyphs on her arms stirred and jumped in the flickering light. "Gellica says she has a mother. I am a woman. Therefore, I'm her mother." Her lips curled down in a disappointed pout. "Really, Detective. Am I the only person in this city with a uterus?"

"Right. It's completely common for bosses to sneak into their employees' homes and sit around in the dark. Though that's more the actions of a jilted lover."

"Now you're even farther afield than before. Gellica is mine. But she's neither daughter nor lover. She's something else entirely. And you . . . " She paused. "You don't need to know what that is." She stepped closer and her anger showed in the crackle of her voice. "You're such an uppity little man, Carter. A low-class shit-kicker who tries to share the stage with his betters. Even Gellica is out of your league, and believe me, that's saying something."

I rubbed the back of my neck. "Could be. I've always run with a bad crowd. Which reminds me." I decided to throw out one more feeler. "What's Harlan's little friend Heidelbrecht got on you? He's awfully confident that you won't move against his boss while he's in town."

"Heidel . . . ?" She stopped moving, though the breeze from the window billowed the curtains, and for a moment it looked like she had wings. "How do you know who he is?"

"I'm a detective. I detected it."

"He's in town." She said it with no inflection. "Where is he?"

I looked at the whiskey, but held off. "Hard for me to say, being the low-class shit-kicker that I am. I wouldn't want to play out of my league."

Her tattoos lit up like neon signs during happy hour, and I knew I'd pushed too far. In the space of a breath the breeze swelled into a gale as it snaked around the room, scattering papers and knocking paintings from the walls. I started to turn, but I was struck by something invisible. It hit me below my left armpit, hard enough to actually throw me from my chair. My leg flew to the side and struck the coffee table and the remaining glass sailed in slow motion, precious amber liquid spilling out as it went. I regretted not taking a taste.

I landed on the carpet and the tumbler landed a few feet away. The thick shag kept it from breaking. I wasn't sure my ribs were so lucky. I tried to stand, but the wind moved so fast it snatched the breath from my lungs even as it kept me pinned facedown to the carpet. Plush fibers tickled my nose as I managed to turn my head enough to see a little of the room. The ambassador's shoes entered my vision as she walked past me. On the edge of my peripheral vision I could see her dress hanging perfectly smooth. Not a single pleat was ruffled by the wind.

Over the rushing din I could hear Paulus's voice. "I don't know what to say." Her tones were velvety, acting the diplomat even as she crowed over me. "But I'm afraid that it seems like we're at something of a loggerhead. Do you know what a loggerhead is, Detective?"

I mumbled something that was meant to insult her family tree, but the words didn't make it past the carpet threads. Paulus's heel dug into the base of my skull. There was no getting out from under her. My limbs were held fast, as though a giant hand locked them in place.

Her voice got softer, more gravelly, yet still cut through the whirl of the wind. "Well," she said, "I suppose it doesn't really matter at this point. Our relationship won't be repaired by a vocabulary lesson, will it?"

Ice cubes clinked against glass as she drained her whiskey. When she spoke again the wheedling was gone. "Let's wrap this up quickly, shall we? Tell me what you know about Heidelbrecht. Did he kill the Squib?" She pressed down harder with her foot. "Did he send you here?" Rage crept into her voice. It felt like my skull was about to crack open with the pressure. "Where is he?"

The sound of a lion's roar echoed through the room. Paintings shook on the walls, or at least it seemed like they did to me. From everywhere at once there was a noise like the final rush of water down a bathtub drain. Immediately the pressure was off my back. Paulus's shoe was still pressed into the back of my head, but I could move again. I twisted, snaking out my hand and grabbing her by the ankle. I turned my head and looked up, just in time to see the punch coming.

She hit me square in the forehead, which is not exactly textbook form, but it got the job done. My bell rung, I let go of her ankle and was rewarded by a kick to my chest, though blessedly without much behind it. She hit me again, then again. Her punches were untrained but vicious, rage-filled blows that wracked me with pain as they landed on my already swollen and bandaged face.

A second roar rumbled the floor and walls. Paulus cursed and stopped her assault. "This better be good," she snarled. With a swift step she strode over me and was gone.

I was immensely grateful. *Nicely roared, whoever you are.*

Another door opened. I struggled to get up, but failed. A figure hustled toward me, but from my position on the carpet the face wasn't clear in the television's glare. I blinked. Taking a second beating in as many days made it hard to focus my eyes, but my rescuer was dressed in a black so deep and uniform that it seemed the very fabric of darkness had come to life. I was pulled to my feet, but my legs buckled. The deep bone pain and reopened wounds combined to swirl my senses and cloud my mind. I thought I was going down into the carpet a second time. Then a shoulder propped under my arm and held me steady, bearing my weight as I was helped from the room. My head lolled to the side, and I inhaled a breath of expensive perfume undercut by something else, something feral and musky. It was a primal scent, like the big cats' section of the zoo.

We left the house by the front door. I reached for the entry vent, but the warmth of the god beneath the Mount was far beyond my reach.

My savior helped me down a few houses, then tucked me into a recessed doorway. I caught a fleeting glimpse of a dark figure retreating back toward Gellica's home. My rescuer seemed more one of the living shadows that Guyer had spoken of than a real person. Was it Gellica? Had she been there the whole time? And if so, had she trapped me, or was it her who helped set me free?

Head spinning, body aching, I pushed forward. Beaten and dazed, I oriented myself using the pull I felt for the Mount. I didn't tell myself I was imagining it, just abandoned myself to its truth. I stumbled back toward the car, leaning on buildings and street signs for support as I went. The smart move would be to go home, then consult with the folks at the Bunker in the morning. But I've never shied away from pressing my luck.

Judging from Paulus's reaction, I needed to see what our local mad scientist had to say for himself. And I needed to get there before Paulus got her hands on him.

33

I SAT OUTSIDE THE UNREMARKABLE building that housed Heidelbrecht's lab and stared it down. It seemed the good doctor was relocating. The gate stood ajar, a cargo van parked halfway through the opening. The van's rear hatch stood open, and the grounds around it were staged with metal filing cabinets and cardboard boxes. Trash and loose papers stuck on the inside of the fence, as if the packing were happening so fast that speed had trumped precision. All in all, it looked considerably worse than the last time I'd seen it.

Of course, I was in no condition to criticize. I'd glimpsed my reflection when I'd gotten in the car and it wasn't pretty. Dark circles under swollen eyes, blood-caked bandages where Paulus's blows had torn open barely closed wounds from my last visit to this lab. If I saw myself from a distance, I'd probably arrest me just on principle. I suppose I should have changed the dressings on my wounds. Instead, I angled the Hasam's rearview mirror so I wouldn't have to look at myself.

My pager buzzed. Code 25: Report in to Dispatch.

I figured Bryyh wanted to make my advisory role even less active, now that Talena was under arrest. I dropped the pager on the passenger seat. Better if I didn't know.

On the seat beside the pager was a pad of paper missing its top sheet. Time was short, but I had run a quick errand before returning to Heidelbrecht's lab. I'd dropped a letter in the mail, addressed to Ajax and containing nothing but his name and a short message. *Thanks for recommending that Dinah McIntire track,* it said. *I'll let you borrow the new Daizey Chainz album sometime.* Back in my apartment that album was on my turntable, and the cardboard jacket sat on the shelf, holding a file with everything I'd learned from Flanagan, Paulus, and more. If something happened to me, at least the kid would have a shot at unraveling the mess and saving Talena. Not that it was likely. But when the deck's so heavily stacked against you, sometimes your only choice is to go all in.

Sudden motion at the lab caught my attention. The front door swung open and a man emerged, with a face as bruised as my own. My old friend Knuckles was carrying boxes of files to the van in the driveway. I killed the engine on the Hasam and strolled up to the open gate. Sliding along the side of the van I glanced around cargo doors. Knuckles had gone back inside, closing the front door behind him.

I slipped my suit coat off and held it ready while I scooped a fist-size rock from the debris along the fence.

When Knuckles reemerged, I threw my coat in his face, blinding him just long enough for me to follow-through with the rock. He dropped quietly. I retrieved my jacket and his revolver. Things go so much easier when they don't see you coming.

Popping the front door open, I peered down the hospital-clean corridors. I couldn't see anyone, but I could certainly hear activity. The dogs in the lab were going berserk, and the barking echoed off the hard surfaces of the floors and walls, providing a repetitive, chanting refrain as I dragged Knuckles in by his ankles and dumped him through the first unlocked doorway I could find. I figured I'd whacked him hard enough that he wouldn't be a problem for the short time I'd be in that nightmare factory.

I took a deep breath. The scent of cinnamon was in the air. I headed toward the lab with my gun drawn.

Passing through stainless steel entry doors, I found the lab in disarray. Broken beakers and test tubes were scattered over the floor, and every step I took crackled with the crunch of broken glass. But even that was barely audible over the barking that had gone on nonstop since I'd entered the building.

The dogs were frenzied. Or rather dog, singular. One brindle mutt had been freed of his plastic muzzle and torn his defenseless cage mates to shreds. An aerosol canister lay in the far end of the cage, its top gone. It looked like it'd been bashed into something before coming loose. The dog pressed himself against the chain-link of the kennel, long strings of drool lolling from his mouth, his entire body convulsing with the force of his barks. I looked in his eyes and only madness stared back.

Motion to my left caught my attention. Heidelbrecht was on the other side of the kennel, close to the entry gate. He held a brief-case in one hand and, ludicrously, a goldfish bowl in the other. The gap-mouthed fish peeked out at me from behind a tiny plastic castle. For a second, we simply stared. Then Heidelbrecht slammed the briefcase and fishbowl on a nearby table, and dove for the kennel gate. He pulled and it swung outward, providing him a minimal amount of protection against the mad dog. But it was enough.

The dog ignored Heidelbrecht and sprinted toward me, hoarse barks and slobber preceding its charge. I carried two guns but I didn't fire. I can't explain why, other than to say that it wasn't the dog's fault that he was there, and maybe I remembered the frightened, hopeful looks in their eyes the first time I'd seen them.

I grabbed a high-backed stool and held it in front of me, legs pointed at the dog like a lion tamer. The dog kept coming, trying to get past the confusing array of stool legs. I backed up slowly, keeping a lab table to my back, looking for a way to contain him.

A low voice spat out an obscenity, and I risked a sideways glance to the doors. Knuckles walked in, wobbling on his feet. He'd recovered faster than I expected. The dog snarled and abandoned me for this easier prey. It intercepted Knuckles with a leap, slamming into his chest and taking them both to the ground. The barking ceased, only to be replaced by the sound of tearing cloth and flesh, then Knuckles's screams echoed off the hard surfaces of the lab walls and floor, one more victim in that building which had heard so much suffering.

I let the stool fall to the floor and looked for Heidelbrecht.

The table where the mad doctor had set the case and the fish was now bare, except for a ring of liquid where water had sloshed over the side of the fishbowl. Beyond was the door to a small office attached to the lab. I ran in, pushing the door open with my shoulder. There I found Heidelbrecht cramming the briefcase with file folders, the goldfish bowl perched on the table beside him.

He looked up and saw me, eyes wide and panicked over the artificially calm lower half of his face. Despite that, he never stopped packing. I took a slow step forward, closing the door behind me.

"So," he said. "You're the man who was here two days ago. Correct?"

"No." I showed him the barrel of my .38. "I'm the man who's here today. Put your hands where I can see them."

Heidelbrecht complied, raising his hands in the air. He sat behind a box-shaped metal desk with no pictures or mementos. The whole office had been decorated to favor record-keeping over comfort. One of the few windows in the lab was behind him, letting in light but not allowing for much in the way of scenery.

"I don't believe it's a good idea to stay here." His eyes bore into me, intense and impassioned above a mouth as rigid as a Mollenkampi's jaws. "It's not entirely safe."

"What's the matter?" I said. "You think Harlan Cedrow might not show up and rescue you?"

"He and I have parted ways."

"Divorce rates these days are shocking."

The doctor's head tilted and he stared at me, unblinking.

"I know you," he said. "After poor Flanagan was arrested you were in the papers. Harlan asked me to pull any file involving you." He let out a burst of laughter, and his voice stepped up a half octave. "It took some searching," he said. "But we turned it up."

Heidelbrecht leaned back slightly. I tensed, but he seemed to be enjoying his revelations.

"You had a profile in the Care Center files, but it was tied to another patient. Janet . . . no, no. Jennifer. Jennifer Michaels!"

I didn't respond, but he seemed to like what he saw in my eyes. "Practically your whole life story in there," he said. "Information is a very powerful thing."

"Information is exactly why I'm here," I said. "What are you doing in this place?"

"I think it would be unwise to discuss that with you."

"Wouldn't be wise to keep your mouth shut, either."

"Now, now. Let's not indulge in idle threats." He lowered his hands slightly, in what I suppose he thought was an attempt to be calming. "I can hardly be killed while under arrest."

"Who's under arrest? We're just two private citizens having a conversation. And if you were to turn up dead, it'd be with your bodyguard's bullet in your head." I pulled Knuckles's weapon out of my jacket pocket.

The maniac scientist sat back, apparently unsure if I was serious or not. That made two of us.

"We were trying to save your city," he said.

I thought of the slathering dog outside, and the destroyed lives of Jermaine Bell-Asandro and his family. I thought of Garson Haberdine's remains scattered over a hotel room, and of Talena handcuffed to her hospital bed. I had to fight to keep my finger light on the trigger.

"Talk," I said. "Explain it to me."

"May I?" He looked at his hands, still raised between us. I nodded.

"Put them flat on the table, directly in front of you. Don't move them."

He lowered his hands, and began his tale.

"Technically I am a consultant to the Cedrow Care Center's research department. But as you can see"—his eyebrows danced as he looked left and right—"I operate rather independently. A specialist of the highest order," he said, "I was brought in to rectify the cowardly and ineffectual measures of the CCC before me. Small people with small ambitions."

"Wait," I said, forcing my voice to stay level. "The Care Centers. Harlan was using them as what—a petri dish?"

"In a way," he answered. "Terminal cases are excellent subjects for controversial methodologies. Because if something goes wrong . . ." He shrugged. "But as I said, the Care Centers were run by amateurs using pale imitations of my techniques. They had no hope of finding what Harlan wanted."

I tried to stay focused, not letting myself dwell on the implications. I had to get as much information as I could.

"And what was it that Harlan wanted?" I asked.

"Oil."

"Bullshit." I kept my aim steady. "There's no more oil to find. What did he really want with you?"

He snorted. "Cedrow believes he's the savior of your city. Wants to preserve Titanshade, to keep it the center of the world petroleum market. He hired me because his work at the Care Centers failed, and he needed my expertise. You see, I am the world's leading authority on manna-based biological modifications." He paused, as if I would be impressed. When I didn't respond, he sighed and continued.

"In any case, it was these techniques that confirmed the presence of oil on his property. A reservoir large enough to keep the heart of the town pumping. He was delighted, of course. The oil that saved the city would also save his company, prolong his family's reputation, blah, blah, blah." He lifted a hand, opening and closing it like a talkative puppet mouth.

"On the table," I corrected, reminding him who had the gun. He dropped his hand, and I continued, "I still don't buy it. The wind farms will bring him so much money—"

"It's about his family name, and this town of fools. The deal was being forced on him by the AFS. He had a choice—sell his properties or Rediron would be shuttered. And most of his buyout would be in the new wind farm company stock. All of that will be worthless once he produces the oil."

"There is no more oil!" I snapped. "Geologists have been searching for years—"

"Not with my techniques. The methods I pioneered have succeeded where all others failed." Heidelbrecht reached up to stroke the nonexistent ends of his painted-on mustache. "Untapped reserves that lie beneath the ice. Far deeper than anyone has looked before."

I shook my gun side to side in a "no" motion, and he dropped his hands with a roll of the eyes and a sigh, a curiously whispering sound as it crossed his motionless lips.

"Harlan was delighted with the results," he said. "Even more so when we found it on the oil field most dear to his heart."

"Then why the Hells isn't he already drilling?" I asked.

"Of course he's drilling! It takes time to drill that deep, to locate reserves and set up a well. You see why he had to stop the Squibs, don't you?" The doctor pressed down on the tabletop, leaning into his story. "They were buying up all the smaller reserves. It was merely a matter of time before they got to the one that housed the oil. And then they would build windmills on it. Such delicious perversity! Like spinning tombstones on the hopes of Titanshade."

He pronounced it oddly, breaking the stress to make it sound like *Titan's hade*. Everything about this man put me in mind of hade, the trickling sound of hidden snowmelt. The superstitious might hear in it the voice of a lost spirit, but more practical minds knew it for what it was: A sign that their surroundings were more treacherous than the surface would indicate.

"So Harlan needed more time," I said, "to slow down the deal."

"Precisely! He needed a distraction."

"Something to push the negotiations back," I said. "Something that might even turn public opinion against the Squib deal." I eyed the doctor. "And I'll bet you had a suggestion for what to do."

"It was a perfect opportunity!" His eyebrows shot upward, reaching for the sky even as the lower half of his faced showed no movement at all. "A scandal would work wonders for our time line."

"And a dead Squib would be a scandal?"

"A dead negotiator with connections to prostitution, who was murdered in a most dramatic fashion?" His tone grew smug. "Well, you saw the papers. Harlan's man Flanagan found a member of the

Squib delegation who was prone to exposure, and made the arrangements. Harlan took it from there."

"This had nothing to do with Haberdine taking core samples on the oil fields?"

"Was he?" Heidelbrecht mused on the idea. "It would hardly matter. The reserves discovered by my techniques are far deeper than any core sample would detect." He rolled his eyes. "Besides, I had much more pressing matters to attend to. Core samples," he huffed. "Really."

"But you didn't just kill Haberdine," I said. "You tore him to pieces. That couldn't have been just for show."

"Quite correct. Our primary test subject was a local boy—"

"Jermaine," I said. It seemed like I was always reminding people that the dead had names.

"Yes," said Heidelbrecht. "We transitioned him from acting as a dowsing rod to acting as a—"

"Wait," I interrupted. I remembered Nina Bell talking about her nephew being used as a guinea pig: *A scar-faced doctor injected him with rainbows.* "Jermaine was how you found the oil?"

Heidelbrecht nodded, talking over me. Once he got going, he couldn't hold back the pride he took in his work.

"The subject functioned perfectly. Infused with a manna/petroleum mix in his system, he acted as the needle of a compass. But instead of being drawn due north, he was pulled toward the hidden stores of oil far beneath all predicted reserves."

My skin prickled as I pictured a teenage boy with manna in his veins stumbling across the ice fields, hovering over reserves of liquid treasure far, far beneath his feet, drawn to it inexorably.

"I'm simplifying the procedure, of course." Heidelbrecht tottered back and forth in a fit of self-congratulation. "As I said, I'm the greatest mind in the bio-manna field. You couldn't keep up if I gave you the full explanation." He froze, as if regretting his words, and eyed my gun. "No offense intended."

He needn't have worried. I had too much on my mind to be concerned about an insult from a sociopath with a PhD. I tried to remember all the times I'd imagined the pull of Jenny's bones on my own. Was that real? Was there some remnant of her on the Mount, pulling me toward her? Had the treatment that gave Jenny such solace been a dry run for Jermaine's suffering? I felt my anger rise and forced myself to think of something else. I focused on the man in front of me.

"You didn't answer my question," I said. "Tearing Haberdine apart. That wasn't just to delay the talks."

"Correct. The attack on the Squib diplomat brought the added bonus of providing additional raw materials for our study."

Raw materials. Jermaine would have left the murder scene covered in . . .

"Blood," I said.

"Viscera!" Heidelbrecht's voice brightened. "There was some improvisation involving a barrel of liquid, and it had the side effect of preserving most of the residue. Tremendously useful. We removed the subject from the brine—"

"Which is when he escaped."

That was why Jermaine's clothes were wet when he showed up at his aunt's house. He'd been smuggled out of the Eagle Crest in Haberdine's half-empty barrel of romantic brine to avoid leaving a bloody trail. His clothes had still been wet and stunk of the stuff when he turned up at his aunt's looking for help.

Heidelbrecht seemed uncomfortable. "We didn't anticipate his ability to get loose while he was still under the influence of the inhalant. It was unfortunate and unprofessional.

"You must understand, searching for material buried at such

depths required the procedure to be very"—he hesitated, his stubby tongue darting out to wet motionless lips—"aggressive. We had to use a level of manna that might be considered unusual. Combined with effects of the Squib smell there were unintended alterations to the subject's temperament."

Alterations like inducing homicidal frenzy and a paranoia so powerful that he killed his own family.

"You used him up," I said.

"We made a sacrifice for the common good."

"You used him up for the common good." Keeping my gun pointed at him, I asked, "Why the aerosol canisters?"

"They were my fee. As I said, cost is my major limitation. In exchange for helping Mr. Cedrow find his oil, I was able to synthesize the particular qualities of the Squib pheromone, and will be able to place it up for auction. However . . ." He pointed at the boxes and packing materials. "Since your last visit, our operation has been shut down. Apparently Ambassador Paulus learned of my presence here and I'm afraid that I'm at risk of—"

I waggled the revolver, keeping his attention focused.

"The canisters," I said. "Where are they now?"

His shoulders fell. "Harlan took them. I don't know where he went or why he wants them, so don't bother asking. But they're tremendously valuable."

If Harlan was getting increasingly desperate, I could only imagine what he wanted the canisters for. "And the Therreau? Putting your product in their carts?"

"Testing, of course. Harlan Cedrow's deep connection with the local religious zealots was very useful. I was able to perform a series of A/B tests for effectiveness before proceeding with pressurization into the canisters. The Therreau move about the city almost unnoticed. The most dangerous things are often invisible."

He waggled his eyebrows. "And as the enhanced protests created even more of a disturbance, Mr. Cedrow was happy to fund the process."

There was a twitch of movement over Heidelbrecht's shoulder. Framed in the window behind him, a dark figure appeared then faded back into the shadows.

I gave Heidelbrecht a simple, "Don't move," and ran back into the lab. I pushed myself flat against the wall beside one of the larger windows, giving me a wider view of the yard. Black-garbed men and women hustling from shadow to shadow, the distinctive markings of an SRT squad just visible if you knew where to look. On the far edge of the property I saw a Mollenkampi I knew well. Angus was barking orders into a walkie-talkie.

A crash from inside the lab brought me around again. Heidelbrecht stood outside his office door, foot still raised from kicking over a barrel. Liquid gushed out of the barrel as it rolled across the lab. With each revolution it revealed the stylized orange and black flames of its warning label: Flammable.

I raised my weapon, but hesitated to fire when there could be armed cops with twitchy fingers outside the windows. The good doctor struck a match and dropped it in the liquid. Flames danced across the spreading pool and leapt up to the barrel. Heidelbrecht ran back into his office.

He called out, "Time to fly, Fritz!" and slammed the door shut.

34

I REACHED THE OFFICE DOOR a second behind him. The handle wouldn't turn. Locked. I put my shoulder into it, but it didn't give. My face was beside the paperback novel–sized window that looked into the office. Heidelbrecht's scarred face appeared behind the glass, inches away from mine. Our eyes locked, then the pane went black. I kicked the door once, twice. On the third kick it flew inward, and I stormed inside.

He was gone, files and goldfish along with him, as if he'd never been there at all. I didn't know how he'd done it, but he'd left me standing alone with all the evidence of Harlan Cedrow's insanity, about to be discovered by cops who may or may not be on the take, and may or may not be gunning for me. And that wasn't even my most immediate problem.

The barrel of flammable liquid was still unloading its contents, shooting out a geyser of flame as it rolled about the room, setting everything near it ablaze. Waves of heat buffeted across the room, and a gray haze was quickly collecting across the ceiling of the lab. There was a fire extinguisher at each end of the lab, and I could easily reach one, put out the flames before they grew out of control. But I didn't move.

The SRT squad circled the building, and any of those cops could be the ones feeding information to Paulus. If they found me there, my career would end quickly and loudly. The only thing that would make it worse would be a corpse on site.

Which is when I remembered Knuckles.

Farther back in the lab, the corpse of the hulking guard was in the same shape as the dogs in the kennel. The surviving dog was on the floor, worse for the wear after its tangle with Knuckles. It looked like he had two broken legs but he kept pulling himself forward, leaving a smeared trail of blood behind him as he crawled away from the flames. His jaws snapped open and shut, his tongue lolled out of the side of his ruined muzzle. The tongue itself was half chewed off, as if it had gotten in the way of the dog's assault.

I couldn't leave him to the fire, but I couldn't risk a gunshot from my own weapon, not with the SRT about to overrun the place. I holstered my revolver and reached for the cylindrical red fire extinguisher on the wall. Walking up to the dog, I approached him from behind and used the heavy metal extinguisher to put the poor thing out of his misery. Then I dropped the extinguisher on the floor and walked past the flaming barrel, leaving it untouched as I prepared for the onrush of my fellow officers.

When the kick came to the front door, I stayed in the storage room. I needed a little bit of luck, and for the first time in a while I got a break. As the first wave moved down the hallway, I used the connecting storage room to stay put, letting them sweep past me. That was when I got lucky; the smoke alarms chose that moment to kick in and trigger the sprinklers.

Everyone in the lab area was suddenly sprayed down with water, throwing the search into chaos. The fleeting moment of confusion gave me an opportunity to slip out of the storeroom and into the deserted hallway. As quietly as possible I slipped through the doorway. Right into the path of a detective doing a follow-up sweep.

A voice barked out a harsh, "On the ground!"

Hands on head, I went to my knees. "Police!" I said. "I'm a cop!"

I risked a peek over my shoulder. I recognized the Mollenkampi who had a bead on me. My luck held out. It was Ajax.

He dropped from his firing stance. "Carter? What are . . ."

"Long story," I said. "I'm going to stand up, don't shoot me."

"I had Dispatch page you. You never responded."

I remembered the page that came in as I'd sat outside the building. I ground my teeth in frustration.

Calls came from the direction of the lab. The SRT team would be falling back any moment to guard the perimeter while the fire department was called in. The flames must have been spreading because the sprinklers overhead kicked in as well, spraying us with pressurized water.

Ajax grabbed my arm and pulled me back the way he'd come. "Why the Hells are you here?" Water soaked us as we spoke, covering our heads and trailing down our faces. A trickle seeped in through the corner of my mouth; it tasted of rust.

I ignored the question. "What triggered this raid?"

"I didn't ask. Kravitz roused everyone and said we were hitting this place. We're serving a warrant for some ugly mug with a scarred face. He said it falls under the Squib killing, but I'll be damned if I know how."

We exited the building, almost tripping over SRT members as they fell back. No one noticed me in the confusion.

"Kravitz," I said. "Then he's the one."

"The one what?"

My head throbbed. I massaged my temples as I walked, remembering Kravitz's tics and beard-pulling. Were they the signs of a detective chafing under a high-profile case, or indicators of a cop buckling under the pressure of an external agent?

"He's been reporting to Paulus," I said. "She's behind this."

"Behind what?"

"She's got some history with the turkey doctor working for Harlan. I saw her tonight, too." I avoided his eye. "Not on purpose—it doesn't matter anyway. She's not working with Harlan. She said she only wants to resurrect the talks."

"You believe her?"

I nodded. "Mostly. She's chasing power, and the wind farm deal helps her."

We reached the perimeter of the lot. He looked at me. "Who set that fire?"

"The guy you were sent to find," I said. I didn't say that I'd chosen to let it burn. Ajax gave me a long look, eyes narrowed over his emotionless, oversized jaws. His right mandible twitched, then he looked away.

"Get out of here," he said. I started to argue and he cut me off. "We can't let anyone see you who knows you weren't with us when we left the Bunker. I'll meet you at your apartment."

I still hesitated and he gave me a shove. "Go!"

I broke away, rolled under the loose section of fencing, and was gone into the night. I knew I'd just stolen something from Ajax, but whether it was his pride, his faith, or his friendship, I couldn't say.

Back in the Hasam, I collapsed in my seat and took inventory of what I had going for me. It didn't take long to build the list. All the evidence in the lab was going up in smoke. I'd trashed our best shot at getting a clean conviction because I'd gone in too fast and hot. I'd put other cops at risk, and I'd let Ajax risk his own skin to save mine.

There was one other thing I knew: I couldn't stop. Not now.

Harlan was going down. His pet psychopath Heidelbrecht was going down. Gellica and Paulus and any other official bought and paid for by Rediron funds—they were going down as well. I'd burn the whole damn city if that's what it was going to take.

The howl of a siren echoed down the street and a fire truck whipped by, its lights painting the buildings red and white in turn. As it lit up the interior of the Hasam, I turned the key in the ignition and headed in the opposite direction.

35

IN MY APARTMENT THE NIGHT was blessedly silent. For a moment I could breathe, and pretend that the noose wasn't tightening around my neck. That illusion, and the silence, was shattered by a knock on my apartment door. I walked over gently, avoiding the two spots where I knew the floor squeaked, and put my eye to the peephole, expecting to see Ajax.

Instead, I saw Gellica.

The fisheye lens of the peephole distended her face, pulling her nose and mouth forward like a wolf's muzzle. My conversation with Heidelbrecht had convinced me that it had been Harlan who was behind Talena's poisoning, but the oilman had known exactly what buttons to push in order to convince me to take the flask. Gellica still had to answer for that, and for the subsequent persecution of Talena. I opened the door.

I said, "I wasn't aware that you knew where I lived."

"You're in the phone book," she said. Her arms were tightly crossed. The thin fabric of her linen suit wasn't adequate warmth this far from the Mount. "Are you going to let me in? It's cold out here."

I stepped aside and let her walk into the apartment. I closed the door and flipped the deadbolt home before following a few paces behind.

"Pretty ballsy move, coming over here alone," I said. "After what you did to me."

Gellica stopped in the middle of my living room, between the stereo system and threadbare couch. She half turned, looking at me over her shoulder, the white of her suit set off by the purple silk of her neck scarf.

"And you're pretty cocky for a guy who got beaten half to death in my house," she said. "You're heavier than you look, by the way."

The shadow figure had been Gellica. She'd drawn away Paulus and carried me to safety. I leaned against the wall near my stacked milk crates filled with vinyl records and newer 8-track tapes.

Eyes closed, she shook her head. "You have no idea what that's going to cost me."

Anger swelled in my chest.

"You have any idea what your scheming and controlling boss is costing me?" My voice cracked, and I tried again. "Someone almost died because of it. Someone with absolutely no connection to you or your boss. I certainly would've died if Harlan Cedrow had his way."

"I know." Her hands clasped together. "And I'm sorry. But I had nothing to do with it."

"You're telling me that when I came to your office with that flask—"

"It was just a flask you left behind. I didn't think twice about it."

I'd never really believed she'd done anything to the flask. It just didn't seem her style. Betrayal, though. That was a real possibility.

"You asked what rig my old man worked on. Why?"

Her eyes were on the ground and she idly kicked at one of Rumple's toys. "Because I wanted to know," she said.

I squinted, as if I could see the truth if I only looked hard enough. Heidelbrecht had pulled Jenny's file and practically gotten my entire life story. Maybe he hadn't needed Gellica's help. I threw another accusation at her.

"You've got someone inside the Bunker," I said, and waited for the denial.

"Of course we do. Information is the currency we deal in. There's not a politician—or a cop—in this town who doesn't have insiders and informants on their payroll. And no one has more information than the ambassador."

"Paulus." I spit the name like a curse, and Gellica let it sit in the air between us. A car drove past, slats of light spilled through the blinds, playing across our faces. For an instant we were painted in strips of black and white, no areas of gray. So unlike the real world. Then it was gone.

"I asked her if she was your mother," I said.

Gellica turned, eyebrow raised. "And?"

"She denied it."

Gellica looked away, a halfhearted smile tugging at her lips. She wiped her hands across the fabric of her pants as if she were brushing off crumbs, then turned back to me with her eyes open wide.

"That's true as far as it goes. I was created by Paulus, of Paulus, to serve Paulus."

My flesh crawled, though I couldn't say why, and for a moment I longed for the comforting weight of a gun in my hand.

Gellica drew a deep, courage-gathering breath. The kind of breath a lover takes before telling you they've been unfaithful. The kind I used to take before breaking bad news to a victim's loved ones.

"I was made of her flesh," she said. "Nurtured and grown in her home in the Hills. Of a dozen brood mates, I was the only one to survive."

I wasn't sure I'd heard her right.

"Brood mates?"

"When the world was rich in manna, some sorcerers were rumored to have learned how to create a homunculus, a living being crafted from their own flesh and the raw essence of manna. A child of magic."

"Uh-huh." I walked past her, through my living room and into the kitchen. "And you're one of these humonocle things?" I poured myself a water. I didn't offer her one.

"Homunculus," she said. "No, the manna cost to create homunculi is too great, and the skills are long lost in any case. Paulus managed to find someone, a bioengineer with mad ideas—"

"Heidelbrecht." It seemed I couldn't get away from that lunatic. "At the lab, it was like he just . . . evaporated."

"From what I understand, that's a habit of his." She said it with a hollow laugh.

I took a drink of water. "Oh?"

"Heidelbrecht created a new procedure incorporating manna and somatic cell nuclear transfer. And that technique created me. I'm a takwin. Part clone, part homunculus." She lifted her chin, and a touch of irony crept into her voice. "I am the highest blend of science and sorcery."

"So Paulus *is* your mother."

"No. She is me. An earlier version of me. I am her directly, with no interference from a father. All my chromosomes, all my genes are from her. Shaped and powered by sorcery. I am a blend of Paulus and the raw essence of manna."

"The raw essence of manna?"

She gave a solemn nod. "Yes."

I wiped a hand across my mouth. "That's the stupidest thing I've ever heard."

Gellica blinked. Her mouth worked soundlessly for a moment before she managed to get out, "Excuse me?"

"You expect me to believe that magic is your daddy?"

She stared.

"Oh, come on," I said, anger creeping into my voice. "You grow up and your mother tells you that you never met your dad because she made you with forbidden magic, and you believe her? Your father is some middle manager, a one-night stand Paulus regrets." I set the water down and pointed at her. "You're not the 'blend of science and sorcery,' you're the result of blending too much vodka in the punch at the annual office party."

Gellica was silent a moment longer, then reached over to the table lamp that sat beside my couch. She tilted the lampshade, causing her shadow to jump up the wall. She took several short breaths, enough of them that I worried she was hyperventilating. I stepped forward, but stopped as the color began to drain out of her. I don't mean she got pale, I mean that her entire figure, body and clothes, turned gray, then progressively darker, like someone cranking the color adjustment on a television set. While she faded to a shadow, her shadow grew more vibrant, and flexed. It was no longer matching her movements.

The former shadow hunched over, then stretched out across the wall. Its mouth opened. But instead of stopping where a normal jaw would stop, the shadow jaw continued to drop impossibly low. The shadow's jaw fell to the middle of its chest, widening and revealing a mouthful of shadow teeth. The shadow was now the same shade of gray as Gellica herself, then it was paler, moving toward white. The dark shape that had been Gellica crossed its arms while the white shadow on the wall dropped to all fours. And then it *roared*.

A great gust of hot wind shot past my face, smelling of rank meat and leaving me stunned and speechless. From the apartments around mine I could hear muffled yells. I stood, stunned, as she and her shadow reversed the process. Her suit brightened back to white, and Gellica regained her normal chestnut brown complexion.

She twisted a lip. "You were saying?"

"A homunculus, huh?"

"A takwin," she corrected.

We sat side by side on the fire escape outside my apartment, legs dangling over the edge, staring out over the city as it hustled below us. Drivers laid on their horns and swore at one another as jaywalkers darted across slowed traffic like minnows passing a pack of sharks. I'd loaned her a spare coat to hold off the chill of the air.

"But"—I shook my head—"how is that even possible? Even when the world was filled with manna, stuff like that didn't happen. You're talking fairy tales."

Gellica looked at me, the glare of streetlights reflected in her eyes.

"Do you remember the first time you heard about the Titan? When you were taught to say thanks every time you walked outside?"

"No," I said. "I suppose I was too young to remember."

"You were told the kids' version, I'm sure. The one that gets recited by parents while putting up Titan's Day decorations." She sighed. It was a soft, wistful noise set against the sounds of the city night. "That version's nice. All about the gift of heat that allows the city to exist in the middle of the ice desert. You don't hear about the blood and suffering that comes with sacrifice until later."

"Maybe kids should have a grace period before they need to deal with reality."

She held a rail in each hand, looking through them like a toddler in a crib.

"My point," she said, "is that sometimes fairy tales are true. And a lot bloodier than you've been led to believe."

I wasn't sure what to say, and finally ended up with, "That's tough."

"That's growing up with Paulus."

I grunted an assent, and asked, "So why are you telling me this? This has got to be a state secret or something."

That got a grim laugh out of her. Even with everything, I still liked it when she smiled.

"No states, just me. And Paulus." She pursed her lips. "I only told you because I need you to believe me right now. All my cards are on the table."

"So you'll level with me?" I asked.

She nodded. "Ask me anything."

"Does Paulus control Harlan?"

"No. Harlan isn't an easy man to control. She had no idea that it was him who killed the Squib diplomat. When we got the news about Haberdine's death she was . . ." She hugged her arms close, chilled by the cool air or the memory of Paulus's reaction. "Furious doesn't cover it. The killing set the entire project back months, if it hasn't already sunk it."

"But once she was presented with the situation . . ."

"She made the best of the hand she was dealt."

"By pointing us to Lowell and Cordray."

"We decided to sacrifice a couple of expendable envoys already marked for disposal. Well worth it, if it meant stabilizing the situation and removing the blackmail threat."

"Threat? How much of a threat could a handful of candies trying to protect themselves be?"

"It wasn't. Not to her. But some of the city's politicians have been getting burned. Find someone to hang for the crime quickly, with salacious details, and you prevent panic and bring the negotiations back online at the same time. Besides, you met Lowell and Cordray. The world's better off with them behind bars, or at least out of our hair."

"But I pursued Flanagan, so you changed the plan."

She nodded. "Lowell and Cordray were instructed to implicate Flanagan. It didn't really matter who we blamed, as long as they were caught and convicted. Like I told you when we first met, all we wanted was for you to make an arrest."

My stomach knotted. I ignored it. "And when that fell through, your plan—"

"Paulus's plan."

"Fine. Paulus's plan was to hang the Squib killing on Talena." I watched Gellica when I said it, and I saw her wince. I hoped that meant she had a conscience, and maybe carried some regrets. "So why the raid on the lab?"

"For Heidelbrecht. Once you told her he was in town, she put out all her feelers. Our man in your department said a detective pulled the file on some muscle, and it mentioned a connection to Heidelbrecht. We had him run with it."

I'd asked Hemingway to pull a report on Knuckles's ID card. When she did, it tipped the location of the lab.

"That man of yours in the department," I said. "Kravitz?"

"Yes."

"He's looked half dead since he took over the Haberdine investigation."

"The ambassador makes a lot of demands." Her eyes drifted to the skyline. "Lots of demands."

"What's she have on him?" I asked. "I doubt it's just greed."

Hemingway hesitated. "I can tell you, but . . ." She rubbed her chin. "Let's say he's in over his head, and now he's trying to protect his family."

I decided not to push it. One set of lost causes at a time.

"Okay," I said. "So when I found your boss was sitting in your house alone—"

"Waiting for me," Gellica said. "She wanted to talk privately, away from the rest of her subordinates."

"So she sat in the dark?"

"She said she was watching a movie when she heard someone come in through a window. She stayed to see who it was. It's not like she can't take care of herself."

When I didn't answer, she shrugged. "Power and wealth can lead to some unusual behavior."

"Well, she did seem obsessed when I mentioned Heidelbrecht's name." I didn't point out that I still had the bruises and aches to prove it.

"He broke some kind of agreement by coming here," she said. "I don't know the details, and I'm smart enough not to ask."

I rubbed my temples. The layers of corruption and betrayal were astonishing, even to someone like me who'd known Titanshade politics my whole life.

"I still don't get why Harlan went to bat for Flanagan," I said.

The metal railing creaked as she leaned back to look at me,

surprise written across her face. "Because Flanagan was innocent. Harlan helps people he thinks need help. It's what the man does. Or did, anyway."

My jaw dropped. "Help people? He's running around with aerosol cans of Squib smell, and I have no idea what he's going to do with them. He's murdered and bullied his way into power—"

She held up a hand. "I can't tell you how his conscience works. But he was born to power. And for most of his life he spent a fair amount of time and money aiding people who he thought were in need. Maybe it's religious, maybe it's psychosis, but it's the way he is."

"So why are you here?"

She took a breath. "To make you an offer. Find Harlan. Stop him, and find someone to hang the Squib killing on. Do that and the evidence against your blackmailing friend will disappear."

My pulse picked up. Finally, I could see a way to pull Talena out of the mess I'd created.

"Paulus will do that?" I spoke carefully. "Last time I saw her she was ready to kill me."

"She's got no choice. There's no one else left. The Bunker's in chaos. The discovery of Heidelbrecht's lab is causing a complete rollout. In the middle of all that, how many of your colleagues are willing to risk their careers to chase down one of the most influential men in the city?"

"Your boss can manipulate everyone in City Hall. She has full control of the police department, the fire department, and anyone else I can name," I said.

Her grip tightened on the rails of the fire escape. "Who are currently trying to lock down an entire city. I can pull some strings and get you a support team, but that's the best we can do."

"Call in the feds," I said.

"You honestly think there's time for that?"

I didn't. There were some drawbacks to sitting at the icy crown of the world, one of which was that you had to take care of your policing on your own.

"Tell her to go herself," I said. "Do it on her own."

"She's powerful," said Gellica. "But she's not a fighter." Her lips pulled down. "She leaves that for others."

"She seemed like a decent fighter when I was pinned facedown to the carpet," I said. "But I take your point."

"Besides, she's got her hands full keeping things together here. You may not like her, but everything she's done has been to keep this situation from blowing up even more."

I didn't have a smart answer. Probably because I knew she was right.

"Paulus is in damage control," she said. "Weaponized Squib blood? It's got to end before more people die. Right now the ambassador's making phone calls. The danger that those canisters pose is being made clear to the brass at the Bunker and in City Hall, without any mention of Harlan himself. Full emergency services will be all over the city."

"He won't be in the city," I said. I remembered Heidelbrecht's insistence that there was more oil to be found beneath Harlan's fields. *The one most dear to his heart.*

"Best guess?" I said. "He'll be at the original Rediron drill site."

"Then that's where you need to go."

I squeezed my legs, first one then the other, trying to find some relief from their continual ache. A fool's errand.

"And if he's holed up with a team of hired guns?" I asked. "How do I bring him in without an army?"

"I don't know. And neither will you until you go there and find out."

My cheek settled against the rough metal of the fire escape.

Past the safety rails the city buzzed and thrummed. I looked down on all the people.

"I wonder how many of them are worth saving," I said.

"I didn't get the impression that you worried about that too often."

"I don't," I said. "But I'm wondering it now."

"Does it matter? Would it change what you're going to do?"

"Not really."

From inside the apartment, I heard another knock on my door. This time it really would be Ajax. I looked at Gellica.

"I'm guessing you'll want to be leaving," I said.

"The fewer people who see me the better." She stood and started to slip out of my overcoat.

"Keep it. I'll either come for it, or it won't matter."

She took a few steps down the fire escape before looking back up at me. "I hope you get through this alive, Carter. I really do."

"That makes two of us," I said, then climbed back inside and opened the door for my partner.

Ajax hadn't gotten more than ten paces into my apartment before a tan and white ball of fuzz streaked toward him from below the dining room table. Rumple jumped onto the back of the couch and nuzzled my partner's hand.

"He's always had despicable taste in people," I said.

"Well, he does live with you."

Ajax rubbed the sensitive spots behind Rumple's ears, getting a low purr in return. It occurred to me that the cat had been nowhere to be found during Gellica's visit.

Jax said, "The raid on that lab turned up—well, I guess you have a pretty good idea of what we found."

I nodded, noncommittal.

"The whole department's mobilizing," he said.

"I kinda had a hunch you'd say that."

There was a metallic clang from outside, like the spring-loaded latch of a fire-escape ladder popping back into place. Ajax's head snapped around. Two long strides took him to the large living room window, the one with the broken blinds that I'd been meaning to fix for the last few years. He pulled the blinds back with two fingers and glanced into the street.

"Probably just a ghost," I said.

He turned away from the window, doing his best to ignore Rumple's continued weaving in and out of his legs.

"Probably," he said. He straightened the lampshade that Gellica had tilted for her transformation.

I pointed at the phone in the kitchen. "You oughta call in and request us a snow-runner from the West Garage. I've got a feeling we're headed for the oil fields."

36

GELLICA MUST HAVE STOOD BY her promise, because we arrived at the Titanshade PD West Garage to find we'd been assigned two snow-runners. A two-seater for me and Jax, and larger transport for the SRT squad. We had a five-person squad as support, and the sergeant in charge was Korintje, a cop well-known for bravery and levelheadedness in tight spots. It had taken some time to get everyone assembled, but by the early morning, we'd gotten the job done. Korintje had sleep in her eyes, and she and her team stifled yawns as we briefed them, but I felt good about going in with an experienced crew.

We were loading up the vehicles with SRT equipment and enough fuel tanks to make it out to the Rediron fields and back, when one of the garage supers came over. He wore an oil-stained blue work shirt with "Roy" sewn in white thread over his left breast.

Ajax and I made our way back to Roy's small office, and found Korintje already on the phone. She was talking quickly, a creeping note of aggravation driving her voice higher as she spoke.

"I don't know," she said. "I got woken up by a call and told to be out here and meet two detectives."

She saw us come in and her mandibles opened and closed. A clear "help me" sign.

"Hold on, hold on. I'm putting you on speaker."

She jabbed the hands-free button on the phone and set the receiver down.

"You there, Cap?"

The voice that answered was not happy, and was no longer talking to Sergeant Korintje.

"Carter and Ajax?" Captain Bryyh's voice boomed over the tinny connection. "What in the Hells are you doing taking one of my best SRT squads out of town? Are you not aware that we're in the middle of a bioterrorist threat?"

"Cap," I said. "That's exactly what we're trying to—"

"What you're doing," she said, "is diverting resources from finding this psycho Heidelbrecht and his insanity gas."

I winced. Paulus had been effective in sounding the alarm, but her desire to keep Harlan's name out of things had been too effective.

"Korintje," Bryyh demanded, "who called you with this crap?"

The sergeant ran a hand over the tortoiseshell-colored plating on her head. "Detective Kravitz."

"At what point did 'detective' start to outrank 'captain'?" said Bryyh. "Because last I checked, my badge says 'captain.' And in addition to lousy hours and an ulcer, having 'captain' on my badge means that I get to tell people what to do. And I'm telling you, Sergeant, to not leave that facility."

Korintje looked to us for help.

Ajax spoke up, talking loud and calm. "Captain, we've got good information that the canisters are located at a Rediron drilling facility—"

"Did you just say Rediron?" If it had been possible, I think Bryyh would have crawled through the phone lines and strangled us. "Carter, did he say Rediron? No, he can't have said Rediron, because I told the two of you to leave the Harlan Cedrow angle alone." She was talking fast, leaving no way to get a word in during her rant. "I have a densely populated city that I need to protect. We are going to secure the safety of our people first, and worry about the ice plains after that."

I scooped up the phone, making my appeal directly into Bryyh's ear.

"I get that. Honestly, I do. But, Cap, I know where the canisters are, I know who has them. Let me go out there and end this." I may have overstated my level of certainty, but something I said must have clicked with Bryyh, because she let me keep talking.

"You wanted me on this case for a reason. You trust me, or at least you did." I didn't review all the reasons I'd given her lately to withdraw that trust. "Let us do this. If we get there and get in trouble, we'll radio back. But everything in me says that this is the right play."

There was a crackling silence while I could hear deep, angry breathing. Then she told me to put her back on speaker.

"Alright," she said. "Carter and Ajax can go on their hunting expedition. Korintje, I need you down in the city. Can you spare one body to go with them? It's your call, Sergeant."

Korintje hesitated. Tactical teams rely on cohesiveness to be effective. She was being asked to give up a lot. After a long moment, she shook her head.

"I can't break off just one person," she said. "It's got to be all or nothing."

And just like that the strike team evaporated. It seemed we were back to my usual streak of bad luck.

When Bryyh disconnected, Korintje stood and let out a low, whistling note of apology. "Sorry," she said. "Maybe you can find another crew to break loose?"

"Will we do?" The voice came from the door to the small office. There, leaning in the doorway and grinning like fools, were Myris and Hemingway.

Ajax stood. "I made some calls," he said to me. "In case anyone else wanted to tag along."

I managed to not embarrass myself by jumping for joy.

"I think we can make that work," I said.

Once we got the snow-runner—we only needed one, now—we headed northwest, onto the ice plains. At first I briefed the others, telling them what they needed to know about the canisters and my fears about Harlan's plans. Even so, I didn't tell them about Gellica's transformations. Maybe I thought they wouldn't believe me. Or maybe some things are too private, even for fellow cops.

We drove for hours, until the buildings of Titanshade receded and only the dark, jagged shape of the Mount remained on the horizon. Away from the city the stars were bright, and the blue and white swirls of the crescent moon were visible until the late morning sun broke the horizon and chased it away. We watched the sky and fell into the uneasy silence that sooner or later overtakes every long drive.

Eventually Myris and Hemingway were snoring in stereo from the backseat. Ajax drove while I did my best to relax and let my body rest. I ran the radio tuner up and down the dial, searching for something worth listening too.

I'd finally managed to get WYOT to come in when Ajax asked, "You really think Harlan Cedrow's holed up here?"

The sunlight reflected off the ice fields as they whipped past, bright even through the heavy tint of my sunglasses. The cold out on the ice plains was a death sentence, and the white/blue glare of the ice an absolute. With no glasses a wanderer on foot would be almost blind, every bit as doomed as someone without proper clothing.

"Yes," I said, before walking it back. "I think so." I looked at him. "We'll find out."

"And there's no chance Paulus is just playing us?"

Ajax kept his eyes on the road. His sunglasses didn't perch properly on his head, a common problem for tiny Mollenkampi ears. To make them fit he'd looped a couple rubber bands between the ear hooks on the glasses, creating an elastic band to keep them in place. He had bent over backward in so many ways since being assigned to babysit me.

"Pretty sure," I said. "When she had me planted face first in the carpet she asked if Heidelbrecht had killed Haberdine. That may have been a play, but I don't think so." It wasn't exactly definitive, but it was the best I could do. A little bit of deduction and prayer that I wasn't about to get us all killed on some wild goose chase.

I spun the tuner again, passing a couple of decent songs to settle on a disco station. Ajax glanced my way in surprise, but I settled back in my seat, content to let the drum machines and synthetic strings wash over me. Jax smiled, and tapped the wheel in time to the beat. The signal grew weaker as we drove, but we let that station play until it dissolved into the hiss and snarl of radio static.

We passed fabricated structures pockmarking the sides of the road like blisters erupting from the skin of a fever patient. We passed ancient pull rigs, designed to be attached to the backs of trucks, brought out on the ice decades ago by fools trying to strike it rich. They were all frozen in place now. The owners had abandoned them or walked off and froze. It wasn't unusual to find corpses from time to time, frozen solid and exposed by a shift in the winds. A solid blow with an ice ax could shatter those bodies just as thoroughly as their long-dead dreams of wealth.

Finally we came closer to the Rediron holdings. Pump jacks moved in the distance, giant hammers swinging against the snow-covered earth, forcing an ever-lessening stream of petroleum out of the earth and into Harlan's coffers. To the west a series of drill derricks stood tall, continuing their search for the oil that Heidelbrecht had promised was there.

We rumbled past in the snow-runner, Myris and Hemingway, Ajax and me. Team Carter all accounted for. We kept driving, not slowing to investigate the newer rigs or stopping to reconsider the wisdom of our quest, until we reached the oldest of the Rediron sites, where generations ago the first transformation of Titanshade had begun.

When we arrived at the compound there was no guard at the gate, but we slowed anyway. The security shack was mostly a formality, as were the roads themselves. A snow-runner could go where it pleased, plowing its way through the loose snow on top of the ice plains. Of course, the driver would have to rely on blind luck that he or she wouldn't encounter any ice-covered crevices, crusty surface giving way as soon as the snow-runner's weight touched it. The real protection out on the ice plains didn't lie with fences and guards, but the naked hostility of the environment itself.

The guard shack here was empty, but orderly. Someone had left their post, but had taken the time to close up properly, even putting a "back soon" sign in the window, a false clock face with blue plastic hands that indicated the guard should have returned hours ago.

The snap of Hemingway's gum broke the silence.

"Does this shack tell us anything we didn't know before?" she said.

"No." Ajax squeezed the steering wheel. "Not really."

"Then let's not sit here staring at it," she said.

We drove on, deeper into the rig camp. The buildings got smaller, the ice thicker on their roofs. The lack of ice on some of the buildings and machinery meant that someone had fired up the thermal wiring. This place wasn't merely a museum piece, it was a functioning drill site.

The service road led to a parking lot, a rough structure to give shelter to any vehicles parked temporarily. Anything staying at the compound for more than a day would be stored inside a heated garage bay. The short-term lot stood empty except for our snow-runner and one other vehicle, an oversized luxury runner that required an ostentatious display of wealth simply to rev the engine. It had oil money written all over its custom interior.

Ajax parked our runner, and the four of us peered at our surroundings. Cops rarely came out this far, and our reception was uncertain. The rigs were far past the boundaries of the city and the jurisdiction of our badges. Anything short of a murder would be dealt with by the crews themselves. And even the homicides we knew of were just that—the ones we knew of.

The compound was made up of a dozen one-story structures, an old-time drilling well to be run by a handful of workers rather than a modern rig that could house a hundred. The buildings were squat things with corrugated steel walls and steep-pitched roofs that had survived decades out in the ice plains. But what was shocking was how well-used it all was. Rediron was still operating this site, as old and as certainly tapped out as it was. If I'd had any doubts about what the mad doctor Heidelbrecht had told me, they evaporated like morning mist. Harlan was searching for the oil that would preserve the city as he knew it.

We were there to stop him.

37

I TURNED IN MY SEAT. Both Myris and Hemingway were peering out the windows as they struggled into their heavy outer coats. Bulky things that constrained movement, there was no surviving on the ice plains without them. Once her coat was on, Myris checked her thick over-mittens. Their pleated fabric had a center flap that allowed gloved fingers to emerge and access her weapon, a compact 9mm submachine gun. Best used in close quarters, it was the standard meat and potatoes of SRT squads. The weapon was on loan from Korintje, who'd said it was the least she could do.

I pointed at it. "You got a light for that thing?"

She looked at me and adjusted her thick sunglasses. In the rig compound there were enough dark shapes that the ice glare was reduced, but for the next hour or so the horizon would still be painful to look at.

"Some of those buildings will be powered and heated, others will be cold storage. And dark," I said. "You'll want a light as we go in and out of them."

"Fair enough." Myris reached up to her vest and pulled out a flashlight. She clipped it to the handrail on her weapon, where it secured with a snap. Whatever she pointed at would be illuminated. Eyes crinkling, she said, "The sergeant sent me out with all the accessories."

Ajax fiddled with the CB, but couldn't raise a signal. He read out our position and intent anyway, half following protocol, half as a prayer.

Hemingway snapped her gum. "So are we going in?"

Ajax answered. "Always scope out the perimeter," he said. "Get your establishing shot. You can learn a lot at a distance. Or so I've been told."

"Keep your hand on your weapons, but keep them out of sight," I said. Our heavy thermal jackets were identical, and it was easy enough to drape a fold of material over our arms. "No need to alarm anyone until they make a play."

We left the runner, and made our way to the garage next to the parking lot. A sturdy structure with bay doors large enough to allow large drilling trucks to enter, it was deserted, though heated and lit. A half-full thermos of coffee sat on a workbench.

We reentered the cold and moved toward the next set of buildings. It was a long, silent walk, marked only by the crunch of snow underfoot. We moved slow and steady, eyes roving, ready to respond to any kind of activity, friendly or otherwise.

The next building was tool storage. Poorly lit and with limited heat, it consisted of two rooms of organized materials, and a repair station.

That's where we found the first body.

A human roughneck hung from the ceiling, a thick chain shoved through his abdomen and twisted back and around to encircle his neck. The few bulbs in the shack left the room mostly in shadow, and Myris's flashlight beam swung across it, revealing and hiding details in turn. The light illuminated the dead man's heavy cold-weather overalls, the oil-stained dirt beneath his nails, the gas mask that obscured his face. My blood chilled as Myris's light swept across the tank on the roughneck's back. I pointed it out to the others.

"You see that?"

Ajax stared at it, then glanced around the perimeter of the room again.

"That's from the lab." I looked out the window. "If Harlan gave it to his whole crew, there could be another dozen madmen running around out there."

Hemingway swore. "You think the whole crew is gassed up?"

I indicated the twisted form of the corpse. "Does that look like self-defense to you?"

Myris swept the room with her light, illuminating the corners to be sure no surprises were waiting for us.

"Okay." Her voice had only the faintest quiver. "So we go back to the car and radio in."

"If we can get a good signal. If we can make it," I said. "If they can break anyone away from the lockdown in the city."

"We need reinforcements," said Ajax. "We can't control a crowd, especially not if they're in some kind of Squib rage."

Through the grime-covered window I saw movement. "Two o'clock," I whispered to the others.

A figure in a breathing apparatus limped between buildings. The roughneck carried an ax and his head swiveled continuously back and forth, a beast tracking his prey. Abruptly he stopped, threw back his head and arms, and bellowed like a gladiator in an arena. His war cry was muffled by the mask, making the sound even less recognizably human. A moment later more shapes appeared around the edges of the other buildings. Some of them shuffled but others bounded, moving in great leaps like oversized rabbits.

Ajax scanned their mounting numbers. "I don't suppose they're going to get their heads straight any time soon."

"Kinda doubt it."

From a distance came the sharp crunch of metal and glass being destroyed.

Hemingway motioned to us. "Stay here," she said, and dashed to the outer room of the toolshed. I followed behind. Peering over her shoulder I could just make out a snow-obscured figure on top of our snow-runner, beating it with what looked like cinder blocks in each hand. As I watched, he struck one of the tracks. A hydraulic line burst with a loud *whuff* and a spray of pressurized fluid.

Jogging back to Ajax and Myris, I broke the bad news that we wouldn't be driving back as planned.

"I count eight of them out there," said Jax. "Plus the one on the car, and that guy." He indicated the man hanging from the ceiling of our small sanctuary. "How many workers do you think they had here?"

"A dozen," I said. "Maybe more. But we should plan on another five or six roaming the grounds. As well as Harlan and his goon."

A scream rent the air. Across the yard two of the maddened roughnecks began to fight. They rolled over one another, clawing and growling. There was a quick movement, and one of them twisted the other's head with an almost inhuman strength. The sound of the neck bones snapping didn't make it through the corrugated steel walls, but I felt it in my gut. In all the stories of Squib smell I'd heard, there'd never been anything quite like this. Whatever Heidelbrecht had done when he'd bottled the Squib smell had also made it more intense.

Ajax shuddered. "This is not good." He looked at me, then at the chain-wrapped corpse. "So if that hose gets loose on that canister . . ."

"It won't," I said.

"Right. But seriously, though. If it does—"

"Then knock me out. You don't need to kill me, just incapacitate me long enough to get me clear of the fumes. A little secondary Squib stink never killed anyone."

Ajax didn't laugh. He and Myris exchanged a look, and he was about to say something else, but Hemingway had rejoined us.

She cursed softly. "Why did they put on the masks?"

"Safety drill?" I said. "Who'd pass up taking a break from work to try out some new equipment?"

Myris adjusted the shoulder strap of her weapon. "Makes sense," she said. "And now that they're on, the workers probably think of them as safety items. They'll wear them until the gas runs dry."

I peered through the window at the men driven mad by Harlan's gas. "Maybe we can wait them out?"

Outside, the whole group of roughnecks crowed with joy as the victor of the fight dragged his victim's entrails across the yard, leaving a crimson gash through the snow. As they bellowed their approval, flames erupted from one of the other buildings.

"Or possibly not," I admitted.

Hemingway pulled her gum out and stuck it on the side of the repair station's workbench.

"Well we're not getting out in the vehicle we came in," she said. "We either need to find another way out or find a more defensible building."

It was hard to argue with that. Ajax stretched his legs, keeping warm in the bitter cold. "Okay. What's the most secure building in this compound?"

"Probably the doghouse," I said.

Myris looked away from the madness outside. "What?"

"It's what they call the operations center. It'll be right about . . .

there." I pointed at a building with only slightly nicer finishes than the rest of the compound. "That's where the supervisors and suits decide what they're going to screw up next."

Jax checked out the building. "Oh, yeah, your upbringing doesn't show at all."

"You said operations center," asked Myris. "Would they have a radio that could reach Titanshade?"

"It should," I said. "The trick is getting to it." I looked at the others. "It's a dangerous walk, but it's our best bet."

Ajax adjusted the hood on his thermal coat and sighed. It was a low warbling note that spoke of determination and acceptance.

"Then let's do it," he said. Myris and Hemingway traded a look, then each nodded their assent.

"That's it?" I asked.

"Yeah," said Hemingway.

"No discussion of the many reasons this is a bad idea?"

"Would it matter?" said Myris.

I shook my head.

Ajax shrugged. "Then let's not waste time on it."

Stepping forward, Myris said, "Alright. I'll take point. You three stay tight to my back. Watch the rear and flanks. We'll skirt around that clump of them and head for this doghouse."

I didn't answer, other than to whisper a curse. The others followed my gaze out the window. Across the yard one of the roughnecks—the one who'd taken to jogging around on all fours— was headed straight for our shelter, face contorted behind the plastic visor of the gas mask. Myris and Hemingway faded into the shadowy corners of the room, while Jax and I pulled away to the sides of the window, each of us pressing our backs to the wall and hoping that the roughneck would lose interest before he reached our shelter.

There was silence for long enough that I let out my breath, then a *thunk* against the wall directly behind me. A pause, then another *thunk*. Something was striking the outside of the building right below my waist.

I glanced at Jax. He was checking his revolver.

Thunk.

I checked my weapon as well.

Thunk.

My partner looked to me. I nodded.

We both stepped back, weapons raised, to face the window. On the other side of the glass what looked like the entire rig crew stared at us, in various levels of damage and insanity. Directly in front was the one with the ax. He stared in at us, and we stared at him. In his left hand he held the head of the man just killed in the square.

Thunk.

The head crashed through the window, and the tide of enraged roughnecks followed. I fired and the ax man jerked, then jerked again as Ajax hit him as well. He dropped as the other crewmen rushed past him, keening and gibbering meaningless noises.

We retreated, keeping distance between us and them. In the storage shed the pistol reports were deafening, and a loud buzz quickly filled my ears, turning down the volume of the screams and gunfire to a low roar.

Hemingway stepped beside me, and Jax backed toward us. Myris's shots came in quick bursts of three, clipping the floor of the shed, where the impacts sent splinters of plywood spraying up into the press of roughnecks. A disciplined, well-trained reaction to subdue a crowd. It would have worked against most mobs, but the roughnecks weren't just any crowd. Each of them was physically imposing, and even without the effects of the canisters they had the kind of strength that comes from a life of hard labor. With the added effects of the Squib canisters not even the fear of death could stop them. They came on, and the warning shots turned to takedowns, striking their feet and legs. The front row pushed onward, numbers behind pressing them forward, chanting nonsense syllables as they swung improvised weapons in the confined space of the toolshed

We fell back, Myris trying her best to lay down suppression fire as the rest of us dropped toward the door. I kept one hand on Myris's shoulder as I retreated, allowing her to back up at a measured rate.

One of the roughnecks almost reached Hemingway on her right, but I squeezed off a round that caught the man in the hip, shattering the bone with an impact that should have dropped him to the floor. But instead of falling, the roughneck pawed at the wound, seemingly more confused than anything. He looked back at me, face twisted behind his plexiglass mask, and shuffled forward, swinging his useless leg alongside him, blind to the pain. He probably would have kept moving forward if he hadn't been clubbed aside by another roughneck, eager for his own chance at our throats.

There were two quick pops behind me. I risked a glance, and saw Ajax firing at two shapes that darkened the doorway. The workers had blocked our retreat.

Myris screamed, and her shoulder jerked in my grip. I spun around to find her fighting off a roughneck who clawed at her with what looked like a fistful of nails, pushing aside her hood and tearing into the plating along her skull. She tried to scramble away, stepping on my feet as her disciplined shots turned wild. Automatic fire sprayed the ceiling, and Myris's flashlight illuminated the dead roughneck hanging from the rafters swaying to and fro as he was struck by errant bullets. Tightening my hold on Myris's shoulder, I stretched to the side and fired into the man attacking her. The roughneck let up for a second, long enough for Myris to push him back and finish him off with a burst into his stomach. She was free, but the right side of her face sported long, bloody gouges from her skull plates to her biting jaws.

She nodded her thanks, and resumed laying down fire. Muzzle flashes lit her profile, and blood glistened as it seeped across her face.

Above us the dead man chained to the ceiling observed the chaos with gouged-out eyes, and I told myself that I'd imagined the metallic pings of bullets hitting his canister, that the smell of cinnamon was all in my head.

Someone bumped into my back. I jumped, loosening my grip on Myris, and found Ajax directly behind me, backing away from the shapes at the door. I tried to provide support in two directions, and failed at both. There was a tug, then Myris's shoulder was no longer under my hand.

Her screams started even before I turned back around. Myris was dragged down and away by multiple hands, each of her limbs stretched in a different direction. One arm twisted, turning and bending unnaturally. When it snapped, the shattered bone created a bulge in the middle of her coat sleeve. She cried out, desperately screaming unrecognizable words. Maybe the names of parents or lovers, or maybe it was only screams of agony. The sound was terrible, until someone got a hand over her throat. Her biting jaws still swung, silently fighting, then suddenly stilled as another roughneck brought a wrench down on her head.

I unloaded my gun into the crowd. I wasn't trying to incapacitate any longer. Fear and rage had eliminated any remnant of discipline. Two more roughnecks dropped. That left three in front of me, and two behind. Cinnamon burned my lungs, and a surge of adrenaline coursed through me. I felt a smile spread across my face.

I pulled a speed loader out of a flap on the side of the heavy jacket, thankful that they were designed to make such actions easier.

A roughneck bore down on me before I could reload. He swung a piece of scrap lumber pulled from a doorframe, twisted nails at its end gleaming in the beam of Myris's flashlight as it bounced crazily across the floor. I dodged the swing, but he caught me with a shoulder. I dropped my speed load.

I shoved the man back, bringing up my other hand in a tight uppercut, using my revolver as a blunt instrument, feeling the impact as it struck his jaw. My broken finger twisted in its splint, but I barely registered the rush of pain that followed. Instead, the taste of cinnamon flooded the back of my mouth, like being force-fed a pastry. My stomach knotted and I hit him again. I kept hitting him long after he stopped moving. Then I turned to the rest of them.

There are moments after that I don't remember. I know I ran forward, I remember the impact as one of the workers ran into me. I know that I walked away from that fight and I suspect the other guy didn't, but I don't know anything more than that.

I do remember the next one, the short guy, built like a fireplug. I remember the arc of his arm as he swung a hatchet up at me. I remember Jax suddenly appearing between him and me, and I remember pushing past even as he crumpled around the impact of the hatchet. I remember watching the worker hit the floor and lie still, and seeing Jax hit the floor while I kept moving. And I remember laughing—*laughing*—at the joy of it all.

I spun, looking for more attackers, but none of them were on their feet.

I turned back, and saw a Mollenkampi sprawled on the floor,

his back against the wall, legs sprawled out in front of him. A human woman lay near him, cradling her head, bloody blond hair sticking to a wound on her temple.

The Mollenkampi looked up at me, gasping, bleeding while he pushed himself between me and the human woman. He fumbled with something in his hand, pushing small cylinders into larger ones. My nostrils flared as I breathed in the scent of his blood. It didn't have the flavor of cinnamon, the irresistible tang of Squib blood, but the sight of him made me rage nonetheless. My hands were trembling, but I wasn't sure why. I flexed my fists and felt something sticky and thick clinging to my knuckles. I knew enough not to look at them.

I took a step toward him.

Another.

He was talking, but I couldn't make out what he was saying.

I realized I knew him.

He was a college kid. He'd stood beside me when he didn't have to, when so many others hadn't. His face was alien, foreign. My teeth ground together and hatred surged inside me, a sensation so strong it felt like it was clogging my throat and racing up the sides of my head.

One more step. My hand was in the air. He was disgusting; he was my friend.

I hesitated, a long moment while I couldn't take my eyes off his exposed throat and the hole there that kept talking, talking, talking . . . It was too much for me to process. I rushed forward. His arm came up but I was already past his prone form, stretching and jumping through the window the roughnecks had shattered.

Outside I hit the ground hard. I pulled to my hands and knees and my stomach clenched, disgorging my most recent meal of coffee and candy bars.

I scooped up clean snow by the handful and wiped it over my mouth, feeling it melt and wash away the vomit. But the sense of horror remained. The scent of cinnamon was gone, and with it the fog in my head began to lift. I was lucky the exposure had been brief. I risked a glance behind me.

Myris was dead, Hemingway badly injured. She and Ajax were down, still in the shed. Jax was so fast, but with his arm injury, he hadn't been fast enough. At least he'd been conscious, and still moving when I left the shed. I didn't know if Hemingway was affected by the Squib smell, but I couldn't risk going back while the broken canister still pumped out gas. My only choice now was to go for help.

I squinted and felt for my sunglasses. I'd lost them in the fight. Luckily the glare wasn't as bad in the compound, where the buildings broke up the vast field of white ice. My revolver was on the ground. I picked it up, emptied my spent shells and reloaded. I had six rounds in the cylinder and another six on the remaining speed loader in my pocket. It'd have to do.

Struggling to my feet, I forced myself to move toward the doghouse.

Thunk.

I turned. On his hands and knees, the roughneck who'd alerted the others to our presence backed up, then threw himself into the storage shed again.

Thunk.

His gas mask was shattered, jagged pieces of plastic visor tearing deeper into his mangled face with each new pounding. One eye was already gone. His teeth were exposed in sections, where he'd chewed away his lips.

Thunk.

His jaws worked up and down as he backed up. I could see the small nub of a tongue in the back of his mouth, the rest gone like the dog's in Heidelbrecht's lab. I wondered if he had a family, a kid at home.

Thunk.

Someone waiting for his return.

Thunk.

Waiting like Jermaine Bell's family had waited for him.

Thunk.

There was a crack and something in my hand kicked backward. I looked down and saw the chill wind tear a wisp of smoke from the barrel of my revolver. The weapon given to me to serve and protect the people of the city. Dully I registered that I only had five shots left in the cylinder.

My stomach clenched again, but there was nothing left for it to reject. So I faced the doghouse and started walking again. Somewhere, in the back of my head, I knew I'd hear that thunk until the day I died.

38

THE DOGHOUSE WAS CLOSER TO the pump jacks and drill rigs. Outside the sound was deafening. Inside the insulated walls of the office it was muted to a dull thrum.

I walked into the entry area, a desk and reception spot that was traditionally deserted in most rigs. They all had areas like this—reception desks, filing cabinets, and fake plants, even though most rigs only saw a few visitors a year.

I walked around the desk, intending to head down the hallway, just as Harlan's Mollenkampi bodyguard came around the corner. Ammon held a gym bag in one massive hand, shirttails sticking out of the unzipped end. He saw me and froze.

"Look, I just want to get outta here," he said.

I had the drop on him, but we were too close for comfort; a gun is a distance weapon, and I like to be far enough away that my opponent can't lay hands on me, but close enough that I can't miss. I inched back, to give me more of an advantage, but stopped as I felt the metal corner of the filing cabinet press against my thigh.

Very slowly the big Mollenkampi raised his hands, gym bag dangling from one of them. "This is bat-shit crazy, and I don't want any part of it." He inclined his head further toward the hallway. "Harlan's down there. I'll lead you to him. All you got to do is let me walk."

I was tempted. I really was.

"One question," I said. "About Jermaine."

"Who?"

My jaw clenched hard and my decision got easy.

"The kid whose lungs you filled with Squib smell," I said. "The one who was driven mad and set loose on the Squib diplomat. The one someone shoved into a barrel of brine to get out of the hotel."

The big guy was silent.

I said, "Because the Squib's echo said that there was a cop in the room. Which to me meant Flanagan, but really any big, intimidating guy with a fake badge can look like a cop, when you get down to it. Flanagan had a soft spot for the kid, and might not have gone through with it. And you're a better choice, anyway. Everyone knows that Mollenkampi aren't affected by Squib smell. A Squib would be much more comfortable letting a Mollenkampi into the room than a human, and you'd have been able to keep your head and smuggle Jermaine out of the Eagle Crest without being seen."

He breathed deep, in and out, not answering me.

"So all that makes me wonder . . . have you got a fake badge tucked away in that bag, Ammon?"

The gym bag hurtled through the air, spoiling my aim.

He closed the gap between us while my gun was pointed away. With long strides he was on me quickly and grabbed hold of my other arm. He struck my elbow with his other hand, trying to bend my arm backward, maybe break it. It almost worked. As it was, I fought to track the barrel of my revolver back to his center of mass.

I got off a single shot. He staggered, but stayed on his feet. I couldn't tell if I'd grazed him or missed completely. He hit me again, and this time my revolver tumbled from my hand, bouncing against the file cabinet and onto the carpeted floor.

Pressed against the file cabinet, I lost my balance. Free arm windmilling for stability, my hand fell on a sheaf of folders. I clenched my fingers and hoisted the folders in the air. Papers flew between us. The big guy slowed for a moment. Even pros can't suppress an instinctive flinch when something unexpected comes at them—at the very least they need a fraction of a second to identify what it is and decide whether to react.

And I used that moment to dive for my weapon. Before I got there a size thirteen wingtip caught me in the shoulder. Unlike his boss, Ammon didn't dress in the vestment of the roughneck.

He came at me with fists balled and biting jaws spread wide. His suit coat fanned out behind him, like a hero in a comic book panel. He moved like one of those four-color heroes as well, a big guy used to letting his size intimidate people—no strategy, all show.

Same as when I met him at Harlan's office, he gave no thought to protection for his neck. I swung upward with an open left hand, timing it with a slight step to the inside, aiming for the soft flesh of his throat. I intended to end this fight quickly.

It was a good plan. I don't know if he saw it coming and reacted, or just happened to tuck his chin at the last minute. Doesn't matter. The result was the same.

Hitting the oversized jawbone of the Mollenkampi was like punching a cannonball. My hand skittered over his tusks and between the toothy ridges beyond. My broken finger twisted again, the splint breaking open as I screamed and my knees buckled.

The only good thing was that Ammon was surprised enough that his fist didn't connect. It whistled past me, a minor distraction compared to the agony that engulfed my hand.

The shattered splint caught on one of the thug's tusks, holding the edge of my left hand in the crushing vise of the Mollenkampi's biting jaws as they clamped shut. My pinkie and ring fingers snapped with a wet pop. Pain shot up my arm, numbing and biting in turns. I smelled blood in the air, and there was a second tearing pain as the Mollenkampi pulled backward and the bones of those fingers pulled apart.

His jaw mandible flicked out wildly, digging its claw into the wound, and stars danced across my vision. There was a sudden, vicious force as one of those wingtips connected with my knee, and I went down. The added weight was enough to tear the remaining flesh. When I hit the ground two of my fingers were still in the Mollenkampi's biting jaw.

I pulled my wounded hand tight to my chest and waited for the follow-up blow. It didn't come. I looked up to see Ammon bent over, head swinging from side to side, scrambling in his biting jaw with first his mandibles, then his hands, trying to dislodge my severed fingers while a chain of musical obscenities streamed out of his speaking mouth. I scrambled on my hands and knees, reaching for my lost revolver. Blood pumped across the carpet from the two stumps on my ruined left hand, and I fought waves of nausea as I crawled forward.

I dove the last few feet, stretching to grab the gun with my right hand. My fingertips brushed against it, almost closing when two strong hands grabbed the back of my jacket and lifted me into the air. The gun stayed on the carpet and I was flipped onto the reception desk. The wind huffed from my chest, and I was suddenly staring at the fluorescent overhead lighting while Ammon's big hands fought for purchase around my throat. I tucked my chin immediately, buying a precious few seconds of time.

Ammon was to my left, trying to get a grip on me like a homicidal masseuse. I kicked and writhed, sliding on the loose papers scattered over the desk, but I couldn't shake free. His grip was strong and he had leverage. Either he'd get underneath my chin and reach my windpipe, or he'd dislocate my jaw and get to me that way. I kicked again and waved my still-bleeding hand in the air as a desperate distraction. It didn't work, but my other hand found something on the desk, underneath all the papers and folders. A letter opener.

I struck with no plan, no forethought about target placement. Just a desperate thrust as I blindly jammed the point of the opener into the tissue of his left bicep and twisted, doing my best to open up the wound. I felt the grind of the metal blade on bone, and I snarled in satisfaction, knowing that I was at least hurting him. Big Ammon howled, and his left hand fell away. I pulled the opener out, somehow keeping my grip on the now blood-slicked handle. I swung again, this time stabbing his right arm. This strike wasn't as deep or wide as the first, but it did its job. He jerked back, letter opener still impaled in his muscle, and swiped at me with his injured left arm. There wasn't nearly as much strength behind it now. I flopped off the desk, too stunned to get my feet under me. I hit the carpet, screaming as I landed on my injured hand.

Opening my eyes, I saw my gun no more than two feet away. I crawled forward. Twenty inches. Twelve. Six. Almost there.

Ammon appeared around the other side of the desk. I kept going. He took two long strides toward me. Bloodstained metal glinted in his hand. He'd retrieved the letter opener. But with one more stretch forward, I reached my goal. The familiar feel of my service revolver nestled in the curve of my palm.

He dove at me with the bloody letter opener raised, but I'd brought a gun to his knife fight.

I left him in the reception room of the doghouse, a .38 caliber hole in his forehead.

All oil rigs are required to have emergency medical kits on hand, prominently displayed and easily accessible. It's a hazardous profession, and crushed fingers aren't an unusual occurrence on those giant metal skeletons. In all my life, I'd never been so grateful for a legal requirement as when I tore the white and red plastic box off the wall and dumped its contents in front of me. I kept telling myself that it wasn't as much blood as it looked like as I coated what remained of my fingers with clotting powder and wrapped them with enough gauze to form a plug. I followed that with more bandage wrap, pulling it tight and trusting the powder and the pressure to stabilize the wound. It was an amateur operation, but at least I wasn't going to bleed to death. It didn't even really hurt until I was done, and the adrenaline started to fade. Then it hurt like all the imps in all the Hells were after me.

There was a small packet of painkillers in the kit. I cracked the bottle open and shook several into my mouth. I didn't have the saliva to swallow them whole, so I crunched them between my insignificant human molars. The bitter taste made my jaw ache, but I trusted that the pain relief would kick in, and moved deeper into the doghouse.

I walked through the main office doors and found Harlan Cedrow, the scion of industry, the great-great-grandson of Rediron Drilling's founders, sitting at a desk with his back to the door, pecking inexpertly at a typewriter. I paused before entering. The room rocked from side to side, and the doorjamb was a steady hand supporting me. A winter coat draped over the back of his chair, and there was no sign of anyone else in the room.

"I heard the gunshot," said Harlan. "Was that a mere warning, or did one of the men get through the front door?"

"I'd say it was a pretty severe warning shot." My voice cracked as I spoke. I kept my left hand elevated, my right arm cocked and my revolver tucked close to my chest as I aimed it.

He turned, the spring on his chair squeaking a meek protest. Behind him, the office's picture window looked out over the ice plains, and it lit us both with the waning light of the day.

"Detective Carter." He placed his hands on his desk, one of them conveniently close to the intercom. I didn't have the energy to tell him it was useless.

He shifted his hand, pressing the intercom, and called out, "Ammon!"

I gave him the best smile I could summon under the circumstances.

"He and I already talked." I showed him my heavily bandaged left hand. "Good thing I shoot right-handed, huh?"

The color drained from Harlan's face. I gestured for him to get up with my head, leaving the barrel of my revolver pointed at his chest. He walked around his desk and paused by the picture window. Behind him the derricks and drills were still in motion, pumping impotently at dry reservoirs and bedrock.

"You're going to lie down," I said. "And put your hands over your head."

He licked his lips. "I just need a little more time."

I almost laughed.

"It's done," I said. "Don't you know when it's done?"

"Nothing's done until I say it's done!" His nostrils flared and his lips pulled into a tight, pale line. "They're going to let this city die unless I save it."

"They?"

"Them! Paulus and the mayor and the AFS and the Squibs. Every moneylender and bureaucrat who cares more about a dollar than about Titanshade, than the people who live here." He went to one knee and raised his hands to the sides of his head. Fingers quivering, he pleaded his case.

"All those people," he said. "Not one of them understands what I'm trying to do."

"They think you're planning to set the canisters loose in the city," I said.

On his knees Harlan looked at me, eyes twitching. "But you knew better."

"You don't want to hurt the city," I said. "You want to save it."

He nodded. Slowly, tentatively. A deliberate up and down motion of his head.

"But," I said, "you're also willing to take some losses along the way, aren't you? Haberdine. Stacie and Jermaine. Even your own men." So many lives destroyed in his quest to preserve the status quo.

"Sacrifices," he drawled. "For the greater good. We had to buy time. Enough to make the strike. The memory of those men will be cherished by future generations."

I started to shake my head, but it hurt too bad to move. I managed a false grin and my best eight-fingered-man tough guy routine.

"No matter how it shakes out," I said. "You'll be rotting in prison. No one's gonna cherish your memory."

Harlan swallowed, Adam's apple bobbing up and down. "That's

as may be. But I ask you this: If the AFS can be assured that there's no end of oil to be pumped from below us, will I be in chains? Or will I be placed in charge of this vital national interest?"

"You're wrong," I said. But I couldn't help but wonder: how much destruction would the government forgive if it saved an entire economy? Hadn't worse things been swept under the rugs in politicians' mansions before this?

I tried to keep my breathing slow and controlled, but I kept getting hotter. The room shifted unsteadily around me as I ran my damaged hand over my head. The bandage stopped at my wrist, and it was soaked in thick sweat as it came away from my forehead. I swallowed. It'd all be for nothing if I went into shock now.

I waved the gun at Harlan. "Turn around, and get on the floor," I said.

He complied and I took a step toward him. Not thinking, I pushed away from the doorframe with my left hand, and the stumps of my fingers erupted with pain. Closing my eyes against the pain, I let out a crack-voiced scream as I fell back into the doorframe, left shoulder hitting it and supporting my weight.

My head swam and black dots squirmed on the periphery of my vision. Each breath came fast and shallow. I dropped my head down, crouching and steadying myself. If I passed out now, I'd never wake up.

I took a deep breath and closed my eyes before exhaling. I suddenly had the sense of time passing. I forced my eyes open and was surprised to find myself sitting on my ass. My mouth had a pasty, bitter film in it. I looked up, trying to find my prisoner.

Harlan was almost on top of me, crossing the room in long, gangly strides, snarling and full of messianic rage. I brought the revolver up and had to put weight into the act; it felt like I was moving through molasses. I fired, twice, not bothering to aim. The gunshots were accompanied by the sound of shattering glass, neither of which did my headache any favors. My vision clouded again.

I tensed, ready for Harlan's assault, but what hit me instead was a biting blast of cold wind. Ice and snow bit my cheeks, the cruel nature of the landscape forcing itself into the room through the now-shattered picture window. Harlan was gone. Beyond the window I could still see his tracks on the fragile top surface of the ice.

I suppose he ran because he wasn't thinking. I can't claim that same excuse. I knew it was suicide, but I'd come too far, and too much depended on ending it.

I followed him out onto the ice because I'm a cop. I followed him onto the ice because he'd killed or been instrumental in the deaths of dozens of people, and in the bizarre experiments at the lab. I followed him because I didn't trust the system that had fought me at every step of the investigation. I followed him because he'd almost killed Talena, and might still send her to prison. I followed him because every fiber of my being ached for justice, for judgment, for vengeance.

I crawled through the broken window of the doghouse and followed Harlan's footsteps toward the derricks and pump jacks, illuminated by the cold and dying light of the setting sun.

39

MY PURSUIT WAS A STUMBLING, wounded run. The only sounds on the plains were the crunch-crunch of my boots on snow and the incessant whir of dead wind scraping over ice. I told myself that there were no voices in the wind, no lost hade whispering in my ear, luring me from my path. Instead I focused on the man ahead of me. Harlan Cedrow ran, and I gave chase. And the chase brought us inevitably closer to the skeletal shapes of the Rediron rigs.

We ran between the derricks and pumps that his family had built generations ago. We ran through snow that stole our vision and wrenched the breath from our lungs. The thick thermal gear was difficult to move in, for me and surely for him as well. With every step I gained on him, and with every step he knew there was less chance of escape.

I closed in on him not because I was faster, but because we both knew he had nowhere to go beyond the drills. To run blindly onto the ice plains was suicide. So we circled round the encampment, moving inexorably toward the derrick in its center, the oldest on site. Old as it was, it was taking part in Harlan's mad hunt, too. Still moving, still searching after all these years, trying to pry its fingers deep into the ground beneath the ice, trying to force the very rocks to give up their secrets. I slowed my pace, knowing he'd turn in there. For a man who filled his office with pieces of oil-industry tradition, this symbol of family history would be an irresistible beacon.

This close to the towering machinery, the blossom of grease and petroleum smells was overwhelming. Ice and snow have no scent, and aromas are slow to emerge in the frigid cold. In the odorless waste of the ice plains, approaching the derricks was like walking into a bakery.

As I moved, I struggled to reload my revolver. I had two live rounds in the cylinder, and six more sitting useless in my pocket. A good way to get killed. One hand mangled and bleeding, the other crippled by painfully numbed fingers, I couldn't even breech the cylinder. I was still struggling when Harlan came around the corner of the rig.

Heavy worker's clothing kept his torso warm, but his unprotected face and scalp were a bright pink splotched with the pale tinge of early frostbite. But he did wear gloves, and that had allowed him to salvage a jagged piece of rebar. He crouched low, peering at me from around one of the fuel tanks, set back a safe twenty yards or so from the drill tower itself.

I was tempted to take a shot at him, but I resisted. It was a likely miss, and a wasted bullet. I stared him down instead.

We were both breathing hard, the smokestack condensation of our breath whipped away by the wind.

I yelled, forcing my voice over the noise of the equipment. "You're under arrest!"

I could have said something more, something clever designed to play to his ego and force him into making a mistake. But my energy was fading, the sun was setting, and I just plain didn't care if he listened to me or not.

I didn't expect him to start laughing.

"Arrest me?" Numb lips slurred his speech like a drunk on a bender, but it didn't stop him from running his mouth as much as ever. "Well, I can't have that, Detective. This is the second age of Titanshade, and you and I need to save this city from outsiders."

I took a slow step toward him, then another. Drawing closer to firing range.

"The first age," he said, "was when my forebears arrived at this place. An oasis of warmth in the cold, a haven to practice their religion."

I kept moving, closing the gap between us while he talked. But he faded back, faster on his feet than I was.

"The second age," he said, and the wind stole his words, making it sound as if he was in more than one place at once. "Came with the discovery of oil beneath the ice. When my family raised Titanshade from nothing. A piece of trivia about the northernmost city in the AFS, and they turned it into the heart of the world's economy!"

The wind swelled, pelting my eyes with snow and ice. Eyes watering, I squinted, trying to focus. He was gone.

I turned, pivoting back and forth, trying to get a fix on his location. The sun was fading fast; the surroundings were going to dusk, and only the crown block at the top of the rig remained bathed in sunlight.

"We make, and they take," Harlan called out, but I couldn't tell if he was ahead of me or to the side. "The world runs on Titanshade's blood. I have a duty to protect this city, to protect my family's heritage. I'll not let the second age of this city end on my watch."

Snow crunched behind me. He'd managed to circle around.

He closed on me much faster than I expected. The rebar in his hand darted toward my face like a fencer's rapier.

I wrapped my left arm around my head, protectively folded in like a chicken wing. When the rebar struck, the pain was white hot. I couldn't tell if my arm had broken or not. Either way, I knew I wouldn't stand against another strike.

He was too close, my gun out of position. I fired, knowing it would go wild, just trying to force him back, to give me room to get a proper bead on him. Instead he hit me again, this time across the back, a heavy overhand blow that sent a ripple of pain crashing over my shoulders and down each arm. I couldn't take it, and both arms went numb.

My revolver fell, striking the ground with a small thunderclap—the impact had discharged it. Chill air snapped as the bullet whipped past my face. I'd come within inches of being killed by my own weapon. The shot's recoil sent the revolver sliding across the ice.

Harlan pulled his arm back, winding up for the finishing blow, when the ice rumbled beneath our feet. For the son of a roughneck, it was an unmistakable sound. I couldn't help it—I looked at the rig.

On a drill as ancient as that one, whatever blowback preventer had once been installed was the better part of a century old. Or maybe it never had one. Either way, when it did strike, it *blew*. The ice seemed to shrug beneath us, and there was a whooshing sound as the pressurized liquid sprayed a hundred feet in the air before scattering and raining down on two small men paused in the middle of a fight for their lives.

Harlan threw his head back and let loose a scream of joy.

"You see?" he crowed. "Treasure found at the greatest of depths!" Arms out, Harlan spun around, reveling in his vindication. Far below anything that the geologists had said was possible, the rig had struck a reservoir. He was right after all.

And he was still a killer.

I dove at him while he was distracted by his victory. We collided and the rebar fell to the snow with a crackling thud.

He swung his hands wildly. We were both so exhausted, so constricted by our coats, we fought almost like children throwing tantrums. One of his hands slapped across my face, turning my head. A few feet in that direction a dark object lay on the white of the ice plain—the rebar.

I shoved off of Harlan and scrambled for it, scooping down to get a good grip as the cold metal seared my exposed hands. I turned to him, holding my prize, while the strike roared like a jet engine behind us.

Ten feet from where I stood Harlan was doubled over, hands on his knees, breathing heavy and staring at me. On the ground beside him was my gun.

For once he didn't run his mouth. He picked up the gun, pointed it at me, smiled, and pulled the trigger.

There was only a click as the hammer fell on a spent shell. He stared at it, shocked at this simple failure. I charged and he had just enough time to look back at me, mouth open, as I swung the piece of rebar as hard as I could. It struck his temple with a sound like a rain-soaked paper bag ripping open.

He dropped, and I let the rebar fall from my hand. I didn't need a medical examiner to tell me that Harlan wouldn't be getting back up again, now or ever. It was over.

The well's geyser still arched skyward, and the stream dissipated as it fell, tiny iridescent drops, shimmering in the short-lived winter sun. I looked back the way I'd come. My tracks were already disappearing in the shifting snow.

I turned a slow circle in place, trying to locate the doghouse. The radio was in there somewhere. I just had to make it back and call for help.

The patter of drops from the geyser sounded like the applause of an invisible crowd as they fell on the ice and snow around me. I allowed myself a smile. I'd done my job, the sun was setting on this whole nightmare, and the only question was whether I had the strength to stumble to shelter and keep warm until the cavalry arrived.

I tried to orient myself to head toward safety. The ice plain was coated in a wide circle by the strike spray. Iridescent drops colored the snow where they landed, and my clothes glistened with streaks of color. I don't know how long I stared, denying the reality of what I was witnessing.

Harlan and his disfigured genius Heidelbrecht had pumped Jermaine full of manna and oil, intending him to be drawn to petroleum reserves like a compass needle points due north, or an ancient whale could home in on a destination from across the ocean. It almost worked. They'd simply found the wrong treasure. There was only one liquid that shimmered like that, and it wasn't oil.

I fell to my knees and threw my head back, watching the manna rain down around me.

In the fading sunlight the glittering iridescence formed an uneven, impossible rainbow across the wide bowl of the sky. Staring up at the display, my coat's hood slid off. The manna wet my head and coated my eyes, my hair, my face. It mixed with my tears of exhaustion and wonder.

Drops of manna traced curved paths over my cheeks and ran into my mouth. There was a pinch on my tongue then it melted away, like cotton candy. There was absolutely no flavor.

40

IT WAS TWENTY-FOUR HOURS BEFORE anyone left me alone in the hospital. I was questioned, debriefed, and quizzed by so many bureaucrats and shrinks that I lost count. They wanted to know if I knew about the manna strike in advance, if Harlan had known, if I had used the manna to save myself, and then they wanted to step through the whole thing one more time.

What they really wanted to know was if I was some kind of secret sorcerer or just the luckiest man alive. Exposure to that amount of raw manna was unprecedented. Some of my interviewers thought it may have partially cauterized my fingers, working with the clotting agent I'd already applied. Others conjectured that manna may have been what kept me warm and awake long enough for the rescue party to find me.

It was all theory. No one knew for sure what it would do to me, or to the land around the strike. For all they knew the entire region was a toxic natural disaster. So the questions kept coming, as fast as I could tell them I had no answers.

Bryyh finally put an end to it. She didn't say anything to me, but her voice barked orders and insults outside my room and next thing I knew I was being told to get a good night's sleep so we could start again in the morning. Once the pencil pushers were gone I checked myself out of the hospital. There was an old friend I needed to visit.

The first thing I did was find someone who knew the far side of the Mount. I'm a city kid; I can navigate a maze of side streets and back alleys but stick me in a ravine and I'll wander lost for days.

It took more doing than expected. Turns out there's not much call for hiking among the boneyards and sky burial grounds on the northeast side of the Mount. But cash talks, and early the next morning my newly acquired guide and I set out.

We drove as far up the Mount as the winding funerary roads allowed. When the roads ran out we hiked in silence, my hired guide shooting occasional, furtive glances at me and my disfigured hand. Word of the strike on Cedrow land was getting out, and there wasn't any avoiding my name being linked to the whole mess. That meant headaches for me and the TPD, but that was a worry for later.

Now Jax, he'd benefit from the attention. Hemingway, too. A boost to their careers and their names in the papers. The whole thing was enough of a feather in their caps that they could keep their heads down and cruise to a pension on that alone.

Of course, pensions weren't an option for Myris. I picked up my pace on the trail, trying to burn off the shame of her death. One more life sacrificed for the greater good, one more grieving family to be consoled.

At least Talena was safe. With Harlan dead, Paulus had no reason to pursue a scapegoat for the killings. On her own, Paulus might have simply left the kid to rot in the system, but Gellica would help see that the charges were dropped. It was one bright spot I could focus on. I'd fulfilled my promise once more. Jenny's daughter would be safe, the wolves kept at bay.

It always came back to Jenny. She'd been my lodestar for over a decade, no matter how bad each of us had screwed up. And I was drawn to her still. She was the reason I'd come to the far side of the Mount.

It took the better part of daylight to make the hike, even with the guide's help. We stepped between boulders and loose dirt, treading carefully from one ankle-breaking hazard to another, the steady crunch-crunch of our boots the only sound. My newly acquired companion grew more nervous as the day moved into twilight, but I pressed on. Eventually I found what I was looking for between two desk-sized boulders.

That trial at the CCC hadn't been as well-intentioned as I'd thought. Whether they knew it or not, the doctors who eased Jenny's pain by sharing it with me had created a manna bond between us. A bond that held fast even beyond death. My bones ached for no medically sound reason, and I felt a pull toward the Mount that no one could explain, all because Harlan Cedrow had used terminally ill patients in his mad search for oil.

Even if they knew the plan, I doubt the doctors had thought it would last. It'd surely never occurred to anyone that the sky shepherds might leave something behind. Until I learned how Jermaine Bell-Asandro had been used as a living dowsing rod, I'd never known I needed to look. Now there was no doubt I'd found what I'd come for; I could feel it in my bones.

Pulling the objects from between boulders, I felt the sarcoma that scarred their surface. The jagged, biting spines erupting from two femurs and a hip bone that had caused Jenny so much pain. A pain I'd carried with me long since it had ceased to trouble her.

Dropped by the shepherds after Jenny's sky burial, they'd been caught between the rocks for years. I might never have found them, if not for the relentless, painful tug that led me there. It was time to break the link. Time to let the past rest.

I could have cremated them, brought them back to town for disposal. But Jenny was a traditionalist.

Setting a fist-sized metal bowl on a flat rock, I struck a lighter and gave spark to the incense inside. Then I formed the bones in a pyramid around the bowl, letting the smoke wrap around, through, and then above them. The scent would alert the condors circling overhead that an offering awaited.

I stepped back and encountered the sudden, bleak realization that I had no idea what to do next. I didn't have a speech ready, and I've never so much as touched anything resembling insight or wisdom in my life.

All I knew was that I missed her. That I'd always miss her.

In her final days we weren't back together, at least not romantically. We'd each burned that particular bridge to cinders. But we were united as two best friends, going through her treatments and pain together.

For all the bad times, I was lucky to have known her. So I said the only thing that made sense.

"Good-bye, Jenny," I said. "Thank you." Voice catching, I bowed my head. "Thank you so much."

I pressed two fingers to my lips then held them in the column of smoke, sending a prayer and a kiss aloft with the incense.

A long moment later I walked away. Above, too far to be seen, the sky shepherds began their slow, spiraling descent from the darkening sky.

On the trail back to the funerary roads we moved as fast as we could. Neither my guide nor I wanted to be caught outside on the

Mount at night. Still, when we came to a low rise I stopped to catch my breath and scanned the horizon.

From the other side of the Mount the lights of Titanshade created a glowing haze, outlining the jagged edges of the Mount at the periphery of my vision. To the north and east the ice plains continued as far as I could see, frozen and indifferent to the struggles of those who walked the Path.

But to the south was something new. Dark shapes with piercing headlights traveled in columns stretching far into the distance. From my vantage they looked small, beetle-like and unstoppable, an endless stream of troop transports and camouflage-wrapped trucks. A military convoy from Fracinica and the other city-states that made up the AFS, on their way to secure the new national interest.

The third age of Titanshade had arrived.

ACKNOWLEDGMENTS

WRITING IS A SOLITARY ACTIVITY, but turning a manuscript into a book is far more than I could handle on my own. What follows is an incomplete list of the friends, family, and collaborators who helped bring *Titanshade* to bookshelves. My sincerest thanks to the people on these pages, and my sincerest apologies to anyone who I may have inadvertently left out.

My parents taught me storytelling and provided me with unwavering support. I could write an entire book simply on the ways that they helped me grow and learn, but one quick example will have to suffice. When I was young I played with tiny knights and dragons, creating adventures on the living room floor that I described to my mom. She wrote them down, spacing out the sentences so that I could copy her handwriting on the lines beneath. She taught me to write by copying my own stories.

Mandy Fox is my lodestar. She is collaborator and coach, critic and best friend. I'm never as happy as when I'm with her, and I plan on staying by her side for as long as she'll have me.

Nat Sobel read my short story in Darusha Wehm's excellent Plan B Magazine, and thought I might have a novel in me. Turns out I did, but I only found it through the encouragement and guidance of Nat and the rest of the team at Sobel Weber: Judith Weber, Siobhan McBride, Sara Henry, and Adia Wright.

Another huge thanks is due to my editor, Sheila Gilbert. I couldn't have asked for a better match. Sheila immediately saw the fun and intrigue lurking in Titanshade, and helped push this novel over the finish line in the best form possible. DAW has been amazing to work with, and I'm forever grateful to Sheila, Betsy Wollheim, Katie Hoffman, Josh Starr, Leah Spann, Jessica Plummer, Lauren Horvath, and Mary Flower.

If you picked up this book because of the amazing cover, it's because of Chris McGrath, who is not only an incredibly talented artist but a patient and thoughtful collaborator. Chris took the time to read the text and ask questions to get the feel of the book, while still bringing his own artistic flair. They say you shouldn't judge a book by its cover, but with artwork like his on the front of my book, I don't mind if you do.

The novel itself was born out of a 90-minute flash fiction challenge on the Liberty Hall site. I owe a huge debt to the participants and to Martin Waller and Mike Munsil, who made the machine work behind the curtain. My challenge cohorts that week were Christine Lucas and Pixiepara, who both provided feedback and encouragement to move ahead.

Throughout the process I leaned heavily on my fantastic local writers' group, Writeshop Columbus. The guidance and gentle correction I received there has been fantastic, and the retreats gave me a chance to hone my craft. Special thanks to the Writeshoppers who reviewed my early versions. They include Brian Justus, Jordan Kurella, Sandra J. Kachurek, and Jerry L. Robinette.

In addition, my online Novel Buddies Stephanie Lorée, Setsu Uzumé, and Jodi Henry each served as sounding boards, cheerleaders, and drill sergeants at different parts of the process. Thanks, guys—I couldn't have done it without you!

As the book neared its final stages, I also received input from beta readers including Megan Myers, Decemae Yangkin, and Laurence French. They pitched in long after the point when it was difficult for me to distance myself from the work, and I'm immensely grateful for their help.

In addition, there are countless booksellers, writers, and readers who provided encouragement and incentive to carry on. If you showed interest when I mentioned I was writing a book, if you told me you'd buy a copy (even if you were only being nice!) or if you found this book and enjoyed the characters and world of *Titanshade* . . .

THANK YOU!